REVIEWS AND PRAISE FOR

THE SECOND LAW

LYNN DAYTON THRILLER #3

THE SECOND LAW is a Lynn Dayton thriller revolving around a new challenge in Lynn's job as a top refining executive working in the busy San Francisco Bay Area. What seems like a puzzling computer glitch could turn out to be sabotage, and too many false alarms are undermining the safety warning system of the refinery, among other odd problems. Only this time the siren's warning isn't another false alarm, but a portent of the biggest disaster Lynn has yet to face: one which has roots in China and connections with California's oil history.

... a spellbinding story that moved between the San Francisco Bay Area, China, and New Orleans, exploring the special talents and interests of a host of intersecting characters whose lives are all dictated by special interests.

The result is a compelling thriller that's hard to put down, absorbingly powerful in both characterization and plot and filled with satisfying twists and turns that introduce readers to the world of not just refinery safety and operations, but high-stakes international intrigue between groups holding special government interests at the heart of their actions.

Readers who enjoy stories of mystery, murder, mayhem and espionage will relish the intricate, complex yet highly accessible series of events **THE SECOND LAW** unfolds.

—D. Donovan, Senior Reviewer,
Midwest Book Review

THE SECOND LAW

LYNN DAYTON THRILLER #3

L. A. STARKS

Nemaha Ridge Publishing Group, LLC
Dallas, Texas

Starks, L.A.
The Second Law/L. A. Starks
(Lynn Dayton Thriller #3)

Identifiers: ISBN 978-0991110728 (ebook), ISBN 978-0991110742 (trade paperback)

Dayton, Lynn (Fictitious character)-Fiction 2. Thrillers-China-Beijing, California-San Francisco, and Louisiana-New Orleans

First Print and E-book editions: October, 2018 by Nemaha Ridge Publishing Group, LLC

*Dedicated to my family and to the 300th anniversary
of the city of New Orleans, Louisiana*

AUTHOR'S NOTE

All mistakes are mine. While most organizations mentioned in this book are real, their people and policies are fictional. Security protocols and systems are disguised or changed.

CHAPTER 1

SAN FRANCISCO

Today's problem seemed simple but had turned lethal. Lynn Dayton, TriCoast Energy's top refining executive, swore to herself as she wove in and out of traffic on the Bay Bridge. Running a refinery like the one in the East Bay was dangerous enough when everything worked. It could be deadly if equipment was screwing up. *Surely it's an equipment malfunction, not someone sabotaging the operations?*

With her was her former mentor—now TriCoast's chief troubleshooter, Reese Spencer. He was puzzled, too. The best the company's expert engineers and computer scientists could suggest was the ubiquitous "computer glitch," with no clue about the source.

"Computer glitch" could mean anything from an erroneous line of code to a critical valve failure.

Reese talked through his reasoning. "Seems the increase in accidents correlates with higher-than-normal turnover for this refinery."

"Correlation is not causation," Lynn told him, twisting to adjust her lean, five-foot-nine runner's frame to the cramped driver's seat. *The computer snag could infect our other refineries and put even more people at risk.*

Similar to other California industries, TriCoast's refinery was camouflaged from the highway and public behind hills. After a final turn, spiky distillation towers and giant product tanks appeared in front of them, arrayed in sections like city squares. Flocks of starlings that had roosted on warm equipment during the night now rose in a black cloud and winged westward toward the bay.

They carded through the front gate and parked as close as possible to the low-rise headquarters building. Since they would be walking past hazardous pumps, Lynn pulled her blond hair into a ponytail to avoid catching it in any rotating equipment.

"Glad you're here." Refinery manager Curtis Zhang showed them to an unadorned office.

"There's no easy pattern to these hiccups yet these problems have been going on for weeks. Your thoughts?" she asked.

Zhang shrugged, clearly exasperated. "I sure as hell wish I had answers, but I don't."

"You hire good engineers and operators," Lynn said.

"But the pull from salaries, bonuses and stock options of tech companies is like trying to escape Jupiter's gravity," Zhang replied. "Or else we hire them, but then they get admitted to one of those ten-week coding boot camps that doubles their salary. So no reason to stay here."

"We have tech opportunities everywhere at TriCoast," Lynn said. "We just need to get the word out."

"Hell yes," Zhang agreed. "The East Bay has always been industrial. So we're using AI, drones, the Internet of Things and driverless vehicles. You name it, we're applying it."

"I don't worry about turnover as much as the safety of our people," she said.

"This refinery's statistics show few accidents until recently," Reese added.

Zhang nodded and introduced two people who'd joined them. "Shirley Watson is our human resources VP and Juan Rojas, our safety and environmental VP."

Shirley's handshake was firm, her smile warm and pleasant.

"Yes, we're concerned, too," Juan added. His six-four, two-hundred-pounds-plus frame suggested he could readily convince people to follow his safety and environmental directives.

"We're always adjusting operations to compensate for problems, so we've avoided a major shutdown so far, but it's only a question of time," Zhang continued, echoing Lynn's thoughts on her drive across the Bay Bridge.

She motioned toward the door. "Shall we?" The five each clipped hard hat straps under their chins. Zhang directed them to one of the multi-story distillation towers.

Most of the refinery's equipment—its tall cylindrical towers, vast drums, pumps, and blocks upon blocks of pipe—was out in the open air. They walked asphalt "streets" from one section to another. Everything was run by trained, unionized operators and technicians stationed in a half-dozen small control buildings. The crews they met were agreeable and attentive but had been on the job less than four years. Their short tenures were unusual for TriCoast. At Lynn's other refineries, experienced hands stayed for decades.

They stood next to a 130-foot-tall vacuum distillation tower shaped like a booster rocket before liftoff although with a larger diameter and stubbier profile.

A klaxon blared. The *woooo* of the alarm pitch started low and became higher and louder.

We gotta roll! "High-pressure!" Lynn shouted. She pointed to a nearby control room.

They ran inside. The room's walls and ceiling had been built to withstand earthquakes and blast pressure waves.

A few minutes later, the klaxon stopped.

Her group was greeted with curious looks from the four operators already inside and others who'd taken shelter. Operators were men and women who controlled the pump systems and enormous oil processing towers. They monitored gauges and alarms to keep equipment from getting too hot, too over-pressured, or too full.

"We heard the alarm," Juan said, his voice tight.

The lead operator looked at her screens and shook her head. "I don't see the source. Just another false one."

Relieved, Lynn and the rest returned outside.

"Could the problem be randomized corrosion? We had a bad incident resulting from high-sulfur crude making excessive sulfuric acid." Although she was talking about one of her Texas refineries, corrosion problems were common in many manufacturing plants. "We didn't find it until after the acid gnawed through a line. A hydrogen sulfide gas leak killed four people."

"I read about that in a company alert," Zhang said.

"We train hard on safety and inspection," Shirley replied, her eyes narrowing. "But the risk of so many false alarms is crying wolf syndrome. People stop responding as fast as necessary. Or at all."

"You've checked to see if systems have been hacked?" Lynn asked. Most plants had experienced attempted computer intrusions and had set up defensive software.

"I'm sure we've been hacked. After our own people couldn't find anything we brought in software consultants, but they haven't found the source, either," Juan said. Impatience roughened his voice.

"Same kinds of failures on the same units?" she asked.

Juan shook his head. "No pattern to either the false alarms or the real ones."

"When we drove in, we saw starlings," she said.

"Yeah, damn birds and their shit," Curtis Zhang replied. "Don't think they're the cause, though."

A high-pressure alarm on a nearby pump blared, sounding like the earlier one.

Lynn looked around for what might have triggered the alarm. *False again? Shirley's right. Easy to stop reacting to alarms when they're so frequent.*

Zhang shook his head and pointed to the concrete building they'd just left.

Lynn shouted over the alarm. "Back to the control room, everyone. Let's move!"

Zhang led, followed by the others.

Shirley hung back, looking for anyone who might be lingering.

Lynn yelled as the alarm kept wailing, "Shirley, you can't save anyone else if you don't save yourself. C'mon!"

The air above her head felt cooler, then warmer, as she ran through shadow stripes from pipe racks five feet over her head.

They heard a distant explosion, as if a vessel or pump had ruptured. Her stomach dropped. She knew all the normal rumbles and rushing sounds a refinery made. This wasn't one. A split-open vessel meant the worst kind of trouble.

"Run!" Shirley shouted.

"You, too!" Lynn replied, waving Shirley forward.

Although they wouldn't be able to see any invisible hydrocarbon gases, leakages could explode once they crossed an ignition source, or even just heat from an engine exhaust.

Lynn looked back and caught a whiff of rotten eggs. Hydrogen sulfide! *This could be as bad as the Centennial accident.* Over a year ago, finding the cause for a gas leak that had killed four people led her to an international plot to sabotage Houston refineries.

The shaft of a big gray pump nearby whined as the pump spun out of control. Its bearing housing started to knock so hard the pump shook. Bolts loosened on the casing as the pump increased rotation speed. Finally, the automatic shutoff triggered.

But the pump's silence didn't mean safety. She knew extra friction from the pump grinding out of alignment had caused its metallic parts to overheat well above their already-hot temperature of three hundred and fifty degrees. Despite its safety design the pump's cooling fins might not dissipate the heat fast enough.

Forty yards behind her, Shirley grabbed the shirts of two men who seemed to think they were hearing another false alarm.

They're too close to that overheated pump! "Run!" Lynn shouted.

Shirley pulled the men toward the control room, a furious look on her face. Lynn turned and started toward her to help, but Juan and Reese yanked her back.

In an instant an invisible mass of gas met the overheated pump.

A wall of fire erupted.

With a roar, an inferno the size of a boxcar flashed over Shirley and the men.

Lynn's horror was deepened by a scalding blast of heat.

Shirley and the men screamed. One tripped. Shirley pulled him to his feet and they ran far enough to roll on the ground and extinguish their burning clothes.

But the fire back-flashed to the original source of the gas leak, sparking smaller fires along the cement where hydrocarbon liquids had collected.

"Someone turn off the fucking flow!" Lynn shouted.

"I did!" Zhang said.

"Fire's called in!" Juan said.

"Extinguishers!" Lynn shouted. *Can we even put this monster out?*

"Oh my God! Oh fuck! Oh God, I'm dying!" one of the men screamed.

Lynn gritted her teeth. *The worst nightmare. Stop! Focus!* She grabbed a fire extinguisher from its outdoor stand.

She hoisted the fifty-pound cylinder.

PASS. She remembered the acronym. She pulled the pin, aimed the hose nozzle toward the base of the fire, squeezed the handle, and swept the nozzle back and forth. The canister didn't seem to get lighter but her hands began freezing as she released compressed carbon dioxide.

Reese, Zhang, and Juan followed her example.

Shirley and the men kept crawling forward. Lynn advanced past them towards the flames, using her elbow to shield her eyes and face from the ferocious heat. The fire was smaller but still a deadly inferno.

Cinders sprayed. Despite her jacket and hard hat, she felt pinpricks of heat as cinders burned through her clothes and found unprotected skin.

We need to clear a path for ambulances.

The fire shrank as she emptied her fire extinguisher and the flames closest to them were quenched.

She shook feeling back into her nearly frozen hands.

Smaller fires burned on the ground and platforms thirty yards away. Lynn moved to shield the three victims from more flare-ups.

"Reese!" She pointed. Reese dowsed the smaller fires.

Ninety seconds after she had grabbed the first extinguisher, she heard the wail of arriving ambulances. *Thank God.* As they pulled up close and braked, she and the others ran to tell the paramedics what had happened.

The medics surrounded Shirley and the two men. They pulled off constricting clothing and placed masks on the victims to deliver humidified oxygen. The medics elevated the legs of each to lessen shock, then attached IV lines.

Lynn was horrified at the size and depth of their injuries. The left side of Shirley's face looked as if someone had punched her in the eye and streaked her cheek with black and red paint. Her neck was blistered and a giant hole gaped through her workpants where the fire had left third degree burns.

Lynn smelled burned flesh and controlled an urge to gag.

She shuddered, remembering too well the day her own father had come home early from work with loose white bandages on his chest and arm.

The next day, when her mother changed his bandages, he grimaced and perspired. Lynn saw with horror that the bandages were protecting his reddened and charred skin. He'd been unable to hug her for months.

This was worse. *My fault. I knew the goddamn computer glitches were trouble. I shouldn't have trusted Curtis Zhang and his folks to fix the problem without being involved myself. Now three of my people might not even survive. God, they look terrible.*

The medics lifted the victims onto gurneys and three ambulances rushed them to the burn center.

Mutual aid fire trucks—a volunteer group of men and women from this refinery and plants nearby—rolled up. Firefighters jumped out and shot foam at a few fires that had kicked back up.

She watched until she was sure no new fires would start. She exchanged glances with Reese hoping he would nod reassurance, but he looked as stunned as she felt.

They regrouped inside the control room with Zhang and Juan.

"Your clothes are burned. Sure you're okay?" Reese pointed to brown scorch marks and holes in her blouse and jacket. Lynn nodded as she smoothed ointment onto her heat-blistered hands and neck.

Zhang, Juan, Reese, and the half-dozen operating technicians gathered around her. Tears blurred her eyes as she remembered Shirley's dash to save the others, and the burns they all suffered. "We have to find out who's behind this. And fast," she said, pounding her fists. "It can't happen to us again. Ever."

CHAPTER 2

BEIJING, CHINA

Cong Li shared space Silicon Valley-style on the floor with his employees. But Chinese-style, only his twenty-square-meter office had a window and a door. He'd returned to the country of his birth to build a fortune with his new company. Everything was on schedule, even his wife's pregnancy. Though not a princeling, he was rich enough not to care whether she had a girl or a boy. He even discouraged his wife from getting a sonogram, reasoning while a boy would be strong, a good reflection on Cong's manhood, a girl might be easier to raise. Girls were valuable, too, since they were rarer than boys. His wife was touring the United States, another part of their long-term plan.

His clothes were better than those of his employees. The cotton was a denser weave and the shoes a finer grade of leather.

Outside, power lines knotted in a tangle in the perpetual brown smog covering this hustling city of over twenty million.

The window had not been well sealed into the wall even when the building was new. Since then, more of the plaster had chipped away. Water seeped in during a rain. At present, hot air and screeches from car brakes and truck horns drifted five stories up into his office.

He didn't hear Comrade Jin enter his office until the rustle of her dress caused him to look up. She had already seated herself on the other side of his desk. Mei Jin was the Fourth Department superior he saw most often, although he knew she reported to others more senior. Her severe expression told him nothing. He noted her eyes had been surgically widened and softened since he'd seen her a few months before.

"Greetings, Comrade Li."

"Hello, Mei." Cong fingered his ivory amulet, worn smooth at the edges.

Only the slightest twitch of her enamel-red lips signaled displeasure at his casual reply.

Like other Chinese businessmen, Cong free-lanced for the government and the military. As appeared would be the case with Mei Jin now, he sometimes took direct assignments. Otherwise he evaluated what might be needed, skimmed data from overseas, and offered the results to the Chinese department or government-owned company who would pay the most. Usually they bought the information.

"Cong, when you studied in the United States, we ascertained you were more mature than many of your classmates. While they admired the Silicon Valley innovators, you remembered the great strengths of the Chinese people."

They had monitored him more than he had realized. He gave his familiar summary of Chinese competitive advantage. "Our people can reverse-engineer any item from a cell phone to Italian shoes and set up a manufacturing factory in a week. Good businessmen control and source all inputs locally, even as small a feature as ballpoint pen tips. We offer the items for half the original price and can still obtain a forty percent markup."

Another twitch of her lips, but this one matched a smile in her eyes. "Mathematics, guided learning, and imitation, which earned you admission to Tsinghua and success in the US, are indeed your strengths, Comrade Li."

Cong inclined his head, appreciating the praise but wary of what Jin intended. "Thank you. I am honored by both your words and your presence."

"Tell me what you have been doing." Her mouth barely moved as she spoke. Cong surmised she'd adopted this mannerism to hide her teeth, which were an unappealing gray color.

He was reluctant to describe to her his group's projects. Such information was important for later trading. His mind raced to think of a simple example. "We have an agreement with several Chinese energy companies. They provide us low-value research which we publish online. Anyone who accesses the research downloads a back door allowing my group to see where the research is sent, how it is applied, and whether technology breakthroughs are made. We get data on a few new users each day."

Mei Jin was impassive. "A waste of time for so little result. Your company is one of tens of thousands in China, Russia, and Eastern Europe. Yet no one has yet bettered the Russians' capture of 1.2 billion addresses and passwords."

"Yes, Comrade Jin." Her reference to the vast number of his competitors was a reminder of her power. "We are humbly pleased to have accessed internal codes of search companies, computer security firms, military sites, electric utilities, and others."

As one example, his group had embedded in instrumentation control at TriCoast's San Francisco refinery. So far their methods remained undetected. He had directed a series of incidents as proof of concept. Cong was now considering several offers for the TriCoast data and his ability to disrupt its San Francisco refinery operations at will. He would not tell Mei Jin about the refinery intrusion because she would insist on getting the information while paying as little as possible. Due to her well-connected government bosses, she could enforce any request. He considered other news he might offer. "Last night I tuned into Stanford's computer science MOOC, massive open online course. Since the curriculum is free, I did not have to hack in."

Mei Jin turned toward him to listen. *Stanford* was golden in China.

"However, since the MOOC is less exclusive it is now less useful. Two hundred thousand other people around the world started the course with me. Perhaps twenty thousand will finish and two hundred will take the certificate test."

"Will you?"

"Perhaps, but I find the MOOC of interest primarily for its data about my classmates."

He watched her face as he told her how much he liked the pictures of the Stanford campus in each lecture because in them, the air was clear. The confession could get him in trouble.

Coal had made China one of the world's largest economies. However, since its byproduct of soot and smog was not filtered out, unlike elsewhere, high concentrations of airborne coal and ash particulates often closed roads and airports. They also injured and killed people—especially the very old and the very young. It was a reason, along with land acquisition, labor disputes, and forced demolitions, behind the hundreds of protests each day. Although the Chinese government denied the finding, officials were aware of science showing China's coal use had also worsened air quality in the western United States.

Addressing the subject of coal pollution, however, was forbidden.

So he startled when Mei Jin said, "Comrade Li, clean air is one of the subjects I, rather than you, should speak about."

How long a jail sentence had his frankness earned him? Could he regain Mei Jin's trust?

"China requires a much larger supply of clean-burning natural gas," Cong said. "Comrade Jin, perhaps there is a method by which we could get the United States to sell more natural gas to our country."

"But China's biggest long-term natural gas supply contract, for billions of *kuài* and trillions of cubic meters of gas, is with Russia," Mei Jin said, still speaking with her lips barely moving. "My comrades would like you to work with the Russians."

She stood and motioned him forward, whispering with sour breath, "We will walk now."

Cong Li suspected his office was bugged but he had never found a listening device. Mei Jin's request to converse outside confirmed he should continue looking.

They lit cigarettes and smoked, then walked out of the building.

Mei Jin had expressed displeasure at his frankness about clean air in the mildest way. However, Cong feared this manner the most, for it could mean the most severe punishment. The punishment had two parts: his parents, who had already been identified, would be watched for a thousand tiny infractions, any of which could merit a prison sentence. His own punishment would be a different kind of prison—he would be "disappeared," to later show up on television confessing corruption and asking for forgiveness. His projects would be given to another company, his own company would be disbanded, and he would be subject to the same Internet limitations of his countrymen. He might never see his wife again.

But to Cong's quiet relief, Mei Jin had two proposals. In the end, Cong would accept them both.

"In the first proposal, you are to continue to *research* energy companies for two objectives."

At his surprised look, she said, "You have no secrets from us, nor should you try to keep any. You are to get offshore Gulf of Mexico bidding programs to assist Chinese companies so our companies can use them for bidding or sell them if we are not allowed to bid. Your targets are to include BP, Shell, ExxonMobil, TriCoast, ConocoPhillips, and smaller companies. Indeed, the smaller the company the better."

"My group is capable of this and I am honored you have made the request of us," he replied. Cong could embed further by obtaining company directories with as many addresses as possible—both home and corporate. Often companies allowed employees to use their own phones and computers, which were less secure. He would bring together his programmers and give them their instructions. Where security software was installed, his company would find a way through. Like they had with TriCoast, they would get in, watch, and collect a daily data drip.

"You are also to target these companies' refineries," Jin said. "Yes, we are aware of your successful intrusion into TriCoast's San Francisco refinery. Our offer is fifty thousand *kuài*."

Who had told Mei Jin? Cong realized one of his group must have been required to inform Jin or her superiors at the Fourth Department. "Comrade Jin, your bid is far less than such ability is worth. We have been offered a hundred times as much by others."

"Comrade Li, you do not understand. You are not allowed to accept other offers. You should not have solicited them. And I do not need to remind you, I am certain, of the alternative."

No, she did not have to remind him. He could provide her the software or he could refuse. If he refused, they would take it and he would go to jail. His family would be targeted.

They reached the end of the block and turned north.

Mei Jin's second proposal was different from anything Cong had done before.

"You will be working with a Russian. With full knowledge of the Fourth Department, you will be paid by the Russians. The project is a path that binds us closer to Russia," Mei Jin explained.

"What will I be doing?"

Jin looked sideways at him, her face still unreadable. "The project will be to interfere with US and Norwegian ships and non-Russian suppliers sending natural gas to Europe."

"Pardon, Comrade Jin, how does this benefit China?"

"Think. Then tell me. If you do not understand, then perhaps I have made a mistake by choosing you and your group for this work. If so, I will take up with my superiors the need to find others."

Cong's thoughts galloped. *Yes.* "China benefits because if Norway and the US cannot sell natural gas to Europe, they will have to sell more gas, and even more cheaply, to China. Our country continues to need and want the gas to power the country as we switch further away from coal. The Russians benefit by continuing to own the European gas market without interference from other suppliers."

"To use American slang like what you must have encountered, you will be the brains and the Russian will be the muscle."

Cong understood but pretended he did not. He knew Jin hated the capitalist contamination she needed from him. "Explain what you mean, Comrade Jin."

"Comrade Cong, this new group will be separate from your company." Mei Jin flicked her cigarette onto the sidewalk and crushed it with her foot. "In addition to the Russian, the other people who join will also be from other countries."

Cong hid his fear as he realized the characters and cultures of the other team members—if the team was even real and not just a Fourth Department snare—were unknown and therefore unreliable. Worse, Mei Jin had outlined a massive scope and responsibility for this unreliable team he was to head.

Cong was trapped.

Mei Jin had assigned him a deadly Second Law Project, named for the thermodynamics rule that all isolated systems degenerate to chaos.

While Second Law Projects could bring enough wealth and safety for three lifetimes, they were often suicidal for all involved.

CHAPTER 3

Lynn pulled on athletic clothes at 6:30 AM and thought about the day ahead. Reese had arranged a morning run with a Stanford professor he knew, saying the professor could recommend the best cybersecurity firms.

A former Navy pilot, Reese had turned around three other refineries. Lynn had called him a few years ago when TriCoast's board of directors approved acquiring a second Houston refinery. She'd counted herself lucky she'd been able to hire him as a troubleshooter, and he had headed the refinery until she found a permanent manager. Reese continued at TriCoast as an interim manager and problem-solver even though, to Lynn's boss's chagrin, he wasn't a TriCoast lifer.

West across the interstate, the vista of pleasant Santa Cruz Mountains mocked her despair. She wondered what she or Reese Spencer or Curtis Zhang or anyone else at the refinery could have done to prevent yesterday's deaths. *All we can do now is stop any more.*

She began the run from the hotel a few miles to the fenced-in entrance. *The Dish* was shorthand for a hilly running path near campus looping through almost four miles of scrub, including a jog near its eponymous radio telescope. As she ran, she remembered the heartbreaking end to the prior day.

After getting emergency contacts for Shirley and the two contractors, Lynn, Juan, and Zhang each went to a home, gave the grim news to spouses, and took them to the burn hospital where the victims were being treated. Lynn drove Shirley's wife, stopping several times so the petite woman could lean out of the car and throw up.

"How could you let this happen to her?" the woman sobbed. "She's everything to me."

"She tried to save two other people. She's a hero," Lynn said.

"I don't care. I just want *Shirley* to live," the woman cried. "We've only been married a few months."

In the hospital's waiting area, one member per family was allowed into the ICU. Each came out crying.

Lynn slipped away to call Mike Emerson, TriCoast's CEO and her boss, then resumed waiting with Zhang, Juan, and Reese. They prepared and sent a short text about the accident to everyone at the San Francisco refinery.

Lynn and Reese had a friendship beyond one of colleagues working for the same company. Although he was much older, Lynn had been acquainted with and liked him for over twenty years, ever since she'd been a penniless engineering student on scholarship living in New Orleans with flying cockroaches. Reese had been her college-appointed mentor, old enough that he'd known Lynn's father. His hair still bristled at the same short length as it had when she'd met him.

When the ambulances had rolled in, the best burn doctors and nurses in San Francisco had rushed to sedate and intubate the three victims, starting them on morphine drips for their excruciating pain. Each was wheeled into the ICU for further evaluation and treatment.

But their burns were too extensive. The smoke and heat inhalation damage to their lungs was too severe. Shirley and the two men she'd tried to save slipped into comas.

Doctors came out of the ICU and beckoned to the petite woman and the other two wives.

Meeting with them one-on-one, the doctors explained that despite the victims' health and young ages, with the smoke inhalation and burns over seventy percent of their bodies, they would not survive. In fact, they were already brain dead.

The doctors asked each wife for permission to take her spouse off life support. The women's cries reverberated from behind closed doors, through the hallways, and into the ICU waiting room. The horrible, difficult finality came when doctors asked the women if they were willing to donate their spouses' organs.

All of the family members were ushered into the victims' rooms to be with them when life support was removed.

Lynn, Zhang, Juan, and Reese kept vigil in the ICU waiting room. Lynn and Zhang wiped away tears. Juan sat, grim-faced. Reese knotted and unknotted a handkerchief.

When the families left later, some accepted hugs from the four. Others glared. More than one warned of lawsuits.

Shirley Watson's wife was the last to go. Lynn reached for her, hoping the woman would accept a hug. She did.

"She was so brave. So strong," Lynn murmured.

The petite woman shuddered with a sob. "I can't believe she's dead! I can't!"

"May I accompany you home, or is there someone who can stay with you?"

The woman looked at her. "Our families were never chill about our relationship, even after we married. But maybe my sister … …"

Once the petite woman arranged for her sister to stay with her, Lynn walked her to a car waiting just beyond the oversized glass doors of the burn hospital. The doors wheezed open automatically, ready for more gurneys.

"I'm so sorry," Lynn said.

The woman leaned against Lynn and sobbed. "Find out what happened. Find out why Shirley's dead."

Already breathless from remembering those terrible hours, Lynn arrived at the entrance to the Dish path and found Reese parked nearby. In answer to her question he said, "I'm in decent shape for an old guy, but I'm not joining you on the run. You looked at Frank's bio?"

Lynn nodded. Frank Chin was a computer science professor with a long list of students who'd started Bay-area companies. He sat on the boards of several.

"You know cool people," Lynn said.

"I do." Reese's face broke into a smile. "And a heads-up Frank will tell you using the Stanford Linear Accelerator or anything else on campus to research our problem is verboten. Place is green energy only and the university gets more than half its electricity from solar power. But all we want is a name or two of good cyber-security firms."

An Asian man in a dark blue tracksuit arrived a few minutes after Reese left. "Lynn Dayton?"

Lynn nodded. "Dr. Chin?"

"Call me Frank. I was concerned I would be late," Frank said. "One of my undergraduate advisees was ticketed in the spring for BUI and I was up last night texting with her about the charge."

"DUI?"

"BUI. Biking under the influence."

Lynn laughed.

Frank looked at her. "If you rode a bicycle, you'd understand why BUI is dangerous. Bad enough the students think laws of physics don't apply to them. They all ride without helmets. Anyway, woman's a brilliant coder. When Zuckerberg visited our intro computer science class, she was one of the few who impressed him."

Lynn and Frank started running. The path was jammed with dozens of other runners and walkers in groups of two and three. As they settled into a comfortable pace Lynn said, "Dr. Chin . . .

Frank . . . I believe Reese mentioned our interest in cybersecurity and in battery tech."

"Who are you using now for cybersecurity?"

When she told him, he shook his head. "You want ShireSafe, or Firefight. The one I like best is KS."

"KS?"

"The initials of the founder: Kanak Singh." They shortened their strides to avoid stepping on dazed—or fearless—black squirrels sitting motionless in the path.

Chin continued. "His company is very good, intuitive, plenty of AI in place. He has an office in Palo Alto and another in San Francisco."

"We'll call him. Can you put in a word for us?" Lynn asked.

He nodded and they slowed to climb a hill.

"And we have one of our brightest people we want to send your way to learn about battery technology," Lynn said. To her own ears, she sounded abrupt but Chin seemed to appreciate directness.

"Your company is an oil company. You don't even have a solar research lab. I can't help you except to send you our published carbon capture research, which is the only subject I teach related to hydrocarbon energy."

"We're interested in all forms of energy."

"You want to dominate other areas?"

Lynn took an extra-deep breath of exasperation. "No, jeez. Of course not. We want to understand them. One of our highest-potential people, Dena Tarleton, will be working on battery storage."

"I can't conduct a class for one. How can she help *me*?" Frank had increased his pace as they topped a rise in the path. The sun angled higher. More squirrels crossed in front of them, noses raised inquisitively.

"We want to know what works, what's available, efficiencies, cost, the best technology," Lynn said.

"You're from Texas." It was a statement, not a question. "Texas has wind and solar farms and its own intrastate electric grid. We have a SLAC-Stanford program looking at grid stability for the two other giant US grids as they bring on solar and wind sources. Everything works at the same frequency and the grid operators want to avoid surges or drops in power. Maybe Dena can give us insight into the Texas grid."

Lynn wiped away sweat. "Yes."

When they reached the gate where they'd started, Chin shook Lynn's hand. "You may put Dena in touch with me. I will answer her questions and she can supply me analytics on the Texas grid. You should also expect a funding proposal from me."

"Of course."

Chin walked away toward campus just before Reese arrived. "How was your talk?"

"He's dubious, but he's in on battery tech if we send Dena his way. And the security firm he likes best is KS, named for its owner, Kanak Singh. Kanak will be expecting us to text for a meeting."

Later, in a parking garage near the KS office, Lynn and Reese shook hands with Curtis Zhang and Juan Rojas, who'd driven southeast from the refinery to Palo Alto. Both still looked as drained as Lynn felt from the loss of Shirley and the two men. They crossed the street and entered a tech incubator warehouse. At clusters of desks and computers, the hum of new, growing companies was palpable.

A floppy-haired, twenty-something who looked like all the others in the room stood to greet them, nodding at Zhang. "I'm Kanak Singh. We're out of this space next week and into a bigger and more secure office we're subletting from ShireSafe. I reserved the conference room."

Eyes looked up from screens as the group made their way across the warehouse. Kanak waved them into a small room whose space was taken up by a table and six chairs. He closed the door and said, "There's an irony about the openness of this space since we're a security company. We're looking forward to fixing that with our move."

The room was so small they were knee-to-knee around the table.

"Thank you for having us," Zhang said.

"We prioritize all recommendations from Frank Chin. He's brilliant. Now, I can't give you any takeaways—no paper, no flash drives." Kanak's tone was relaxed and low, as if little excited or distressed him. His was the calm demeanor for which Lynn had hoped. "We'll give you background on security. Frank Chin tells us you have already consulted with one company. Whom?"

Curtis Zhang provided the name.

Kanak said, "They're not bad, but they're not as experienced as we are. Frank alluded to your situation. Tell me more."

Zhang gave a few seconds of California oil history. In the mid-1800s, Californians had seen natural oil and asphalt seeps in Santa Clara, San Mateo, Marin, Santa Cruz, and other counties. Yale chemist Benjamin Silliman pronounced them commercial. To lift and process the asphalt, and soon the oil, dense forests of pump jacks and refineries sprouted in the late 1800s and early 1900s.

"You can still see the pump jacks in Bakersfield and on Los Angeles hilltops," Kanak agreed.

Even with little drilling in the twenty-first century California remained a big oil producer, Zhang explained. Heavy, sour crudes carried the names of the places they'd been discovered: Kern River, Torrance, Huntington Beach, Wilmington, Long Beach, and Beverly Hills. Later, oil discovered in Alaska and Latin America was also shipped to California refineries to fuel California cars, trucks, and airplanes.

Then Lynn spoke and Kanak made notes. "We have five refineries in four states. We just sold a sixth. Overall, TriCoast generates about fifty billion dollars a year in revenue, depending on oil, natural gas, and gasoline prices. No surprise our refineries are targeted nonstop by a variety of outsiders—they're large concentrations of infrastructure and millions of barrels of oil, pure energy designed to combust and burn."

Lynn nodded at Zhang, who explained further, "We run about a hundred and fifty thousand barrels a day of crude oil at our San Francisco Bay refinery. Used to be all California crude from the San Joaquin Valley and Los Angeles that we pipelined in. Then we added Alaskan and Middle Eastern crude by ship. Now we also get some crude in from Canada, North Dakota and Wyoming. We make CARB gasoline, a big chunk of what's used in the Bay area," Zhang said. He finished with a bitter remark. "Refineries are places for masochists. The state punishes us when we're successful—they don't want us to expand—and punishes us when we're unsuccessful—if one of our units goes down and there's not enough gasoline or diesel."

Kanak looked up in surprise at Zhang' angry tone.

Lynn explained, "You have to realize we're mourning the three people we lost yesterday."

"I'm so sorry," Kanak said.

"We always want our refineries up and running," Lynn said.

"What we're seeing are bumps in our operation," Zhang added. "Like the systems are being probed. But no one can find the damn source. We can't tell if the problem is the alarm software, the instrument control software, or something else. Little anomalies show up at random times. We'll see a bump or pressure release when we haven't made any changes to our temperatures, crude mix, or pressures in any of our vessels."

"Just the one refinery?" Kanak asked.

"So far just the California refinery in the TriCoast system. Our refineries elsewhere aren't experiencing this. But other California refineries have had problems, too," Lynn said.

"I'll give you my boilerplate," Kanak said. "What I tell everyone first is, don't expect to prevent an attack, no matter what system you're using. Start by assuming you've been breached. The only question is whether or not you're aware of the intrusion."

Juan nodded. "The statistic I've seen is three-fourths of oil and natural gas companies suffered at least one successful cyber-attack in the last year."

"There are viruses and attacks directed at companies such as yours. US energy companies are targeted at least as often as banks. AnonGhost attacked international energy companies to protest the use of US currency in oil trades. The OpPetrol and Shamoon viruses were directed at energy infrastructure, like pipelines."

Lynn felt a chill in her gut. *Nothing announced, only silent attacks.*

"Attackers used to "spray and pray:" send out a generic virus across the network and hope it penetrated several places. But now intrusions are precise. The attacker studies a company and designs a specific attack," Kanak explained.

"We've outlined our problems at the refinery. Will you assist us?" Lynn asked.

"Let's talk about what I see from what you've told me," Kanak said. "First, I did some research before our meeting. I agree with you this is deliberate. And the pattern you're describing is neither random nor tied to normal equipment aging or maintenance."

"What do you mean, not random?" Zhang said. "Sure seems so to me."

"These incidents are occurring during your day shift hours and at the San Francisco refinery. Upsets are occurring on certain control systems and equipment. The incidents are infrastructure-focused, not financially-focused. And no one has contacted you claiming responsibility or asking for a ransom payment."

Juan shook his head. "Kanak, 'incident' is the wrong word to describe a disaster resulting in the deaths of three people. And you're still not explaining enough of a pattern."

"On the contrary, what I've expressed are important parameters because they limit the problem."

"But who? And how do we stop it? That's all that matters," Lynn said.

"You've nailed the approach," Kanak replied. "Once you have *who* you have an idea about motive. Who benefits by being able to shut down part or all of your refinery at will? While I won't rule out anyone, this is more likely a state actor or someone somehow connected to one, not a free-lancer. I doubt you're facing an Eastern European or Nigerian trying to grab money through credit cards or ID theft. My company would start by determining every individual and organization with physical or electronic access to your systems."

"We could be talking about hundreds, thousands-" Zhang said.

Lynn interrupted, "All the more reason to start now. I assume you can? You have a plan-of-work contract? What kind of budget are we looking at?"

Kanak leaned forward. "Yes, we're booked but we always are. I'll shoot you our standard verbiage. I can carve out resources to start right away." He named a cost four times what Lynn had expected to pay.

Juan, Zhang, and Reese looked at Lynn for her decision. She said, "I can't lose any more people to a fucking computer virus, someone playing footsie with our systems, or whatever the hell this is. Let's roll."

CHAPTER 4

BEIJING

Displaced villagers protested outside of Cong's building. He stopped a few times to stare at them, surprised at their naiveté and their willingness to violate *Zhongyong*, the Confucian doctrine of the mean which valued equilibrium, moderation, and avoiding excess—especially emotional excess—above all.

He hoped to emulate the successes of the older generation: start a business, make money, emigrate to the US or Canada. He remembered what his wife had said after she learned her visa had been approved. She was packing a single suitcase with her clothes of richest reds and yellows. "I have missed Rochester. I worry about leaving you. But husband, I am excited to breathe the clean air of the US again." If all went as promised, she would still be in the United States when the time arrived to deliver their child.

Here the coal dust sickened everyone, young children and grandparents most of all. Clean air was an advantage above all others Cong wanted for his baby-to-be.

His group hung out in Garage Café in the Zhongguancun tech district after hours and preferred bloodless computer work to protests. Although the Chinese internet firewall was high and deep, with implicit approval—never explicit—he and his company circumvented barriers using a virtual private network, or VPN. His company's hacking expertise was extensive: as he'd told Mei Jin, they'd broken into and embedded in the information architecture of military sites, federal agencies, electric utilities, software companies, retailers, computer security firms, and even a bank.

In the US one could invest in a business, get a visa, and success wouldn't trigger intrusive questions. By contrast, the exact shortcuts necessary to succeed in China became the shortcuts by which one could later be accused and imprisoned.

So Cong was both glad and wary when Comrade Mei again appeared in his office. She sat on his desk and leaned in close to him, smelling of rancid cooking oil and the rot in her mouth.

He pulled away from her, already exhausted at having to appear attentive as she moved even closer to him with her unpleasant smell and abusive, hard-edged requests.

"I have come from the ten-year planning session. There is even more urgency for your work." She licked her gray teeth. "As the biggest energy user in the world, our need for all energy sources is enormous. But oil reserves and production from our own national companies is reduced. The corrupt executives who are the cause of this embarrassment will be dealt with."

"Yes, Comrade Jin. My company has focused on your first request for US company and commodity data," Cong said. And if she didn't need it, the data would be salable to one or more Chinese oil companies. But he did not say so aloud.

Comrade Jin got up from the chair. "Come here." Together they looked at the protestors outside. She turned to him and snapped, her breath close and foul. "Foolish cretins. You would never betray us by showing pictures of these protestors to others. Or sharing our secrets outside of the country. I can trust you?"

"Yes."

"Comrade Cong, for our plans we also need a man with both Islamist and oil shipping connections. We have developed several such contacts in South Sudan through our national companies' work there. You will call one."

Despite US financial aid in separating Sudan from South Sudan, China had become the true beneficiary of the changed geopolitics. Among the million Chinese in Africa, thousands sought fortunes in South Sudan. China encouraged the resettlement and its own trade with the region by providing weaponry and money for roads, schools, hospitals, and dams—both in Juba and throughout the country. China also deployed soldiers to United Nations peacekeeping forces to help guard the oilfields and Chinese workers. Not a coincidence, China bought as much as eighty-five percent of South Sudan's oil exports.

"We find South Sudan is eager to do whatever is necessary to assist the sale of several million dollars a day of its light crude to us. Such crude can no longer be sold to the Americans since they have billions of barrels of their own."

"There are rumors of great unrest in South Sudan," Cong said.

Mei Jin stared at him without speaking. Unfiltered world news was off-limits to ordinary Chinese.

He shrugged, worried at her reaction. "Probably untrue."

"Perhaps your sources are better than mine. Perhaps you don't need my help."

"I do need your assistance. Are you acquainted with such a person as the one you described?"

Mei Jin hesitated, then wrote a name and number and handed the paper to him. "Matak Abdullah is a human resource recruiter in South Sudan. He speaks English. Call him now. Now!"

She spit on his carpet. As she left, she closed the door with a loud bang.

Cong considered the five-hour time difference between Beijing and Juba and judged Matak was awake. This was all official business, so Cong didn't hesitate to use the cell phone Comrade Mei had given him. She would want a record of the communication.

"I am speaking to Matak Abdullah?"

"Yes sir, you are."

"I am Cong Li. I am calling from Beijing. A mutual friend suggested you would be able to hire men for a project for me."

"Yes, yes."

Did Matak already know the project? Had Comrade Mei already told him before even coming to his office? "You have many friends in the Philippines with special talents."

"I do, I do."

Cong preferred to stay calm, but the man's repetitiousness was annoying. "I am calling you because I understand you have performed well for us in the past. I expect similar expertise this time."

"Yes, once I have your money, yes."

"You must find for us two *believers* who are ready to achieve their life's mission. Philippine seamen who are working together on an oil tanker bound for the southern United States. On a VLCC."

Matak's voice became slower, more deliberate. "There are dozens of such men."

"They are to be paid the going rate for their sacrifice. For the honor of doing this thing."

"Yes."

"And second, you must make and get a bomb aboard the tanker. One triggered by a cell phone call circuit detonator with backup detonator triggered by GPS coordinates. There will be no payment until the bomb is aboard."

"This will require a much higher price because this is a much more difficult project than I had been led to expect."

Cong let his patience slip. "Who has talked to you before me?"

"I cannot tell you. They would kill me."

"Comrade Mei Jin?"

Cong's question was met with silence, so he said, "I will confirm the increase in payment with Comrade Jin. I will make the initial payment. Please find and contract the seamen."

Cong sat back in his chair. He didn't like Matak's eagerness to please nor dealing with a man about which he knew so little. He could identify the strengths and weaknesses of those who worked for him in his company. But he had no idea if Matak could keep a secret, or find the experienced seamen. Most of all, he was angry at his lack of control over the man: Matak would be reporting every action to Mei Jin. The Second Law project was just starting and it was already stickier and more difficult than he had expected.

In a cramped, noisy apartment on the Philippine island of Mindanao, Liamzon ate the last bite of his mother's chicken adobo he ever expected to taste. There'd be plenty aboard the tanker, but only her recipe had the ideal mix of cloves, peppercorns, vinegar, sweet soda, and garlic. Only she simmered the chicken in soy sauce long enough.

After he wiped his mouth and stood, Liamzon hugged his diminutive mother, a hug he hoped would stay in her memory. Her arms locked around his waist in return.

"*Nanay*, I do not want to leave you. You will be okay?"

She smiled at him. "Yes. I'm proud of you. You have your honest job. Not hiding in the jungle like the crazy men."

He didn't have the heart to tell her he believed the crazy men would be the ones to accomplish a great future for the Philippines. They wouldn't have this argument today. He shouldered his bag, left the apartment, and stepped outside into musty humidity to catch one of the colorful jeepneys to the airport.

Liamzon and his cousin had oil tanker endorsements qualifying them to work as engine room cleaners. Despite armed guards everywhere on Mindanao, they'd reveled in a week of shore leave. Tanker traffic was heavy so they'd had no problems finding work. No curriculum vitae to text or email, no biding their time in Manila waiting for their cell phones to ring in the middle of the night. More time to flirt.

He answered his phone "Allo, Matak."

Matak Abdullah was a South Sudanese to whom they'd been introduced several months ago by the local Abu Sayyaf leader. He was a warm, congenial man who'd paid Liamzon and his cousin twenty thousand pesos each when they were first recruited.

"You are doing well? Your voyages are going well?" Matak asked. After Liamzon and his cousin earned their licenses, Matak Abdullah had helped them pay for seaman's courses in Manila and at the University of Cebu. They earned the STCW-95 certification permitting them to crew on ocean-going ships. Like their countrymen, they were men of the sea. Many worked on cruise liners, but serving people, especially non-believers, was not for him.

"We are. Each day my cousin and I think of you, and thank you," Liamzon said.

"Liamzon."

"Yes."

"Listen to me. You are good engine room cleaners."

"We are, thanks to you."

"Now it is time for the lives of you and your cousin to be greater than those of engine room cleaners."

"We are happy with what we are doing. What more should we do?" Liamzon asked.

"You should pay back what has been spent on you," Matak said.

"What would you have us do?"

"Liamzon, you and your cousin will retaliate for the death of Abu Sayyaf commander Abu Sulaiman."

"Sulaiman. He was a great and courageous leader," Liamzon replied.

"Yes, and he was killed nearby by infidel US soldiers. But are you truly ready?" Matak asked.

"*Inshallah*, I can speak for my cousin. We are."

"Ask him. I will remind you, you are to prepare a suicide video or podcast to be given to your family and posted after your death."

"Perhaps I am not as prepared as I should be," Liamzon said.

"Are you afraid of dying? You do not seem to me a coward," Matak said.

"And I am not." But what they were to do in the name of avenging Sulaiman was breathtaking.

"Liamzon, you will be rewarded with paradise. For your heroic action, your mother is guaranteed to follow you there when she dies."

"My mother is important to me. She is all I have."

"Your mother and your cousin's mother, your aunt, will also be rewarded on earth. Each will be paid four million Philippine pesos."

About eighty thousand US dollars, the payment would provide his mother with the security she needed for the rest of her life. And he would have given it to her with his own life. A life completed with honor for avenging the death of Sulaiman.

"Matak Abdullah, may I consider your request? I want to be sure in my heart I am worthy of such an honor."

"You must tell me your decision by the time you reach Saudi Arabia. And Liamzon, now because I have asked you, understand there is only one answer. Others, except for your cousin, cannot be told our plans."

"I would not tell any others."

"Correct. Nor would you be allowed to."

After a flight from Davao to Manila's Ninoy Aquino International Airport, Liamzon and his cousin settled into the clean, wide seats of the airplane taking them to Bangkok.

"We will be in Ad Dammam soon, in fourteen hours," Liamzon said to his cousin, with a tentative smile.

"Hmm. Yes. You will be ready for all we are to do?" the shorter Filipino asked. His grunting tone matched the sullen expression on his face.

Liamzon reveled in the travel, and was glad to be on the plane with his cousin. Knowing this could be his last, that even greater pleasures might await him in death, made him more attentive to the luxury. "Think, cousin. The shipping company is flying us, ordinary motormen, on Saudi Arabian Airlines."

Despite his normal pessimism, Liamzon's cousin relaxed. "This is a nice plane. Then back to normal life when the crew bus picks us up for the ride to the Ras Tanura docks."

"Matak Abdullah spoke to you also, cousin?"

His cousin looked around to be sure no one else was watching or listening. Then he nodded.

"I told him I wanted this airplane flight to decide. He told you the bomb to avenge Sulaiman would be placed in the engine room? That the bomb is big enough to blow a tanker and any others around us out of the water and kill everyone aboard?"

"Yes."

"And you have already agreed, my cousin?" Liamzon asked.

"Yes."

CHAPTER 5

DALLAS

Lynn's forty-fifth-floor downtown Dallas office was a blue-gray aerie lined with basketball goals of different heights and pock-marked with dozens of invisible corporate land mines. The sun was just starting to rise when, after a red-eye from California, she sat in her office to talk to Mark Shepherd, TriCoast's security chief, along with bulldog-shaped Mike Emerson, TriCoast's CEO and her boss. Mark's shaved head made him appear both vulnerable and tough.

"TriCoast owns oil in a lot of places I don't control. I'm anxious for my people's safety. Barges on the Mississippi, railroad cars in North Dakota, tanks in south Texas, and pipelines," Lynn said.

"You and Mike are about to ask me if you can take ownership of the oil at our refineries, instead of in transit," Mark replied. "The answer is no, unless you want to get involved with fly-by-night folks who may be less safety-conscious than we are."

"But what if a company in North Dakota promises they've stabilized their light crude but they haven't and we experience another Lac-Mégantic?" Lynn asked. A few years earlier an un-manned train full of light North Dakota crude had rolled into the eastern Canadian town of Lac-Mégantic, derailed, and exploded, killing forty-seven people.

"In such cases, the question of who has custody or ownership doesn't matter. Lawyers go after anyone with deep pockets."

"So my best solution is still Dena's group."

Mark nodded.

Fast-rising co-star Dena Tarleton was in the risk management group. As part of her career development, Lynn had asked Frank Chin to help her learn battery technology. "Dena is running operational checks and safety audits of everyone with whom we do business."

"Your coffee looks so good I'm going to step out and get some myself," Mark said. He closed the office door as he left.

Since Lynn had never seen Mark drink coffee, she realized this was his excuse to leave her alone with her boss. She wondered about the subject of Mike's secret discussion with her and ran through her division's safety and financial numbers in her head. *No problems there. Except for the San Francisco refinery.*

"I was hoping to ease into the subject, but I'll get to the point. I'd like to add US natural gas exploration and production to your responsibilities," Mike said.

"You're joking, aren't you?"

He leaned closer. "Just a temporary change."

She put her cup down so she wouldn't spill her own coffee. "You would more than double my workload. If you double my salary, I can consider the possibility."

"That's your only requirement?"

Lynn groaned at her slip. "Three times my base salary plus a fifty percent bonus." *He and the board will never agree.*

Mike nodded and then said, as if he'd read her mind, "I'll get the board to agree."

"Our natural gas reserves are in Canada, Pennsylvania, and Texas. I would need some people to help me with the transition. Maybe I could also reassign Dena from risk management to get a handle on what the gas division needs once she's had her session with Frank Chin on battery technology and electric grids? If," and she held her hand up, "I take the job." Dena was an ambitious woman in her twenties who reminded Lynn of herself but with better clothes and a voice as smooth as an FM announcer's. Lynn thought of her younger sister, Ceil. *Dena's like Ceil would be if Ceil and I shared the same views and Ceil was less prickly.*

"I need your answer in a few days. If you can't add the natural gas division, I'm going to my second choice."

Leaving her no time to reply, Mike got up and opened the office door, motioning Mark back in. No coffee cup.

Lynn laughed at him. "You have to make your stories about drinking coffee more believable."

Mark saluted in agreement.

Lynn stored away the new-job conversation to consider later and turned back to the security chief. "I have your text on defensive training. First of two required sessions at 6 AM tomorrow?"

"You and Mike. Reese. Others. This is your last chance," Mark said. "Everyone else has been through the sequence. You'll meet your new part-time bodyguard there. I've assigned you a male this time, Beau Decatur."

"Part-time?"

"Can't afford full-time. Part-time means when you're out of the country, or somewhere in the US where you could be in danger or are high-profile."

"And does he know about—"

"Yes, we've told him what happened to your last bodyguard. Lucky for you he still agreed to take the job."

Lynn flinched. Her previous bodyguard had been killed while protecting her. But having Decatur around her husband and her step-children could be complicated. "So he won't be with me 24/7?"

"Only the times and places you, he, or I think necessary," Mark said.

She looked at both men. "I've hired Kanak's company to help us with the San Francisco refinery problems but I need an information technology pro assigned to refining full-time. Mike, are you good with that? My budget will cover the cost."

"Yes. Sounds like you need more people with cybersecurity expertise working onsite too," Mike said.

Mark leaned back without relaxing. "IT is always under-staffed but I may have the man for you. An outside guy already working with us. Patrick Boudreaux. Fortunately, Patrick will be there tomorrow morning, too."

Pretty damn convenient, Lynn thought. *But whatever.*

A knock sounded on the door, and Mark opened it to Reese Spencer and a man Lynn had met a few times, Arch Webber. Arch was about the height of a jockey. Lynn had heard his name mentioned as a star player in TriCoast's company soccer league.

"We heard you two were in and wanted to catch you, talk some Louisiana matters," Reese said.

"We're wrapped up for now," Mark asked. Including Reese and Arch in his glance, he said, "See you tomorrow morning. 6 AM."

Bulldog Mike Emerson looked annoyed. He'd told Lynn many times he thought Reese Spencer was too old for TriCoast. "Shouldn't you be somewhere on a golf course, Reese, collecting Social Security?"

Lynn's cheeks burned with impatience. "Damn it, Mike. I hate to put on a show for Arch but Reese is good. He's done well in every job I've given him and he's helping me figure out what kind of glitch just spun out our San Francisco refinery enough to kill three people. Before last week he was backing up Kim Garvey at Marrero as the refinery's operations VP."

Reese shrugged and smiled. "And Marrero is why I thought you two should meet Arch ahead of the next big Gulf of Mexico lease sale. Among his many talents, Arch is our top lease bidding specialist, and he's put together the strategy for the blocks being of-fered. A lot of them are oil-prone and they're in areas that already have offshore pipelines. Even though Marrero has a lot of sources, oil from offshore Gulf of Mexico is always worth our while since it's so nearby."

Like other scientists and engineers at TriCoast, Arch had turned his triple petroleum engineering, statistics, and computer science degrees from Texas A&M into money-making expertise for the company.

Mark turned to Arch and said, "Have you cleared everything with David?"

Arch said, "Yes, and with Dena, who's been assisting him." David Jenkins was TriCoast's sunburned exploration EVP who spent as much time in the field as possible. He was the one whose budget would pay for the tens or hundreds of millions of dollars of lease costs, and then the billions for drilling any blocks they won in the offshore bidding.

Arch winked at them. "Dena's a hell of a soccer player in the TriCoast intramural league. I've wished she was on our team every time we play hers. And I hang out with David whenever I can. Everyone treats him like a pasha since he's got so much TriCoast money to spend."

"Arch, what you're talking about bidding on these leases isn't chicken feed," Mike interjected. "Two hundred million dollars? Wasn't that the last number I heard?"

"We won't win all of them," Arch replied. "But based on the production of the blocks near the ones for sale, I've developed new bid algorithms to give TriCoast a fighting chance against Shell, ExxonMobil, and the others."

"Sounds like an advantage for us," Lynn said. "Is your work secure?"

"Air-gapped on a laptop without an internet connection. I back everything up on company computers with special passwords and security."

Lynn thought of the computer-related headaches that had escalated so horribly to the deaths of three people. "Our biggest concern right now is computer security. Our bid strategy is worth millions to us, and to others. You need to harden your security even further. Some group infiltrated our San Francisco refinery control system and caused such big operational jolts three people wound up dead."

Arch looked anguished. "I heard about Shirley's death and the deaths of the two men she was trying to save. Awful. Of course I can bump up my computer security another few notches. I'll do it."

On the way home from the early-morning discussion to her new husband and step-children, Lynn drove past the East Dallas gingerbread house her father lived in until his death. She and Cy had rushed to hold their wedding last fall in a location her frail father could attend, so they'd married in her father's backyard.

He had died a few weeks later.

His house had been in a gentrifying area near White Rock Lake, a favorite neighborhood for a mix of immigrants and young professionals. Lynn had sold the house, but she still drove through the neighborhood occasionally. *As if I'll find my father here.*

Her own house, the one she had lived in before marrying Cy, was a few blocks away and still on the market with no offers. She drove past it, too, and confirmed the yard had been mowed. The realtor had suggested to Lynn she lower the price, but she'd been unwilling to do so. She turned her car toward north Dallas. She still couldn't think of Cy's house as hers, but she ached to hug Matt and Marika, her step-children. And a hug would be only the beginning with Cy.

Cy had landscaped his house with bald cypress trees, red oaks, crepe myrtles, big-leaf caladiums, and St. Augustine grass. When Lynn parked in the driveway of the mid-century ranch, eight-year-old Marika was in the side yard, climbing the ladder to a zip line attached to the largest branch of a red oak. She grabbed the bar and careened several feet above the lawn, then jumped off at the end. Her face sported peanut butter dimples where she'd apparently pressed half a sandwich against her face.

She hopped over to Lynn on one leg and hugged her waist, leaving peanut butter spots on Lynn's jacket. "Lynn! Lynn! Guess what I did yesterday! I ran into a brick wall!"

Lynn gasped. "Are you okay? What happened?"

"I was running fast and couldn't stop."

"And the wall turned out to be pretty solid, hmm? Did you think maybe you'd go through, like a super-hero?" Lynn sighed at how quickly Matt and Marika learned, and yet how much they had to experience. *Like, crashing into a wall.*

"Yeah. Maybe. But I'm okay."

Cy and Matt met her at the door with enthusiastic hugs.

Three-year-old Matt's big eyes peered up at her. "Cows hurt."

Cy, understanding his son's code, lifted Matt to his shoulders. "He means his calves. We went to the park and someone did a lot of running to keep up with his sister."

Lynn knelt down next to Matt and brushed his dark hair with her hand. "You're too cute."

"Coot," he repeated. She tickled one still-plump baby leg. He grinned at her.

After dinner, games with Marika, and Lego-building with Matt, Lynn motioned Cy aside.

He raised his eyebrows.

She whispered, "Yes later, but right now I need to talk to you. Mike's offered me a new job with even more responsibility." After she explained, she said, "I'd be gone from home more. Can you and the kids handle longer absences?"

"Yes. And if not you, whom? Henry Vandervoost? Do you think he'd do a better job?"

She shook her head. Cy had named her European counterpart, and nemesis.

He put his finger to her lips. "I hate to bring this up but … "

"Since I'm in a good mood now, when am I going to drop the price on my house to get a buyer?" She laughed. "Cy, think of my place as a condo. We could get a babysitter here for the kids and go spend the night there. In fact, why can't we move there? Why do I have to sell my house instead of you selling yours?"

"Lynn, the past is *literally* consuming too much space in your life. We've talked about this. You're fond of your old house, yet you've had someone taking care of it for the last several months. Meanwhile, Marika's school is near this house, *our* house. So is Matt's day-out program. And yes, please believe I'm glad Hermosa has been able to step in and help with Matt and Marika. She took amazing care of your father. You're traveling quite a bit, which I understand, but I'm not in favor of uprooting us and moving several miles away from the schools with which I'm familiar."

"You're ignoring the shops and neighborhoods with which *I'm* familiar?"

He shook his head. "I understand selling your father's place so fast was an emotional wallop, but . . ." He showed her the book he was reading: *The Professor's House* by Willa Cather. "Man can't leave his old house. Splits from his family over the house."

"You see parallels to our situation?"

"This is a seller's market. You could drop the baggage, the responsibility. You've already sold one house." Cy smiled at her.

"But that was my father's," Lynn said, hearing the protest in her own raised voice. "You're talking about my place now. And in the battle of the books, here's what I'm reading." She showed him a copy of *House of Sand And Fog*, by Andre Dubus III.

He nodded. "A grim one, for sure. Guy kills himself and his wife over a San Francisco house. But Lynn, listen to me. The house you're standing in right this moment is yours. You need to let go of the other one, for us. We're your family now."

Too early the next morning, Lynn and Mike met a dozen Tri-Coast employees at an outdoor training facility situated between a city golf course and a cement plant. Mark Shepherd and Patrick

Boudreaux would be leading Lynn, Mike Emerson, Reese Spencer, Arch Webber, Dena Tarleton, and others in an active security briefing. The "active" part they were preparing to learn.

"So you thought if you kept ducking these training sessions we'd forget you?" Mark asked them. "No such luck. But you get the prize for being the last group."

Beau Decatur looked as if he'd been a football linebacker, followed by hard military training. He shook her hand, his own twice the size. "Glad to meet you, Lynn Dayton."

"And I, you. Listen, will you … ?"

" … be covering the husband and kids, too? Not unless all four of you go to Saudi Arabia or Yemen."

She nodded, relieved to keep some privacy for her new family. Another connection flashed in her mind. "You have the same last name as Stephen Decatur, the sea captain who defeated the Barbary pirates for the US in the 1800s. There's a street in New Orleans named for him. Distant relation of yours?"

He shrugged. "Could be."

When she introduced herself to Patrick Boudreaux, he nodded at her, then turned away. *Patrick's an angry man.*

"Some of you have bodyguards," Mark Shepherd looked at Lynn and Mike. "But they may not always be by your side. Remember, a person is not suspicious. What could be suspicious is the activity he or she is engaged in."

"Many of TriCoast's operations are in remote areas. Additional security measures are a matter of course," Patrick added. "These places are difficult to protect. Terror groups are aggressive and unpredictable. Many would like nothing more than to hold you hostage, along with TriCoast and the US. These folks often have access to sophisticated weapons. They use electronic and social media to communicate. They can assemble instantly."

"The day will only get warmer, so let's take five," Mark suggested.

Lynn and Mike handed out sports drinks. When she saw Arch, she said, "Have you been to the Marrero refinery?"

"A few times."

"Can you meet us there? We have a number of topics to cover and I want the managers to hear your thoughts on the next several Gulf of Mexico sales. We're always looking for the best crude sources. Your bid strategy may yield us some good-quality Light Louisiana Sweet."

"I don't want to give away too much of our strategy," Arch said.

"And I don't want you to. Just talk in generalities, so the managers can plan their future crude oil slates. We always want the lowest-priced crude of course, but we get synergies when TriCoast refining can do business with TriCoast E&P."

Reese and Dena joined them. "Remember Arch agreed to ramp up security on the lease bidding programs," Reese said.

Lynn nodded. "Can't be too secure. We could have virus or malware spreading from our San Francisco refinery. Arch, I don't like the idea of backing up your work on the corporate computer system."

"I've been considering the necessary modifications since you asked. I'll make them in the next few days," Arch said.

Lynn shook her head. "Make those security modifications ASAP. Tell me as soon as they're done."

Arch nodded. "Will do." He smiled at Dena and said, "I still want you on my soccer team."

She grinned. "Maybe next season."

They tossed bottles into a garbage can and regrouped around TriCoast's security chief to continue the training.

"How do you spot a weapon?" Mark asked.

"If the clothes hang oddly," someone answered.

Mark nodded. "We're not talking fashion faux pas. You may see the weapon, or its bulges or outline. The person might have a knife or brass knuckles, not just a gun. Look for jacket sag. Often someone will palm a weapon—he or she will run a knife blade up an arm or leg for concealment. Or the person may walk awkwardly, or not bend his knees because he has a gun or knife in his boots or shoes. And then there's the touching. Just like people touch their hair and faces, someone with a concealed weapon will touch or adjust it often."

"Sounds like a lot to look for when I'm just trying to keep myself safe," Lynn said.

"Be observant," Patrick said, staring at her as if his eyes could burn holes. "Always."

Lynn tried not to draw back from Patrick's glare. *What's his problem?*

"We'll start locally, here in Dallas," Mark said. "What do you do if someone pulls a gun on you?"

The answers came with nervous laughs. "Say a prayer … hope your will is drawn up … hand over your wallet … time for martial arts moves."

Patrick drew a gray plastic gun and aimed at Dena's head. Several people gasped.

As if they'd practiced, Mark narrated. "If you don't remember anything else, remember to stay calm. What happens if Dena freaks out?"

Patrick nudged Dena. "Your cue."

Dena started screaming until Mark held up his hand. "What do you think a man with a gun to your head will do?"

"He'll panic. And you can't predict how he'll react," Lynn said.

"Ten points for Team Dayton," Mark replied. "Now, Dena, look him in the eyes."

Dena stared sideways at Patrick.

"What happens now?" Mark asked.

"She's getting a good look at him so she can identify him," Mike Emerson responded.

"Yet if you identify someone by skin, hair, and eye color, you've reduced the number of suspects to just millions of people on the planet. I'll explain in a minute. Why the eye contact?"

"So he sees her as a person?" another man suggested.

"Yes," Mark said. "In most cases, the gun is for leverage."

Patrick pushed the toy against Dena's head and said, "Money."

"Robbery is what you're most likely to face," Mark added.

"How could I not panic if someone has a gun on me? I have to assume he'll shoot," Lynn said.

"If he wanted you dead, you would be. So use those brains and figure out what the guy wants. This one is obvious. He wants your money." Mark handed Dena a red purse.

Dena said, "Ugly. Not my brand. But I can pretend."

"What do you do?" Mark asked her.

Dena threw the purse behind Patrick and ran away from him.

Mark shook his head. "No. Now you've freaked him out. Back, please."

When Dena resumed her place, Mark said, "Let's repeat the scenario."

This time, as she raised her arm to throw, Patrick put the toy gun to her shoulder and said "Bang!"

Mark looked the group. "Simplest is best. Hand over your wallet or your purse. Slowly. Tell the person each step beforehand, and make each move *slowly*."

Dena pantomimed his instructions and said, "I never liked that purse, anyway."

Mark smiled and the others laughed, except for Patrick.

"Okay, now's the time to stare at him. What are you looking for?"

"Height, weight, clothing, eye and skin color."

Mark shook his head. "We get the same description for everyone: 'six-foot, one hundred and seventy pounds, wearing a sweatshirt.' He'll change clothes, like you do. Look for something unusual—scars, marks, or tattoos."

Dena stared at Patrick and winked. "So how did you get the scar on your face?"

Patrick put aside his prop gun and looked at the people gathered around him. He touched a ropy scar beside his ear and said more than he'd said in the last half hour. "Roadside bomb in Afghanistan. Lost five men there, another to suicide once we returned."

The group solemnly dispersed.

Patrick motioned Lynn aside, twenty yards away from everyone else. "Do you know who I am?"

"Patrick Boudreaux, security specialist."

His mouth set in a grim line. "My sister's name used to be Jean-Marie Boudreaux. You knew her as Jean-Marie Taylor." So Patrick Boudreaux was the brother of the woman who had been murdered in Lynn's Houston refinery.

"Oh my God. I'm so sorry." Lynn looked down. *Nothing can bring Jean-Marie back*, she thought for the thousandth time. One of Jean-Marie's killers was dead and the other one was on trial.

Patrick was silent, as if to avoid saying the harsh words that seemed to be at the top of his mind.

"Can you work with me? I'd understand if you couldn't," Lynn said.

"Let's see what evolves. If you or I think I'm slipping and not focusing, I'll be out of here. Let me be frank, Lynn. You were the one running the refinery when Jean-Marie was murdered. Even though you weren't the killer, you were in charge of the man who was. So her death is your fault, too."

Lynn shook her head. "We all thought the world of Jean-Marie."

"And what good did that do?" Patrick asked bitterly. "Bottom line, you screwed up by not investigating the man behind the crude switch scheme fast enough. When my sister started asking questions, he killed her! You should have been faster off the mark."

"Patrick, he tried to kill me, too. Look, I've got a lot of lives at stake here, and in San Francisco. Again, are we going to be able to work together, or should I hire someone else?"

"We'll see, won't we?"

"Not good enough. You need to decide now. If the answer is no, then walk away."

He paused, then nodded and stood his ground. "You're right. The blame for her murder is on the killer and his accomplice. For Christ's sake, my business is spotting safety risks. How could I have missed the signs? Now my own sister is dead. I'm at fault, too."

Lynn shook her head. "It's the fault of Jean-Marie's murderer and his accomplice. Not mine. Not yours."

CHAPTER 6

As EVP of five TriCoast refineries, Lynn required the Marrero refinery near New Orleans to benchmark itself against TriCoast's larger Houston refining complex. Both shut down when hurricanes and floods occurred. The Marrero refinery had closed ahead of Hurricanes Katrina and Isaac, but not everyone evacuated. Some lost their lives when their neighborhoods flooded; most lost their homes. Yet like New Orleans' Ninth Ward, its Lakeview neighborhood, and further away in Galveston and Houston, Marrero had rebuilt.

Reese drove Lynn on the Huey P. Long Bridge across the wide, muddy Mississippi River upriver of the French Quarter. Refinery manager Kim Garvey met them after they cleared the security gate. She and Lynn were similarly dressed in khakis, white shirts, blazers, and steel-toed shoes.

"You've been keeping Reese in line, I hear," Lynn said, referring to Reese's position as Kim's second.

"Quite the reverse. Reese is teaching me everything about running a refinery." Kim nodded at Reese. "Glad to have him here."

Lynn was pleased Reese had been able to back up Kim as refinery manager but worried that either Kim was not learning the position fast enough or she was downplaying her ability. Both would lead to problems. She filed the thought away for a later private discussion with Kim.

Her stomach contracted with anxiety after she was introduced. A speech to two thousand potential oil suppliers had been easier; this audience was more important. She adjusted her clip-on microphone and turned to face four hundred Marrero refinery employees. Kim and Reese stood to one side. The room was large and humid: summer in Louisiana made the ever-present exhalation of nearby marshes even more noticeable. The marshes waited in stillness, like people did, for the arrival of summer hurricanes.

Headhunters were creating a flood of a different kind by bombarding her employees with texts, tweets, and emails. A multibillion-dollar surge in Gulf Coast expansion meant everyone was desperate for the expertise represented by the four hundred people in front of her. No matter what she said, a few would trickle off to other jobs in a week or two. But she didn't want to lose a single one.

"I'm pleased to speak to you today. I want to share what the company's good news means in terms of increased opportunities for you at TriCoast.

"We've completed our integration of what used to be the Centennial Refinery with our major, existing Houston refinery, giving us six hundred thousand barrels per day of crude oil processing there. With your refinery here handling another three hundred thousand barrels per day, TriCoast retains a solid market share of Gulf Coast refining. Our gasoline and diesel exports have tripled and the company's new ethylene cracker just started up.

"What this means for you is new opportunities—opportunities to learn in your current positions, opportunities to take your expertise to other parts of the company, and of course, opportunities to grow and progress with TriCoast, to both expert-level company-wide consultants and to management. The simple fact is, with our growth we have more to manage."

Many in the audience smiled and nodded when she said, "I'm sure many of you have been approached for jobs with other companies, including our competitors. While I can't make guarantees, your long-term future at TriCoast is promising. I also want to remind you of our new-hire referral system. If you recommend a new employee to us and we hire him or her, TriCoast will pay you a minimum bonus of ten thousand dollars, half on hiring and half after the new employee has worked at TriCoast for a year. For some jobs, like welders, the payment is larger. So if you have friends, neighbors, or acquaintances you think might be a good fit for us, get in touch with Kim and her staff and let's get them here."

She concluded and took questions.

Then she motioned to Kim and Reese. "Can't wait for the walkthrough you two promised me," Lynn said. "Okay with my message yesterday about a few people joining us?"

"Sure. I've been working with Reese. Patrick and I are both Coast Guard reserve, so we've crossed paths at the base a few times. Fill me in on the others," Kim said.

They walked to the lobby. "Dena Tarleton is one of our high-profile senior analysts in risk management," Lynn said. "You may see her promoted in a few months. Arch Webber is a federal lease bidding specialist, now working for my colleague, David Jenkins, the man who always muscles in on my budget. Arch is proficient in statistics and game theory, so he winds up heading a number of interesting projects. He's done great work for me on corrosion probabilities and risk minimization."

"Arch Webber and I go back to before I was at TriCoast," Reese explained. "When I worked in New Orleans full-time we used to catch a few beers together and eat soft-shell crabs whenever he was in town. He's a good guy."

"And let me tell you what you may not have heard about Patrick Boudreaux," Lynn said.

"Yeah?" Kim asked.

"Has his own risk management firm. In fact, he and Mark Shepherd have been leading the last round of self-defense training, so I've met him. We expect to hire him, among others, to fix security issues in our San Francisco Bay refinery. A heads-up: he'll ask aggressive questions you may not like."

"Boudreaux. With that name and as a fellow member of the 8ᵗʰ Coast Guard Reserve, he's from around here. I think I've seen him before. I'm sure I have." Kim looked thoughtful.

"Yes. And he's the brother of Jean-Marie Taylor." Jean-Marie had been a New Orleans native to the core, and Lynn pronounced her name as Jean-Marie had. *John-Marie.*

"For real? She was one of my best friends, in or out of the company. I couldn't believe she got killed over there in Houston."

"Boudreaux was quick to tell me he blames me for her death."

"*Cher!*"

"He's also one of the best risk managers and IT jocks in the business according to Mark. So I hope he changes his mind about me," Lynn said.

"You knew Jean-Marie well?" Kim asked.

"Not until we acquired Centennial. She was one of its executives. I was a few years behind her at Tulane."

"Roll, Riptide!" Kim chanted the cheer of a college team locals followed with the same rowdy enthusiasm they showed for the Saints. A Louisiana State alumna, Kim followed with "Geaux Tigers!"

There'd been plenty of evidence of Jean-Marie's brilliance at Tulane's engineering school. Her name was on achievement plaques throughout its hallways. "When I met her at Centennial, she was a good safety and environmental VP."

"You're shaking," Kim observed.

"I'm still angry at the assholes who killed her," Lynn said. *Always will be.*

"I heard you fought one and he fell into a storage tank and drowned. For true?"

"I'll have to wait until the trial of the other man is over to say more."

"Got it," Kim replied.

Dena and Arch joined them. Arch's short stature required him to reach up to shake Kim's hand.

Kim asked, "We don't need golf carts to get around the refinery, do we? You all are okay hoofing it?"

Although the subtropical humidity and mid-afternoon clouds promised rain, no one would admit to wanting a ride, air-conditioned or otherwise.

The front end of the three hundred thousand barrel-per-day refinery was divided into two parts—one to handle sweet, or low-sulfur, crude, and the other for sour, or high-sulfur, crude oil. After distillation and treating, the end products—gasoline, jet fuel, and diesel—from both trains would be the same and would meet the same demanding chemical specifications, interchangeable with products from any other east-of-the-Rockies refinery. The Marrero refinery also exported gasoline and distillates to fuel-hungry Central and South America.

Out of habit, Lynn glanced at the refinery's flares ten stories above them. They burned at their normal height. No operational upsets. *Good.*

Patrick Boudreaux caught up to them just as they passed through the security gate from the office to the acres of refining hardware. When Lynn introduced him to the group, their expressions grew serious. *They don't want another consultant looking over their shoulders.* Dena looked at Patrick as if she were remembering Saturday's drill with the plastic gun.

But Boudreaux had none of the insecure, boisterous arrogance of hired consultants she'd seen many times. Indeed, he appeared leery of showing too much enthusiasm.

"I'll open by saying you guys handled the recent flooding well," Patrick said. He held up his hand. "Yes, you have plenty of experience, but your drills paid off."

"Nobody hurt, no lives lost, not much equipment damage. We were back online as soon as the water receded," Kim said. They walked the road toward one of the massive catalytic cracking drums.

"I'm sure you hear about other refinery accidents. As always, there's more than one factor," Patrick said. "But often, explosions are traced to vaporizing leaks reaching too high a concentration."

"My people walk the pipes and check the vessels each shift," Kim said. "We do another check running material balances around the refinery and each major unit."

"Good. But most accidents happen on start-up or shut-down, just like most airplane accidents happen on takeoff or landing. Same idea, big transition of a complex system," Patrick said.

Dena bent forward to listen.

"You're talking about . . ." Reese nodded at Patrick and he returned the nod.

Before Patrick could explain, Arch said, "Kim, excuse me, but do you have test-to-failure going on?"

"What do you mean?" Lynn asked.

"Maybe I notice because I'm shorter, but so far, every pressure gauge I've seen on this unit is broken." A broken pressure gauge could lead to leaks and even fires and explosions in the high-temperature, high-fuel environment around them.

"What?! You're not a refinery engineer. You must be reading them wrong," Kim said.

"They're broken. I couldn't read them if I wanted to," Arch replied.

The group backtracked and saw indeed that five pressure gauges, each four feet off the ground, had been smashed.

"And there's who's wrecking them!" Arch started running toward two people fifty yards away, just as they slammed wrenches onto another gauge. Pieces broke off and clattered to the ground.

"Goddamn. I *know* them," Kim said. "Let's go!"

Lynn, Kim, and the rest of the group caught up to Arch, ran with him, and confronted the man and the woman with the wrenches.

"Carl, Amy! Stop! What the hell are you doing?" Kim said. "Carl and Amy are with our onsite maintenance contractor," she said to the others.

"Just what you told us to do," Amy answered. "Test to failure for all the pressure gauges in the refinery."

Kim appeared so angry she could barely speak. "I would *never* tell you to do such a test! What the hell are you talking about?"

Carl said, "But you called us last weekend. Or called the company. Gave those instructions. We thought they were kind of strange, but our manager said you said you wanted to get started on the weekend, get the test done quick. See how the refinery withstood a front-line failure."

Lynn and Reese looked suspiciously at Kim.

"That is such incredible bullshit. I never give those kinds of instructions. Did your manager record the call?"

Amy looked chagrined. "I imagine he did. I'm sorry. We thought we were doing what you wanted us to do."

Kim shook her head. "No. No such test. Look, best thing you and Carl can do right now is to leave the premises and stay away until we find out what happened."

Amy and Carl nodded, not speaking, and were soon out of sight past the security gate.

Kim looked at Arch. "I'm glad you spotted the broken pressure gauges." Then her face changed. "Holy hell, had they told you what they'd be doing?"

Arch's ears turned red. "No. Just lucky to be short, I guess."

"We should be glad he did spot them," Lynn said, her mind racing. *Is Kim lying to us?*

Kim wheeled around and yelled at Patrick. "I thought I could trust you since we both did reserve duty together but maybe I don't know you at all. Did you just set us up with this fake-instruction bullshit on my refinery's gauges?"

Patrick took a step back from her and shook his head. Then his expression got darker. "But before you cool off, let's discuss other things you could also be overlooking, if you're like everyone else."

"Time fucking out." Everyone watched and waited as Kim jogged several yards away, stood, and stared at the ground.

Lynn looked at Reese. His raised eyebrows told her they agreed. *Kim needs more training in managing situations like these without losing her cool.*

Expressions grew serious. TriCoast hired the best graduates of the best engineering and business schools, people accustomed to performing well and leading any group of which they were members.

Just as Lynn was preparing to tell Patrick to go ahead and talk, Kim walked back to them. "Sorry folks. I care about the lives of everyone here. I'm going to ask Arch to help me get to the bottom of those crazy instructions."

Patrick took a conciliatory tone but his message was harsh. "Kim, you and I have seen a lot of situations in the reserves. Now, I'm walking in off the street here into your refinery, but your cybersecurity is Swiss cheese. Your docks aren't secured. Your crude sources aren't verified. Neither are your people, especially your lateral hires who don't come right out of school."

"Hang on," Reese started.

Many of my most effective hires, like Reese Spencer, have been laterals. And I sure as hell trust Reese, Lynn thought.

"Excuse me," Patrick said in an annoyed tone of voice that really meant *excuse you.* "I'm not finished. Your coker hasn't been turned around in three years—"

"But the coker hasn't needed a turnaround," Kim interrupted.

"You're paying me for my time. If you interrupt me, you're paying me more," Patrick said.

"So let's hear you earn your money," Lynn replied.

"You're doing business with companies you haven't vetted. You may have currency and bank losses you're not even aware of. Besides what we just saw with the bogus instructions on destroying pressure gauges for a so-called test, you haven't done a top-to-bottom valve bypass check in years. You could have an emergency release and have ten bypass valves not working the way they should. I doubt shift handoffs are being correctly communicated, and you're behind on your operator cross-training."

Reese made notes on a tablet. Kim was red-faced. Lynn wondered if Kim and Patrick would avoid one another at the next Coast Guard reserves meeting.

"And I won't even take bets on this last one, Lynn," Patrick said, turning to her. "No one else in the company understands what your refining group does or your importance."

"Yep," Kim said. "This walkthrough is over."

Lynn heard the strain in Kim's voice and decided she would address her own concerns later. "Arch, Reese, let's go over the security changes."

Later, as they gathered in a conference room, Lynn poured iced tea.

"I've been in New Orleans helping Kim run this refinery just long enough to gain ten pounds," Reese joked.

"Jeez, I gain twelve every time I'm here for a conference," Arch said. "But I have several favorite places. Tell you what. Let me take you to dinner at Jacques-Imo's Café in a few weeks. I'd suggest going tonight but no way can I get a reservation so fast. Maybe a few weeks?"

"New Orleans' cooking is the best!" Lynn said, remembering how even on a student budget she'd been able to eat well, from muffulettas to gumbo, beignets to red beans and rice. "So before I drown in saliva, Arch, tell us what you've done, or will be doing, to secure what's on your computer, including the algorithm and the lease bidding strategy."

He pointed to a small black case. "Physically, I keep the laptop with me most of the time. It's always locked. I'll take the back-up off the corporate system, do a tape back-up instead. I'll get blockers for the USB ports. Get some extra shielding for the cables. Replicate everything onto a second laptop. Change passwords. Re-encrypt the data."

Reese smiled. "We'll buy dinner at Jacques-Imo's."

CHAPTER 7

NEW ORLEANS

Matak Abdullah shivered in a New Orleans hotel room he was unable to warm. He'd made a long flight to New Orleans to stay at this hotel, Arch Webber's hotel. He was much better as a recruiter than as an assistant, but the payment he'd gotten erased his doubts.

His special cell phone rang. He'd received it from Cong Li with instructions to use it only for Cong and a few others.

The number was blocked, no surprise. "Stay close. We're going out tonight in a big group. This could be our opportunity to get Arch Webber's computer and to eliminate him as a witness. You've tested your keycard hacker?"

"I have. It works here. Have you obtained what we will use?" Matak asked.

"I have the poison."

"And I brought a knife, if we need one." Knives were easier to obtain, and to get into US hotels than guns, Matak had learned. And quieter.

"It will be late. I will get you. We will enter his room before he does."

He was anxious to finish the assignment and get back to South Sudan from this cold, cold room.

In New Orleans, the cardinal directions of north, south, east and west describe highways, but the meaningful directions are *upriver* or *downriver*. In a free-flowing manner, the Mississippi River anchors the city. The city in turn pays homage to the river: its streets conform to the river's sinuous turns. The exception is the old French Quarter, Le Vieux Carré. Its streets—Toulouse, St. Peter, Dauphine, and the rest—sit on a Cartesian grid dating from the 1800s, reflecting French origins.

The Quarter's tight streets and dense hotels, bars, restaurants, and residences had been designed for walkers and horse-drawn carts. Today, the same streets trapped automobiles and delivery trucks in regular jams. The area's studied seediness was a place catering to tourists on a drinking holiday. Its residents had seen everything and they made money from its less hardened visitors.

More of the city's culture was revealed in its architecture and streets, including nine streets named for each of the Muses.

But the city's cultural history wasn't on Patrick Boudreaux's mind.

Instead, he thought of his sister, who had been murdered at the Houston refinery she worked at after Lynn Dayton's company bought it. Of all the fucked-up stuff he'd dealt with, losing his sister was by far the worst.

As a risk manager, Coast Guard reservist, computer white hat, and EOD specialist, Patrick Boudreaux had personal contacts within the FBI, CIA, and DOE's office of cybersecurity and energy security. Since returning from Afghanistan, he'd worked many emergencies. Despite the lucrative offers, he'd almost turned down recent TriCoast assignments precisely because he still held Lynn Dayton responsible for his sister's death. The issue of Reese's age also made Patrick question Lynn's hiring skills, though to her credit she stood by Reese, as she did with all her employees. *All except my sister.*

His friend, TriCoast security chief Mark Shepherd, had persuaded him to take on the multi-pronged security training and investigation project. Patrick was finding Lynn as straightforward and warm in person as Mark had described. But so were many psychopaths he'd met.

His sister, Jean-Marie Boudreaux, then Jean-Marie Taylor, had entered the refining business at a time when it was rare for women to do so. Married and divorced soon after, his sister had put in long days and slogged through the inevitable resistance to female supervisors, becoming head of safety and environmental projects for Houston's Centennial Refinery. Last year, she'd been killed by one a fellow executive-turned-mercenary after she started questioning him on the sources of crude oils. Some were crudes he had corruptly substituted for a more expensive kind so he could pocket the difference. The man later fell to his death in a storage tank while attempting to kill Lynn Dayton. His accomplice was now on trial.

But why did Dayton live when my sister—with all her Louisiana survival skills—didn't? Surely Lynn wasn't in league with my sister's killers. But even if not, she must have been negligent.

Lynn owes me, and she's the first to say so. The sympathy in her eyes when she talked about Jean-Marie seemed genuine to him. She had remembered the bar his relatives opened in Houston, NOLA-in-Exile.

Now more lauded for its food, the bar had changed its name to Big Oyster—the aphrodisiac double meaning was intentional—and added branches in Baton Rouge, Lake Charles, Lafayette, and with an enormous celebration, finally in New Orleans' French Quarter. Many offshore platform workers made Big Oyster their first stop when they took their two-week shift leaves. In fact, it was so well-regarded an oilman's hangout Patrick's relatives often broke up fights between rival contractors looking to hire salt-water-weary toolpushers for stints in North Dakota, West Texas, and Pennsylvania.

It didn't escape Patrick's notice that Lynn had urged everyone to meet tonight miles away from the Marrero refinery at Big Oyster.

Lynn hoped an evening with business friends at a bar might smooth the roughness of Patrick's blunt analysis. She also hoped to learn who had called in the bogus, dangerous meter destruction test, since Kim protested she hadn't. Fortunately, Patrick, Kim, and Reese were all willing to join her for at least an hour. With Arch and Dena, Lynn figured on a tab for six. She had just the place.

Lynn's bodyguard had not accompanied her to the refinery but joined the group in the Quarter. Decatur wanted to nix her going—too many people, too unprotected.

Lynn protested. "I have to work; I have to talk, do business. And when I was at Tulane I spent so much time here drunk and sober the street map burned into my memory."

"I still don't like it," Decatur said.

As a compromise, he drove her to the edge of the Quarter and they parked near Canal. When they walked down Bourbon Street toward the Big Oyster, Decatur mentioned he and Patrick Boudreaux had trained at the same gun range. "So I can vouch for the man."

"If you vouch for me to him," Lynn said.

He nodded. "Of course. And I've told the New Orleans Police Department I'm here. Professional courtesy. I've got friends on the force."

The street smelled like yesterday's wash water, a hot, stinky, leftover stew of beer and dirt. Performers in costumes jostled them on the sidewalks. The streets were clogged with college students, drifters, and tourists from across the globe. Music poured over and around them signaling the beginning of dozens of outdoor parties. Lynn smiled. Like the song's lyrics, she *had* missed New Orleans.

As they turned right on St. Peter and neared Jackson Square, more buskers and performers thronged the street. Most had dogs. Every few yards a new voice sang a different tune.

She and Decatur met everyone else at Big Oyster's prime street-side tables, the result of a quiet word between Patrick and his uncle, the owner. The first round was on the house for the same reason.

When she sat down Lynn said, "Looks like nothing's changed. Everyone hangs out in one quadrant of the Quarter. We should call it the One-Sixteenth."

Several people laughed but Arch asked, "What do you mean?"

"The quarter of the Quarter most people see is from Canal to St. Peter, and from Bourbon to Café Du Monde and the Riverwalk."

"For true. The rest, like Dumaine, is more interesting, quieter. Sometimes more dangerous," Kim said.

They debated whether the Mississippi River was at its widest in New Orleans or in St. Louis until several people checked their cell phones.

"Neither. Alton, Illinois," Arch said.

"Only if you don't count the lakes," Reese said, and punched him in the arm.

"Well, here's where you dump the bodies," Kim said.

"What do you mean?" Lynn asked. *How grim.*

"The deepest part of the Mississippi River is right over the levee there, between Governor Nicholls Wharf and Algiers Point. Two hundred feet."

"Hate to dive in," Arch Webber said.

"You'd be in the Gulf of Mexico before you got very deep. The current's strong," Patrick told them.

Kim said, "Yeah, I always like to see how people respond to my invitation to go fishing after I tell them how often people get lost in the bayous outside of town."

They watched the promenade around Jackson Square. People shuffled and stopped, sweated and swore. In the midst of the wet, bald heads, beach hats, and limp hair, a white, lacy parasol floated over in their direction from the Cabildo. The woman holding it looked as if she never allowed the sun to touch her skin. She came to their table and looked quizzically at them. Patrick's uncle hurried over. "May I present Madame Taliesin?"

The woman offered a soft, cool hand to each of them.

Patrick's uncle continued. "Madame Taliesin is one of our neighbors. She paints faces for collectors' dolls. They are exquisite, and the dolls sell for exquisite prices."

"Would you like to join us?" Lynn asked.

When the woman nodded, Patrick's uncle said, "I'll bring you your usual."

They added a chair to the group and as they drank, she told them stories of her decades in the French Quarter, stopping from time to time to powder her pale skin. Her "usual," Lynn noted, was a double Scotch on the rocks.

When Patrick's uncle offered everyone at the table a second round, Patrick said, "He had offshore men in this afternoon who bought drinks for the house for four hours straight. And he always serves a lot of the jazz players late at night after their sets. They're good customers."

At midnight, they crossed the street to Café du Monde. After waiting in line several minutes, they secured tables near the stairway to the Riverwalk. Soon, waiters brought their orders of milk, coffee, and beignets—fried, sugary doughnuts.

Kim, who had decided to stay with them much longer than the single hour she first planned, said, "They don't even ask you how much powdered sugar you want. They just heap it on."

"Reminds me of your approach to safety," Patrick murmured.

"What the hell did you just say? If you've got a criticism, speak up," Kim said.

Arch and Reese shifted in their seats.

"I'm saying, you don't have good control of your refinery, just like you don't have good control of that sugar spoon," Patrick said.

"I've been there three months, you've been there an hour, and you're telling me your eyes are better than mine," Kim said evenly, a fierce look on her face.

Patrick shrugged. "You might say so."

"In all the times I've worked with you, been taught by you, at the Coast Guard reserves at Plaquemines, I've never seen you act like such a jerk."

"Different place, different roles," Patrick said.

Arch spread his hands as if to quiet roiling waters. "Patrick, you're going to give us all indigestion. Can't this wait? Plus, Kim hasn't been running Marrero for very long."

"Inexperience is no excuse," Patrick said. "Reese has been advising Kim, and he *does* have experience."

"What are you saying?" Lynn rubbed her fingers together to get rid of the sticky powdered sugar.

"Times have changed. Security has changed. Kim needs to catch up her refinery, *your* refinery," he said, looking at Lynn. "Where were the safeguards to keep a couple of contractors from smashing pressure gauges, thinking they were following Kim's orders? Why didn't they check the order with someone? Why didn't they think for themselves to figure out something was wrong with the request?"

"We have to trust one another, inside and outside the company," Arch said. "If we don't, it will take twice as long to get anything done."

"But trust can be misplaced. Sometimes, all of you shouldn't be so quick to trust everyone."

"Let's call it a night," Lynn said. *So much for a friendly bonding evening with Patrick Boudreaux.*

New Orleans' late-night warmth was liquid against Arch Webber's skin. He'd drunk twice as much as usual. Just a few of the French Quarter bars, t-shirt shops, and oyster dives had closed. Music continued to flood the streets as if hurricane waters had never been there and would never come again.

The group had finished a last round of drinks at the Big Oyster, courtesy of the tough-talking consultant, Patrick Boudreaux, whose uncle owned the place. Then they'd gone to Café Du Monde. At one point in the evening he'd pulled his wallet from his suit jacket to pay and someone—he didn't remember whom—put it back in his pocket for him after he almost left it on the table. After Patrick's unpleasant criticisms at Café Du Monde, half of the group departed. He'd stayed and placed a second order.

Later, cell phone pictures and French Quarter cameras would show that by two A.M. the TriCoast group had split to their hotels or cars in twos and threes.

At tomorrow's pre-bidding conference he'd exchange stories, talk prospects, and build more of the personal bonds handy for trading oil properties at the next oil and gas exposition in Houston, Pittsburgh, London, or Dubai.

It was humid as hell. Webber leaned against an elevator wall while it climbed twelve floors. Why'd he asked for a room so far up? The elevator was spinning and he held his breath. *Let me make it to my room.*

The women in the TriCoast group were colleagues and thus off-limits. The Quarter held no other girls to score—at least not ones who wouldn't cost him several hundred dollars or have some disease, or really be a man in drag, or be in the midst of a sex change one direction or the other.

At the door to his room—was it 1416?—he fumbled through his wallet for his card key. He banged his head on the door, then slumped against it when he couldn't find the card. He looked through everything again. He didn't want to go back downstairs for a new card, not when he was feeling so sick.

To his surprise, the door eased open. Not questioning his luck—these rooms were never unlocked but what the hell—he slipped in and headed for the bathroom.

By the time he came out, he felt better but still dizzy.

A woman—or was it a man?—with a white parasol stepped from behind the blackout drapes. Arch didn't see the other person hidden in the drapes.

Webber squinted. "Shit. You scared me. Aren't you … "

"Nothing to fear. Yes, Madame Taliesin."

Webber squinted again. "No. Didn' I see you before with …." but his brain was too fogged to complete the sentence. "How'd you get in?"

"Same way I always do," the familiar-looking stranger said, holding up Webber's hotel card key. "You gave this to me."

Had he? Webber couldn't remember. The hair on his neck prickled when Madame Taliesin said, "A nightcap?"

He slumped into a chair at the small desk. Arch shook his head but couldn't clear it. Madame Taliesin turned and added water to a glass. Was there something else in the glass? He couldn't see. Too dim.

Another, much deeper, voice, sounded behind him. "Yes, you want a nightcap."

When Arch turned his head to see who had spoken, two rough hands clamped around his ears and turned his face back to the front. The fingers on the hands, the only thing he could see, were dark brown.

"Your drink," said the woman, putting what looked like a glass of water in front of him.

"What do you want?" Arch asked, putting the glass to his lips, pretending to sip and setting down the glass. He could see his phone, but it was too far away to reach.

"Your passwords," said the voice behind him.

"I'm too drunk to remember them," he said, which had the merit of being true. He flinched when one hand moved from the side of his head and brought a long knife to his throat.

"Just start your computer. I'm sure they will come to you," said the person who looked like Madame Taliesin. The person's voice sounded familiar, but everything from the last few hours ran together.

Sure enough, when he turned on his laptop, muscle memory took over and his fingers typed the passwords.

"Say it now. Slowly," the man with the knife commanded.

"F-O-R-T-U-N-A-&-8-8," Arch said, feeling the man's knife on his throat at each syllable. He spelled out the other passwords as he delved through various layers of encryption. It would be easy enough to reset them later.

Silence overtook the room as Madame Taliesin stared at the screen. *Something's wrong with her looks*, Arch thought. *Like someone in drag pretending to be her.*

TriCoast's offshore bidding software popped up on his screen. Madame Taliesin nodded.

"So you have what you need. Take the computer. Let me go. I'll pretend I never saw you," Arch hated the pleading tone in his voice. He had no leverage except their pity.

When Madame Taliesin unplugged the computer and put it in its case, Arch's hopes flared. But the knife hadn't moved from his throat.

"He can go?" the voice behind Arch asked.

"No," Madame Taliesin said.

Turning to him, Taliesin said, "Arch, your choice is simple. The knife or the drink. I understand the knife is painful, especially if our friend here drags out the killing as he likes to do. If I were you, I'd finish the drink."

Maybe it's only water. They'll leave and I can call 9-1-1. I can drink real water to flush it out. The knife was held to his throat as he drank. *Maybe it is water.* He couldn't taste or smell anything else.

Suddenly, he felt excruciating pain in his legs and arms. Every last nerve in his body was on fire. He stomach clenched and he vomited. He looked at Madame Taliesin. "You lied about the pain!"

"Hmm. So I did."

Arch curled into a ball trying to ease the pain. Pain everywhere in his body. *Jesus God, just let me die.*

Within a few moments, his heart stopped and his wish was granted.

Nodding his head, Matak Abdullah said to Taliesin, "This computer will be most valuable. I will tell the others you have passed my test to join our Second Law group and share in its riches."

"Thank you." In a voice even Matak found chilling, the person dressed like Madame Taliesin continued, "there are only a few things in this company I want, and I don't have them yet."

The melting New Orleans dawn presaged a fierce afternoon sauna.

But the heat didn't penetrate the double-paned window of the anonymous hotel room overlooking the Mississippi River. Even if it had, the man atop the double bed near the window could no longer feel it.

After tapping twice and announcing herself, the housekeeper parked her heavy cart near the door and entered the room. She never knew what she would find behind the doors. Usually it was a man or a couple on the evil side of a hangover, but this one was supposed to have left already so she wanted to get the room done. She touched the cross on her neck, waved her entry key, and the lock clicked.

The door swung open to a vista of the river.

The man on the bed stared at the ceiling, his mouth wide open. She shouted and stumbled backward into the hall, pushing her panic button to summon hotel security.

A broad-shouldered security officer appeared and opened the door. The housekeeper looked in behind him. At first it appeared the man on the bed was a passed-out drunk like so many others she'd seen. The smell of vomit was in the air.

But his chest was as motionless as the furniture.

CHAPTER 8

NEW ORLEANS

Lynn's assistant had booked her hotel a few days before. With a doctors' convention in the city, the ground-level suite in which Lynn spent the night was expensive, one she could never have imagined when she was a penniless student. The suite sported polished hardwood floors and original paintings hung on exposed brick walls. A reconditioned wooden baggage cart from the docks found new life as a table. Robust air conditioning overrode summer's heat. Outside, landscaped ferns lunged out of the ground toward the swimming pool, but the tips reaching the water had turned brown from chlorine.

The shortcomings of the room's charming hardwoods and street-side location became audible at 4:00 A.M. Single-paned windows meant outside noise bounced in and then off the floor and walls. Women's voices screeched in high, unpleasant octaves as bars emptied late. Then delivery trucks rumbled, rolling early.

Between Lynn's developing hangover, the clatter through the walls and windows as loud as if she had bunked down in the middle of the street, and partiers yelling phrases with a dozen variations of "fuck," New Orleans before dawn felt less than magical.

Lynn had returned to sleep when the chime of her cell phone stung her ears. She panicked. A call so early meant a family emergency.

So at first, she was relieved to hear Decatur's voice.

"Sorry to wake you but NOPD just called me. Housekeeping staff found Arch Webber dead in his hotel room. They called me since he worked for TriCoast and they knew I was here."

"Oh my God! That's terrible! Has his family been notified?"

"Yes, his parents and his two sisters have been told. NOPD is still collecting evidence but they say he appears to have been a robbed by a person he knew. Someone he let into his room and had a drink with. His money and computer were taken, not his cards or ID. Of course, he had all kinds of information on his computer."

"How did he . . ." Lynn started to ask.

Decatur answered her question before she finished. "Not clear. No signs of attack although his face and extremities suggest he was in pain when he died. He'd already had a lot to drink. Hotel cameras show a woman with a white parasol going into Webber's room before he arrived."

"Madame Taliesin?"

"Apparently. She was followed in by an African or African-American man. NOPD got decent security pictures of him—he must not have expected cameras—and NOPD is putting out a BOLO or be-on-the-lookout. If he's international, INTERPOL will issue a Red Notice on him, too. The reason I called is the police are questioning a person they want you and me to see. They've got someone who lived across from Madame Taliesin picked up on another charge."

Lynn called Reese, who'd been a long-time friend of Arch's, and told him the news. The air between them was silent for a while. Reese finally said, "I just can't believe it. Man didn't have an enemy in the world. He was a good man. It's so unfair. His family knows?"

"Yes. They've been notified. Why don't you join me and Decatur at NOPD's office?" She gave him the address.

When Lynn, Reese, and Decatur arrived at the New Orleans' police precinct office a half hour later, Lynn was reminded of New Orleans' bleaker side. There could be a down-on-your-luck aspect to this particular bend of the Mississippi River. She felt it today all through her body.

Decatur introduced Lynn and Reese to his friend, freckled Sergeant Ryan O'Shaughnessy.

O'Shaughnessy looked at Lynn and Reese and said, "You've been to a crawfish boil or two, yeah?"

They both nodded.

"Ever watch them critters?" O'Shaughnessy asked, then answered his own question. "The crawfish are put into salt water first so they clean themselves out. Means they vomit. They crawl on top of one another to try to get out. How this place feels after the weekend. I wish we were in the middle of Mardi Gras, believe it or not. Then the pre-meds are all over the place, dripping with energy, looking for people to help. That's when those students learn the reality of dealing with schizophrenics is different from studying neuroscience in the classroom."

"I remember those times," Lynn said. "Ryan, Reese is my friend and colleague—he was my first boss when I was in school here and he was running a plastics plant. He works for TriCoast now."

O'Shaughnessy fist-bumped Reese and said, "Sure. We crossed paths a time or two when he worked in New Orleans. I helped him with a few situations."

"Like Lynn, Arch Webber was my good friend," Reese said. "I can tell you before you ask me that he didn't have any enemies, none he ever mentioned."

"So cutting to the chase," O'Shaughnessy replied, "I wondered if when you last saw Webber and Madame Taliesin, you might have seen Gail, too. She was arrested last night for assault. Says she found her husband in bed with a transsexual, she beat them both up, and her husband had to go to the hospital in an ambulance since his kidney damage was so bad. Tells me she's a nursing student. And a temp at Gonzo Go-Go. Also claims she was so drunk she draws a complete blank on the whole night, except she's sure

Madame Taliesin was walking around with someone last night on St. Ann, maybe with Webber after they left the Big Oyster? There's a man at Charity Hospital with damaged kidneys who fits the description of her husband, but so far we don't have evidence to match the rest of her story."

O'Shaughnessy opened a door and went in.

Through observation glass, she, Reese, and Decatur could see and hear O'Shaughnessy question a slumped-over woman.

"Gail, who gave you the black eye?"

"I don't remember. But this is from my husband." She proudly pulled down her collar to show a dull, red hickey.

"Same man you put in the hospital?" O'Shaughnessy asked.

"Maybe." The woman looked up with a cagey expression.

"What about Madame Taliesin? When was the last time you saw her?"

The woman appeared agitated. "Last night. Like I told you already. At St. Ann near Jackson Square. Where is she now?"

"She lives across from you?"

"Yeah."

"You say you saw her with someone else last night. Can you describe the person?"

The woman's hair swung into her eyes as she shook her head.

The police officer showed her a picture of Arch Webber. "Did you see this man?"

"I don't remember." Gail shrugged.

"Gail, you have to try to remember." The officer's voice communicated urgency.

"Stop asking me questions," Gail said, and pounded her fists on the table. "I'll have the ghost of Chicken Man put a hex on you. You can't hold me here." She stormed out of the room.

After a beat, O'Shaughnessy nodded and left the room, too, rejoining them.

"Chicken Man? A name I haven't heard in a while." Lynn looked at O'Shaughnessy.

"Who's Chicken Man?" Decatur asked.

"Dead now, but used to practice voodoo in the Quarter. Quite a character, and I've met a few. Back to my original question. Do any of you remember seeing Gail last night, or at any other time?" O'Shaughnessy asked.

Decatur, Lynn, and Reese shook their heads.

"Please stay in touch so I can find you."

"Officer O'Shaughnessy, thank you," Lynn said.

"I want justice for my friend," Reese added.

"We want to find and prosecute whoever killed him. It sounds awful but the killer could have just been after our bidding models," Lynn said.

"Everyone hacks these days. Killing a man is a tough way to steal secrets," O'Shaughnessy replied.

Lynn and Decatur left for the Marrero refinery. Once there, they gathered together everyone who'd gone to Big Oyster the night before.

The group glanced at one another and then at Lynn and Beau Decatur. As she told them about Arch Webber's death, she, Reese, and Decatur watched for reactions from each. But the same shock, anger, and sadness showed on every face.

"Arch Webber is…," Kim stopped and looked sick. "I mean, *was* supposed to run the Gulf of Mexico lease bidding in a few weeks."

No one had seen Arch last night after leaving Café du Monde. No one mentioned Madame Taliesin.

After they left, Dena waited behind to talk to Lynn. "Arch was so awesome. I really feel bad. He must have been killed for his computer. He was safeguarding it, and us."

"Hell, everything specific to TriCoast was backed up in the cloud and on other computers. And it's password protected, although passwords don't stop everyone. No one should lose his life over data," Lynn said.

Dena shook her head.

"David Jenkins or one of his guys will step in for Arch. I'll call him when I get to the airport. Maybe you can help, too, Dena. Jesus, poor Arch."

As Decatur drove himself and Lynn from Marrero to the Louis Armstrong Airport, Lynn realized that as Arch's boss, David might already have heard the news. She dreaded talking to him because he already considered her a Typhoid Mary.

Arch had been prepared to represent TriCoast at a Gulf of Mexico lease bidding sale worth hundreds of millions of dollars to the US government and to companies competing for prime deepwater drilling locations. With David Jenkins and TriCoast's geo-seismic team, Arch had evaluated every block, calculating the company's best bidding strategy for each. *Had a competitor or a foreign company tried to buy TriCoast's top-secret bidding numbers from Arch and then either killed him when they got it, or killed him because they didn't?*

She punched in David's number. When he answered, she said, "David, I have bad news."

His voice cracked. "Lynn Dayton. Why are people always getting killed around you?"

CHAPTER 9

BEIJING AND COPENHAGEN

The text from Matak Abdullah was coded to alert Cong to pick up the call from the unidentified number.

"Mr. Cong, we were successful. The Viper and I planned the killing of Mr. Arch Webber as you suggested and we have completed it. I have his laptop. I will download its contents and send them to you."

"Good. You will be paid the rest of what you are owed," Cong said. "What did you think of the Viper? Is he capable?"

"Viper was dressed as ugly old drunk woman, a good disguise. There are many he-she and she-he in New Orlean, so I don't know what Viper is."

"You didn't take off the ugly-old-woman disguise to find out?"

"No time. But the Viper is strong, with low voice."

"What happened to the woman whose clothes Viper took?"

"Knocked out with a smashed bottle, Viper said. Left in an apartment. Probably bled to death."

"You aren't certain?" Cong could already hear Comrade Jin's tirade at that loose end.

"I trusted the Viper. Viper gave me the address, a street called Iberville. But like I said, no time to check. We waited a long time for Arch. I had to leave immediately to get out of the country."

"Tell me the address where the old woman is supposed to be dead. I will have a more reliable person check it," Cong said.

Matak did not respond to or chose not to recognize the menace in Cong's voice. Cong committed to memory the location Matak told him and said, "Wait for my next communication."

He jogged down five stories of stairs to get to his appointment with Comrade Mei Jin.

She was already at the tiny coffee shop when Cong arrived, her mouth set in an angry line. "I have argued with ten people already for your chair."

"I apologize, Comrade Jin."

"Okay. Okay, first. I approved your travel to Copenhagen but I must ask why."

"I am meeting the Russian, Vikenti Andreev. The Baltic Sea area is familiar to him and he does not have to travel far. He suggested it," Cong said. In truth, it was Cong who had suggested Copenhagen and Vikenti who had agreed.

Cong rushed ahead. "I just spoke with Matak Abdullah. He has been successful in obtaining the computer with the bidding information we want. He will send it. Regrettably, the computer owner did not survive."

Mei Jin's expression didn't change as she leaned close in the tiny coffee shop. Her foul breath added to the stinking miasma of Beijing's dirty air, a gritty smell that could never be shut out. But Cong moved nearer, to hear her whisper.

"You are wrong. Matak was not successful. Yes, he retrieved the computer. Yes, the computer owner was eliminated as a witness. But Matak's image is now on several hotel security cameras. And you did not tell me he would be accompanied by another person, some ugly old woman."

Like you, Cong thought, but didn't say.

His stomach sank. Hotel security cameras. And now Mei Jin knew about the Viper, an asset he had hoped to keep secret.

"Matak was unaware of the cameras. He is unfamiliar with American hotels."

"A weak excuse. *You* should have expected. *You* should have prepared him. *You* are incompetent. And why involve another person? Further incompetence."

As a bonus, another of his traps had sprung a few weeks ago. Someone at TriCoast had come to him. By clicking on links and a brochure in the China Power website, a TriCoast user had downloaded a keylogger. When the surfing indicated a few hops onto more personal sites, Cong realized he could target TriCoast from the inside by snaring this person for his Second Law group. So he did. The person or people called themselves The Viper. The Viper had already proven helpful, as he explained to Mei Jin.

"This person was not an old woman. It was someone called *the Viper* who came to me. The Viper got Matak into the room because the Viper could break through the hotel door lock system and the Viper dressed like someone the computer owner knew."

"Who is the Viper?"

"The name the person uses, Comrade. I believe the Viper is American and appears to work at one of our target companies, TriCoast Energy."

"How did this person find you? It could be an ambush." Mei tossed the stub of her cigarette into her coffee cup. Cong tried to ignore his feeling of revulsion.

"The Viper connected with me by one of our own snares. We post as China Energy and gain automatic access to the security clearance of anyone who downloads China Energy information. When I contacted this person—"

"—or spy agency, it could be," Mei said.

"Correct, Comrade Jin. I am not certain. But I believe the Viper's actions show him or her to fit perfectly in our Second Law Group. The Viper could also help on our TriCoast projects by showing us additional, better ways into its systems."

"The Viper, even with a TriCoast address, even with a disguise as an ugly old woman, could be a mask for a teenager trying internet doors. He could be quite willing to appear to fall into your snare, even to help Matak, so he can catch you. Most likely, it is someone from an international security agency, like the CIA, or the SVR. Perhaps it is even this Vikenti Andreev you are going to Copenhagen to see."

Cong leaned away from her and said, "Or it could be a simple, naïve person as we so often find. This has been an effective snare. I will stay where I already am, in TriCoast's systems, and see what else the Viper brings me besides assisting Matak in obtaining for us vital oil bidding data."

Mei Jin's lips parted to show her gray teeth. "We will not be responsible, or even acknowledge you and your company, should this Viper come after you or expose you."

As he had told Mei Jin he would, Cong traveled to Copenhagen to meet the Russian, Vikenti Andreev. Vikenti was the Russian counterpart the SVR and Mei Jin of the Fourth Department had assigned to the Second Law group. Their initial discussions would be face-to-face.

Mei Jin sent him the hotel security photos without saying how she got them. He saw one with the Viper dressed as the old woman. Surely the Viper was not Vikenti, he thought.

Vikenti had asked for a large initial payment, which Cong had arranged through his Russian backer. Cong had no intention of paying further if possible. He didn't trust his fellow Chinese, let alone a non-Chinese.

The weather was overcast, but it was the gray of rain and wind rather than the yellow of coal sulfur. They met near the Rosenborg Castle moat. Vikenti looked nothing like the Viper, Cong was relieved to see. His black hair was gelled into a flattop with fenders and he lugged around profoundly overdeveloped shoulders.

Cong introduced himself. After a couple of questions and head-shakes, they decided to use English. Cong was uncomfortable with the decision, though not the language itself, because he knew most of the people around them spoke English as well or better than they did Danish.

So instead of buying tickets to enter the castle as he had planned, Cong motioned toward the gardens outside. The gardens didn't allow bicycles, another reason for Cong's choice. Since arriving in the morning, he had already just missed being hit by several black-suited commuters on electric bikes when he misread a traffic light and stepped off a cobblestone sidewalk onto a smooth asphalt bike lane.

Cong expected Vikenti to test his leadership in one or several ways—strength, loyalty, arms, finances, or intelligence.

"I was surprised when I was asked to meet you," Vikenti said. "We normally use only Russians. But I was told I could teach you much."

"I am sure you are correct," Cong said, happy to have already found the man's weakness—his vanity. "But of course my group and I were responsible for the power surges that melted security computers in the United States. And the ransomware attack on one of the world's the major shipping companies, headquartered here."

"I don't believe you." The Russian ambled.

"I'm sure we could compare notes on many such exploits. But we have another mutual interest. China is Russia's biggest customer for natural gas. And yet we are finding many others who also wish to sell us gas."

"We could stop supplying you. We have customers in Europe and Asia." Vikenti smoothed his hair, then wiped the gel from his hands onto his pants.

"But you have competitors who also want to sell gas to your customers in Europe and Asia. Norway, Algeria, Australia, and now the United States," Cong said, calling Vikenti's bluff.

Vikenti's forehead creased beneath his flattop hairstyle but he said nothing.

Cong pressed the point. "Your country wants to keep selling gas to us because your long-time customers in the European Union, including even tiny satellites like Latvia and Lithuania, are looking for other suppliers besides Gazprom. This they do with the encouragement and support of the traitorous United States."

"With whom China does not hesitate to trade," Vikenti said, spitting onto the grass.

"The US is attempting to block Gazprom's newest pipeline from Russia to northern Europe and encouraging Europe to reduce its dependence on Russian gas."

"We, Russia, want to scare these other sellers—the US but also Norway and Algeria—out of the European markets we have always supplied. For decades, we loyally supplied. We must scare the Europeans into buying only from Russia," Vikenti agreed.

But Cong knew Russian gas was high-priced, much more expensive than gas supplied by the US. Moreover, Gazprom cruelly reminded any protesting customers in its forty-billion-dollar European market of their dependence. With the flick of a switch, Russia's Gazprom could and had cut off midwinter heat to the Baltics, Bulgaria, and Germany. Russia had even financed environmental organizations to protest shale gas drilling anywhere in Europe. All to maintain the continent's dependence on Russian gas.

"We are also aware of our reliance on your country. Russia supplies our small refineries. Sometimes we buy more oil from you than from Saudi Arabia."

Vikenti nodded with satisfaction.

Time for the last stroke to the man's vanity, Cong thought. "I am well-placed enough to be told our leaders' concerns. After investment debacles in Canada and Venezuela, China prefers doing business with one of our largest fellow powers, a country understanding of my country's needs."

"This is a nice stroll and you make honey with your words but you are wasting my time. Why did you invite me here?" Vikenti asked.

"Gazprom supplies Europe by pipeline, while the countries competing with you supply by liquefied natural gas terminals, correct?" Cong wanted to lead Vikenti to the inevitable conclusion.

"Yes."

"So to meet Russia's objective of Gazprom remaining the single seller of natural gas to Europe, you need to create an incident or two of strategic sabotage that appears to be an accident. This has already been approved by your government."

"What does China get from it?"

"Nothing," Cong lied. Fewer gas terminals would mean cheaper natural gas prices, which would benefit China. "But we need development plans for US natural gas fields. China's Fuling Field in the Sichuan Basin resembles US gas fields, so drilling plans from companies like TriCoast would be most useful for our planners."

If Vikenti couldn't extract plans online, Cong would ask the Viper. It would be a test. And if the Viper couldn't get development plans, Cong was sure his group could obtain them. He thought about the tens of billions of US-dollar Chinese investments made by the national companies and the Chinese wealth fund: oil sands in Canada, North Seas offshore, refining in Portugal, drilling in Oklahoma and in South Texas, oil and gas interests in Brazil, Syria, Uganda, and Kazakhstan. Many had been profitable. Many had shared expertise voluntarily, others involuntarily. Chinese organizations had already learned much from his and others' technology acquisitions.

But better to make Vikenti work for his side of the deal.

"Where should I start?" Vikenti asked.

"You should investigate several regasification ports to determine which is most easily approached and eliminated. Perhaps your first target should be Lithuania. Or Poland."

"Easy. Are we finished?" They had reached the corner of the castle garden at Kronprinsessegade and Gothersgade.

Cong considered the loose end Matak had left him, the old woman whose clothes the Viper had taken and who was supposed to have bled to death. He stopped Vikenti and pulled him away from the path. "My superiors recommended you, yet they did not inform me of all of your abilities. In addition to the bombing of the liquefied natural gas terminals, we need to eliminate people who may have learned of other secret plans. You have done such work?"

Vikenti Andreev nodded. "Many times."

"There is an old woman in New Orleans, in the USA. She interfered with our operations. She was to have been killed, but I'm not certain she was. Here is the address at which you should find her dead body. If she is not dead, kill her."

CHAPTER 10

DALLAS AND NORTHERN CALIFORNIA

After long sessions with the New Orleans authorities, Lynn returned to Dallas on a TriCoast company plane. But even the sleek Gulfstream 500 was no match for roiling thunderstorms that delayed her arrival until 1 AM.

The next morning she told her husband about Arch's death.

"This and the three in California. Are they related?" Cy asked.

"I have no idea. The hotel got a picture of a man going into Arch's room, so it seems possible he could be the killer. But weirdly, he was accompanied by this local, older woman we met, a long-time French Quarter character. No idea how they're connected, or if they're connected to the California deaths. But the simple fact is Arch, who was a good man with no enemies, is dead, too."

"You still want the bigger job adding the natural gas side of things you've been offered? You're already so high-profile. After your news of Arch, I'm worried you could become even more of a target."

"I want to find the causes of the four deaths before anything else," Lynn said.

"Why doesn't Mike offer you oil drilling as well as natural gas, since oil and gas are produced together?"

"General conflict of interest since I buy oil for our refineries. Yes, David Jenkins and I will work together since most basins contain both oil and gas. The biggest area of both cooperation and conflict is the Texas-New Mexico Permian Basin since there's so much gas co-produced with oil there." David was the executive vice president in charge of domestic oil production.

"So Mike thinks David would jump ship and you wouldn't?"

"He doesn't want either of us to leave, but he seems to think David is more likely to."

"Is your job coming out of David's territory? Is he going to be pissed?"

"Yes, but no. One of our drilling execs left, so David's getting his responsibility, too."

"Have you considered other offers? Maybe there are other, safer companies, where you'd be less public."

"I've gotten calls for twice the money and large ownership percentages, so I'm being offered even more public positions." She hesitated. "At TriCoast, I know and like, or at least understand, everyone. People are honest and everything's fair. I've had opportunities other companies wouldn't have allowed me. Of course, things could go sidewise next week."

"Lynn, we're your family and we love you."

She nodded.

"You can't yet identify how or why these deaths occurred, but Arch's seems especially suspicious. I'm concerned a crazy person would want to make a point by injuring or killing you."

"Cy, I love you, and I love the kids. But if you love me, you have to understand how much my job means to me. Always has. Don't hold me down. Don't back me into a corner. Don't make me choose between the job and you. Not if you really love and understand me."

He shook his head. "I'm not asking you to choose. But maybe you'll be safer with your new bodyguard, right?"

She nodded.

Clouds hung in the sky like bunches of grapes. Mark Shepherd, TriCoast's security chief, and risk manager Patrick Boudreaux were leading this second safety training session. In the late, hot morning Lynn drove to the same place the group had met before, an outdoor location in northwest Dallas. The Elm Fork shooting complex was nearby, but they wouldn't practice with firearms until later.

Before the session began, Lynn sat in her car and reviewed emails while waiting for the others. Her eyes were drawn to one sentence on Cy's risk factor list. "We depend on our key management personnel and technical experts, and the loss of any of these individuals could adversely affect our business."

Arch Webber's death was far more than a business risk. Reese had said Arch had no enemies. If not, then the motive had apparently been to steal TriCoast company secrets. When her buzzing phone showed Reese's number, she knew Arch was on his mind, too.

"You're at the training session?"

"Yes. Where are you? Aren't you supposed to be here?"

"I am," Reese said, "but I decided to stick around New Orleans, talk to the police some more. Arch was a good friend, and I still just can't . . . " he choked and then finished, ". . . believe it. I want to be informed and keep the investigation moving."

"Will you be able to join me in San Francisco, then?"

"I'll fly straight there later today and meet you tomorrow."

"Sounds good, Reese. But I won't make your excuses for missing this training session."

"No worries. I'll be sweating as much here as you are there."

Everyone had gathered on the training ground, ready to begin.

When Lynn joined them, she said, "Before we start, I need to tell you something. We lost a great guy yesterday in New Orleans, Arch Webber. The police are investigating. Reese Spencer has stayed behind in New Orleans to help NOPD with the follow-up, and any questions they might have."

All looked shocked at news they hadn't yet heard, then grew silent.

Remembering Patrick Boudreaux's argument with Arch, Lynn let her glance linger on Patrick as she spoke. "We've met with the New Orleans police. If you remember anything unusual, something you think might explain Arch's death, please tell me or Reese and we will pass it along."

Patrick stared back. "I can disagree with someone without escalating to violence. Don't you dare suggest otherwise."

Lynn wondered if he was protesting because he was telling the truth, or protesting because he was lying.

"Okay, we're all here and everyone remembers everyone from last time." TriCoast security chief Mark Shepherd slid his hat to the side and wiped his brow. The temperature would be a hundred degrees by the afternoon. "I want to talk about knives first, guns second. An assailant with a knife can throw it. He, or she, can also get in fast and close. Decatur, could you demonstrate?"

Beau Decatur showed them a twelve-inch sport knife. "Hunters have them, lots of people do. This one has a decent heft, a sharp point. Everyone get behind me and to one side or the other."

Once all were in position Decatur said, "A pro with a knife aims for a flat surface." He gestured toward a hay bale about ten yards away. "You see the bale over there. But a back or a chest could also be a target."

"Who are you calling flat-chested?" Dena asked with mock annoyance. Everyone laughed.

Decatur winked at her and said, "You want a flat surface because otherwise the knife can ricochet back at you. You want the knife to spin, so grab it by the handle. Keep your thumb on the top so it doesn't over-rotate."

They moved in as he demonstrated the grip. "Now, just like golf or ultimate Frisbee or any other sport, you have to visualize, so visualize the knife sticking. Square up your shoulders, start your throw with your arm above your head, and release it with your arm pointed toward the target. Don't snap your wrist."

He went through the motions slowly, then drew his arm back. His arm whipped past his head and he released the knife. It spun cleanly toward the target and stuck several inches into the center of the bale.

"Nice!" Lynn said.

"I want all of you to practice. Even if you've never thrown a softball or a baseball, you can do this. For safety, we'll use a single knife and go one at a time."

After a half hour, when everyone in the group could hit the hay bale, Mark said, "We also want to demonstrate close work. This is why a knife is so dangerous."

Decatur sheathed his demo knife. "The lesson here is it's easy to get close, or for others to get close to you, and do a lot of damage." He and Mark demonstrated several moves and holds. To Lynn, most of them seemed to end with the sheathed knife at Mark's throat. She wondered how much she could trust her new bodyguard.

Mark had the group pair off and they practiced.

The mid-morning heat was sweltering by the time they took a water break.

Then Mark said, "Change of pace. Let's do a shooter scenario with a couple of females. Lynn, Dena."

They stepped to the center of the circle and fist-bumped.

"Dena, you're the hostage taker and Lynn, you're the hostage. Pretend Beau Decatur isn't with you." Mark tossed a plastic gun to Dena and she caught it.

Dena grabbed Lynn's arm and put the plastic gun to Lynn's head in a quick, sure move.

"Dena needs Lynn as a means to an end, as leverage for whatever she wants. Maybe money and a free getaway," Mark told the group.

"Five million and safe delivery to Belize on a corporate jet," Dena said.

Everyone laughed.

"Shouldn't I scream?" Lynn asked.

Patrick took over. "No. For two reasons. First, if you start talking, everyone's stress level goes up, especially us males."

More laughter.

"Second, police will be around quickly. You want to be quiet so you can hear what they say. And another thing. Lynn, or anyone in her situation, stay as far from your assailant's head as possible."

"Because?" Dena asked.

"Why do you think?" Patrick said.

"Oh. If the police have to shoot, they'll aim for the head," Mike responded.

"Points for Team Emerson," Patrick said.

"Let's run through the scenario without the police. Now what?" Beau Decatur said.

"So is this where I try to get her to talk?" Lynn said.

Mark nodded. "Ask her about a shared topic, or what does she believe in. Why she's doing this. Defer to your captors and their intelligence. If you connect, you might make it harder for them if they're deciding whether or not to kill you."

Lynn turned to her pretend assailant, feeling the plastic gun dig into her scalp, and said, "So, Dena, uh, how are your folks?"

"Wrong question." Dena's face hardened and her tone was as icy as January.

Lynn stiffened. "So what's the right one?"

"Lame," Dena said scornfully.

The group watched, then Patrick continued, "Okay, Lynn and Dena, at ease. Back to the circle."

Dena's face transformed and she said, "Aw. I wanted that jet trip."

"Now we're getting to kidnapping, the most serious situation. Look around you. Northwest Dallas," Mark said. "You're within a few miles of valuable real estate, but it doesn't make things safer. If anything, high-wealth and high-power areas expose you to more risk. This location on Luna Road is one of thousands of places nearby to dispose of a body, and bodies have been found here."

Several people looked around and shuddered. Lynn remembered her own experience of being kidnapped at TriCoast's Centennial Refinery. *I was lucky to live.* She tried to focus on Mark's words but her mind kept replaying Jay's assault. She had survived only because in his rush to attack her he'd fallen past her into a crude oil storage tank.

"Your kidnapper wants money or wants you dead. He doesn't want sex—makes it too easy to identify him. Although as an aside, you should avoid traveling on foot alone, especially you ladies, or if you've been drinking. And wear shoes and clothes you can run in."

Mark tossed the plastic gun to Patrick and motioned to him and to Mike Emerson, TriCoast's CEO. Patrick held the gun to Mike's head. Although she knew it was make-believe, Lynn flinched.

"Try not to get into a car. If you do, you may be driving to your own grave," Mark said.

Despite the heat, Lynn shivered. Forcing her into a car was what Jay Gans had done.

"You okay?" Mark asked her. Everyone else was staring. "You lived this. Feel like there's anything you can tell us from your experience?"

"I got in the car with him. He had a gun." Lynn's voice was low.

"Yet you survived."

"Luck. Adrenaline," she said.

"I'll take those every time," Mark responded, then spoke to the whole group. "You'd be amazed how well your brain can function in life-threatening situations."

The feel of Dena's plastic weapon and seeing Patrick pretend to hold Mike brought back the memory with extreme clarity. *His gun against my head. Deep breaths.*

Mark addressed Mike. "Look past his shoulder as if someone's there. Then you can run."

Mike did so. Patrick looked at him and shook his head without turning. His hold tightened.

"Or stand your ground and don't get into the car," Mark said.

Patrick pushed the gun at Mike's head and said. "Bang. Now you're easier to carry."

Mark interrupted. "You guys didn't plan this too well, did you? The TriCoast board better have succession plans in place."

Mike's smile was a grimace.

"Once you're in the car, can you jump out through the opposite door or window?" Mark asked.

Mike patted his barrel stomach. "No."

Mark Shepherd wiped his brow. "Okay, here's the plan. Listen to what I'm saying, since you're used to giving directions instead of following them. Once he has you driving in the car and he tells you to drive to the cement plant between X and Y on Luna Road from your mansion in Las Colinas, what do you do?"

"I drive fast to the nearest police station," Mike said.

Mark nodded. "Yes, or to a crowded parking lot or another busy place. When you get there, slow down, ram a parked car and bail out. Kidnapper's smacked with an air bag and you're gone."

Sweating in the rising heat, Lynn, Mike, and the rest of the group took a short break and then continued their training, now more urgent on the news of Arch's death.

When they practiced defending against a potential kidnapping, Lynn chose Patrick as her opponent. *This could be my chance to get him to talk.*

They squared off. She whispered, "Everyone heard you argue with Arch. Where did you go after you left us in New Orleans?"

He got behind her, grabbed her collar and yanked her against him. "I didn't kill Arch but I should worry you," he whispered, "not for what I'll do, but for what you don't know about me."

Even with a gun made from plastic, Patrick looked threatening enough for Beau Decatur to move toward her. She shook her head at Decatur and he stopped, watching them. Lynn couldn't see Patrick but she turned her head and spoke over her shoulder. "So where did you go that night?"

He said softly, "Home, for Chrissakes. You're the one who fucked up the situation—you should have figured out Arch was in danger."

How dare you blame me! But instead, Lynn said, "Let go of my arms. I want to face you." When he did, she turned around, locked onto his gaze, and spoke. "Patrick, believe me, if there'd been any way to figure out Arch was in danger, I would have done whatever it took to save him. And if you thought he was at risk, you should have been at his side. When I need you, I need to be able to trust you. Completely. If you're not on my side, and Tri-Coast's, if you don't feel loyalty to this company above and beyond a paycheck, tell me now so we can find someone else."

"I'm on your side." In a calmer voice he continued, "And while we're practicing, remember elbows, knees, and eyes."

Mark and Patrick demonstrated advanced Krav Maga defenses. "First try to de-escalate. If you can't, then remember *anything* can be a weapon. If you can't get away and you can't get your attacker's weapons, these moves might be your last chance. But don't count on them saving you."

The session closed with firearms training at the nearby gun range. Lynn realized she'd need many more hours of practice to improve her aim.

The TriCoast company planes were booked, so Lynn waited at DFW's airport for a commercial flight to San Francisco. Just as she settled into her first-class seat, her phone buzzed with a text from a New Orleans phone number. "Call me. Ryan O'Shaughnessy."

While other passengers boarded, she punched in Officer O'Shaughnessy's number. "I'm on a plane waiting to taxi, so I may have to cut off. What have you learned?"

"Does the name Matak Abdullah sound familiar? Maybe someone TriCoast worked with overseas?"

"No. Why?" Lynn looked around and kept her voice low.

"INTERPOL helped us identify the man on the security cameras who went into Arch's room before Arch died. Was killed. Guy's from Africa, South Sudan."

TriCoast's list of suppliers flashed in her mind. "It's an oil-producing country but we don't buy from them so I don't know anyone there."

"Man's a fixer and a recruiter for all kinds of operations, including Chinese companies. He recruits from Africa, the Philippines, all the countries ringing the Indian Ocean. He's got connections with terrorist groups."

She turned to the airplane window and made her voice even quieter to stifle a gasp. "I have no idea how Matak would have been acquainted with Arch."

"I wish INTERPOL had identified him faster," O'Shaughnessy said. "He's already slipped out of the country."

She reviewed what she knew of the San Francisco computer malfunctions that had ended up killing Shirley Watson and the others. "Does Matak do business with cybercriminals?"

"We don't have anything specific, but likely yes. Cybercrime is everywhere, and criminals get into any business they can."

A flight attendant announced cell phone shutdown.

Matak Abdullah. She and Reese would meet with Kanak Singh in California. *Countries around the Indian Ocean. What are the odds Kanak's heard of him?*

After another long evening flight, car ride, and restless night in a hotel bed, Lynn met Beau Decatur in the hotel's lobby the following morning.

"You don't have to run with me," Lynn said.

"You were attacked last year while running, weren't you?" Decatur said.

"Only once in all the years I've run."

"Got my orders from Mark Shepherd. The company's got too much invested in you. Don't take it personal."

"Of course not." *So I'm less replaceable than usual these days?*

"We can warm up with stretches," he suggested.

"You're my personal trainer, too?" Lynn was annoyed.

The morning was cool but foggy, so they wore reflective jackets. She kept a slower pace, Decatur at her side, as she strained to see more than a few feet ahead. The sidewalk was uneven. Curbs jutted out unexpectedly and she slipped a few times on damp pavement.

As they turned onto a slender two-lane road with no sidewalk, they stayed left to face oncoming traffic. Decatur flipped on a headlamp. Cars and trucks, including electrics and hybrids, crept up behind them noiselessly, their lights the only warnings. Once or twice, Decatur pushed her left so they could both get out of the way of speeding drivers who hadn't expected runners on the road.

Despite the fog and traffic worries, she felt better after running five miles along the Bay and back.

Decatur drove Lynn and Reese to the East Bay refinery. As he drove, she made and answered calls with her refinery managers around the country, staring out the window at the industrial landscape. The history and size of northern California's infrastructure, starting with the Gold Rush and continuing through the Transcontinental Railroad and the development of its port, surprised her because it was so seldom noted. She realized she had expected only software companies.

In Curtis Zhang's office, she and Reese greeted him and Juan Rojas. Decatur waited in the hallway. The few adornments in the sparsely-decorated room featured Chinese silk tapestries of red dragons and framed pictures of Zhang taken with family and friends in China. Lynn filed away the observation as she changed mental gears. "I didn't see the flocks of black starlings roosting in the equipment when we drove in this time. So before we get to the serious stuff, how's the falcon and falconer?"

"We started a few days ago. So far, so good." Zhang smiled. "Juan has a huge soft spot for birds."

"Crows especially," Juan said. "They live forever and they're smart. It's why I'm not a big fan of wind and solar energy. Too many rips in the cosmic fabric."

"Meaning?" Lynn asked.

He grimaced. "I can't stand the wind turbine blades dicing up thousands of birds a year and solar arrays roasting thousands more. The birds are attracted by the bright shiny mirrors, fly up to them, and it's all over. The hawks zip along looking at the ground for prey like drivers looking at their cell phones. They never see the turbine blades going a hundred and seventy miles an hour and they get crunched."

"Juan and I met with the falconer the first night," Zhang said. "He showed me how he uses a laser to light certain areas. He released the two falcons and they scared off the starlings. My concern is the cost. Guy says they're thousand-dollar birds. But the happy result is no stinking bird poop sliming the equipment."

"Once he's done, if the starlings come back, we may get the newest toy. Vineyards and farms have been using robotic falcons," Juan said.

"Who gets to fly it? Did you just get a dozen new applicants for maintenance engineering?" Lynn asked, smiling.

"And to top it off, no refinery upsets in the last few days," Zhang added.

"Good news," Lynn said.

" But causation or coincidence?" Reese asked.

"I'm not questioning my luck. Going to three funerals in two days was damn sobering," Zhang replied.

He opened the door to Kanak Singh, the cybersecurity company founder.

"You asked for an in-person update," he said, "so I'm stopping by on my way to Berkeley." He shook hands with everyone in the room.

They invited him to sit but he replied, "This won't take long. First, we've been monitoring and you haven't had any upsets or intrusions in the last few days."

"We were discussing it. Sounds crazy, but we've got a falconer and his birds chasing our birds away. Maybe the falconer is the solution?" Juan asked.

"I'll note it," Kanak said. "But I expect whoever penetrated your systems from the outside has taken a few days off."

"You described spear phishing last time," Lynn said.

"We still think spear phishing is the probable source of the breach. A couple of other possibilities are IP proxies and Google dorking. There are sites where you can get IP proxies so when you log in, you appear to be logging in from another area. Kids sometimes use it to get their test scores early, and so forth."

"And Google dorking?" Juan asked.

"An intruder looks for unprotected infrastructure and tries to hack into it. It was done with the Bowman Avenue Dam in Rye, New York, for instance. An Iranian hacker found an open computer controlling the dam's gates and other functions. The dam was very small, used just for flood control. More good fortune, the gates had been manually disconnected, so he didn't cause any harm. The hacker was found and prosecuted. But nuclear installations, chemical plants, refineries like yours, infrastructure, banks, the New York Stock Exchange—everyone's cybersecurity and industrial control systems are constantly being tested by intruders."

Lynn shook her head. "Kanak, we've encountered something else very specific, and wondered if you knew anything about it. Or *him*, I should say."

Kanak tilted his head, waiting for her question.

"Have you heard of a ring of South Sudanese cybercriminals? In particular, someone by the name of Matak Abdullah?"

"Everybody tries everything, but the Eastern Europeans, the Chinese, and the Russians are the most proficient," he said. "South Sudan? No. Matak Abdullah? No. Why?"

"We don't want him to realize we captured his image online, but the New Orleans Police Department has identified him as a person of interest in the killing, possible homicide, of one of our employees."

"I'm sorry to hear about another TriCoast death." He winced. "I know tens of thousands of people offline and online. I haven't heard of Matak."

"Don't advertise his name. He can't know he's been identified," Lynn said to Kanak as he left.

After waiting a few moments, Lynn asked the others, "What do you think of Kanak's company so far?"

"They've done more control systems projects than we typically see here in the Valley. Their customers include defense contractors, airplane companies, and a few refiners and petrochemical companies," Juan said.

"But what about his slow pace and all the options he hasn't checked yet?" Lynn asked.

Zhang shook his head. "He's prioritized us. He'll get us an answer soon."

"We needed the answer two weeks ago, before our folks were killed," Lynn said. She wished desperately she could turn back the clock and prevent their deaths.

They regrouped in a conference room next to Zhang's office. It overlooked the entire refinery, including its rail yard.

Lynn gestured at the line of black tank cars. "Juan, safety is *your* job but I can't stop myself from worrying about dangers to everyone at TriCoast. Where are you on railcar flammability training?"

"Right now we have very little oil coming in by rail. To answer your question, rail safety is up to the carriers themselves," Juan said. "They're the ones who file with the states and cities on the oil they're shipping, when, and by what route. In the past, since we have our own mutual aid firefighting crew for unusual and risky fires and explosions like the one we just had, we asked the cities to stand down if we had an incident. But lately we've put more time into practicing with nearby municipal fire departments for large hydrocarbon fires."

"How many jurisdictions have you trained?' Lynn asked.

"A dozen. We have another couple dozen to go. The San Bruno group is already up to speed since they're trained to deal with airport fires. The other refiners have helped coach first responders, too. Like I said, we've got a big mutual firefighting capability."

A steady chanting broke through their concentration.

"Hey hey ho ho. Oil fracking's got to go"

"Spoil the oil. Stop the trucks."

Zhang looked out the window and sighed. "It's our turn."

"How often do you have protestors?" Lynn asked.

"They're on a calendar. Sounds weirdly professional but they negotiated with us. Two days a week."

Lynn was concerned about danger to outsiders. *I'm already worried about the safety of the employees here, and they're the professionals. They're safety-smart in ways the protestors might not be.*

Everyone else joined him at the window.

Juan explained, "Much as we invite them to our community education seminars, some still think all oil is the same gunk that trapped mammoths in La Brea Tar Pit."

"And others think it means either the *Beverly Hillbillies* or sucker-rod pumps right on top of one another like La Cienega

Drive," Lynn said. The century-old image would loom large as long as the bobbing horsehead pumps remained visible to the filmmaking headquarters of Los Angeles.

A knot of two dozen protestors stood behind a banner, blocking the refinery's tanker truck exit.

"They could be dangerous to themselves as well as people coming and going from the refinery, like our truckers," Lynn said. It wasn't unusual for protestors to literally cross the line between free speech and trespass. She wondered why they had focused on TriCoast.

As if he sensed her question, Juan said, "We're in the rotation, remember? Twice a week they show up here."

"This isn't good for our folks, or for the drivers trying to stay on schedule," Zhang said. "We'll call the police."

"Let's go down and ask them to move off the TriCoast property first." Lynn didn't expect trouble but was glad to be with a group.

"I don't think you should confront them," Zhang said to Lynn.

"We won't confront. We'll talk," Lynn replied. She turned to him. "You have to live with them all the time. I'll take the lead. They can yell at me for a change."

Decatur stayed near her.

Outside, they approached the banner-wielding protestors. A line of eight tanker trucks stalled behind the gate, unable to exit without hitting a protestor.

Flanked by Decatur and Zhang, Lynn walked toward a neatly-dressed woman holding one edge of the banner. "This is a safety problem for you and for us. Could you please move off of TriCoast property?"

The woman looked at her phone and smiled. "So you're the head bitch?" She spun her phone around. It showed photos of all of TriCoast's senior executives.

Lynn felt a chill at their preparation. Then her anger rose. "Sure, *sweetie*. She would be me." *Anger is a losing tactic*, she told herself, taking a deep breath. Decatur moved in closer to her and she sensed his presence. With him at her back, she felt freer and calmer than she might have otherwise.

"And he's your meat bag?" The woman taunted, tilting her head at Decatur.

"We can call names all day, but you and your group are breaking the law," Zhang said to her.

Another man who also appeared to be a leader let go of his section of the banner and stalked over.

"You got a problem with us exercising our First Amendment rights to free speech?" His voice was bitter.

"No. What I have a problem with is you and your people endangering yourselves, my people, these truck drivers, and the train engineers. *That's* a huge problem for me. You need to move out of the way and tell the people on the tracks the same thing," Lynn said.

"How you gonna make us, bitch?" the woman said.

"If you don't, the police will. Get off of our property now," Zhang said.

Lynn was both reassured and impressed by Zhang's calm. Dealing with protestors was clearly a regular exercise for him.

"So you two are the good cops and soon you'll call the bad cops? I'm so scared," the bitter man said.

"You need to move off of our property, now." Lynn gestured behind her at the truck drivers lined up behind the gate. "These people are trying to make a living, do their job. You need to let them do it."

"Not when they're polluting the planet," the man said. He started coughing. In unison, everyone else holding the banner coughed with him.

"Move off of our property," Lynn said. *So much for the repetition theory of negotiation.*

The man interrupted his coughing to say, "I can't hear you."

Lynn nodded at Zhang and Decatur. They rejoined Reese and Juan to the sound of a new chant.

"*Oil bitch gotta go. Oil bitch gotta go.*"

Four squad cars pulled up.

"I already called the police," Juan said. "Our own experience and my friends at other places say they're the only authority this group pays attention to. Even then not always." He flexed his shoulders, appearing ready to defend the whole group if the nearest protestor threw a punch.

As officers got out of their cars the group rotated and slow-stepped onto the sidewalk outside the TriCoast refinery gates, keeping their banner aloft.

Zhang waved and dropped his hand in a "go" signal to the security guard, and the guard opened the gate for the truckers.

Decatur drove Lynn and Reese through the refinery gates an hour later.

The protest group was still there. Many shook their fists and others flung roofing tacks onto the street in front of them. Decatur swerved to avoid the tacks.

Hope they didn't the same thing to the truckers. She called Zhang to tell him about the tacks.

She was taken aback by his snarled reply. "Goddamn protestors. One of these days a couple of them will wind up dead." Then he softened his voice. "I hope you know I'm joking."

CHAPTER 11

VIENNA

One of Cong's Fourth Department contacts arranged for him to use a house owned by Gernot Insel, a mysterious consultant who appeared to work both sides of many fences. When Cong arrived, he found the sleek house in Wien 13, the Hietzing district—minimalist, of post-modern design with horizontal planes, boxy glass-walled rooms, and white furnishings—familiar, if anything ten times the size of his Beijing apartment could feel familiar.

Vienna itself was so far east it could have been in the old Eastern bloc. The city was a secular oil business mecca doubling as OPEC's open-air shopping mall. For Matak, Vienna would be a bitter reminder of OPEC's power to bankrupt his country.

Indeed, although Matak Abdullah had already traveled to the literal Mecca, Cong had picked Vienna—a sophisticated, tolerant city, the pinnacle of the learned Western world in the early 1900s—with Matak in mind. Vienna was a city where cultures and espionage repeatedly crossed. Coming from South Sudan, Matak would find the place extraordinary, even more than New Orleans. Electricity was always available to everyone, not only for a few hours a day and only to the elite. The background of oil negotiations in Vienna would relax Matak. South Sudan's oil production was largely sold to Cong Li's Chinese colleagues. Most South Sudanese people themselves used firewood and charcoal to heat and cook.

Vienna had additional significance to the Islamist Abdullah. This was the center of the western world that, but for the help of Polish King Jan III Sobieski, would have been conquered by the Ottomans in the second siege of Vienna in 1683. So while there had ultimately been no military takeover, Vienna today appreciated the cash the Islamic world brought to its coffers. With strolling, costumed Mozarts, balls, music, and unattainable society levels, the city induced envy in non-Europeans, who would never belong.

This was supremely useful to Cong as a point of manipulation with Matak.

He was already a risk, just as Cong had feared about the non-Chinese members of the group. When Cong asked him for access to as much of TriCoast's computerized bidding data as he could obtain, the idiot hid the fact he couldn't hack well. He instead acted as if the Second Law group was a club with a violence test for entry.

Cong learned the news of Matak's picture on several New Orleans' hotel and street cameras had been immediately reported. Both a US 'be-on-the-lookout' and an INTERPOL Red Notice for Matak meant law enforcement officers across the globe were looking for him.

However, in addition to TriCoast's offshore bidding models, Cong needed information on the resources the South Sudanese man had recruited for the oil tanker.

The next day Cong examined the red brocade, velvet, and mahogany in the Hotel Sacher sitting room while he waited. Everything was decorated in layers—armoires, chairs, sofas, walls. To Cong, this spoke of static history. In China, no one had time to decorate, much less in such elaborate style. In China, the landscape and the buildings changed by the hour as the country chased growth.

"*As-Salam Alaykum,*" Cong greeted Matak. He nodded toward the breakfast room. A waiter evaluated them and offered a table, neither the best nor the worst. Cong had chosen the Sacher Hotel to overwhelm Matak—*see, this is our capability*—and from Matak's satisfied grin, he'd accomplished his aim. They chose the buffet and made several trips. Cong himself marveled at a room lined with floor-level wooden rails placed an inch away from the wall to keep guests from bumping chair legs on the moldings. He thanked Matak for the TriCoast bidding models the Sudanese man had sent. Then Cong gave into an impulse and said, "I thought you would be able to get this information online, without getting the computer itself."

"But I did obtain it for you."

"It cost more than it should have," Cong said. The man had to realize his picture was out to law enforcement and security officers everywhere. Cong himself would not be able to see Matak in person again after today.

In mid-morning they walked through the extravagant shopping along Kärntner Strasse. Every ten meters or so groups of women clad in black burkas sat together. To Cong's eye, the groups looked like large ravens, although he expected their presence heartened Matak. Most of the conversation around them was in German, except for the frequent, costumed Mozarts distributing playbills.

Cong paid after Matak, with great deliberation and much help from retailers, bought clothing and trading goods for his return trip. He scanned the stores and streets to determine whether or not any of the store security officers or Viennese police recognized the South Sudanese man. None seemed to.

After a while, they took a taxicab to Prater Park. Matak had mentioned he was from a tribe of expert horsemen and he would far prefer to ride even an old nag of a trail horse to watching the trained, prissy Lipizzaner stallions. "They are a waste of good bloodlines."

They rented horses and rode the sloping trails of the big park.

After they returned the horses, they crossed a bridge over a busy street and railroad tracks enclosed in a canyon of high fences to keep out pedestrians, then walked through a hotel to an industrial portion of the Danube River. Matak finally told Cong what both had traveled so far to discuss in person. Matak had recruited two Philippine seamen. They were cousins. The first was named Liamzon and the name of the second was unpronounceable. They would soon be aboard a Saudi Arabian oil tanker headed from Ras Tanura for the United States Gulf Coast. Later, once they were near or docked for unloading at the Louisiana Offshore Oil Port, Liamzon would detonate the bomb. His cousin would be certain Liamzon carried out the plan and coerce him to do so, if necessary.

"There is a word. Autopilot. The plan is on autopilot now," Matak said.

Cong nodded. It was the kind of destruction for which he had hoped. Mei Jin would approve. He asked questions about the Filipino seamen's training and ability to blend in, all of which Matak answered.

Seeing his agreement Matak said, "But I talk to my friends and I think you are underpaying me, particularly since I have now delivered the contents of the TriCoast computer to you."

"Your friends are Somali pirates?"

"There are many businesses in South Sudan," Matak said, neither agreeing nor disagreeing. "What I'm doing is worth twice as much."

"You put us all at risk. People around the globe are looking for you. We have an agreement. To consider paying you more, I need contact information for the seamen and the terms of your agreement with this Liamzon and his cousin. I need to verify your truthfulness."

"It was harder to find the seamen traveling on a tanker to the United States. Fewer unloading there now. And there is your reputation to consider. I am sure you would want my friends—who can identify the businesses and homes of your many Chinese countrymen who have moved to Africa—to consider you a fair and generous man," Matak said.

Cong was displeased with the direction of the conversation, although he was not surprised at the man's stupidity, stupidity Matak had already proven. Cong had not expected his Second Law colleagues to be honest. But he could not stomach threats, no matter how amorphous, against the tens of thousands of his countrymen scraping out a living on the African continent. And the BOLO and Red Notice attention to Matak had now made any association with him far riskier.

"I am listening. I will have to make your case to those who employ me. They are the ones who provided the money for your flight, your stay at the Sacher Hotel, and your purchases. To do so, I must have the contact information."

"Why? So you can cut me out?" Matak said scornfully.

"No. To persuade those who pay me to pay you more, they will require further documentation. How will you be communicating with the seamen? How often? What are the exact instructions you have given them?"

Matak looked at him and decided to cooperate for the bigger payout. "Email in Liamzon's mother's name. Every few days I send a recipe and he responds with a word or two. My instructions are so simple a donkey could follow them. He has a cell phone detonator. As a backup the bomb can be detonated just by proximity to certain GPS coordinates. You would be wise to be in touch with your superiors soon."

Matak displayed only a touch of arrogance, but it was too much for Cong. He considered his options. Matak was bigger and probably armed. Cong had a knife, but it would be insufficient. Fortunately, few people were out mid-week.

A couple of swans floated by on the river.

"We should ride the horses one more time before you return. They did not appear to be getting enough exercise. Maybe we can gallop them this time," Cong said.

They walked back through the hotel and onto the pedestrian bridge. No one else was around. Cong asked Matak about his taste in women. "You are outside of your country. You can tell me."

"Blond, tall, Danish," Matak answered.

Cong checked his phone for the time.

"And you?"

Per the schedule he had earlier obtained, Cong heard the train whistle three hundred meters away.

"Did you not hear me? Or do you have pictures to show me?" Matak asked.

"Pictures, yes," Cong said. "Let's stop here while I find the right one."

They paused in the middle of the pedestrian bridge while Cong pretended to thumb through his phone.

"She must be special, to be so hidden," Matak said.

The whistle sounded much closer, just behind the bend. Cong could hear the churn of the train's motor. He leaned against the side of the bridge and motioned Matak closer toward him, pointing to the picture on his screen of a beautiful face framed in blond hair belonging to a stunning, slim, long-legged nude.

As Matak reached toward the phone, Cong kneed Matak in the crotch.

Just as the shock of pain and surprise registered on Matak's face Cong put one arm behind the man's back and bent down. With the other hand he grabbed one of Matak's legs.

He flipped Matak over the side of the bridge onto the tracks just before the train crossed below them. High fences on both sides of the track below the bridge trapped the South Sudanese man.

Cong walked off the pedestrian bridge toward the park.

Matak screamed as he anticipated the horror of his death during the last few seconds of his life.

CHAPTER 12

Lynn, Dena, Patrick, Decatur, and David flew to rainy Pittsburg in a Grumman Gulfstream IV. TriCoast's corporate jet was also jammed with engineers and geologists. Lynn reviewed her notes.

The very first successful oil well—indicated by the presence of oil seeps—had been found in Pennsylvania. It was also Yale chemist Ben Silliman who determined the oil could be separated into fractions by boiling range. He showed it to be a moneymaker, just as he later would in California. One of the fractions, kerosene, began replacing whale oil in lamps. Ironically, using kerosene for illumination was eventually replaced by natural gas, which was in turn replaced by electricity.

Silliman's results enabled Colonel Drake to get financial backing and in 1859, Drake and his Pennsylvania Rock Oil Company drilled the first commercial oil well, in Titusville, Pennsylvania.

Nearly a hundred and fifty years later, TriCoast and several other companies had confirmed the existence of a giant natural gas field, the Marcellus Shale, after two professors had estimated it held an unbelievable trillions of cubic feet of natural gas. Like its competitors, TriCoast had acquired and drilled acreage in the eleven hundred-mile-long play, focusing on sweet spots in southwestern and northeastern Pennsylvania. Day-one production rates from the new horizontal drilling were up to thirty million cubic feet, a level of success once impossible from onshore US wells.

She heard a few words of conversations around her in with the dry, understated tone of optimism.

"The Marcellus looks like the Barnett in Fort Worth except with green grass and trees."

"Great rock. Really great rock."

Lynn was glad the five of them would be seeing Dwayne Thomas. She'd met Dwayne when she had urged TriCoast to buy the Houston oil refinery at which he worked. He'd been skeptical of her and her company at first, yet they had ended up working side-by-side to save their refinery from an explosion. She found him resourceful—a common compliment was Dwayne could hold a plant together with nothing but baling wire.

Lynn had asked him to oversee construction of processing plants needed to make the Marcellus natural gas saleable. The gas in this area was "rich," which meant when the gaseous methane was produced out of the ground, heavier gases such as ethane, propane, and butane came along for the ride. Since pipelines and customers wanted to transport or burn only standard methane cleaned up to precise specifications, the other gases had to be stripped out and sold.

Two-carbon ethane was split from the one-carbon methane and both were pipelined to the Gulf Coast, Ontario, or liquefied and shipped in a sort of virtual pipeline to Swiss-owned chemical plants in Norway, Scotland, and elsewhere. New two-hundred-yard-long China-built Dragon class ships carried the gases overseas. Lynn thought the lean ships did resemble dragons. With a hop, skip, and jump, ethane moved from southwest Pennsylvania via pipeline to a refinery-turned-terminal and dock at the Marcus Hook industrial complex on the Delaware River south of Philadelphia, and on across the ocean to Europe.

Hundreds of similar processing plants existed in the world, but until recently none had been needed in southwestern Pennsylvania. Now, giant pipelines and billion-dollar chemical plants were being built to use the gas and liquids, the first in the U.S. in decades. The situation had flipped from not enough natural gas to having so much its price in Louisiana was higher than in Pennsylvania, a reversal.

Lynn had recommended Dwayne for this assignment constructing natural gas liquids plants, expecting it would lead to more opportunities for him.

After the company plane landed, they rented a car and Decatur drove them south through rolling hills.

They found Dwayne onsite near a half-acre pad of dirt, comparing machine-drawn paper plans to a diagram on his iPad. His hardhat was pushed back on his head and the real estate of his black jacket was split between the yellow, red and blue diamond Steelmark logo for the Pittsburgh Steelers and the stylized lone star longhorn of the Houston Texans.

"So Lynn, whadya think of ol' PA? Can you believe I landed in another town called Houston? Looks like the one in Texas, too, except it's a lot smaller and has hills. No hurricanes, either." He pronounced it *hurrikins*.

Nearby was a tall platform topping out several feet above the trees. It looked like a Six Flags bungee jump.

"It's good to see you." She smiled, and introduced Dena, Patrick, and Decatur. "And you've met David."

"You know what happened to Lynn's last bodyguard?" Dwayne asked Decatur. Lynn winced.

"Heard all about the woman's death while she was protecting Lynn before I took the job, yes," Decatur replied.

"So Lynn, you came to do real work instead of going to wuss meetings in Washington or Europe." He gave her a warm handshake, his mitt-sized palm more than covering hers. Then he shook hands with the others.

"Someone has to eat those five-course dinners," she replied.

"Well, cut me in. Hey, I heard you ran into protestors at the San Francisco Bay refinery. The 'energy for me but not for thee' crowd?"

She nodded. "How are the contractors treating you?"

Dwayne smiled at David. "Not to Steelers tickets. Main thing is they have plenty of Pennsylvania shale experience so we're on schedule." As if cued, his phone rang. Despite his quip about the storybook Pennsylvania landscape, his ring tone was a clip from Little Texas' "God Blessed Texas." He let the call go to voicemail.

"David and I reminded TriCoast's board of the size of the play," Lynn said.

"We've got four hundred thousand acres to search but the seismic is telling us a lot. We've been blessed with good rock up here." In his born-again Baptist phrasing, Dwayne was saying the shale, "the rocks," beneath their feet had high natural gas and liquids content. Other industry references were to golf—religion of another kind. The rocks containing the most gas were the "fairway" of the play; one company had even chosen Fairway as its name.

"Let me show you around." He included the others in his glance. "We'll be hooking up our wells to these plants as fast as Lynn and David can drill them and as fast as we can build the plants." He pointed at the four-story structure of a drilling rig. "There's the closest mother well. It'll have eight laterals off of it. TriCoast's got another ten child wells waiting on tie-in. When we're done with our first phase, we'll have cryogenic plants capable of handling eighty million cubic feet a day, along with five compressor stations and fifty miles of pipe."

The report Lynn and David had prepared for TriCoast's board of directors had identified the Marcellus as having from 160 to over 500 trillion cubic feet of gas in place, with at least ten percent, or up to fifty trillion cubic feet, ultimately recoverable. To put it into perspective for the board, they explained fifty trillion cubic feet was so much it could cover all of the United States' natural gas needs for two years. Estimates of the Marcellus field's value started at $150 billion and skyrocketed higher. The Marcellus was also close to natural gas markets, a valuable accident of geology, history, and population: two-thirds of the US population lived within a 350-mile radius of the field.

"The pipelines to the northeast are coming along, right?" Lynn asked. Dena and Patrick listened. Decatur had stepped away to make a few calls.

Dwayne shrugged. "Sort of. Big dollars to build them without any guarantee they'll be used. Yes, everyone gets excited having enough gas for heat when a few feet of snow land on Boston, but the worry is much of the year the lines would be empty. No one can stay in business that way. I sure sound like Bubba whine, don't I?"

"Bubba wine like wine coolers with barbecue?" Dena asked with a grin.

"Bubba whine, like whining because the gas price is low," Dwayne admitted.

Lynn laughed. "You've never been much of a whiner. You're making the rounds of the utilities? They're big gas buyers."

His eyebrows lifted. "We have tough competition from coal, but we're selling more to those folks. For them, it all comes down to dollars per BTU. At these low prices, we're competitive. And gas is cleaner, big sales point."

When Decatur rejoined them, Lynn told the group, "I stay in touch with Vandervoost. He's telling me the Germans, the Austrians, the Poles, and the Eastern Europeans would rather not have Russia controlling whether or not they have heat in the winter the way they do now. He says the EU is dying to get gas from a non-Gazprom supplier."

Dwayne stared at her speculatively. "Vandervoost always gives you trouble, always wants to take over your job. Why is he helping you now?"

"I think he's honest about wanting to get his own damn winter heat from someplace other than Russia. Speaking of danger, you heard Arch Webber was killed?" Lynn asked.

Patrick pursed his lips. Dena and David stared at the ground. Decatur stared at each of them in turn as if looking for signs of guilt.

"Yeah. Damn shame. Any leads?" Dwayne asked.

"We're trying to figure it out and NOPD is on it," Decatur said. "The hotel had a video of a man entering Arch's room."

"And you? Have you seen anything strange lately?" Lynn asked.

"Glad you mentioned it. There's something I have to show you," Dwayne said.

He guided them to his computer. "Our security contractors sent this over. See this guy? They'd never seen him before. He's not the one on the hotel video in New Orleans is he?"

Lynn looked and saw no resemblance. "Your intruder is light-skinned. The one going into Arch's room wasn't."

Dwayne said, "So, he's poking around last night. Three A.M. Somehow he disabled all but one camera, yet its video is decent, even in the dark. The thermal imaging was operative, too."

She looked at the video. While it was short, some of the man's features could be discerned. Big, bunched shoulders. Elvis Presley hairstyle. "He left one camera working and doesn't seem worried someone might get a look at him. It's as if he's taunting us, or threatening us."

"Where was this taken?" Decatur asked.

"Near the first compressor station. It feeds two of the biggest pipelines in the Northeast. But see, he just walks around," Dwayne said.

"At three A.M.?" Patrick said.

"Yeah."

"Did our security people challenge the guy?" Lynn asked.

"Yes. The man said he was local, couldn't sleep, was out walking. He left at their request." Dwayne said. "Climbed into a white pickup."

"I'll follow up with them," Decatur replied. "Anyone get a plate number?"

"Yes. The security guys ran it. Out-of-state rental. They're getting a name on it now."

"I'd bet bogus," she said.

He nodded. "So, want me to tell the cops to beef up patrols here?"

"Yep. And send the video to Mark Shepherd," Lynn said. "He has access through his law enforcement network to new facial recognition software and some huge database. Let's see what he comes up with. Run the idea of more of our own patrols past him. At a minimum we'd better look at getting a different security company."

Lynn worried that yet another TriCoast operation, and more of her people, were being threatened. The TriCoast group gathered around Dwayne before heading to their nearby hotel. Patrick Boudreaux asked about running trails.

David said, "Sounds good but remember, bears roam around here."

"David's right," Dwayne added. "I've seen 'em early in the morning. They actually killed one field worker, and we've heard of other encounters. Just don't get near cubs or between a mother and her cubs. That's when attacks on humans occur. And don't carry or wear anything smelly, especially not food. They're paws-and-jaws eating machines."

"Eating. My kind of work," Dena whispered to Lynn.

Lynn smiled. Dena didn't look as if she spent much time eating.

"A few more rules while we're on the subject," Dwayne said. "Don't go anywhere alone. The bears weigh two hundred pounds on average but some weigh six hundred pounds or more. They can run faster than you think, over thirty miles an hour. They're your height or taller. If you meet a bear, don't run, don't scream, and don't make any sudden moves. Just make yourself look as big as possible."

Before splitting up at the small town's largest motel, the Tri-Coast group agreed to a five-mile run the next morning.

In her room, Lynn video-chatted with Cy and the kids. When she was finished, she felt as lonely as a rock.

She switched on her computer and cell phone to answer texts and emails and watch a webinar on drilling technology David had recommended.

At one A.M. she was awakened by the sound of tense voices in the hall outside her room. She couldn't identify them except to hear one was lower than the other. *We're not the only ones staying here, but could David or Patrick or Decatur be arguing with someone?* Just as she got out of bed to hear better, the voices moved away into silence.

The following morning Lynn, Dena, Patrick, Decatur and David met in the bright, cool northern morning light. All wore jackets and sweatshirts. As a precaution, a man at the motel's front desk gave them bear bells. Lynn and Decatur carried cans of bear spray, too.

Within a few hundred yards, the road away from the motel was surrounded by dense forest. Lynn tried to see into it past the underbrush. *A giant clawed paw could reach out and swat one of us off our feet.* They ran on the main road through town and then onto the trail Dwayne had recommended, their bells jingling. He'd told them the trail ended at a high clearing. From there they could turn around and run back.

When they got to the clearing, everyone fist-bumped and stared at the view of the surrounding hills and forests.

Dena pointed. A bear with two cubs ambled onto the trail forty yards away, blocking it. A second, smaller trail to the west offered another exit but crossing in front of the bears could draw them toward the group. In every other direction the drop-offs were a hundred feet or more, so any jumps could result in broken legs or worse.

The cubs walked closer on all fours. Their mother stripped bark and ate, oblivious. A thin drizzle started.

Two forty-pound balls of fur and inquisitiveness edged toward the humans, sniffing the air. Then they disappeared from view.

"Where are they?" Lynn asked.

Thrashing noises sounded nearby. Two pair of black, inquisitive eyes and two short, stubby cub noses poked out of the bushes twenty yards away, making noises like children chuckling.

"Holy shit!" Dena exclaimed. "You guys are cute but don't come any closer."

Decatur and Lynn edged between the cubs and the group. The cubs continued to stare and sniff, locking their gazes on the strange creatures in front of them.

Patrick said, "Remember, no screaming or running,"

"Screaming is exactly what I want to do!" Dena whispered.

The cubs inched even closer.

Patrick pointed to the sow, who had now noticed her cubs were gone. She sniffed the air for her cubs' scent and started grunting.

"She's headed toward us!" Dena sounded panicked.

The sow appeared to weigh eight or ten times as much as her cubs, a killing machine made even deadlier by her maternal instinct, just as they'd been told.

The sow followed her cubs' scents to their location twenty yards away and huffed at them. Then she turned her head to look at the humans. Lynn could see the bear's enormous paws, her heavily-muscled jaws and her furry snout. *Thank God the cubs haven't moved right up to us. Yet.*

The sow sniffed, as if she winded them. The cubs' bright gazes followed their mother's and one of them whimpered.

"Check your pockets again," Lynn said. "Does anyone have anything?"

Each person unzipped pockets and reached in.

"Goddamn," David whispered angrily. "There's nothing in my pockets but they sure as hell smell like bacon."

"No sudden movements. Take off the jacket and give it to me," Lynn whispered. "Patrick, cover me." She stood up as tall as possible, stretched out, took the jacket, and walked ten yards away from the group and toward the sow, her bear bell jingling. She had one hand on the jacket and one on her bear spray.

I don't want to die.

She dropped the jacket and backed toward the group, watching the sow, who was watching her.

"Let's go on the other trail," Decatur whispered. "If we move slowly, we can get to it."

The sow and her cubs began to lope toward them. Lynn and the rest of the group eased onto the westward path out of the clearing. Patrick took the lead with Lynn and Decatur at the rear, closest to the bears. It took every nerve she had not to run.

Then the sow put her nose to the ground and snuffled toward the discarded jacket. When she pawed through it, her sharp claws tore at the pockets. She chewed on them and shredded the jacket into tiny ribbons.

"Fuck. That could have been me," David said.

The group stumbled down the path. After an eternity, they reached the intersection of the trail with the paved road.

"Okay, we can run now," Patrick advised.

Their relief was palpable as they sprinted toward town.

Lynn wiped drizzle from her face. *Was David really so careless or did someone smear bacon in his jacket?*

CHAPTER 13

NEW ORLEANS

At Officer O'Shaughnessy's request, Reese met him in the French Quarter to search Madame Taliesin's apartment.

"We have Madame Taliesin on camera going into Arch's hotel room," O'Shaughnessy said. "Remember when you, Lynn, and her bodyguard watched as I interviewed Gail? Gail was the nearby neighbor who'd put her husband in the hospital with a kidney punch. She told us she saw Madame Taliesin that night. No one else has reported seeing Madame Taliesin since. I have a warrant to search her apartment. Since you were a friend of Mr. Webber's, I thought you might recognize anything of his in her apartment, maybe something Madame Taliesin left behind."

"Was Madame Taliesin an anti-oil activist? Maybe out to get anyone she could find associated with TriCoast or other energy companies?" Reese asked.

"She's a local character, a longtime alcoholic like many here, but no, I've never seen her or heard of her attending protests of any kind. Some people with addictions, and Madame Taliesin was one despite her high-toned exterior, have all they can do to put one foot in front of another day after day. But I could be wrong."

Madame Taliesin's apartment was located near Jackson Square, where Reese and the TriCoast group had met her and where Gail had reported seeing her later.

The building's owner directed them to through a courtyard to a two-story structure which had been slaves' quarters more than a hundred and fifty years earlier. While renovated to Vieux Carré building code so the exterior looked as it had two centuries ago, the building's apartments now boasted princely rents.

"I haven't seen her for a few days but that's not unusual," the burly owner said.

"What about her neighbors?" O'Shaughnessy asked. Reese wondered if the owner would say anything about Gail and the punch she'd landed on her husband.

The owner shook his head. "Everyone here is so transient. Madame was the exception—she's lived here for years. Most come in, pay the two months' rent I require, then after another few months come up short. They skip out or I throw them out. Happened with the people on either side of Madame."

No mention of Gail, which seemed odd to Reese. By the look O'Shaughnessy gave him, he'd noticed the omission, too.

The burly owner knocked on an orange door to a second-floor apartment. "Madame? Madame?"

When no one answered, he opened the door with a key attached to an orange-colored ribbon. "Madame?"

No answer.

"If you'll wait outside," Officer O'Shaughnessy asked the man. "This could be a crime scene. Madame Taliesin was photographed entering the room of a man who was murdered. We need to limit the number of people in her apartment."

"But I own this building!"

"Please stay outside," O'Shaughnessy repeated to the building owner, including Reese in his directions. The men reluctantly complied.

O'Shaughnessy stepped in and cleared each room. He returned to the orange door and nodded at Reese. "No one here. You can come in." He shook his head at the building owner. "Sir, please continue to wait outside."

The inside of the apartment was so spare it appeared Madame Taliesin spent as little time in it as possible. In one corner, an iPod sat on a stack of vinyl records. A rime of dust covered a glass-topped table.

O'Shaughnessy nodded toward the door. "No need to have him in here. It's possible he could have helped Madame Taliesin attack or kill Arch. She's a small woman. Although he doesn't resemble the man on the hotel video."

Reese drew his arm in a big circle. "Nothing, let alone protest literature. I don't even see books or a computer or a phone charger."

"Check out the kitchen."

A trash can rattled with empty liquor bottles. Full ones lined the shelves. O'Shaughnessy pulled on gloves, opened the refrigerator, and pointed to a bottle of white wine. "She was provisioned for a hurricane party, not much else."

Although it appeared no one had been in the apartment for a few days, Reese was careful not to touch anything. "There's nothing here I recognize as belonging to Arch."

"She doesn't seem to have been here in the last few days. Certainly no white parasol. Maybe she's staying with friends."

When they left, O'Shaughnessy gave the building owner his card. "Call me when Madame Taliesin returns."

Madame Taliesin awoke on her back in a room lit by a small lamp and a sliver of sunlight poking through outside shutters. The light seeping in told her it was late afternoon.

Her head hurt. When she felt it, her hand came away sticky and brownish-red. Despite the closed floor-to-ceiling shutters, she could smell the Mississippi River nearby.

She groaned. The dinner at the Big Oyster. Very generous with the drinks there. She'd be going back.

As she slowly awakened, she realized only her head hurt, nothing else. *Thank God.*

She didn't remember coming to this place, not at all. But she did remember what happened the night right after the big dinner in Jackson Square with all those lovely people . . .

Madame Taliesin folded her white parasol, crossed Decatur Street and stumbled as she walked on St. Ann toward her apartment. She waved as she passed her neighbor, Gail, not surprised to see her out on a warm night like tonight. Gail was the one who beating up her husband every time he cheated on her. *She's going to kill him one of these days.* A slight, hooded figure caught up with her as she turned the corner at Jackson Square.

"I don't have anything for you," Madame said, expecting the familiar supplication.

"I don't want anything. I thought maybe I could buy you a drink?"

"Have I met you before?" Madame Taliesin peered through the dark, squinting alcohol-rheumy eyes to look at a young man who was keeping his face hidden. Or was it a woman? Madame Taliesin decided. Man. It didn't matter. A drink was a drink. "Wouldn't hurt to check back in with those nice people at Big Oyster."

They turned left at the corner of Jackson Square and walked in silence towards the Big Oyster.

"Closed," Madame Taliesin announced regretfully.

"We're not far from Bourbon. Something will be open there," the young man said.

They turned right at Toulouse. Madame Taliesin peered around. "Martin. I mean Martina!" she yelled to another friend, who waved back.

"I know everyone here," she told the young man. They turned left at Bourbon. Despite the young man's friendliness, Madame Taliesin was relieved to get back to the busy, commercial lights and music.

After a few more blocks and several of the strip clubs, she was getting impatient with her companion. "So where are we going?"

"These places are expensive. I don't want to pay extra for the shows," her companion said. "But I know a good place."

He guided her to another side street off of Bourbon. "You'll like it. It's closer to the river."

"You're wearing me out for these free drinks," Madame Taliesin said. "I'm almost sobered up, which I never want to be."

"This bar's over by the river. They don't skimp on the alcohol."

Madame Taliesin stopped and planted her feet. "No. Too dark."

He pulled a bottle from his jacket. "So keep me company and let's sit on the Moonwalk. You can help me finish this."

"You done dragging me around?"

He smiled. "I am."

They crossed Decatur toward a dark parking lot. The last thing Madame Taliesin remembered was the smash of the bottle against her skull and terrible, terrible pain . . .

She looked around the bare room. Her white parasol was gone. She never set it down. It must have been taken. Stolen.

She was dressed in clothes of a type she didn't own—a pair of sweat pants, a button-down chambray shirt, and running shoes. She tried to remember what had happened after the bottle smashed against her skull.

Nothing else came back to her. Could be a concussion, or could be near-normal since she passed out most nights.

What had happened to the young man with her? She hadn't seen him hit her, but he must have been the one. Why? And when, dear God, could she get another drink?

When she tried to stand, she fell. Her ankles were wrapped together with cord. Her left hand was tied to a chair with a droopy knot. Her right hand, the one she'd used to check her head wound, was free.

As small and weak as she was, it appeared whoever had bound her up wasn't worried she would be able to untie herself.

She worked the knots loose with her free hand, shook out her feet to get blood flowing, stood, and peered around the dim room. She tried the door but it was locked from the outside.

She needed a drink. No reason to wait here.

As she'd noticed before, the set of tall, narrow windows—more like doors—stretched from floor to ceiling and appeared to open to a balcony. She searched for a heavy object to break the windows but then spotted their hand cranks. She tested one and a long skinny window began to creak open.

This was too easy. Assuming it was the young man who'd cracked a bottle over her head, maybe he thought she'd died. Or maybe he didn't want her to die—he just wanted her clothes, shoes, and parasol. That could be a weird motive in other places, but not in the Quarter.

She opened two side-by-side windows inward. She waited but no one yelled or tried to stop her. Then she pushed open the outside shutters. Light shafted in and she saw she was in a room as plain as her own apartment.

No time to study the interior decorating. Gotta go.

She stepped out on a wooden platform hemmed in by an iron-lace balcony, a traditional French Quarter second story. She looked up and down the street. Decatur. Not too far from Iberville. A tougher part of the neighborhood than she liked.

The ugly clothes might help her. She gingerly swung one leg over the iron lace, held on with both hands, then swung the other leg over. Her toes gripped the ledge. She checked left and right and saw no cars coming on the street below. She hesitated a moment. *Broken ankle for sure.*

A man appeared underneath her, and spoke in a Russian-accented voice. "It appears I arrive just in time. I catch you. Jump."

She let go of the balcony and crashed on top of him.

He helped her to her feet. "Nothing broken."

A few other people nearby clapped.

"You are a brave woman to jump."

"I was trapped. I had no choice. And thank you, sir," Madame Taliesin said. "For true thanks, will you join me in a drink?" When the time to pay came and she didn't have the money, either her favorite bartenders would take her credit or this man would pay.

"Of course. But let me take you to a place I just found. We can get a bandage for your head there."

"What is your name? I'm Madame Taliesin."

"I know who you are. My name is Vikenti Andreev."

Everyone knew who she was, so it didn't surprise her when this man did, too.

He directed her to a nearby bar, one she often avoided as too rough for the refinement of Madame Taliesin. The bartender said, "Lots of blood, but a small cut," and applied a bandage.

Madame and Vikenti chatted and laughed as evening turned into late night. He matched her drink for drink. *Those Russians.*

Well past midnight, he helped her to her feet. "You live near? I walk you home."

Outside the swinging doors, he steered her left onto Iberville, toward the river.

She shook her head. "This isn't the right way."

"It is. Do you need I carry you?"

"No."

"Yes, you do." As they passed a dark courtyard, he pulled her into it.

Madame Taliesin never saw the knife that cut her throat. Andreev severed her vocal cords first. Her eyes widened in terror but her scream was soundless.

He unfolded and unzipped a canvas bag he had stashed earlier in a corner of the courtyard. He rolled her into it. The bag was large enough and she was small enough he could hoist her body onto the dolly he had also hidden.

He rolled his cargo downriver along French Quarter streets. A few blocks past Café du Monde, he slid into the shadows. Finally, he reached his destination near Governor Nicholls Street Wharf.

Andreev tossed the bag into the Mississippi River.

Her body might get lodged there or it might disappear into the Gulf of Mexico. It did not matter. He had disposed of the problem.

CHAPTER 14

NEW ORLEANS

Kim Garvey reported for Coast Guard reserve duty. Although she was physically away from her job managing the Marrero Refinery, the responsibility was on her mind.

Indeed, it was the trouble-maker at her Marrero job, Patrick Boudreaux, in *his* volunteer job as a government risk manager, who briefed the reservists and recruits on where they were headed when they boarded the cutter. "I'm going to talk and then go to your stations. One place you'll be patrolling is the Louisiana Offshore Oil Port, or LOOP. The Coast Guard's Bertholf cutters—on which you're riding now—will improve your duty."

As they got underway, Patrick explained LOOP was eighteen nautical miles offshore Louisiana, or twenty miles south of Port Fourchon, which he pronounced *FOO-Shon*. "It's in deeper water than any other harbor, a hundred and ten feet. It can handle over a million barrels a day of imports and another three hundred thousand barrels a day of Gulf of Mexico crude. The offshore terminal is three mooring buoys in a hundred and ten feet of water.

"Although there are over three thousand oil tankers worldwide, only the biggest ones come here. So, tankers offload oil at LOOP. It's piped to storage onshore at Clovelly, twenty-five miles inland. Clovelly has eight underground salt dome caverns capable of storing sixty million barrels. Then the crude is piped to the refineries and petrochemical plants on the Gulf Coast and up into the Midwest.

"For those of you who always inquire about size,"—at this, the man next to Kim snorted—"the largest of these tankers has an 85-foot draft, is more than a quarter-mile long, and transports four million barrels of oil. The ships are imaginatively named: VLCCs and ULCCs for Very Large and Ultra Large Crude Carriers."

He handed around a graph whose peaks and valleys drifted downward from left to right. "With all the shale production, there's less need for imports, so volumes through LOOP are now around a few hundred thousand barrels a day, a third of what they used to be. However, we expect the volumes will ramp up again when the platform is re-piped for oil exports, not just imports. So LOOP will remain a critical piece of infrastructure. While it's civilian, in a way it's part of our national defense."

Kim knew the shale guys at TriCoast like David Jenkins were happy to be exporting oil, but as someone whose biggest cost was oil, she wasn't excited to have more competitors from South American or Asian refineries. Still, David and Patrick said it helped all of them by encouraging American energy companies. And having stable US suppliers who followed the same laws she did was important.

As they took their stations for the remainder of the trip out, Kim recalled the map mounted on the wall beside her desk. It showed where her refinery's oil was sourced: Saudi Arabia and Mexico via LOOP for sour crude. Light sweet crude came in from TriCoast's production all around the United States, and medium sweet the company produced and traded from offshore blocks in Ship Shoal, South Timbalier, Grand Isle, West Delta, Main Pass, and Breton Sound.

As they got closer, Patrick pointed out a tanker a considerable distance away from a platform. "From the schedule, this one's about to leave. Notice you don't see anything around the tanker but water. It's not pulled up at the platform. It's a mile and a half away."

One of the men with her whistled.

"The tanker connects to one of those three offshore hoses I told you about and pumps out oil. The hoses connect to a single buoy mooring base and the oil goes in a 56-inch underwater pipeline to the marine terminal you see over there. It looks like your standard offshore installation because it is. Got the control platform separate from the pumping platform and away from the pipeline. Easier and safer. We're going to the platforms, not the tanker."

The cutter pulled next to the marine terminal and they climbed the ladder up to the top deck.

Patrick's manner eased as he introduced them to men and women he apparently knew well. He exchanged grins with the maintenance chief, Miles.

"Patrick, how's it hanging?" the large, jolly man in maintenance coveralls asked.

"Top form with this group, Miles," Patrick said. He correctly listed the hometowns and parishes for each new recruit and reservist. For active-duty reservists like Kim, Patrick also included their tours of duty. "Kimberley Garvey, two tours, one each Iraq and Afghanistan."

She didn't expect anything further, but Patrick also said, "Garvey is TriCoast's Marrero refinery manager in her civilian job."

Miles looked at her and said, "So you're always thinking about this oil coming into your refinery and whether us folks out here need anything special like Picou's doughnuts or new fishing lures."

She smiled. "Yes sir, I am. And I will do so in the future, sir. Picou's."

Miles showed them the pumping platform with its giant pumps, power generators, instruments, and laboratory. The control platform was where everyone on the platform lived and worked. "We do rotations, same as every other platform out here." He waved his arm around. "You got your heli pad, your bunks and kitchen, life support stuff if we need it, and tanker traffic control station for those big suckers at the buoy."

Miles looked at the recruits and got serious. "Now if we ever call for you boys and girls, it's like the Macondo fire. It's for damn sure serious and I want you here ASAP."

Decatur drove Lynn and Reese along St. Charles to the New Orleans Police Department's French Quarter station. The sight of vast, green Audubon Park made her miss Jean-Marie Taylor, who had been a fellow Tulane engineer as well as Patrick's sister.

They passed one of the old, wooden green Perley streetcars drifting along its tracks and she wished she had time to ride in it. She remembered standing on the St. Charles median, looking toward the tracks' vanishing point for the headlamp of an arriving streetcar. The streetcars rocked in somnolent rhythm late at night and their sounds were legendary: clicking when the car stopped, absolute quiet when the electric motor shut off and a low rumble when it started up again, the slight bumping noise of the pantograph—an articulating mechanism on the streetcar roof collecting electricity from the overhead catenary.

"You look like you'd rather be on one of those streetcars," Reese said.

"Nailed."

As a student, she had memorized names of the cross streets so different from her Tulsa hometown: Louisiana, Napoleon, Jefferson, as well as streets named for the Graces: Terpsichore and Melpomene. Street names projecting ethereal loftiness and frank lust in the swampy city: *Elysian Fields. Desire.*

New Orleans was an all-sensory experience—from tradition and history to food, music, verdure, and architecture. Lynn relished its neighborhoods: the Garden District to the Central Business District through the French Quarter and Faubourg

Marigny and on into the industrial suburbs. Like the wall once dividing East from West Berlin, New Orleans' Canal Street divided old English and French districts whose histories were embedded in the changes of street names as they crossed Canal, from Carondelet, St. Charles, and Camp to Bourbon, Royal, and Chartres.

They parked a few blocks away from the police station.

"I meet you for ten," is what Officer O'Shaughnessy had said, and he was prompt.

"I have bad news," he said as soon as he saw Lynn, Reese and Decatur. "We found a body in the Bloody Muddy, the Mississippi River, this morning. We're checking dental records, but we're fairly sure it's Madame Taliesin."

"The real Madame Taliesin is dead?" Lynn was shocked. "When did it happen? How?"

"The coroner will fill us in when she knows. At 6 A.M. this morning a shipping company security officer spotted something wedged under the docks near Governor Nicholls Street Wharf. He moved closer, saw a body wrapped in canvas. Got some of the officers on shift and the coroner there."

"Who killed her? It must have been the guy on the hotel video," Reese said. "After knocking off Arch, he must have killed Madame Taliesin."

O'Shaughnessy said, "Could be. We'll get to that. Your group saw Madame Taliesin at The Big Oyster the night Arch was killed, correct?"

"Yes," Lynn said.

"Madame's death makes it even more critical for us to construct a timeline. I have a person I want you to hear, and then I have other news for you," O'Shaughnessy said.

They got up and walked through a warren of old desks and new computers. "Martina claims to have seen Madame Taliesin the same night you and Gail did, but later."

"Just let me clean up, O'Shaughnessy darling." A woman in high heels tottered by. Her wig was askew and her tight shorts showed flabby thighs and a few weeks' growth of hair. "One of the tenants came through last night and absolutely *destroyed* my apartment. Knocked pictures off the wall. Smashed light bulbs. Left enough trash in there to plant *sweet potatoes*. I opened up one bag and a dozen cockroaches came flying out. Took me forever to sweep and straighten."

"You remember where the bathrooms are," O'Shaughnessy said to her.

"Uh humn. But why's the ladies' so small?" She pushed open the door into the women's restroom and projected her deep voice. "Yo. Tranny on the loose. Don't panic, ladies."

As they waited, O'Shaughnessy said, "In my experience she's honest, although her perspective can be different."

"You mean as trans?" Decatur asked.

"Nah. You ask her what time it is and she tells you it's Sunday. Little unusual, but so's this whole city."

They got coffee. After ten minutes, Martina joined them clean, refreshed, smooth-legged, hair coiffed, striding confidently in four-inch heels. "Do I look fabulous?"

"Awesome." O'Shaughnessy introduced Lynn, Reese, and Decatur.

"You one of those businesswomen who finds dinner in the frozen food aisle?" Martina asked Lynn.

"Yes," Lynn said.

"You're a bit old for my taste," she said to Reese. "But you, handsome! Tough-looking," she said to Decatur. Martina turned to Lynn. "Plenty of testosterone in that one. Quite the bodyguard you've got there."

Lynn smiled.

"Martina, Mr. Webber worked with Ms. Dayton, Mr. Spencer, and Mr. Decatur," O'Shaughnessy said. "Martina, bad news. Madame Taliesin has been missing for a few days. We found her body this morning."

Martina shook her head wailed. "She was my friend! She was everyone's friend! She wouldn't hurt a flea."

O'Shaughnessy handed Martina a handkerchief.

Martina's expression changed immediately. "Don't pull that DNA crap on me. I got my own and I'm keeping it." She took out a tissue, blew her nose, and stuck the tissue back in her purse.

"Everything Mr. Spencer and Arch's colleagues tell me suggests it was unusual for Mr. Webber to open the door to his room. You knew Madame Taliesin. Now it seems you might have been one of the last to see her alive. Was she acting out of character?"

Martina wiped away more tears with the back of her hand. "It sucks. After all the good Madame Taliesin did for everyone—the sum of her life, her relationships, jobs, her dolls—it's overshadowed by the last few hours of her life."

Lynn nodded.

"Okay. So, I saw her before I went to do my show. It was a slow night for Bourbon Street, I remember. Then when I was walking back, I saw her walking on Toulouse toward the river. She was with a guy in a hoodie. Not as hot as Mr. Decatur here."

O'Shaughnessy questioned her further. Martina couldn't remember more details but promised she would call O'Shaughnessy if she did.

After she left Lynn asked, "What was the other news you mentioned?"

"Remember the second person in the room? Matak Abdullah from South Sudan? He's dead, too," O'Shaughnessy said.

"What?!" Lynn exclaimed.

"It was a follow-up from INTERPOL on the Red Notice. Matak was run over by a train in Vienna, Austria. He fell from a bridge over the tracks."

Lynn winced. "Can't be a coincidence."

"I'm not sorry for him, since it looks like he killed or helped kill Arch," Reese said. "But why? Why him? Why Arch? What the hell was Matak doing shipping out from New Orleans to Vienna?"

"There's more," O'Shaughnessy said. "He didn't just fall. He was pushed. Pushed off the bridge by another man, an Asian man, onto the tracks."

"So he was murdered but the description of his killer could be any of hundreds of millions," Reese said.

O'Shaughnessy nodded. "The cameras on the bridge don't show much detail. Here's where we're in luck. Anyone could figure out when Matak was shoved from the time and date stamp on the camera pictures. Since the men appeared to be not just from out of town but non-European, local authorities circulated Matak's picture with the shadowy one of the man who apparently pushed him."

"Someone remembered them?" Lynn asked.

O'Shaughnessy smiled and smacked the table victoriously. "More than one. Various retailers on Kärntner Strasse, where Matak and his killer had shopped, wanted to know when they would be back. The clerks remembered because Matak's apparent killer was paying for purchases, very large purchases. Even better, a waiter and a front desk man at the Sacher Hotel, where they seem to have stayed, identified them both by copies of their passports they were required to provide. If we can assume the passport is real and not fake, big *if*, Matak's killer is named Cong Li."

Reese looked at Lynn in surprise. "Cong any relation to our Curtis Zhang at TriCoast or any of the several people working at TriCoast with a last name of Li?"

"I hope not, but you're asking a good question. I'm not sure how we get the answer except by monitoring communications, which introduces a huge privacy problem if it's even possible. It's been explained to me there are about a half-dozen common Chinese surnames, including Li and Zhang, so millions of people have the same name but aren't related." Lynn turned back to O'Shaughnessy. "So has any kind of Red Notice or BOLO been issued for Cong Li?"

"INTERPOL and Homeland Security have his name, so I imagine he's on some kind of list now. I'm sure the Viennese police are involved. Maybe federal Austrian investigators, too."

Later Reese, Decatur, and Lynn met David Jenkins and Patrick Boudreaux at TriCoast's nearby New Orleans office. Lynn, David, and Patrick conference-called Dena and discussed the terms of a Mexican production-sharing contract due for negotiation. Underlying the discussion was anxiety about how many competitors had gotten TriCoast's Gulf of Mexico lease bidding plans from Arch Webber's computer.

"It's late but we need a new strategy," David said. "Dena, you and some of your folks are working on it with my guys for tomorrow, right?"

"Have been and will be," Dena replied.

Lynn, Reese, Patrick, and David, accompanied by Beau Decatur, arrived at Galatoire's in the French Quarter, a formal, established restaurant where only clueless tourists made reservations. The maitre d' asked Lynn if she had a regular waiter. Despite her head shake, when the maitre d' recognized Patrick from his uncle's restaurant, he awarded them a prime table.

They talked strategy for the US and the Mexican bid rounds in the Gulf of Mexico. In the back of her mind, Lynn made new plans.

As they departed the restaurant into the hurly-burly of Bourbon Street, Lynn pulled Reese aside. "I'm calling Kanak Singh in San Francisco to find out if he's ever heard of this Cong Li. Will you find out if Cong works for the Chinese government?"

"Yes. Anything to find out who's responsible for Arch Webber's death."

CHAPTER 15

Vikenti called Cong to update him. "Your suspicion was correct. The old woman in New Orleans was alive. Now she is not."

"I am glad I can rely on your expertise," Cong said.

"Now, for my country's objectives. I have tested the security at the TriCoast Pennsylvania field site. It can be overcome. It would greatly benefit Russia to inflict damage there."

But it would hurt China, Cong thought. He gave an indirect answer. "Delay such an undertaking. Other projects are more important."

At Vikenti's grunt Cong added, "I meant, more important to Russia."

"Yes, that is true. In fact, I am now on my way to Klaipéda. Lithuania has tormented us far too long with its primitive LNG port. It is time to close it and I must do so."

To free itself from relying on Russia's Gazprom for natural gas for heat, Lithuania had opened a liquefied natural gas port at Klaipéda a few years earlier. The port allowed the former Soviet satellite country to import natural gas from any country able to load and ship it in liquefied form. Suddenly Lithuania was buying more than half of the natural gas it needed from non-Russian sources, including TriCoast and others in the United States.

When Mark Shepherd, TriCoast's security officer, asked for an emergency meeting with Lynn, her assistant arranged it.

"What's up?" Sara Levin, the company's chief financial officer, wanted to know when she, Lynn, and Mark sat down together in Lynn's office. "I cut short a call with one of our biggest pension investors." Although people who managed tight budgets could also be restrained in their personal manner, Sara didn't fit the mold.

"Believe me, this is news you want to hear before your investors do," Mark said.

Lynn was surprised when Jim Cutler, special agent in charge from the local FBI office, entered behind Mark. She was even more surprised to see Patrick Boudreaux joining them.

Lynn closed her office door. "Can't be good."

"I'll get right to the point," Cutler said. "TriCoast has a security breach. TriCoast information has been showing up on dark web sites with an offer to sell more."

"Crap, are you kidding? Do Mike and David know?" Lynn was referring to TriCoast's CEO and vice president of exploration.

Mark nodded.

"Show me the site," Sara said.

"It's offline now. In fact, Patrick here was the one who found the site and got it taken down. Your info was exposed for five or six hours," Mark said.

"But for anyone who took a screen shot it might as well be forever," Lynn moaned. "What was posted?"

"A list of offshore blocks on which TriCoast is bidding in the next Gulf of Mexico auction. The 'merchandise' offered for sale were the amounts TriCoast planned to bid."

"Sounds like it came straight from Arch Webber's stolen computer," Sara said.

"Listen, while we closed this site, we didn't find the originating leak or a hack. It's still out there, maybe more than one place. The company is still exposed," Mark explained.

"We traced it through a few layers of encryption to Chinese or Eastern European servers," Cutler added. "And much more *was* being offered."

Lynn thought of the information from O'Shaughnessy about Matak's killer's name, or the name he was using. *Cong Li.* "Mark, Jim, I assume you've heard the Viennese police found Matak Abdullah dead. Matak is believed to be the man the New Orleans' hotel video shows going into Arch Webber's room the night he was killed. The Viennese police also have the name of the man staying at the same hotel with Matak and seen with him there in Vienna. Cong Li."

"Yes, I've heard," Cutler says. "That's part of our case. Cong is Chinese. But so are 1.4 billion other people."

The proverbial needle in a haystack. "So what else of ours is being offered on the dark web?" Lynn asked.

"Offshore bids, past and planned. Refinery upgrades. Engineering schematics. Seismic data. Crude oil sources. Financial and accounting data."

"Damn it! So they—whoever 'they' is—know everything. Where we're going to drill next, our newest sulfur reduction technology, maybe even the earnings data we'd be releasing next week." Lynn turned to Mark. "Is Sansei involved?"

Mark shook his head. "Sansei has broken up." The pan-Asian Sansei group had been similar to OPEC, except composed of oil buyers instead of oil sellers. He added, "You get the Koreans, the Chinese, and the Japanese together with the Indonesians and other Asian countries, and now they're each powerful, especially the Chinese with their giant economy and their multi-country Silk Road initiative. So when they can't agree, they start disrupting one another's economies and spying on one another. No country wants to help another compete to buy the same oil. So no Sansei."

Lynn shuddered. "You said you didn't find the originating hack, or computer zero. Can you identify anything on the location of the breach or breaches?"

"We think the Chinese ended up with at least some of the information. We're working on any other data leakages with Kanak Singh and the folks at his company," Mark said.

"The Chinese have partners for their Gulf of Mexico projects, and they own big chunks themselves. Would they be interested in vacuuming information from us, too?" Lynn asked. She looked down at her hands. She'd pretzeled a half-dozen paper clips.

"They want data and plans from everyone. They've hacked or tried to hack into several energy companies. What's different for TriCoast is they weren't only hacking. They were actually *receiving*. It appears one or more people at TriCoast gave them special access."

"Christ on a pogo stick! Who? And what do you want us to do?" Sara asked.

"Let's start with an obvious question," Cutler said. "Who in your organization speaks Mandarin, is a recent Chinese émigré, or would have a reason and ability to leak this information?"

Lynn looked at Mark. "Curtis Zhang is the only one I can think of. But he's an excellent manager for the San Francisco refinery and couldn't be more attentive to his job." She felt sick at the accusation. "As for people with Mandarin language skills, or Chinese heritage, the group could be dozens or hundreds."

Cutler said, "To save us both time, run us through what you understand about your cybersecurity."

Lynn poured herself a glass of water. "We're members of an oil and gas cybersecurity-sharing hub with two dozen other energy companies."

"One of the seventeen industry ISACs or Information-Sharing and Analysis Centers. No offense, but ISACs are the blind leading the blind," Cutler said.

Lynn looked hard at him. "More than anyone else, the other companies understand all the people in all the countries we buy oil from and sell products to. They're the ones who first described Unit 61938 on Datong Road, in China—a whole building of hackers. They also understand our refining and oil production equipment far better than the FBI ever will, thank you very much. We do keep you at the FBI up to speed and vice versa because we're also in Infragard, which is supposed to be an FBI-industry partnership."

Cutler nodded. "The Chinese strategy is to be every-where—they target every company with trade secrets or intellectual property worth stealing or copying so they don't spend the expense and time of inventing it."

"They're like a giant fishing trawler—hauling in everything and sorting it later," Sara suggested.

"They do exactly that too, in reality," Cutler said. "Off the coast of Africa. Hell on the small fishermen there. But let me give you a specific example. One Chinese hacker was caught when he tried to access a US utility company's systems which would allow him to control pipelines and cut off water supplies. The same group we mentioned, Unit 61398 of the PLA, hacked at least five US companies and a labor union in the steel, solar and nuclear-power industries for information on computers, pricing, and technology. Many hackers are employed by the government but others are freelancers who may take orders—literally, as if from a menu—from the military or state-owned companies requesting technology delivered to them instead of developing it or leasing it themselves. Here again, when a Chinese company says they 'provide information technology services,' they mean they steal corporate secrets."

"So grim," Lynn replied, wishing for ways to stop them.

"We have the same capabilities," Cutler said.

"That doesn't make me feel one iota better," Sara responded.

"The worst case is a hacker taking down electric utilities and water systems," Patrick said. "A Russian group using the names of "Energetic Bear" and "Dragonfly" tried to do so. The Russians have been practicing on Ukraine, taking their power plants offline for hours. They're sometimes successful at remotely controlling electricity grids, petroleum pipelines, electricity generation, and other important energy companies. It's worrisome enough our Department of Energy set up its own cybersecurity and energy infrastructure security response office."

Lynn shook her head. "Terrible, and I'm glad you're already on it. But my problem is right here, right now." *Who killed Arch and stole his computer? Who were Matak Abdullah and Madame Taliesin working for?* NOPD would examine fingerprints and get more evidence from the crime scenes.

She couldn't wait for answers from NOPD or the FBI or Patrick Boudreaux. She would start by questioning Curtis Zhang.

The Alpine, a Liberian-flagged double-hulled VLCC, very large crude carrier, took on its two dozen crew and hundreds of thousands of tons of Arab Medium Sour crude oil at Ras Tanura, the largest Saudi terminal. The Alpine was an average-sized carrier in the Saudi fleet. Its volume of about two million barrels would need twenty-eight hours to unload once it arrived at LOOP, the Louisiana Offshore Oil Platform in the Gulf of Mexico. After the crude was refined into gasoline and diesel, it would be worth more than a hundred and fifty million dollars at the pump.

The ship's common language would be English, according to the German captain, Karl Beyer, under whom Liamzon and his cousin had served on another voyage. After their credentials were checked again by the ship's security officer, they boarded the big tanker, where the odor of hydrocarbons mixed with the smell of the dirty, salty ocean.

The Alpine left Ras Tanura on a clear day. Matak Abdullah had told Liamzon where to position himself once the tanker approached the LOOP terminal. He had told Liamzon's cousin to be certain Liamzon followed directions. But there was no need because Liamzon was so certain the heaven awaiting him would far surpass his earthly life.

He and his cousin were the only ones who knew where the bomb was. He verified its placement twice a day. He checked the cell phone trigger in his locker, which remained undisturbed. A back-up was ready, in case the primary trigger did not work. And the beauty of the back-up trigger, as Matak had explained to him, was it could go off even if he and his cousin were dead.

They would be busy aboard the Alpine until they neared LOOP. Up to the last moment they would spend their time cleaning and maintaining the engines in the excellent, thorough way that had earned them these jobs.

CHAPTER 16

DALLAS AND CALIFORNIA

Lynn was anxious to have Curtis Zhang, her San Francisco refinery manager, answer questions when she prepared for a video chat with him. Mark Shepherd, Patrick Boudreaux, and the FBI's Jim Cutler joined her in her office. Once she and Zhang were connected, she introduced the other three with her. "You know our security chief, Mark. FBI Agent Cutler is involved because this cybersecurity problem could spread beyond our refinery in California. We've hired Patrick Boudreaux to consult with us on risk and cybersecurity because we're short-handed for something so critical. He's helped lead our self-defense training, too." Lynn remembered the sweaty outdoor sessions.

"With these gentlemen here, you're not calling just about operations, I'm guessing," he said. "No recent bumps here."

"No, something different. Or someone, really," Lynn said. "Have you ever come across a man named Cong Li? He's in China, has a computer company there."

"You're giving me well over a billion people to consider, including fifty or a hundred million with a last name of Li," Zhang said. His voice got sharper. "Why, you people think I resemble Cong Li?"

Lynn questioned the wisdom of their four to his one on the video chat. She didn't want Zhang feeling defensive. "No," she said, and shook her head so he could see her disagreement. "I thought you might have met him at a conference or even online since he appears to do a lot of work for, or rather *on*, energy companies."

Cong slammed down his coffee and they could see black liquid slosh out of the cup. "Are you accusing me of letting some Chinese thief into TriCoast's San Francisco refinery system?"

Boudreaux started to speak and Lynn shook her head at him, mouthing *Let me handle this*. "No Curtis, I'm not. We're grasping at straws because you speak Mandarin—"

"—Along with maybe five hundred other people in this company, including dozens who *do* have the last name of Li. Like your engineering manager, Preston Li."

Lynn plowed ahead. "Curtis, here's the detail. Your refinery was disrupted via its control system. Someone got into the control system software. That disaster resulted in three deaths, including your human resources vice president, Shirley Watson. Then Arch Webber was killed in New Orleans."

"I heard about Arch, too. So terrible!" Zhang looked subdued.

Cutler interjected, "It appears he was killed by a man named Matak Abdullah—identified from the hotel cameras."

"Anyone catch Abdullah?" Zhang asked.

Cutler said, "He skipped the country. And before law enforcement could track him down, Matak was killed in Vienna."

Zhang grimaced. "Hell of a lot of killing going on."

Cutler continued, "Yes. And Matak's killer has been identified. Man spent the day with him in Vienna and is on various cameras there. The guy's name is Cong Li. That's why Lynn is asking you about him."

"Given his connection to Arch's killer, it looks to us as if Cong could be in charge of something big," Lynn said. She dreaded saying her next thought aloud. "Maybe official. Maybe for the Chinese government? Bottom line, Cong could be targeting us at TriCoast. So we're trying to figure out why did he start with us? We need to understand the connection and stop him. And if it's the Chinese government, we need to understand their motive."

Zhang nodded. "Let me float his name here, see if anyone else has heard of him. I won't give away why we want to know."

"So Cong could have been the source of the breach into our refinery. Do you have any more ideas as to how it happened?" Lynn asked.

"I've talked to people here—everyone's guess is a random virus. Damn. It's what the people out here call the "Red Queen" effect." We're running as fast as possible but staying in the same place. But I'll look further for any interactions with Cong Li."

"Have you heard from Kanak Singh lately?" Lynn was anxious to know herself yet she wanted it clear to her refinery manager he was in charge of his own refinery. *But can I really trust him?*

Zhang nodded. "I got all the official permissions I needed so I let Kanak Singh get deep into the system. He said he might have found the malware. He wanted to meet in person—didn't want to send anything online. He'll be here this afternoon at 1 PM. 3 PM your time."

"Good. Patch me in on video. I have questions for him," Lynn said. She turned to Cutler and Mark Shepherd and said, "Since that'll be an operational update, Patrick Boudreaux here is the only one who needs to be on the call. If Kanak has vital security information, we'll tell you-"

Boudreaux interrupted. "What should worry you too are your communications. In warfare—"

"—warfare?" Lynn asked, regretting her invitation to include Boudreaux on the afternoon call with Kanak. "Aren't you being extreme?"

"No. They're big systems, under attack," Boudreaux explained. "Several good analogies. In warfare, disabling or jamming the communications system is considered "loud," meaning it's too noticeable. Of course, communication jamming is a useful tool—it appears to have happened against the Ukrainians by the Russians when the Russians took Crimea. But many times an attacker prefers to get into the system and corrupt information. Even though just a small percentage of the data is wrong, the system becomes so unreliable users stop trusting it. And all kinds of communications depend on trust."

"Russia keeps coming to mind," Lynn said. "They supply about a third of the natural gas to Europe. But if Gazprom stops sending gas to Europe, and they've done so from time to time, the Europeans will be jacked up and ready to do whatever the Russians want."

"People without heat get desperate," Cutler agreed.

What do the Chinese want from us? Have they involved the Russians? Lynn thought. *Or the Saudis? What the hell is going on?*

Later in the day, Zhang called Lynn on the company's video chat system. He introduced Kanak Singh to Patrick Boudreaux and Lynn introduced Boudreaux to Kanak.

"Let me explain it's typical for hackers, who launch hundreds of millions of attacks a day, to create problems via what's called 'chaos by small doses.' They don't do a massive takedown, but instead pick away to find security holes," Kanak said.

"This appears to be what's happened to you at TriCoast. Your attacker was able to download a type of malware first identified in an attack in Ukraine, which suggests Russian involvement. The malware is called by two names: *Industroyer*, or *CrashOverride*. It was specifically designed to disrupt industrial-control systems like those at your refineries."

"Wow! What do we do?" Lynn asked.

"The malware receives instructions from and feeds data back to a host system. I'm trying to trace it now. Emphasis on the word *try*. The routings back to the original system are complex and hidden. But I'll pull the string and see if I can get all the way back."

"Will our operations be at risk while you're tracing?" Lynn asked.

"Not any more than they already have been. If anything, since we're monitoring in real time 24/7, you'll be alerted more quickly," Kanak said. "But we don't want them to know we're onto them, whoever they might be. In fact, I congratulate you. It takes most companies several months before they find an intruder in their systems and you've—we've—done it in a few weeks."

Lynn's face flushed. "No congratulations. We have three dead people due to that malware."

Kanak's expression fell. "Right. Of course. So sorry."

"Let me ask you what I've already asked Curtis. You ever come across a man named Cong Li?" Lynn asked.

"There are lots of people named Li, either real or fake names, in hacker world. Name doesn't ring a bell, but it's a huge help when we do our traces. Why do you mention it?"

Lynn explained Cong Li had killed Matak Abdullah after Matak had killed Arch Webber.

"No coincidences in this business. We'll check him out," Kanak said.

"While we're talking security, have you tested your security cameras at the refinery?" Patrick asked Lynn and Zhang.

"No, though I've been told some of our cameras in Pennsylvania were knocked out," Lynn said.

"You should get people to verify them, at least in Pennsylvania, as well as at your San Francisco Bay and Marrero refineries. There's a cheap Chinese-made brand many companies and governments around the world use, but most US government and secure installations no longer allow the brand. The cameras may have built-in back doors allowing hackers to gain access. It's happened before with a huge denial-of-service attack. And get this, the company's owners include people tied to the Chinese police and the Communist Party. In fact this company grew their business with contracts from Chinese government agencies."

"I've heard of them," Zhang said. "In fact, they just opened a research office nearby."

"Sure, let's get our security cameras checked, too," Lynn said. "Curtis, if you'll follow up with your refinery, I'll pass the word along to our Pennsylvania folks and Kim Garvey at Marrero."

"And hey. Minor point but I don't want to forget. We're speaking to all of our clients to say the rumors are true but not much has happened yet," Kanak said. Lynn thought she detected hesitation in his voice.

"You lost me, Kanak. What rumors?" Lynn asked. *Has Kanak's company itself been hacked?*

"ShireSafe has been talking to us about an acquihire."

Well, damn. ShireSafe was a giant cybersecurity firm with a habit of turning down energy company clients. Their stated reason was that they had better projects from the FBI, IRS, CIA, Homeland Security, and the Defense Department. ShireSafe's software helped clients analyze huge amounts of sensitive data to detect fraud, keep data secure, deliver health care, and respond to catastrophes. "By acquihire, you mean they're absorbing your company but you keep working for them?"

"Yes."

"Does this affect your project for us?" Lynn asked.

"No and yes. No because they're not one of those companies with a polyamory club, so we don't have to deal with that distraction."

"Since I don't live in Northern California, what's a polyamory club?" Lynn knew the answer but wanted to see Kanak's reaction.

Even with so-so screen pixilation it was apparent Kanak's skin had darkened in a blush, but he laughed. "They're all over the valley and some companies quietly support them. They're for people who want several lovers, male, female, groups, and so on. Think year-round Burning Man without the desert. You have to have an app to keep track of your . . . meetups."

People like Dwayne would flip out. Lynn nodded. "I can see an in-company polyamory club might be a distraction, and a huge security risk. You said no and yes. So how *does* ShireSafe acquiring your company affect you working for us?"

"Our client list may not completely mesh with theirs."

Maybe I'm just imagining the worst. Maybe I'm wrong. "They're one of those firms with a rigid no-hydrocarbon policy?"

"Yes, I'm sorry. They have long-term leases on a bunch of hard-to-get real estate for offices and hire slews of Stanford computer science grads. They're making us good offers and would put us into one of their SCIF buildings."

So I'm right about their anti-hydrocarbon bias. "SCIF?"

"Sensitive Compartmented Information Facility. A building that resists passive and active attempts to access the information inside. It's locked down and there's no way to get data out. Networks are air-gapped from the public Internet so no signals or information can be transmitted past its walls. It has advanced biometrics for security, walls impenetrable by radio waves, and heavily-protected storage of physical items and digital data."

"But Kanak, you're working for us now."

"Furiously. Twenty hours a day."

She wasn't sure whether or not to believe him. And if she did believe him, it wasn't all good news. The KS engineers would wear themselves out.

"I assume you're the one making the decision?"

Kanak nodded. "I and my board. To answer your next question, if we decide to go ahead, the deal would close in a few weeks. So we can keep working for you at least until then."

The video call concluded, Lynn left TriCoast's offices and drove a few miles to her next destination. Dark mesas of clouds banked in the west. She reluctantly handed the key fob of her Porsche to the Katy Trail Ice House valet—she was always reluctant to hand over her Porsche key—and walked inside to meet Dena for drinks. The bar was near the popular Dallas hike-and-bike trail for which it was named, and its interior rang with clinking bottles and loud, relaxed voices. This was part of her job—bringing younger managers like Dena along by meeting with them outside of the office so they could ask questions in an informal environment. At its simplest, Lynn relished the chance to have a beer with one of her fast-tracked and most capable employees.

They found a booth and ordered Shiner Bocks. Dena took off her jacket and rolled up her sleeves. "Time to get out of uniform. Though we won't really, will we?"

Lynn smiled and shrugged.

"In answer to the question you're ready to ask, yes, I'm happy. I'm starting to understand the culture. TriCoast is different from my last job. There the code was so well-developed we didn't need to explain much to one another. Everything was understood."

"What did you do before TriCoast?"

"Analysis of media companies at Kodiak. Everyone at my level and just above was female, so we were on the same wavelength. Where you stood depended on which companies you covered. The bigger the companies, the higher your status."

"Did you meet Josh Rosen? He's a trader at Kodiak."

"No. It's a big company. He must have been on a different floor. Maybe he's someone famous for fifteen people."

"Meaning?"

"He has a small network."

Lynn doubted it was true of hyperkinetic, hyper-connected Josh Rosen but decided not to argue. "What do you find similar between here and Kodiak?"

"Same Mack-truck-sized egos in the men. Same general sense of entitlement. You took chemistry, too, right?" Dena asked.

Lynn nodded.

"So you remember the only difference between estrogen and testosterone is the placement of the –OH and the =O groups," Dena said, drawing on a napkin. "And I still see men and women trying to shake off their competitors, though they're less vicious here than in New York."

As long as they don't kill one another, like Jay Gans tried to do to me, Lynn thought. "Who do you mean?"

"David Jenkins, for one. Surely you've seen the curl in his lip when he talks to you."

"He has the same expression with everyone. As TriCoast's production chief spending billions of dollars, for a while he was a king of the oil patch. Now he's throttled way back because of lower prices, but his division is still vital," Lynn said.

"So with current good refining economics, you're the queen?"

"Nope. Everything can change tomorrow in the refining biz. We compete at the pump. If another company cuts prices a dime a gallon, we have to do the same."

Dena tilted her head toward a large woman sitting at the bar. "Breasts a little gravity-stricken, don't you think?"

Lynn shrugged. "I hadn't noticed."

"Well, I do find the competition here different than in New York."

"Less?" Lynn asked.

"It still comes down to who can eat the least. But the delta of the standards of beauty between men and women are much wider here. In New York I was likely to run into one of my male buddies at Hermes. Here, the guys think they've got it made if they match their socks. The standards here are more time-consuming for women relative to men."

"What else have you observed?"

"I can assume none of the older, married men are having affairs."

"Why?" Lynn was curious.

"Other than the grapevine? See the hair sprouting from their ears? If a man is sleeping with a woman he's trying to impress, which usually means not his wife, he makes sure he doesn't look sloppy. They get those suckers plucked. It was one of the first things I learned from my father."

"Your father?"

"I came to terms with it a long time ago. My father was physically and verbally abusive. He had a string of affairs—so you can bet his ears were always hairless—but he never wanted a divorce. My mother—well, with three kids and no resources of her own, she had nowhere to go but crazy. She self-medicated with booze and pills."

"I'm sorry."

"Don't be. I played a lot of soccer and had my share of concussions on the field—still get the occasional migraine—but the sport got me out of the house. We kids stuck together and grew up okay, and my mother finally got sober enough, long enough, to divorce him. He'd come crying back to her, but when she was done, she was done."

Lynn nodded.

"All it means is I'm trying to do better with my boyfriend's kids. You have step-children, right?"

"I do now." Lynn's marriage still felt so new she had to remind herself she was married.

"My boyfriend has kids, too. Young ones, two, four and seven years old. Of course, he doesn't have them all the time. He shares custody with his ex-wife. They're darling, but I'm always ready to get more sleep after they've stayed with us."

"I'm getting less sleep myself these days," Lynn said. As a stepmother to three-year-old Matt and eight-year-old Marika, she and Cy often discussed getting sleep by any means possible. *We sound like junkies talking about drugs, but the drug we crave is an uninterrupted eight hours of shuteye.*

Dena continued, "What can you tell me in this bar that you couldn't tell me in the office? It's why we're here, right?"

"No big secrets. We like your work, want you to stay, see you moving up. Oh, and it turns out the man who killed Arch Webber has been killed himself."

"Really? Who was it? Happened here in the US?" Dena frowned and sat back.

"A South Sudanese named Matak Abdullah. He was killed in Vienna. Pushed off a bridge in front a train."

"Who pushed him?"

Lynn leaned forward. "Appears to have been a man named Cong Li. And he may be the one, or one of the ones attacking us. Kanak Singh found files in the San Francisco refinery control software sending data to and receiving commands from outside our system. He pinged them and came up with an IP address used by Cong's company."

"Is he sure?" Dena looked dubious. "You believe a hired-gun third party who's maybe just giving you a name you already have because he's under pressure to produce?"

Lynn's anger flared. *I could slap this woman.* All she said was, "Yes." *Best to go to other topics.* "Do you have any questions for me?"

"I'll be direct. In this company, as one of my former boyfriends would say, do the promotions go to bros before hoes, or is it chicks before dicks?"

Lynn smiled. "Performance. Is our division making money, growing the capabilities of our people, satisfying customers, staying ahead technologically, improving our efficiency, and hitting our safety and environmental targets? Are we better at all those things than our competitors? Hitting those goals isn't limited to men, or women."

"So simple, hunh?" Dena said with a grin.

"Well, there's one other thing, Dena. If you get mad, you lose. If you become afraid, you lose."

After the beers, Lynn felt a pleasant buzz as she drove home. Her step-daughter Marika was spending the night with a friend.

Baby Matt would be the center of her and Cy's attention, until he went to sleep and they could focus on one another.

Cy had turned off the house lights to keep the inside cooler during 100-degree days. A Western red cedar fence surrounding the back yard also helped retain cool air from the trees' shade. "They're spraying tonight for West Nile and Zika mosquitoes. And the black heat stroke warning flag at the gym has been flown so much it's turned gray."

Matt sat in a booster seat at the table. Cy had cut up pieces of hamburger for his son to nibble. After a few recent meals in which Matt had almost choked from eating too fast, Cy was giving him his food more slowly and in smaller pieces.

The little boy grinned a big, gapped smile that lit the room when he saw Lynn.

"Listen. I eating. *Haaaoomp!*"

"You make a great chomping noise!" she said, hugging him.

"Lynn! Do you want a hang-a-burger?"

Cy kissed her and said, "We wanted to wait for you but Matt had to eat. He was hangry."

"Hangry? Oh, angry because he was hungry."

Cy nodded. "And I wish I could get him to eat fish."

"Fish smells too loud!" Matt shouted.

"I understand," Lynn said. She thought of the discussion of cyberattacks—often they were not obvious—they were not 'loud.' *The boy has a future in cybersecurity.*

Matt pushed away his plate.

They occupied the evening with their son's routine of playing hide-and-seek, bathing, building colored brick houses, and reading to him until his bedtime. Fortunately for her and Cy, Matt went to bed early. Marika was starting to fight bedtime.

As they tucked him in Matt said, "You need a hot lava suit if you want to dig to China."

"To dig through the center of the earth where it's so hot?" Lynn asked him.

Matt nodded. In bed, he looked smaller and more vulnerable than when he had been running through the house playing hide-and-seek. She knelt, cupped his face with her hands, and kissed his forehead.

After turning off the light she sat at the end of the bed while Matt murmured to himself.

Cy sat down next to her in the dark and leaned over to kiss his son. "He calls it magic whispering."

Despite her exhaustion, Lynn couldn't sleep. She tossed and turned as images from the day played through her mind. *TriCoast is under attack. By Cong Li and maybe others. Russians? They've already killed four of our people. What do they want? How can I stop them?*

CHAPTER 17

THE CARIBBEAN AND LITHUANIA

Cong had not expected this assignment would lead him to the Caribbean. When he'd gotten word of his destination, he made himself appear reluctant to leave his company and country for a few days. He wasn't.

At this moment he was checking into the finest hotel on the small island of Nevis, the Four Seasons. Palms lined the drive. A generously-sized golf course flanked one side.

Salmon-colored walls of his suite opened onto a deck. Lounge chairs and blue sky beckoned from the pool and beach beyond.

The resort was so big and had so few people compared to Beijing, he felt as if he'd stepped into heaven. But he was here for business. Perhaps this was also Comrade Jin's way of tempting him to complete the Second-Law projects. *You could live in places like these.*

At a four-course dinner, he found himself surrounded by wealthy Europeans and regretted his stay would be short. *Any stay would be too short*, he thought.

The Fourth Department had found many advantages to posting Chinese citizens on this and other islands frequented by North Americans and Europeans. In addition to surveying Chinese-owned oil and products storage tanks, he could also determine who among Chinese millionaires and billionaires was buying property here and in the US. With a passport and citizenship from Nevis, he could travel throughout the region when needed—Trinidad,

Mexico, the Dutch West Indies, Central America, and even West Africa. Best of all—and indeed the reason for original Chinese investment—was the relationship with oil-producing Venezuela and improved access to the United States, especially its Gulf Coast refineries and petrochemical plants.

He was not the Fourth Department's only Nevis experiment. Other Chinese men were traveling alone or in small groups. Some he encountered again at property sales offices around the island, along with Russians and Middle Easterners. In a few unhurried days—so many fewer people than Beijing and such clean air!—he found several attractive properties and purchased one: a million-dollar beachfront lot suitable for a six-bedroom home in a new development. He reassured the property salesman he would be visiting often to oversee construction, although he wondered to himself if once the home was built he would ever be allowed to stay there. His explanation of the relaxed environment, as well as his ready cash and an even more extensive credit line, assuaged any doubts the salesman might have had.

Cong was here for a specific reason. The colleagues working with him on the Second Law project informed him a US cybersecurity professional, Kanak Singh, had somehow found and been able to trace back to them the malware Cong had implanted in TriCoast's San Francisco Bay control system. Moreover, activity on Kanak's movements through their control of cameras at the refinery suggested Kanak had met with Curtis Zhang, the refinery manager, and Lynn Dayton, TriCoast's head of refining.

He would think further about how to eliminate Curtis Zhang in his next attack on the San Francisco Bay refinery. Cong's sabotage of the refinery had also uncovered copies of Lynn's e-mail sent to Zhang, including her plan to rent the same terminals for which he'd already put in a new bid on behalf of the Fourth Department. She had given Zhang the details of her visit to Curaçao, one of three small Caribbean islands near Venezuela.

He phoned his contact at the refinery. "I understand Ms. Lynn Dayton will be visiting you soon. She should have an accident during her visit."

"Yes, but nothing can happen to her inside our gates."

"What do you suggest?" Cong asked.

"Most guests take a side diving trip. You could arrange an accident. Just tell me which charter and I will be sure she and whoever goes with her is aboard."

Cong called Comrade Jin, who promised him a name from her network and a time Cong could meet him.

The second loose end was his fault. When he killed Matak after Matak exposed the group to risk with a murder and then demanded more money, he left Liamzon and Liamzon's cousin unsupervised. Although their instructions were so simple they could execute them without Matak, problems Cong had not anticipated might occur. Matak had been in contact with the cousins every few days.

He was faced with finding Liamzon's email address and sending him a message that wouldn't arouse the young man's suspicion. He had prepared for the first part of the task but not the second.

He began by looking over the brief, cryptic messages he and Matak had exchanged to introduce themselves and then to meet. He didn't see a way to commandeer Matak's email account. He hoped Matak had been greedy and lazy enough to use the counterfeit smart phone to access his email.

When he scrolled through the files from Matak's phone, he smiled. Matak had indeed read email from his phone. The keylogger Cong had installed on the phone had grabbed Matak's email password, which was—no real surprise—*Bugatti*.

He logged in with the password, looked at the sent mail files which included the TriCoast bidding models he had already received, and found the address to which Matak had been sending recipes. Sending the recipes made it appear the messages were from Liamzon's family and functioned like short, 'are you there?'

pings. Liamzon's confirmation replies were brief as well—just "yes this" or "not this."

The recipes did appear to be Malay. Cong did an untraceable search for a similar recipe, found one, and emailed it to Liamzon.

He would watch the account.

Later, Cong caught a small plane to Curaçao. Just past the airport's security exit, he was waved into a Toyota Yaris by a tanned, sandy-haired driver, arranged by Comrade Jin.

He was driven through several kilometers of desert-like scrub. The driver pointed out the island's big refinery. Cong knew it only as the place Lynn was to visit. Their destination was the island's Schottegat waterway where he was to meet the second man Comrade Jin had selected.

The driver pulled over near one of the docks, motioned him out of the car, and spoke to a balding, pockmarked man with mutton-chop sideburns standing nearby. To Cong's surprise, the language sounded like either Dutch or German. The driver pointed his thumb at Cong.

"In English. Comrade Jin has spoken to you?" Cong asked.

The pockmarked boat captain nodded.

Cong pulled out his cell phone and showed the captain a picture. "This woman, and anyone with her, must have a lethal accident. You will be called to give her a tour. It must happen then."

The captain shrugged and smiled. "No guarantees. But the ocean can be rough."

"Perhaps something simple, like an equipment failure. Or your boat leaves while they are swimming without life preservers." Cong pulled out a thick wad of big bills and shook the man's hand while handing him the money. "You will receive the other half when I have proof from you she is dead."

Returning from New Orleans, Vikenti Andreev paced himself. He had hired two of his former SVR colleagues with whom he'd worked many times both inside and outside of Russia. They'd arranged to meet at Kaliningrad, the center of a small Russian land wedge on the Baltic Sea between Poland and Lithuania. It was five hundred kilometers from Copenhagen, where Vikenti had met with the strange Chinese operative, Cong Li.

The SVR colleagues walked around the Lower Pond promenade on a mild August day with temperatures Vikenti estimated at about twenty degrees Celsius. *Warmer than just about anywhere in Russia.*

"You have the auto?" Vikenti asked the taller one. The taller one looked more imposing, but the shorter one had deadlier aim with every weapon.

"*Da.* For you, Vikenti, Mercedes E-class."

Vikenti sighed. "No. Change it before tonight. Not the finest. We want something more common."

Vikenti had waited until the three were together to explain the mission.

"Our assignment is to disable Lithuanian liquefied gas imports. Since imports came from non-Russian sources, we have been forced to lower gas prices to Lithuania and its Baltic neighbors, improperly draining the Russian treasury."

Both shook their heads. All of Russia waxed and waned on the prices of its oil and gas exports.

Vikenti was smart and experienced enough to have doubts, which he explained. "The Lithuanians have safeguarded their regasification terminal by floating it. It is like a giant ship, 300 by 50 meters with a draft of twelve and a half meters."

The taller one smiled at the size.

"The terminal was built by the South Koreans and is leased from a Norwegian company. It is called a floating storage and re-gasification terminal or FSRU. The Lithuanians compound their insult to us with its name: *Independence*."

"*Nyet*. Lithuania must be punished," the shorter one said.

"The floating terminal is permanently berthed at an island in a constricted sound," Vikenti explained. "The Norwegians both lease the FSRU as well as staff and maintain it. They have multiple security checkpoints. The island and waters around the terminal are also difficult barriers to breach. The land side is narrow. On the water side, often an LNG carrier is moored right next to the FSRU, unloading a cargo of gas. All around are catwalks, firefighting towers, loading arms, and so on. So approaching by water is also too risky. And the LNG itself is gas liquefied by cooling it to 127 degrees Celsius below zero."

The taller one said, "We get too close, we could get cold burns. Or suffocate."

"Interesting possibility as a weapon," the shorter one said.

Vikenti agreed. "But actually using LNG to attack would require more complex equipment than we have."

"So how do we do anything?" the taller one asked.

"I am about to tell you. The operators on the FSRU regasify the liquid, then ship it onshore to a high pressure gas pipeline, and then another eighteen kilometers to a metering station, and on to the main gas grid. The gas is measured at the metering station. From there it is sent out to the whole country." Vikenti had memorized the map, so they stopped while he drew it on a piece of paper. Once they'd seen it, he tore the map into small pieces and threw it in a trashcan. "We will penetrate security at the metering station and do as much damage as possible."

The two men smiled.

"You have the Semtex and detonator?" Vikenti asked the shorter one.

The smaller man looked at him maliciously. "You even ask? SVR wanting to buy in Kaliningrad Oblost? Yes. What about weapons? Clothes?"

"Makarovs with silencers. Hardhats and overalls," Vikenti said.

The smaller man frowned. "Not bad."

After dinner near their hotel on Bolshevistsky, they drank a few shots of vodka and made plans for the following morning.

They arose early for the trip.

Vikenti nodded his approval at the replacement vehicle, a Nissan sedan. The taller man drove. No one spoke as they travelled east on the E28, then northeast on A216 to the border crossing at Sovetsk.

When it was their turn in the automobile lane at the border crossing, they stopped at an iron gate. Uniformed guards spoke to each man in the car, staring hard at their Russian passports. Vikenti and his men explained, in Russian, that they were laborers being sent to Klaipėda for building construction. Vikenti had hidden the Semtex under a floor mat, and the detonator parts in the spare tire. The guards looked into the car but saw neither.

At last they were free to cross the Neman River beneath a several-story stone archway flanked by two medieval towers.

The tall man drove them northwest. Russian Cyrillic script on highway signs changed to vowel-heavy Lithuanian. No one stopped them again.

They turned off the main highway before they reached Klaipėda, near Gargždai.

The tall man drove them toward the inland gas metering station.

Vikenti said, "Remember, once we get past the guard, we are looking for the biggest pipelines. The largest is seven hundred millimeters."

The installation had large signs and a double set of fences topped with razor wire. Inside, they could see rows of silvery pipes, the biggest ones feeding through the walls of an enclosed shack on one side, with several smaller pipes exiting the other side.

The tall man drove them to the guardhouse. The two guards, young and fit and clearly promoted above ordinary Lithuanian police officers, eyed them.

"We have been called in to examine for pipeline corrosion and gas treating," the tall man said. Vikenti and the shorter man had their silenced Makarovs hidden at their sides.

One guard looked at the other and shook his head. "You are not on the schedule. Turn around and leave or I will call for a police escort."

Vikenti pulled out his Makarov, aimed it at the nearer guard, and said to the other. "Open the gate or I will shoot him."

The smaller man exited the car, out of sight of the guards.

The second guard pushed a button and the gate began to swing open. Then he reached for and punched a second button. An alarm began to blare.

Vikenti fired his silenced Makarov at the first guard's head, tearing a bloody hole through it. The shorter SVR operative shot the second guard, also in the head. He dragged both guards' bodies behind the security booth and jumped back into the Nissan.

"Drive slowly as if we belong here," Vikenti shouted to the driver over the noise of the alarm.

A few men appeared. Vikenti waved as they drove past. "If they follow us, shoot them."

The taller man drove toward the densest alley of large pipelines.

Vikenti grabbed the Semtex from underneath the floor mats while the smaller man assembled the detonator.

Vikenti held the remote control for the detonator and pointed to the forest of the largest pipes.

The smaller man nodded, took the Semtex, and placed it underneath the giant mass. He attached the detonator.

Once he was back in the car, Vikenti said, "Drive out. We need distance."

A hundred meters later, a man jumped in front of the Nissan. He shouted over the blare of the station's alarm. "Who are you? Stop! Tell me what you are doing!"

Vikenti nodded to the driver and he stopped.

Vikenti leaned out the window and shot the protestor before he could get closer.

After another few hundred meters, Vikenti said, "Ready?"

"Da."

The gate was still open. The security guards still lay where they'd been dragged.

As they car sped out the gate, Vikenti hit the detonator remote.

A loud explosion drowned out the blare of plant's alarm.

The Nissan slowed and they were rocked by a pressure wave.

The first explosion was followed by several more explosions as smaller pipelines connecting to the larger ones ignited and also blew up.

Vikenti said, "We are not going back to Kaliningrad, or the way we traveled here. We have another destination. I will direct you."

CHAPTER 18

CURAÇAO

Lynn met her bodyguard, Beau Decatur, in Miami. From Miami, they were bound for Curaçao, an island near Venezuela. It had once been a part of the Dutch West Indies and was now a country within the Kingdom of the Netherlands.

"I looked at your history. You had a run-in with the Venezuelans," Decatur said.

"When I bought Centennial Refinery for the company. Turned out Centennial had a crude oil buyer who, through a trading intermediary, was buying cheap Venezuelan crude and faking paperwork to pretend it was better-quality. So he was getting a kickback. But our beef wasn't with the Venezuelans."

Decatur looked dubious. "Except for the turmoil. Protests, bread lines, famine. And people have long memories, even about something indirect."

She was so tired and jet-lagged she couldn't reply. She fell asleep until their arrival at Willemstad, Curaçao's main city.

Decatur had reserved a car. He drove out on a road called Franklin D. Rooseveltweg, past intriguing-looking caves. They were soon in a residential area and Decatur gestured toward other thoroughfares names like Winston Churchillweg and Cubaweg. He made a right turn, and behind a fence she spotted the familiarly-shaped giant processing towers of a refinery. They circled around Schottegat waterway. Lined up across the water Lynn saw vivid blue, orange, and pink four-story buildings.

They checked in to their hotel and parted.

After another ten hours of sleep, she woke up in the morning dressed in the prior day's clothes. Grateful for a flexible wardrobe that traveled better than she did, she made coffee, showered, and changed into khakis and a white shirt.

Her object in visiting Curaçao was to evaluate oil and product storage on TriCoast's export routes to Europe, Central America, and South America. Lynn also hoped to talk to engineers at the refinery who had formerly worked in Canada. Refineries on the islands of Aruba and Curaçao had been built by multinational companies more than a hundred years earlier upon the discovery of oil in nearby Venezuela. The one on Curaçao was now owned by the island's government and had, at times, employed up to a quarter of the island's population.

When Lynn and Decatur had arrived the previous night it had been cool and windy, the palm leaves lifting and falling with the circulation of steady eastern trade winds. By contrast, the morning was hot and still. The scent of jasmine flowers surrounded them as they met for breakfast with one of the refinery's executives, Jorge Rosenberg. Their tiled outdoor restaurant overlooked the beach. Its green wicker furniture was the year-round outdoor style favored in the Caribbean.

Even today weather remained an economic key. Good weather meant more tourist dollars. In earlier centuries, the trade wind literally meant *trade*. Absence of trade winds resulted in much slower movement of people and goods across the ocean.

Curaçao's native Arawak population had been taken over by Dutch colonists in the 1600s. It had also, at various times, been a primary Americas destination for Sephardic, Ashkenazi, and other Jewish populations, including Jorge's forebearers. Jorge explained that of necessity, he had learned and spoke four languages: Dutch, Spanish, English, and Papiamentu. At the hotel, pale, blond Dutch tourists and their language predominated, obvious in phrases like *hier drukken* pasted near a cold water spout.

Foot-long iguanas emerged near the table, apparently expecting their ration of toast and eggs. They rested prehistoric bellies flat against the cool red-rock tile, then like the rude houseguests they were, trundled over to each new arrival. Tongues flicked. Snouts rose. A pale-skinned tourist, her shoulders burned pink from intense tropical sun, let them crawl on her as she fed them mango.

Their host shook his head at her. His "*nee*" sounded like *nay*. "Bad idea," he explained.

Lynn didn't have to look twice to agree.

Their drive to the storage terminals took them past the brilliantly-colored European-style buildings they'd seen the night before. At the dock and tanks they could see the match to the specifications they had already received. Although Rosenberg said he had several offers, when Lynn named a price to rent the terminals for five years, he told her TriCoast's bid was in range.

As she'd requested, Rosenberg also introduced them to a small group of the refinery's engineers and finance professionals who had worked in Canada. Each explained anxiety about Chinese partners of the Canadian companies for which they'd worked: the Chinese had downloaded terabytes of proprietary design and operation data. One said, "Don't quote me and don't write down what I tell you. I'll deny everything. But this is something you must understand if TriCoast ever operates with a Chinese partner."

Lynn thought about Cong Li and his murder of Matak Abdullah. *Kanak told us Russian software was used to attack our refinery, but what if Cong's in charge of that, too?*

After a long series of meetings, Rosenberg said, "For you to travel so far and not snorkel would be criminal. Everyone who visits here takes in the beach. *Klein Curaçao*, or Small Curaçao, is good. The waters around it are clear, with many colorful fish. In fact, knowing you would want to see it, one of my colleagues has already arranged a charter for us. He sent me the information yesterday."

"Sounds amazing," Lynn said. She'd snorkeled in the Caribbean on short vacations with friends after divorcing her first husband and before marrying Cy. *But Cy and the kids would love this,* she thought. *They like anything water-related.*

They gathered swimming gear, then drove to and boarded the snorkeling boat Rosenberg's colleague had rented for them. Their quadrilingual host gave instructions to the boat's captain first in Spanish and then in Papiamentu. The captain, balding and pockmarked with mutton-chop sideburns, said little as they began their two-hour trip to the dive location.

Lynn looked at a text she had received from Dena. "*Ping me back once you get this. Re Kanak and our SF refinery: My research came up with a hacking tool like Sakula, the malware used on the OPM computers. The software appeared to be electronically signed as safe but wasn't. Maybe Kanak and I should check our refinery systems for it.*"

Lynn felt helpless at the invisible threads of malicious software taking down very large, very visible refineries. She responded, *Got yr msg. Suggest to Kanak he check our SF refinery for that malware, too.*

As the three of them prepared to enter the water Rosenberg said, "I've been to this area before. Right here it's about four or five feet deep but the current's strong. The best fish viewing is at the shelf. But be aware there's a steep slope down and then a drop off to fifty feet."

The water was so salty it buoyed Lynn back toward the surface.

Forests of purple and brown brain-shaped coral spread beneath them. Velvety black-blue tang swam around rocks and other tall stalks of coral. Decatur pointed to an octopus and Lynn to a squadron of squid.

On the sandy bottom, she saw flatfish with spotted bodies. It was as if dozens of eyes were looking up at her. More fish swayed and rocked with the current, letting the water move them. Some of the fish attracted to the coral were dark electric blue with bright neon spots.

Her mask began to fill with water and the sandy bottom blurred. She kicked up a few feet to the surface, pulled the mask off her head and dumped out the salty water. She tightened the straps. But when she put the mask on and swam, salty water filled it again, stinging her eyes.

Decatur's head popped above the water nearby. "Leak in my breathing tube! What about yours?"

"I haven't tried it yet but water's leaking into my mask." She put her own breathing tube in her mouth, began swimming, and took a breath. She tried not to freeze when her mouth filled with water instead of air.

Instead, she shot to the surface, spluttering and yanking the tube out of her mouth. "Mine, too! And where's Jorge?"

She put her face below the surface of the water, trying to stare through her blurry mask. A pale shape lay on the sandy bottom ten yards away, being towed by the current away from the beach and toward the drop-off.

She flung her head out of the water; turned, and grabbed Decatur's arm. "I see him! He's flat on the bottom about thirty feet away! He's not moving. The current's pushing him toward the drop!"

If he slid over, it might be impossible to retrieve him.

She and Decatur swam closer to where she'd seen him. They dipped their heads below the surface of the salty water and she pointed. Rosenberg's body was splayed out in a starfish shape.

Decatur waved her away and spit out his breathing tube. "Wait here! I'll get him. Get the captain and the boat over here!"

He dove down, kicking hard.

Lynn turned to find the boat a few hundred yards away. "Hey! Hey! Help us!" she yelled as loud as she could.

The boat captain was turned away and appeared not to hear her. *What the hell? What's happening here? Where's Decatur?*

"Captain! Captain! Help us! Bring the boat here!"

Clearing the water from her mask, she put the mask to her eyes but not around her head, and dipped under the surface, looking for Decatur and Rosenberg. She saw Decatur grab Rosenberg's body. Twice it slipped out of his grasp. Finally he was able to wrap an arm around the man's chest. He struggled to swim back to the surface with the body.

When their heads were above water, Decatur said, "Take off his mask and turn his head!"

The rubber strap was tight on his head, but Lynn ripped it off. She felt guilty at scraping the skin on his head but realized he was unconscious. She turned Rosenberg's head to one side. Water dribbled from his nose and mouth but he still wasn't responding.

Decatur gripped Rosenberg's body from behind. "Call the captain?"

"I tried. He's not responding."

Decatur shouted at the captain. "Captain! Help! We need your help now! Come here!"

They could see the captain, but again he didn't turn.

Decatur looked at her, assessing. "We don't have time to get him to the boat. Switch positions with me. You hold him and dog-paddle. I'll give him mouth-to-mouth here in the water. Can you do that?"

"Yes."

Lynn moved next to Decatur behind Rosenberg. She reached around Rosenberg's right shoulder and jammed it between her arm and her side. The water buoyed him up, but his slack body was still heavy. She kept his head above the waves, paddling with her free arm and kicking with her legs to stay in place.

Decatur put his mouth on Rosenberg's and blew hard again and again. Rosenberg's lips looked blue and were pulled back in a rictus of terror.

His body got heavier and heavier as Lynn struggled to keep his head above the water.

Lynn saw Decatur's look of determination as he kept blowing rescue breaths into the man's mouth.

Rosenberg's head came forward and he vomited salty water. He startled.

Then he began climbing on top of Lynn, pushing her down under the surface as he frantically tried to use her body as a platform to lift himself out of the water.

Lynn couldn't loosen his grip. Her step-children had done the same thing a few times in their deep swimming pool, but they were much smaller and weaker. And they hadn't been as panicked.

Rosenberg's legs clamped down on her shoulders and wrapped around her neck as he struggled to keep his head above the water.

She dug her fingers into his thighs, squeezing as hard as she could. *He'll kill me trying to save himself!*

She put her fist into his groin and jabbed. Finally, she was able to pry his legs off of her neck.

She surfaced for air and breathed in deep gulps, paddling self-protectively to stay away a few yards away from Rosenberg.

Decatur said to him, "Hold on. Relax. RELAX! Float on your back. That'll keep your head out of the water."

Rosenberg thrashed his arms and legs.

"Lean back!" Decatur said.

Rosenberg vomited more salty water. "I'm drowning!"

"Put your legs up and your head back. Unbend at your waist. We're right here," Decatur said.

"We won't let you drown," Lynn reassured him.

Rosenberg gasped and then slowly relaxed. He stretched out on his back.

"Here's what we'll do," Decatur told them. "Lynn, you swim alongside. Jorge, I'll tow you. That asshole captain needs to talk."

With Decatur supporting Rosenberg in a swimmer's tow, he and Lynn sidestroked for several minutes until they reached the boat.

The boat captain. "Why the hell didn't you help us?" Lynn shouted.

His head was down and he was silent. He stepped back away from them.

They held onto the sides of the boat and tossed in their fins, masks, and breathing tubes.

As they'd agreed, Decatur was the first to mount the steps in the back of the boat.

He yanked out a diving knife and pushed the captain into a seated position, holding the knife on the captain's neck.

Lynn supported Rosenberg from behind as he dragged himself up the boat's steps and stumbled into the boat. She was the last to climb in.

Once they were all aboard, Decatur tied the captain's hands and feet. "Lynn, you're driving the boat back. I don't trust this guy."

"I haven't driven a boat before," she said.

"You can do it. It's not hard, especially out in open water. See the steering wheel and the throttle on the center console?"

"Yes."

"Grab the steering wheel. Turn on the ignition. Open up the throttle. Take your time."

Lynn did. "Now what?"

Rosenberg stood nearby, ready to help Decatur hold down the captain. "Turn a few times. Get a feel for how the steering wheel and throttle respond. Return the way we came."

Lynn opened the throttle and tested the steering. She turned the boat to head back on the two-hour trip.

Decatur grabbed the boat captain's sideburns and pulled. The man squeezed his eyes shut but said nothing. Decatur shouted at him. "Who told you to fuck up our snorkeling equipment?"

The man shrugged.

Decatur looked at Rosenberg. "Can you translate?"

Rosenberg's smile was the first they'd seen since they'd saved him. "Maybe not those exact words. I'll try Dutch, then Spanish, then Papiamentu."

The captain responded, finally, when Rosenberg questioned him in Papiamentu.

Decatur questioned the captain for several minutes, with Rosenberg translating. The man was silent or shrugged.

"Why did you give us damaged equipment? Were you trying to kill us?"

"Did someone pay you?"

"Did someone threaten you?"

"Who are you working for?"

"Who else have you killed?"

Decatur shouted the questions. Rosenberg translated. Decatur whispered and Rosenberg translated.

"I really want to cross the line with this guy," Decatur told Lynn.

"I understand. But I'm glad you haven't," Lynn replied.

"He's got information we need. I *know* he does."

Decatur started his litany of questions again.

As they neared land an hour and a half later, he told Lynn to throttle down. Decatur moved in closer to the captain and aimed the knife at his eyes.

"We can sit out here forever. And we will. Who told you to do this? Why? When?"

Rosenberg translated. This time the man answered and Rosenberg translated into English. "He claims he was asked to meet someone and when he did, the person pulled a gun on him and told him to give us damaged equipment."

"What was the person's name?" Lynn asked.

The captain seemed to understand what she was asking. He shook his head.

"What did the person look like? Man or woman?" Decatur glared at the captain as Rosenberg translated.

"Woman called. But he met a man. Asian."

Lynn grimaced. "Korean? Thai? Chinese? Indian? Pakistani?"

Rosenberg asked the captain, who murmured something. Rosenberg said, "The captain says not Indian or Pakistani, but he can't tell between the others you mentioned."

"What kind of gun did the man have, or is he telling the truth about a weapon, and the man?" Decatur asked. Without warning he jabbed his diving knife at the man's throat, though he didn't break the skin. "Tell him I will see to it he loses his license and all his customers if he doesn't give us better answers."

Rosenberg looked nervously at Decatur's sudden action, and then asked. The captain looked down and spoke in a low voice. "No, the Asian man didn't really have a gun. Just lots of money. He told the captain he would pay more when the captain finished," Rosenberg said.

"What was he supposed to 'finish'?" Lynn asked.

The captain seemed to understand. He nodded at Lynn, and then turned his glance to include the other two. His voice when he spoke was even quieter.

"He says he was supposed to kill you and anyone with you, Lynn. The man showed him a picture of you," Rosenberg said.

Lynn shuddered. "So he damaged our diving equipment in a way that almost did get *you* killed."

Decatur sheathed his knife. "The captain could have done a lot worse. Giving us damaged snorkeling equipment is passive and low-risk. He had to expect he might not succeed."

"Damn well almost did," Rosenberg protested.

Lynn said, "I don't want to put ideas in his head, but ask him if he really was going to kill us."

Rosenberg translated. The man shrugged and spoke at length.

"He says the man had given him lot of money, even if was only half. His friends told him the Asian man had already left Curaçao on a plane and they would tell him if he returned. And he said when he takes people out on his boat, they are smiling and having fun, and you were, too. He's says he's not always a good man. He does have a gun, but he couldn't kill you." Then Rosenberg snorted. "But he freaking almost did me in."

"Did the captain's friends at the airport say where he was going next?" Lynn asked. "There can't be many Asians traveling through Curaçao right now. Or where he was from? Did they see his passport?"

Rosenberg turned and put the questions to the captain. He frowned, then his eyes widened with a memory. "China!"

Damn. This is fitting together into a big hideous picture. Lynn thought of Cong Li and glanced at Decatur, who put a finger to his lips. They wouldn't alert the captain, who was still maintaining he didn't know the man's name. The captain could turn around and call as soon as they left him. *In fact…* "Ask him for his phone. Let's find out who called him and verify who and where the call came from."

But when Rosenberg translated the request, the captain shook his head, nodded toward the galley, and explained. "No cell phone on the boat. Just a satellite phone for emergencies. The woman called him and the man met him when he was on land."

Once they neared the dock, Decatur gave Lynn instructions for easing in. Rosenberg jumped out and moored the boat. He turned to Lynn and Decatur and said, "There's no way to hold him just because he gave us leaky equipment. The police won't want to investigate. They'll say it was an accident like those that happen to clueless tourists."

"I wouldn't call you clueless," Lynn said to him. "Are you okay?"

"Still shocked. Grateful. You saved my life."

"See if you can find out more about this Chinese man who wanted us all killed," Lynn said.

Decatur left the boat captain tied up. He put his knife near the tip of one of the hairy mutton chops. "Stay away from us. If I ever see you again, I'll kill you."

Lynn was grateful they'd survived the day, and that they'd been able to save Jorge Rosenberg. Everything else she'd learned gnawed at the pit of her stomach. *How big is Cong Li's group and what is he trying to do? Who else is in his kill matrix?*

Lynn and Rosenberg filed a complaint about the boat captain with the local Curaçao authorities. Then she and Decatur endured a long return flight that dropped her off in New Orleans and returned him to Dallas for additional training.

CHAPTER 19

LOUISIANA AND OFFSHORE

Kim was alarmed when TriCoast security chief Mark Shepherd scheduled a sudden video conference with her, Patrick, Reese, and Lynn.

"I called to tell you the Lithuanian LNG import terminal was attacked yesterday, resulting in an explosion. It's been shut down," Mark said. "Kim, you also have an interest here, given your reserve status. The word has gone out to your chief and the active-duty officers."

"Casualties?" Patrick Boudreaux asked.

"Several people killed from the explosions. And at least three shot."

Kim remembered Reese's and Patrick's warnings to her and her fellow Coast Guard recruits a few years ago. *I never did find out for sure if Patrick also works on FBI projects.*

"Who's responsible?" Lynn asked.

"No one knows yet. They're checking border crossings. It might have been a group of Russians."

"Lithuanian LNG," Patrick said. "That's a key installation."

"And it's one of the places we're shipping our Pennsylvania natural gas to," Lynn added. "The Lithuanians are trying to break the stranglehold the Russians have had on them. Russia's Gazprom has a history of overcharging and if countries don't pay what the Russians say they owe, Gazprom cuts them off, even if it's in the middle of winter."

"So given this, for us at TriCoast and for energy infrastructure throughout the US, we're ramping up security," Mark said. "Kim, I think LOOP and everything around the Gulf of Mexico will be getting extra attention from the Coast Guard."

"I've already been notified to prepare for a Coast Guard reserve callout," Kim said. "I can't predict when it will happen except once they say *jump* they mean *now*. So Reese, can you step up for me at the refinery? Make sure you've got the reins in hand before I have to go dark, wherever I'm on patrol?"

"Of course," Reese said. "We can start immediately."

Kim remembered another time she'd heard Reese Spencer and Patrick Boudreaux speak. In contrast to today when Reese was her second in command as she managed the Marrero refinery and Patrick had been called in to consult, then they'd been her Coast Guard instructors.

Kim had entered the Coast Guard after her service in Iraq as an army mechanic but before she joined TriCoast and started rising in its ranks. Eventually she'd gone on reserve status.

The day a few years back had been cool and misty, one hinting at summer's clamminess yet to come. Kim drove from Plaquemine on Louisiana State Highway 1 through the flat wetlands to the day's class and listened to a local radio host telling jokes. *I need some jokes. But tell me the jokes to make me forget dead friends.*

That morning, Boudreaux had introduced Reese first. "Reese has run refineries along the Mississippi River, so he'll talk about high-value industrial targets. And since he's a retired Navy pilot, you Coasties should give him an appropriate welcome."

After the usual catcalls Reese, then as now with his short bristling hair, sat on a table at the front and leaned forward. In a stern, Southern-accented voice like ones Kim had heard from hundreds of other military colleagues, Reese said, "You all do high-risk drug interdiction and deal with crazy, desperate people. What I'm talking about is a potential attack on Gulf Coast or Mississippi River plants and refineries—and there are dozens of them. It's a different scenario but can hurt or kill people. The plants are so big you can't always see the hundreds of people working there, let alone the thousands in the surrounding communities. But they're all at risk."

Just as he sometimes did now, Kim remembered how Reese's voice slowed when he wanted to make a point. "Hundreds, thousands of people."

"Sir, the Coast Guard doesn't patrol the Mississippi River," Kim said.

"While most often you're offshore in the Gulf of Mexico, there's a contingent who gets to—emphasize *gets to*—patrol the river around New Orleans during Lundi Gras, the day before Mardi Gras," Patrick interjected.

Reese continued, "And many of these plants and refineries are right on the Gulf of Mexico, where you do patrol. At the refineries I've run, we worry that if we're attacked externally, it may be invisible—through the wires instead of old-time river pirates or new-age jihadis. However, I've seen plenty of industrial sabotage, so it happens.

"Here's the deal—a fertilizer plant, a refinery—they can become some of the biggest bombs around. The Texas City explosion over seventy years ago was one of the world's largest non-nuclear explosions. It was caused by a fire aboard a ship carrying fertilizer—ammonium nitrate—and it chain-reacted into fires and explosions onto other ships and oil storage facilities. The whole thing killed about six hundred people.

"The Texas City explosion was an accident. But make no mistake. There are plenty of people who want to do us the same harm deliberately. I know, because I've discovered and stopped a few.

"What I want you to do is what you already do, which is to start with Sierra Alpha, or situational awareness. Someone calls you about some random boat near their facility or headed upriver, don't go warp one immediately, but check it out." Reese stopped. "And now Patrick Boudreaux will talk about LOOP."

"I'll cut to the chase," Patrick said. "If you're caught in the middle of a gun battle, you've failed. The Coast Guard tries to identify and intercept threats before they arrive. It's one reason the Guard is effective. You have a culture of thinking forward and planning."

Kim wondered if the rumor about Boudreaux consulting for the FBI was true.

"Do a little math with the price of oil and you can see we're talking about real money tied up in another place you should be aware of, the Louisiana Offshore Oil Port, or LOOP. Oil vessels unload at buoys about twenty miles south of the Louisiana coast. Think a few hundred million dollars a tanker. The Islamic State and Al-Qaeda love financial targets and LOOP is essentially one big bank, operating since 1981. The difference from the past is since the U.S produces more crude oil, LOOP may become bi-directional—taking crude in for the US *and* shipping out US and Canadian crude."

He opened a laptop. "LOOP's security office gave us training files."

As the screen resolved into pictures of what appeared to be open water, Kim said, "It looks like a few buoys bobbing around."

"The buoys mark where the tankers deliver the crude. LOOP security watches these buoys all day every day."

There's a job that'd make you crazy, Kim thought.

Boudreaux showed another picture of what looked like a standard offshore platform. "The security team and LOOP oper-ations are on these platforms, about one and a half nautical miles away.

"What makes this different and why it's been beating ports at Corpus Christi, Texas, and St. James, Louisiana all to hell is LOOP can unload—and now load—the world's largest tankers, the Very

Large Crude Carriers and the Ultra Large Crude Carriers. Corpus Christi might get into the race, though, if they deepen their channels and raise a bridge or two."

After lunch, Boudreaux resumed his lecture, holding up a diagram. Reese Spencer sat nearby. "Since tankers this size cost fifty thousand dollars a day or more to rent, no one wants you to slow them down for inspection if you're merely suspicious. Fuck 'em. If it's suspicious, inspect. The tankers can be from the Middle East, West Africa, the North Sea, Colombia, Venezuela, Ecuador, Mexico, and Russia. All democratic, peace-loving areas who admire the United States and our foreign policy. Not."

"So right, dude," someone behind Kim said.

"We have engineers in here, but this is for the rest of you. At the buoys, tankers offload through hoses connected to a mooring base and submarine pipeline. The oil—now mostly Saudi Arabian, used to be Nigerian, too, but Nigeria's been shut out by all the new US production—flows about a mile and half to the offshore pumping terminal where it's measured and sampled before being pumped onshore to the Clovelly terminal. All you can see on the surface are pipe arrays. From Clovelly it's pumped in a 48-inch pipeline into salt storage caverns—nearly seventy million barrels' worth—that sit about a third of a mile below the Louisiana marshes or else it's pipelined to refineries. Simple, huh?"

Aboard the tanker, Liamzon and his cousin kept to themselves, fulfilled their duties, and waited. Liamzon passed the days at work thinking of the heaven he would enter.

Matak had told him it was likely the captain would be able to monitor any communications. They'd kept their simple conversations in a code Matak had assured him couldn't be broken by outsiders. There had been a hiccup—a couple of days when Liamzon hadn't heard from Matak—but then the conversations resumed. Mainly about his mother and her cooking, which served as his reminder to stay cautious. The back-up trigger was GPS-keyed, so Liamzon didn't worry about getting to it when the time came, if the cell phone trigger failed.

He and his cousin were sure of their mission. He'd been taught about the superiority of the next life. A martyr's death would give him the highest possible standing in the afterlife.

So when he came back after a shift, he was worried to see his bag had been moved. The evidence was slight. Only a few things had been taken out, but they'd been left out, as if the mole didn't fear discovery. Matak had told him to be alert to this possibility. The phone had not been removed.

Liamzon found his cousin. "My bag was moved and items were left out. Remember, Matak told us to watch for this."

"What about the trigger phone?"

"Still there in the same place. But someone must have wanted me to know they suspect me."

"Who?" his cousin asked. "Or more than one person?"

They puzzled over who among the forty men on board it might have been.

"The bag check happened during the day," Liamzon said. "So, a man or men from the night shift."

"But not an officer. Still leaves fifteen men. But it doesn't matter. Even if we get the wrong man, the right man will understand his actions have been noticed."

"And that we are watching him," Liamzon said. "Matak told us what to do if this happened."

"Yes, cousin. So we must do as he said."

On any voyage, sailors formed groups of fragile alliances based on nationalities. The trusts were uneasy, disrupted by any provocation. Every seaman had a knife. It would be suicidal to work on a tanker without one.

In the evening, Liamzon and his cousin waited in their room and Liamzon stuffed a cap in a pocket. Toward midnight, they crept toward the lifeboats and hid behind one. When a junior

Filipino seaman—a man Liamzon knew was also from Mindanao—walked by alone, Liamzon jumped him from behind, slapping one hand over the man's mouth and grabbing his neck in a chokehold. Rather than wait for the man to asphyxiate, Liamzon's cousin pushed Liamzon's knife hand onto the man's neck. The knife sliced the man's neck through all the way to the spine.

As his blood spurted, the man struggled to get free. Each movement showed his shock at the betrayal by Liamzon's cousin, a fellow countryman. He never saw Liamzon.

The young seaman stopped struggling. His body slackened and evacuated. Blood was everywhere.

Liamzon took out his cap and put it in the man's waistband. The captain would question everyone, but all aboard would assume one low-status Filipino had killed another in an internecine quarrel for which the cap was the answer.

However, the seaman who had searched Liamzon's bag would realize his action had been spotted. And that he would be next.

Liamzon headed to his bunk to scrub the blood from his hands and arms.

CHAPTER 20

When Lynn woke up in her Pennsylvania hotel room, she calculated the time in Paris. *Ceil's back from lunch by now.* She texted her sister and was happy when Ceil phoned.

After discussing friends and family, Lynn asked her sister about her work at the International Energy Agency.

"Challenging, but interesting, too. And I hear you've been named TriCoast's head of North American natural gas," Ceil said.

"Whoa! How did you find out? I just accepted the responsibility. It hasn't been announced."

"I have sources," Ceil replied, clearly pleased to have surprised her older sister. "On top of the refinery work? They paying you double?"

"More. So you won't be surprised by my next question. What are you hearing about the European Union's stance on Russian natural gas? It's no secret we have a lot of natural gas here—literally boatloads."

"First you or someone will have to untangle the Russian threat, which is, 'buy our gas at triple the market price or we'll invade you.' At least for some countries. Germany, the Baltics. Word is, they've got enforcers scattered throughout the EU."

"TriCoast can't counter the Russian threat alone."

"No. The US government might be able to, but the EU can't. A few empty ports can take non-Russian liquefied natural

gas—Barcelona, for instance—but they don't have enough pipelines to send it to other countries."

"The Russians are tightening a noose."

"Qatar and Algeria, Mozambique, Russia, and even Australia
expect Americans to stop drilling so they can keep or increase
their shares of the global gas market."

"No surprise," Lynn said.

"I miss you, Lynn."

"Visit us any time. Matt and Marika want to see more of their
Aunt Ceil."

"Oh my God. I'm an aunt now."

Lynn hung up and felt the still-new mix of happiness and
guilt. *I'm a mother. Stepmother. And I'm not with my children.*

She boxed the feeling. She would focus on Cy and the kids
when she was home.

Her next call was to David, the head of oil exploration and
production whose billions in natural gas operations she would
soon take over managing. As they talked, Lynn thought about the
biggest union at her refineries. The periodic negotiations were
amicable enough that the union seldom struck, to the chagrin of
youngest engineers. New engineers never admitted it but many
hoped for a strike so they could wield wrenches themselves and
directly operate the massive towers, boilers, and exchangers.

She had agreed to meet Dwayne at the site of one of the wells
TriCoast was drilling. He gave her the exact coordinates, along
with markers like "a red barn, right turn, and then five miles
on a gravel road." When she made the turn off the highway, she
plugged her phone in for music but couldn't hear the opening of
favorite song since it started out at the same frequency as the road
vibration.

She was pleased she didn't see the black 150-foot-tall rotary
drilling rig until she was about a quarter mile away. The ability
to minimize visual and ground footprints was one reason David
had chosen this contractor. No matter who did the actual drilling,

TriCoast's name was on the sign and she would be the ultimate focus for any complaints.

Small, white trailers formed a half-circle of temporary out-buildings on one side of the large cement pad underneath the thirty-foot-high drilling platform. On the other side was a structure that looked like a heavy-duty sand delivery truck. However, it was propped up vertically so it appeared to be standing on its nose.

"You like our sand pile?" Dwayne asked her, grinning, as she got out of her car. "It does just what you think. The driver drives it here, pushes a few levers, and presto, the unit goes up and we have ourselves a sand storage silo." He waved papers at her, a technical-looking document titled *Control of Onerous Cations*. "It's all about water and sand. Oh yes, and the natural gas we produce, when we can find buyers."

"And cations are onerous because?"

"The water produced with the gas is the saltiest, cloudiest stuff you ever saw. Another reason David hired this contractor. They do a good job cleaning up and recycling the water."

"The contractor is moving millions of pounds of sand and millions of gallons of water around for each well?" she asked. Dwayne nodded. When they could, TriCoast and other companies laid field-wide pipelines to deliver water. She appreciated even more the military veterans TriCoast had hired. All were experienced with large-scale logistics.

"The contractor tries to minimize costs, but it can take more than a thousand truck trips to haul in the equipment, workers, sand, and water for each well. Of course, after a while it slows way down. Once the well's finished, there's only one truck a day, if that."

"How does the type curve on the wells in this zone look so far?" she asked. Once they knew the reserves, the type curve would tell them about how much gas to expect over the following weeks and months. For these horizontal, hydraulically-fractured wells, natural gas production spiked high at first, then declined fast.

"Matches what we expected. The wells pay out in months, which they have to since they cost so much," Dwayne said.

"How's the spud-to-release time?" Lynn was referring to the number of days the rig drilled, start to finish.

He gave her a thumbs-up. "It's in the single digits. In fact, if you'd come a day or two later these mud-eaters, sorry, rotary crew, would be on to the next well."

"Dan was telling me about lateral length."

"Around eight thousand feet. Who'd have thought you could drill down a mile to the pay zone, make a right turn and drill another mile and a half horizontally? We'll go by the offsite drill room, too."

Dwayne introduced her to the contractor's rotary crew and gave her a tour of the rig, shouting into her ear over the noise. "This here's a field-based science."

"What do you mean?"

Dwayne grinned. "We experiment until we get it right."

Lynn got in her car and followed Dwayne's truck as they wound around hills and into valleys. After twenty miles of dizzying roads, he pulled up to a one-story nondescript building flanked by a satellite dish and cell phone tower.

As they parked and went inside, he said, "I wish you could have seen the rig at night. It's strung with white lights. Better 'n a Christmas tree."

At the contractor's control room, they checked in with the shift supervisor and with TriCoast's company man, its liaison for all wells being drilled for TriCoast. The room resembled a trading floor with banks of terminals, except in this case, the operators were remotely watching wells being drilled. Each operator studied several screens, a screen for each well.

Seeing Lynn's surprised look, the supervisor said, "We got about fifteen rigs turning to the right, meaning working. As you just saw, our guys on the rigs are operating and steering the drilling, but we monitor it here. This room is your basic second set of eyes."

Most of the drilling supervisors were young men, with maybe a half-dozen young women. One of the men showed her the scale: the tip of the vertical segment, already drilled to several thousand feet, was short. Then it reached the right-angle turn and the horizontal laterals were scaled logarithmically because they were more thousands of feet long.

She and Dwayne asked a few more questions, then turned to leave.

The supervisor said, "Oh, before you go, you've gotta see the benefit for our employees who work night shifts, weekends, and summers. We all like it."

The supervisor opened a door to a large room with several big sofas. A wall-mounted television screen was tuned to a children's program and several children between Matt's and Marika's ages were watching television, playing on tablets or with toys, or napping. An older woman in the corner smiled at them as she prepared sandwiches and milk. Ceiling cameras were aimed at the children from several directions.

"Daddy day care. The guys, and the gals, too, can bring their kids here when they come to work, drop them off, and keep an eye on them while they get their jobs done. The spouses love it because they don't have to leave their own jobs, and most of them are full-timers, too."

After driving several more winding miles through the Pennsylvania hills they were back at Dwayne's office. He introduced her to Kelly Salant, TriCoast's regional marketing vice president for the natural gas and liquids Dwayne's group produced.

While they shared sugary kolaches and coffee, Dwayne said, "I'm still getting a handle here. Thank goodness Kelly has it all in her head. Pipelines go every which way across the state. Smaller pipeline networks move gas around the state and many of them have been in the ground more than a hundred years. The big

T-pipes were laid seventy years ago to move huge volumes of gas from Texas, Oklahoma, and Louisiana to the Northeast."

T-pipes, Lynn remembered, were big trunklines whose names all started with a T.

"But now," Dwayne continued, "with all the gas we're finding here we ought to rip out a few and start over."

"Some of those pipelines *are* being reversed," Kelly said. "We're shipping gas back west to the Rockies and south to Atlanta. We're fighting over market share in Louisiana, particularly once you can flip a chunk of Texas gas around and sell it in Mexico. And companies are extending the smaller pipelines to take natural gas out of Appalachia. Our biggest issue is TriCoast's gas competes against itself, especially on the Gulf Coast where you've got the Haynesville in Louisiana and the Permian in Texas and billions of cubic feet sluicing down from our fields here in Pennsylvania. Some is being exported as LNG out of Maryland and Louisiana and some is piped to Mexico. The best bets are the Japanese utilities—they've locked in a few twenty-year contracts with us. We get the gas to Maryland's liquefaction plant, the gas gets liquefied, and it's shipped out from there."

Kelly smiled. "We're moving gas to the Gulf Coast for liquefaction and shipping, too. Of course, our competitors have the same idea. And while the Europeans and Asians want to buy what we're selling, we're competing with Qatar, Malaysia, Russia, Australia, Mozambique, and Trinidad."

Lynn nodded. *Same as what Ceil told me.*

Kelly continued, "LNG used to be tied to oil prices, which *used* to be high. But now the price is tied to the supplier's local market. Big problem. In Mozambique, for example, the local market price isn't the oil price, but instead is zero. Zero!" She shook her head.

"We have the same problem ourselves in west Texas with all the gas co-produced there with the oil," Lynn said.

"Right, so *any* revenue, let alone any covering the costs of processing and transport, looks good to Mozambique. Another problem we have with these new countries buying is many don't have a credit track record or are unreliable in making payments. Still, with every ship moving over three billion cubic feet of gas, it's a big boost to demand."

"So global competition is tough. How about competition with coal right here?" Lynn asked. Natural gas and coal competed on price to supply electricity generation plants. The fight often came down to a matter of pennies, although natural gas had the low-carbon environmental advantage.

"We take turns. Coal kicks our butt, then we kick theirs," Dwayne said.

"Other issues?" Lynn asked Kelly.

"In this part of the state, most of the gas comes out with a lot of liquids. It's good and bad, depending on how much processing capacity, pipeline capacity, and demand we have for those. We've seen an uptick in gas processing plants and new natural gas liquids pipelines. And there are a couple of other developments on the LNG side. Instead of massive plants costing billions of dollars and requiring twenty-year contracts, companies are building small-scale container projects. And there are marine applications like at Jacksonville, Florida, and Port Fourchon, Louisiana."

"Port Fourchon. It's not far from our Marrero refinery," Dwayne said.

"Right. We'll ask the people there what they've heard," Lynn replied. She complimented Kelly on her work.

Kelly shrugged and smiled. "Some months our customers chase us, and some months we chase them."

After talking to Mark Shepherd about what Dwayne had seen on his monitors, Mark had arranged for Dwayne and Lynn to meet with the FBI in Pittsburgh. The Pittsburgh office was renowned for its partnership with local companies on issues of cybercrime. The office had joined with companies to form the National Cyber-Forensics and Training Alliance, a group that allowed companies to work with the FBI without having national security clearances. All could call on Carnegie Mellon's computer science experts.

Adding Mark Shepherd and Jim Cutler by conference call, Dwayne and Lynn showed the video files to the Pittsburg Special Agent, explaining why they thought it was more than simple vandalism. He agreed, telling Lynn and the others he would run it through a facial recognition database.

CHAPTER 21

NEW ORLEANS, DALLAS, AND EUROPE

Lynn couldn't clear the anger out of her head—TriCoast secrets stolen, sold, and apparently used in the lease auction she'd just attended at the Superdome. But by far the worst of all, Arch Webber had been killed for them. Murdered.

Lynn called NOPD officer Ryan O'Shaughnessy. She tried to keep her tone calm, but her impatience felt as strong as a lightning bolt. "What have you learned about Arch Webber's death?"

"We're still going through street cams as we have time," he said without prelude. "The last time you saw Mr. Webber was at Mr. Boudreaux's uncle's bar on Jackson Square?"

"Yes."

"We got a club barker who works afternoons and then does shift work as a bouncer and bartender at the hotel where Mr. Webber was found. Said if he talked to you, it might help his memory."

"I have time now," Lynn said.

"He's working the afternoon shift at the Bourbon Street club. Meet me at Bourbon and Bienville. You got Beau Decatur with you?"

"Not today. This was supposed to be a routine visit. No protestors, and I'm not outside of the country," Lynn said.

"You really think New Orleans is part of the United States?" O'Shaughnessy asked.

Lynn laughed, glad for a lighter note. "You got me. But very few places in Louisiana are safer than Bourbon Street." The parts of the Quarter frequented by tourists, and where most of the businesses were situated, were well-patrolled.

She walked from the Superdome to Carondelet, across Canal Street and the neutral ground, and onto Bourbon Street. A few blocks later she was shaking hands with Officer O'Shaughnessy. They made their way through early crowds near a club called Fais Deaux Deaux, then past strip clubs named Stilettos and Temptations. French Quarter clubs catered to all interests and pocketbooks. A few were well-lit and expensive; many were darker and cheaper.

"He said he'd meet you at Centerfolds. You should buy him a drink. Or buy yourself one because then he gets a cut."

"Happy to."

"Tourists and locals can get snooty about the French Quarter, but I think of it as living history," O'Shaughnessy said.

"I don't like the French Quarter, but I love it, if that makes sense," Lynn replied.

"Perfectly."

Lynn's thoughts returned to Arch Webber. "What has the coroner found out about Arch Webber?"

"She's reluctant to release any details before the report is final, but—" he nodded before she could interrupt "—she's given me a few by phone, off the record. We see a bunch of cardiac arrhythmias here, so a cardiac shock was her first expectation. But the evidence from his body suggested some kind of toxin. The standard screen she uses for alcohol, cocaine, and amphetamines didn't find those in his system. She's looking, and I asked her to hurry, for other poisons that might have killed Mr. Webber, even if they're the so-called zebras instead of horses. She did remind me she doesn't have the budget or personnel to do full toxicity work-ups on everyone who croaks in the Big Easy."

Lynn's cheeks burned with frustration. "How can we convince her Arch *really* deserves the full work-up?"

"No worries. I said Big Easy. French Quarter deaths always get full attention. Arch is getting the extra mile from her. So will Madame Taliesin."

In the dim light of Centerfold's, O'Shaughnessy introduced her to Norman Moore, a square-built man with the thick neck of a football player and extra girth indicating a life of rich New Orleans eating. He studied her, satisfied himself of something, then shook her hand.

Lynn gave the bartender enough for two rounds of drinks and a generous tip. But when O'Shaughnessy ordered a soda and Moore a tonic, Lynn asked for a tonic, too.

"Between my two jobs I see hundreds of people every day," Moore said. "Sometimes thousands."

O'Shaughnessy showed him a picture of Arch Webber and one of Madame Taliesin. Moore leaned over to study them in the murky room.

"Him I don't recognize," Moore said of Arch Webber's picture, and Lynn despaired of a wasted trip.

"Hang on. Sure I do. He was at the hotel when I was. He's the guy our cleaning staff found dead the next morning." He looked at them. "Swear to God, the man wasn't in the hotel bar. I was tending. I saw him walk by late, not too late. Looked like he'd gotten enough drinks elsewhere, though of course I would have served him if he'd walked in. But no disturbance from his room while I was on shift."

"But Madame Taliesin. Hell, everyone knows her," Moore said. "Knew her, I mean. She used to stop by here—this club—for the occasional Scotch. She was one of few regulars who always got the free drink. What night was this?"

"She was seen alive the Monday night before last."

Moore shook his head. "Couldn't have been then. I saw her. I remember because Mondays are slow except the one before Mardi

Gras, which is crazy." He stared at the picture of Madame Taliesin again. "What about the person who was with her?"

O'Shaughnessy and Lynn looked at one another. No other person was pictured with Madame Taliesin. Yet Moore was confirming Gail's observation.

"Was it Arch Webber?" O'Shaughnessy asked, holding Arch's picture up again.

"No. Fact of the matter is, I couldn't tell you if the person I saw with Madame Taliesin was a man or a woman. I see lots of trannies here, so I can usually spot them no matter what sex they are that day, but the person I saw with Madame had his face turned away. I think it was a male, though who cares?"

O'Shaughnessy interrupted. "I do. Makes it easier to identify the body if I know the sex, or at least the equipment."

Moore said, "Got it. Anyway, Madame gave me a little wave like she did when the person with her was buying her a drink, but they didn't stop here."

"Do you remember where they went?"

"Turned off Bourbon. Went toward the river."

"Where Madame Taliesin's body was later found," O'Shaughnessy said. "And you're sure it wasn't Arch Webber with her?"

"Positive," Moore said.

"What about your late shift that night at the hotel? After you got off here?"

"I had the, oh, maybe ten to four am shift there."

"Did you see Madame Taliesin there?"

"One thing sticks in my mind. I saw two people, a man and a woman, rush through the lobby about a half hour before Arch Webber returned to the hotel. Then later, maybe an hour after I'd seen Arch, I saw the same two people leave the hotel. They weren't in a hurry then. Funny you ask, because one had on clothes that looked exactly like what I'd seen Madame Taliesin wearing earlier in the evening. They talked for a few seconds outside the hotel, then went in opposite directions."

"But it wasn't Madame Taliesin and Arch Webber?"

"Looked a little like her because of the clothes and the body shape, but no. I knew that woman and her walk and her raspy voice anywhere. Could have been a man. The other person was definitely a man, dark-skinned. What little I heard of his accent, he sounded like a foreigner, not someone from New Orleans."

Lynn nodded. Norman Moore's description of the man matched Matak Abdullah, from South Sudan.

They left Moore at his club as the soundtrack rewound to *"Isn't She Lovely?"*

Lynn and Ryan O'Shaughnessy walked a hundred yards before she turned to him. "So Madame Taliesin was with us at Big Oyster on Jackson Square. Then, Gail saw her with someone not far away, St. Ann and Jackson Square. Martina saw her in the same general area, Toulouse. Moore saw Madame Taliesin with a person at one of the Bourbon Street intersections. Then Madame Taliesin and the person headed toward the river. Next, he sees someone *dressed like* Madame Taliesin and a second person we know is Matak Abdullah go into the hotel where he's doing his second shift. Do you think Norman Moore was somehow involved?"

"Nothing is out of the question. I'll talk to him further. Four sightings," O'Shaughnessy said. "But we don't know who the mystery person was. We can assume he or she got Madame Taliesin's clothes before or after Madame Taliesin was killed. Maybe Madame Taliesin was killed by the person with Matak Abdullah. No report yet from the coroner on Madame Taliesin's death although we understand her throat was cut and she was likely dead before she went into the river. Matak and the second person went to Arch Webber's room for his computer. It wasn't a random robbery. They knew what they were after."

Lynn realized his implication. "So the mystery person could be someone inside TriCoast who knew the value of what Arch had on his computer and wanted it. Matak Abdullah was there to help. It appears the two of them poisoned Arch and then left. We still aren't certain what poison was used, or how Madame Taliesin's body got into the river."

In the evening, Lynn returned to Dallas for the following day's executive committee meeting.

Early the following morning, she and Reese talked in her office. Reese and Dena Tarleton would be making a presentation to the committee as Lynn had requested, about anti-drone technology. She'd asked them to give the talk as a way of reinforcing her support for Reese and of highlighting Dena to other TriCoast executives as one of her highest-potential new hires.

Reese said, "We also need to update the committee on the investigation of Arch Webber's death."

Lynn nodded, just as Dena appeared at the door. "Come in, Dena. You need to hear what Reese will be telling the committee about Arch anyway, though I'd ask you to please keep it confidential."

"Of course I will," Dena said. "I do hope progress has been made. Poor man."

Reese said, "I'll run through a couple of items we've learned per what you've told me: a witness told us a second person went into and out of the hotel with Matak Abdullah, dressed in Madame Taliesin's clothes, but it wasn't Madame Taliesin. We've placed Matak at Arch's room from the hotel cameras. The New Orleans coroner is still working the case but has narrowed it to poisoning—we just don't know which one. Matak, in turn, was killed by a Chinese man we believe to be Cong Li. Moreover, we believe Arch's computer was broken into and our bid data was either used directly by whoever employed Matak or the data was sold and used by other people. That's based on our results at the lease auction yesterday, with so many bids so close—just slightly higher—than ours."

Dena's eyes widened. "Cool! It sounds like you're getting close to finding out who killed Arch. I'll always remember him as one of the best soccer players I ever faced in the TriCoast league."

Reese looked at her. "Arch was a good friend of mine. There's nothing I want more than to find his second killer and anyone else involved. I won't rest until I find them."

In the sunlit conference room a few minutes later, Lynn introduced Reese and Dena to the executive committee and said, "Drones are important in our business, from pipeline and refinery inspection to monitoring offshore platforms. They save lives when we send them into places dangerous for our people to inspect, like distillation tower corrosion or tank manhole covers right over lethal concentrations of certain gasses. But my refinery security team has reported an increasing number of unauthorized overflights from rogue or outsider drones causing problems. This device locates them and jams the signal so they can't fly."

After the presentation, Dena left. Reese stayed to brief the committee about Arch.

But first, Sara asked the question Lynn had been dreading and now would have to ask Reese to keep confidential. "Lynn, while I have you here. More thoughts on downsizing? When will you be ready to start?"

"In fact, I'm fighting right now to keep the people we have from being hired by our competitors. So I want a delay," Lynn said.

Mike brushed a hand as if waving her aside. "So does everyone."

"Refining is more profitable than we've been in a few years. The drilling companies are laying off, so why isn't David's drilling division doing the same?"

"We'll need those people when the drilling picks up." Mike said.

"We need good, experienced people to run our refineries, too. I don't put up with slack," Lynn replied.

"What about in your new area? Natural gas?" Sara asked her. "If you think David should lay off people in oil drilling, you should do the same." She moved a water glass around with her thumb.

I'm boxed in. "We can't do much about price, but we're increasing our sales volumes. I'm expecting a call next week for more of TriCoast's natural gas for Mexico. I went to the quinceañera for the daughter of one of their executives."

Mike smiled. "I wouldn't exactly call that slaving away at the mine face."

"You kidding me? I would," Sara interrupted. "Getting all dressed up in this heat?"

But Sara's next comment made Lynn's stomach drop.

"Lynn, if you can't deal with these layoffs, we'll have to find someone who can. I'm sure lots of other companies would love to hire you. But this is the course we decided on. Either you're on our team or you aren't."

What would happen to Cy if I lost my job? There goes his hope of cutting back at work and spending more time with the kids. But everyone working for me is giving over a hundred percent. I'm screwed either way. "When you compare our profit per employee to every other division, it's clear my folks are more than pulling their weight. There are no efficiency gains by laying off people. Hell, with an average age of fifty, attrition is already losing me more people than I can hire."

Mike's expression was grim. "C'mon and get with the program. Do the layoffs. It has to be this way."

Reese said, "What I have to talk about is worse." He stopped, choked, and recovered. "Perhaps not all of you have heard that our TriCoast employee Arch Webber was also a very good friend of mine. Lynn and I have been in close contact with Officer Ryan O'Shaughnessy and others at NOPD, who are investigating his death. The evidence suggests he was murdered."

Gasps came from around the table. Reese paused to let the news sink in.

"We believe he was murdered for the information on his laptop computer, which disappeared the night of his death. This information we think was sold and we know was used against us in yesterday's Gulf of Mexico lease sale. I can run through the numbers.

"But our real focus is on finding Arch's killers, and also who may have ordered his killing, and bringing them to justice. Two people were in his room. We know one, Matak Abdullah, was subsequently killed in Vienna by a Chinese man, Cong Li."

Heads shook as everyone listened.

"Like I said, we will not rest—I will not rest—until we learn the identity of the second killer. We also have to learn if Cong Li ordered Matak Abdullah to kill Arch. You need to understand that will require us to work with not just NOPD, but authorities outside the United States, which we will do." He said quietly, "As God is my witness, I will stop at nothing to get justice for Arch."

Vikenti Andreev wanted to spend a pleasant few days in Paris before his SVR men and a new set of coordinators joined him. He phoned Cong on a burner phone to confirm his plans for France and Poland, which would require a considerable sum of money.

"No payment. Your sloppy operation in Lithuania is all over the news. The authorities may identify you soon. I have a more important issue. I have received bad news. You must fly to New Orleans. There are more people there you must dispose of."

"You want me to kill someone? Can't you find another?" *I don't want to get on an airplane to go to stinking New Orleans again,* Vikenti thought.

"Vikenti, in Copenhagen, you said this was a skill of yours and you would use it if we needed. We need it. You are being paid extremely well."

"Cong, I will do as you ask. Next week."

"Now, Vikenti."

Vikenti considered himself to be far more than a killer. For example, he knew he was superb at delegating. He sighed at the idea of having to leave Paris.

He used more burner phones to call four industrial explosives experts and two project coordinators he knew from the SVR. While he expected to be at one or the other of the next two sites he had chosen when the projects were executed, it would be preferable for the coordinators to put the projects in motion themselves at the dates and times they considered best. Each group would devise the timing, logistics, explosives amount, and placement for its target.

Vikenti spoke to the first coordinator about the LNG storage and regasification terminals at Dunkerque, near Calais, France and the second about a similar terminal in Świnoujście, Poland. Once they and the explosives experts heard the sums involved, they signed up without hesitation.

He explained they should be prepared to carry out the projects within a week.

By the time he got off the airplane in New Orleans, after far too many hours in the air, Vikenti wanted sleep. He would much rather have been in Paris instead of this backward imitation of it. He wanted to be planning LNG terminal explosions instead of planning how and when to kill people. Too simple, too easy.

As he waited wearily in New Orleans' passport control line, Vikenti's attention was drawn by a noisy brass band playing jazz music right beyond the double pane of glass separating him from his luggage, taxis, and sleep. As he contemplated the fastest methods to find and finish his targets, the joyous-sounding band made him feel as if he was being welcomed into New Orleans to accomplish just that.

CHAPTER 22

LOUISIANA

When Lynn arrived at TriCoast's Marrero refinery the next morning, David Jenkins stopped her in the hallway. "Spare me a minute. We've been talking about drilling. I have an expert who swears lightning strikes show us the location of salt domes and so also the location of oil and gas deposits."

"No offense, but he sounds crazy."

David nodded. "Sure, and many good ideas do at first. The science could support it. Let's you and I go out and see his proof."

"How long will this take?" Lynn was intrigued, but she eyed her schedule of meetings and a screen full of emails and texts. Talking to refinery manager Kim Garvey and security expert Patrick Boudreaux were at the top of her list.

"A few hours. He's not far from here. Over near Bayou Cane."

"David, you have time for this?" Lynn had expected the oil drilling head to be busier.

"Until we see higher prices."

"Is this consultant going to show us salt domes we've already have mapped ourselves? If so, he won't be telling us anything new."

"He can back-verify on existing domes and if it looks good, we can use his idea for new drilling. Plus with a thunderstorm brewing, we may see the guy's theory in action."

She nodded, more interested than she expected. "I'll ask Reese to go with us. What about Dena?"

"I asked her already. She says she'll be stuck downtown talking to NOPD about Arch Webber's death."

NOPD must be interviewing everyone who encountered Arch that night, Lynn thought. *What's the pattern and who are the links between Arch's death and the bid results? Why am I missing it?*

Lynn called Reese and he agreed to go. She knew from past trips the area was marshy. Like much of south Louisiana, the ground was fluid—neither land nor water but an in-between muck. Much of it was wetlands or salt marsh and thus closed to drilling. The question was whether the theory might apply at other locations.

She changed into clothes similar to what David and Reese would be wearing: long khaki pants, boots, a white shirt, and a Rangers baseball cap. *We'll all be in the same uniform.* They left the Marrero refinery in one of the refinery's trucks.

For lunch they stopped at a roadside bar, one Lynn judged would have the best food in the area. Humid air had loosened the adhesive signs advertising bait and they'd tumbled onto the porch. *This weather would be hard to run in. Better than bears on the trail, though.*

Glowing beer signs dominated the bar inside. Pool tables lined the middle of the floor. Low-hanging, low-wattage lights gave relief from the harsh, humid air outside.

They ate fries and soft-shell crabs and argued baseball.

When David excused himself for the bathroom, Reese leaned over to Lynn and said, "You and I need to talk further—as soon as you can get away, in private. You heard me tell the board yesterday that all I care about if finding out who killed Arch. We both know we have at least one insider sabotaging the company. I have some ideas about who they might be."

"Who?" She looked toward the restrooms. "You suspect David? That's why you waited for him to leave?"

"My evidence isn't good enough to give you names yet, but I think whoever killed Arch is tied into not only our bidding problems, but also the refinery hacking."

"If I were taking bets it would be Patrick Boudreaux and his off-the-rack soft nihilism," she said, her frustration boiling up.

"No. My own experience is TriCoast doesn't trust outsiders like me, but it's not Patrick. Of course he's still angry at you about his sister's death—

"—because he thinks it was my fault!" Lynn wondered if Patrick was the inside saboteur, or if he had leaked information to the people who were.

"But he's on your side. More than even he realizes."

David reappeared at their table. Lynn nodded silently at Reese, indicating they would talk later.

Just as Cong had told him would happen, the Viper arranged to get a vehicle delivered to Vikenti Andreev's hotel in the morning. The Viper promised one that would be forgettable because it was a popular Louisiana model.

He hoped for a sports car, so was disappointed to see a truck, a Ford F150. But its air conditioning was solid and he assumed he might need its off-road handling.

The Viper sent him directions to an out-of-the-way storage locker where he picked up a Smith and Wesson M&P15 semi-automatic rifle with a sight and ammunition. The rifle was similar to others he had used; it was a good choice. The Viper had also sent directions to an empty parking lot near the TriCoast refinery in Marrero, from which his target would be coming and going.

He crossed the Mississippi River and doubled back on US 90. Then he saw the refinery and found the location from which he could watch the front gate. He parked and waited, turning off the truck. But the summer heat and humidity was merciless, so he turned the truck back on, idling to run its air conditioning at full blast.

Unlike his killing of the drunken old woman in the French Quarter, this one wouldn't be preceded by time spent in cool, comfortable bars.

He was dismayed to see that after a few hours of idling, the truck was almost out of gas. The closest station was a few blocks away. He despised leaving his post but calculated he still had hours before his target would depart the refinery.

When he returned from filling the truck, Vikenti was surprised to see, much earlier than he expected, his target getting into a truck similar to the one he was driving. Two other people, a woman and another man, were joining him. *If I'd been longer filling up this ridiculous truck I would have missed them.*

The presence of the other two people could present a problem, since only one person was on his list from Cong. He could kill the others if they interfered, but his ears still rang with Cong's criticism of the less-than-perfect Lithuanian operation.

Vikenti Andreev slowed as he followed the target's truck west, continuing on Highway 90, the same highway on which he'd crossed the river earlier in the morning.

After driving several miles, they stopped and pulled into a run-down bar advertising fresh seafood on the side of the road. Vikenti drove past the bar and his stomach rumbled. But he couldn't risk the group spotting him—even chatting him up as Americans were likely to do—by going in. For lunch, he settled on a fast-food drive-through a few miles away, then returned and parked as far from the bar as he could while still keeping a sight-line on the target's truck. As he waited, he attached the sight to the rifle and loaded its ammunition.

In less than an hour, the three were back in the truck. Vikenti followed in his own truck, careful to hang back but not lose them. This became more difficult once they left the highway near Houma and headed onto smaller roads with less traffic.

Trees draped with moss and vines overhung the two-lane highway, and Vikenti struggled to keep the target truck in sight but his own unnoticed. Then it began to rain, and Vikenti slowed further, cautiously avoiding other trucks coming seemingly right at him from the other direction on the two-lane road.

Finally, the group pulled over on and stopped. Even better, they appeared preoccupied with meeting another man in yet another truck. Vikenti drove past, followed the road around a corner, pulled off, and parked. He waited to see what they would do.

The storm that had threatened broke as they neared Bayou Cane.

The highway necked down to two lanes. Water from passing trucks splashed onto her windshield, blinding her until the wipers could clear it, like driving through a car wash.

They saw the consultant's truck and pulled off the road to meet him.

The man was a long-haired, gap-toothed, former research project manager for one of the large oil companies. He said, "Thanks for coming out. You've heard about the correlation between lightning strikes and salt domes. It was a geologist and a meteorologist in Houston who first observed the phenomenon. As the meteorologist explained, 'Heat and pressure in the subsurface can generate electrical currents and cause them to flow... When these currents run into a fault, they don't jump it. Instead, they run along the fault.'"

David confirmed, "So lightning seeks out the areas with the most geomagnetic hot spots, and those tell us where the faults are?"

The consultant nodded.

"You're literally looking for where lightning strikes more than once," Lynn said. *Cool.*

The consultant nodded, his long hair swaying. "You game to see the thing in action? I have just the spot. Let's stand back a few hundred yards or we'll get fried."

"Let's!" Lynn said.

"Storm-chase much? You and your father must have run after tornadoes in Oklahoma, too," Reese said to her. Reese had known her father, so he spoke with authority.

"A few times," she admitted, grinning at the memory.

They followed the consultant's truck down several roads overhung with hackberry, elm, and honey locust branches. The rain had stopped falling and instead hung in the air as hot mist. Sweat ran down Lynn's neck and back, but it didn't cool her.

The consultant stopped, and they pulled their truck behind his. He pointed toward a shelter. It was a big lean-to, covered with an asphalt-shingled roof and open to the air on all four sides. "Watch your step. Lots of quicksand, deep water, and mud."

The vegetation was different here—cypress trees of several kinds including bald cypress, Tupelo gums, and Spanish moss. And much more water.

The consultant said, "In one way, quicksand is safer than you might think. Since it has such a high density, if people or animals get stuck, we won't be swallowed right away. Our bodies are less dense than quicksand. What's bad is getting trapped, though. Then you risk dehydration, burning, or drowning when the tide comes in. No problems for us because we're together and there's plenty of branches to break off and use for a rescue."

Guy's really a good-news/bad-news person, Lynn thought.

"The strikes will be over there," he said, gesturing toward a beaver dam amid the heavy roots and water.

The target truck followed the new truck and Vikenti, cursing, idled for as long as he could. Then he drove the narrow, twisting road.

Fresh tire tracks showed him the direction they'd taken. He wiped sweat from his brow and his hands, worried the humidity might cause his hands to slip. He opened his window, listening for the sound of the other trucks. When he heard them stop, he stopped, even though he couldn't see them. All they'd done, it seemed to him, was drive further on a muddy road into this wretched swamp.

He grabbed the rifle and exited the truck, leaving the door open to prevent making a sound. He ducked behind trees, lifting one shoe and then another from the muck as he slipped closer.

The group of four stopped in front of a roofed shelter. All were dressed similarly, but Vikenti could see one was a woman. He studied the group and identified his target. He decided it might be necessary to wound or kill the others.

Still hiding behind trees, Vikenti moved closer to the target and assumed a sharpshooter's stance.

The storm resumed. Lightning cracked, hitting a cypress near the dam, and everyone jumped. Thunder followed, menacingly, while they laughed at their own scare.

"This shelter will keep us—"

David's voice was interrupted by another cracking sound.

Lynn glanced around for a lightning flash but didn't see one. She turned to see a look of shock on the shaggy man's face.

Two more cracks sounded, like heavy books falling off a ladder.

"Get down!" Reese screamed, pushing David and Lynn to the ground.

Lynn crouched. Through the rain something glinted.

Real lightning flashed again, closer this time.

The consultant lay flat on his stomach, a red stain flowering across his back. Lynn felt for a pulse. Nothing.

"Reese! David!" Lynn reached out to both of the men.

"I think I'm shot," David said. He reached around to touch his shoulder and his hand came back bloody. "Shit, I need an ambulance."

He had to get the wound above his heart.

"Sit up," she said.

Pressure bandage. How the hell do I do that? She took off his shirt. The hole the bullet had made was dark and bloody. She pulled the sleeves out flat and rolled the trunk of the shirt tight. She pressed the rolled shirt against the wound and tied it tight in front with the sleeves.

"Don't faint on me," she told him.

"It burns. Use my phone," David said. "Call 9-1-1."

While she called she checked on Reese.

He, too, was flat on his stomach. His wound was lower than David's, directly behind the heart and probably through it.

Lynn turned him over. Reese Spencer—her father's friend, former Navy pilot, her mentor, and for years her steadiest colleague and friend—looked at her with glassy eyes.

"Lynn, I'm—"

"Shhh. Reese. We're calling for help." A sob hit her throat and she gulped air.

He moved his head. "Run. Get out of here!"

"No way," she said. "You'll make it. We're not leaving you." *Goddamn. No way can a medic get here in time. We're out in the middle of fucking nowhere.*

The lightning was more frequent now, but the shooting had stopped.

Lynn held Reese's hands in hers. Blood dripped from his mouth. He vomited blood. Lynn wiped it off of his face and tried to clear it out of his mouth.

His lips moved but his pulse was thready. He was going into shock.

Lynn put her ear next to his mouth.

"Final flight."

She hated his pilot's death phrase. "No, Reese. Hang on. You'll make it!"

"Tell my wife…"

"You'll tell her yourself. Come on Reese. Stay with me!" She cradled his head in her hands.

His eyes stopped moving. Almost imperceptibly, his body relaxed.

"No, Reese!" Her throat closed so hard she had to remind herself to stay alert.

Who's shooting us? Why? And where the hell is Patrick Boudreaux?

The sound of a vehicle gunning penetrated through her shock. She looked up and saw a truck turn around on the muddy road and speed away.

Vikenti ran toward his truck, anxious to get away before anyone else arrived, particularly law enforcement officers.

He jumped in, shoved the rifle under the front seat, and started the truck. As he turned around, trying not to bog down in the mud, he saw the woman staring at his truck. She didn't move to follow him.

Branches whipped past his windows and he drove on, relieved when he could turn back onto the asphalt highway. Never had he been so happy to see a paved road.

He kept a steady speed to get him away from the swamp but not attract attention, falling in behind a car and two other trucks.

Blue and red lights flashed in front of him as sirens wailed. He imitated the example of the other vehicles and pulled off to the shoulder.

An ambulance and a sheriff's car whizzed past.

He followed the other drivers back onto the highway, then exited on the first road to New Orleans.

CHAPTER 23

LOUISIANA/ATLANTIC OCEAN

Lynn greeted the arrival of the medics and deputy sheriffs with numb shock. It had been too late for Reese and the consultant even before David had called them. *It was too late the moment we walked into this damned swamp.*

Patrick Boudreaux arrived a few minutes later. She glared at him and shrugged off his attempt at a consoling hug. *He could be the killer. I can't let him touch me.*

"I was in the area. The emergency vehicles passed me," he explained.

"Doing what?" Lynn asked.

"It wasn't TriCoast business. Another client."

Her fury and sadness left no room for a considered reply. "Sure. Awfully damn convenient. Sure as hell coincidental!"

"You think *I* killed them? Lynn, I'm sorry for what happened, but I didn't even realize you and they were here. I don't have a gun." He shook his head. "I can't believe I even have to defend myself to you. But of course. Why would you trust me? Why should I trust you? Maybe you got them out here and arranged to have them shot. You're not wounded. Not even grazed."

"If I was the killing type, I'd kill you for what you just said. Reese has been one of my best friends for years. Why would someone want Reese—both of these men—dead? Reese is—was—one of the best men in the world."

Patrick looked at her soberly. "Reese was a good man. We are in total agreement about that. I'm sorry. I know he meant a great deal to you."

His consoling and conciliatory words took her off guard. Raw emotion overwhelmed her and she sobbed. Her tears mixed with the rain on her face. Her mind flashed over the decades she'd been acquainted with Reese, first as a friend of her father's, then as a mentor when he'd hired her for her first real job in New Orleans, and now as a colleague and friend.

When the deputy sheriff arrived, she answered his questions mechanically. The deputy told her she would need to go to the sheriff's office to give a written statement. They would also get a written statement from David once he was cleared to do so by the doctors at the emergency room. The ambulance drivers prepared to take away the bodies of Reese and the gap-toothed consultant.

As she walked to the truck in which she was now the only passenger, her wet shoes became wetter, heavier, and slower, until each step felt like lifting concrete blocks tied to her feet. She shuddered at the enormity of the loss to Reese's family. His wife had wanted him to retire, but Reese had insisted he preferred working. Lynn dreaded the call she would have to make now to Reese's wife. *I shouldn't have listened to him. I should have forced him to retire. It's my fault.*

Who the fuck shot him and why? Jesus. And why the consultant? Was the shooter trying to kill us all? If so, Patrick's right—why wasn't I even wounded?

The tanker had slowed its progress toward the Gulf of Mexico. The captain explained their oil was not yet sold, so the shipper had asked them to take a few extra days until he found a buyer. Several other tankers around the globe were doing the same, basically serving as floating storage. Since more oil was being produced than bought, it had to be stored.

Liamzon had thought his mission would be easier with his cousin involved, but he'd started to doubt his early optimism. His cousin was distant, seldom acknowledging him when they saw one another, and never sitting down for the long talks they'd had in the old days. They often worked different hours, so perhaps his cousin's fatigue explained his recent bad mood. Or maybe his cousin didn't really believe in their jihad, or worse, thought Liamzon didn't believe.

After he finished a late shift, Liamzon ducked down one of the small metallic passageways toward his bunk. Without warning a strong arm grabbed him around the neck and his head was jerked back. A knife tickled his throat. "My cousin, do not forget Matak sent me, too. You must do as I say, or I will tell Matak he can't trust you."

Liamzon wouldn't tell his cousin he was getting regular communications from Matak.

The attacker lifted the knife and Liamzon spun around to face his cousin. The seaman held the knife in front of him, a knife with a blade so long it could fillet large fish. Or him.

"What…"

"I have sensed doubt in you. Perhaps when the time comes you will not do all that is required of you. You seem afraid. Perhaps you love this life too much."

"No! No, my cousin. You are wrong." Liamzon bowed his head. "When I have been quiet, it has been because I have been planning, or because I have been anticipating the life beyond this life."

His cousin's face relaxed fractionally.

"So you see. You do not need to report me to Matak," Liamzon said.

"I see you have your watch." The shorter man brought his own watch up to Liamzon's face, then paralleled it with Liamzon's arm to show the watches were identical. "You know what to do if we are discovered."

Liamzon nodded.

His cousin lowered his voice further. "The phone GPS switch will trigger automatically when we near our destination. Remember, I will be observing you to be certain you are prepared to faithfully carry out your duty." The smaller man sheathed his knife and pushed past Liamzon as he headed toward the bridge.

For Liamzon, the passageway now seemed even tinier and the smell of oil permeating the tanker more sulfurous.

Comrade Mei Jin's pantsuit rustled as she entered Cong Li's office. She began talking as soon as she closed the door.

"I am standing, Cong Li, because I am discomforted. I am discomforted because you have wasted money on yet another trip. I gave you the name of the Curaçao boat captain and you met him to get rid of our Lynn Dayton problem. She is still alive. You failed."

Cong permitted himself one retort. "The captain was not as ruthless as you led me to believe. But we will have other opportunities. I have good news, news that can help you and China earn more foreign reserves and give us a strategic advantage over the United States."

She waited, her mouth closed.

"You recall my group was able to embed itself into the instrumentation control for TriCoast's San Francisco refinery. We have already demonstrated proof of concept by forcing them into an involuntary shutdown," Cong said.

"We made our payment so you would reserve that software for us, so I owe you nothing. And others tell me TriCoast has discovered the malware and is removing it after we saw a cybersecurity expert, Kanak Singh, meet with Curtis Zhang, the refinery manager. Feed from our proprietary cameras at this refinery has also stopped. They must have replaced the cameras." Comrade Jin's impatience was as noxious as her rotting, gray teeth.

"I said I have good news, and I do. The Russian Industroyer software we embedded in their instrumentation control will suggest to them a Russian source rather than us. And our version of it is self-replicating. When removal attempts are made, the malware re-implants and then spreads to any other attached device or software, like a human virus. And more good news—I have been able to embed the virus in two more refineries, as well as a pipeline control system that moves gasoline from the southern California refineries to northern California buyers. So for example, we can reduce the flow—not shut if off because such an action is too obvious, but reduce it. In the weeks and months it takes to repair any industrial equipment in California, we can sell our own gasoline to the needy customers."

Comrade Jin listened without responding.

"But now, in addition, we have been able to code and embed a second kind of malware affecting the refinery's safety systems. So, for example, many of the automatic shutoffs no longer work if we direct them not to." He was pleased at this exponential breakthrough, a result of copying similar software from a Saudi Arabian plant.

Comrade Mei Jin appeared unmoved by this technical advance. "Yes? How does such malware help us?"

Cong Li permitted himself a smile. "Let me show you." He punched a few buttons on his computer and a schematic of Tri-Coast's San Francisco refinery appeared, with boxes and shapes for various processes, and lines between them showing how liquids and gasses flowed from one unit to the next. The Viper had told him when this confidential blueprint appeared for sale on the dark web, and he had purchased it.

Cong pointed to some boxes. "With the combination of software, we disable temperature sensors here and here, at the highest-temperature locations near the bottom of the distillation tower and the coking unit. We also disable the automatic flow shutoff, safety alarms, and emergency cooling water. The resulting explosions will take the refinery offline for days, perhaps weeks or months."

"An interesting concept but how do we benefit?" Despite her scorn, Cong could see Comrade Jin was interested.

"The simplest action would be to ask for a ransom to remove the software."

"Insufficient money for the exposure," Comrade Jin objected. She shifted from one foot to another. She had been standing longer than she expected but sitting would be a sign of weakness.

"Yes. So our own Chinese companies could offer emergency supplies of gasoline, jet fuel, and diesel—at a fair price—to replace what this refinery could no longer make. The US West Coast always has high prices and not enough fuel, so the US government would be ready to pay us a special, and higher price, for us to supply them in an emergency."

Comrade Mei Jin showed her gray teeth in a ghost of a smile. "Good. But Cong, there is a problem with your plan. Our petroleum products do not meet California's specifications."

Cong permitted himself to sit back in his chair. "If there is an emergency, the air quality rules and specifications for our products would be suspended. It has been happened before. With big shortages from a TriCoast refinery shutdown, the local, regional, and federal governments would be forced to suspend the rules again."

Cong knew he had convinced Comrade Jin when she nodded, pulled out her cigarettes, and offered him one.

CHAPTER 24

SAN FRANCISCO

After a sorrowfully exhausting few days, Lynn, Dena, and Decatur flew to California to follow up on the San Francisco Bay refinery problems.

They stopped in Palo Alto to buy the latest thrillers at Books, Inc.

"Now what about dinner?" Lynn asked, glancing at Decatur. He looked as if he was fueled by three squares a day.

"You okay with salad?" Dena asked him.

"Long as it comes on top of a steak," Decatur said.

"We'll skip the vegan places then," Dena said. They found parking in one of the civic garages and a table at Tacolicious. After dinner they walked in downtown Palo Alto. Conversations around them mixed English and a Mandarin-sounding language. The white-light-wrapped trees lining University emphasized laughing faces of strolling tech professionals. *I will never be that happy again*, Lynn thought. *Not after seeing Reese killed in front of me.*

When they checked into their Palo Alto hotel, Lynn did a double-take at the room rate.

"They asked *me* for my first-born child," Dena said.

The following morning, the caffeine lift and smell of eucalyptus outside of Philz didn't change the aggravation of stop-and-start traffic as they drove past venture capitalists' offices on Sand Hill Road.

Lynn thought, *I have to tell Reese about...* and with horror, remembered his death again. Once onto I-280 Decatur had to continue at the same slow pace.

"Damn this traffic! Between watching for the bicyclists and the driverless cars and being slowed down here by all the tech company commuter buses, we'll be a freaking half hour late." Lynn ground her teeth.

"The traffic is always bad here during commuting hours," Dena said.

"No, today is particularly bad. There aren't any alternate highway routes. They don't exist here on the peninsula. The trains are on strike, the concierge told me." It felt good to Lynn to argue, but Dena didn't take the bait.

"You're upset about Reese's death," she said. "I'm glad Decatur is driving."

"Yes. Aren't you upset?" she asked.

"I am. He was one of the few willing to give me plenty of responsibility without constantly checking on me."

Decatur drove them across San Francisco, past warehouses repurposed as gaming and tech company buildings. A line of traffic waiting to get onto the Bay Bridge stretched a mile in front of them. Tankers coasted out in the bay and container ships were stacked as high as buildings with goods from China, soon to be unloaded on east-bound trains and trucks.

"Mark Shepherd didn't have any ideas about who killed Reese," she said, "at least not any he was willing to share."

"It must have been difficult to talk to Reese's wife," Dena said.

Lynn nodded and felt hot tears in her eyes.

Once across the bridge, they exited the interstate and passed wood-shingled houses on hilly streets that rose in sudden, sharp angles. Familiar shields of grass berms came into view and they were at the refinery. Decatur left Lynn and Dena at the front office; he arranged to return within a few hours.

Curtis Zhang and Lynn patted one another's shoulders. He said, "I heard about Reese Spencer. You two were long-time colleagues and friends."

She nodded and looked at him, walling off her sadness, afraid of completely losing her self-control. "Tell me what's going on here."

"Listen, Kim and I both found some of these Chinese-made security cameras we think are a risk, so we've replaced them, and the other TriCoast refineries are doing the same. Kanak's company is still working the hacking angle. They were here yesterday, and I understand you're talking to Kanak this afternoon. One of their infamous meeting-while-moving hikes?"

"They like to walk and talk to cut down on interruptions," Lynn said. "I'll take the excuse for exercise." Despite Zhang's kind words, Lynn still wondered about his connection to China, but wanted to ask in a way that wouldn't shut him down. "Curtis, you remember our earlier discussion. I'm trying to understand any relationships we might have with the Chinese. Have their refineries ever backstopped us for gasoline or diesel, for example?"

Curtis Zhang stepped back. "You trust me to run this huge refinery but you still don't trust me outside of it?"

Lynn shook her head as Dena looked on. "No, I trust you. I'm just wondering how the hell Cong and whoever he's working with got inside." She waved her hands. "Yes. Cybersecurity issues. But often those come down to a dropped password or an opened e-mail. I just can't figure it."

"You underestimate the hackers. They scour everything, all the time, looking for holes. Even in the most thoroughly tested systems they find them. I think that's what happened to us. Can we talk a few California logistics while I have you here?"

"Go ahead." Lynn didn't like the conversation being redirected.

Zhang's tone was defensive. "We can import all the Middle Eastern crude oil we need but we can't bring in gasoline or diesel from other parts of the United States."

"Curtis, you're telling us what we already know." Lynn was impatient. She still felt rubbed raw by Reese's death. "The isolation is geographic because the region is cut off by the Rocky Mountains and the water access to the rest of the US is through the Panama Canal. You're isolated too by regulation because of the tough specs of California's special reformulated gasoline."

"So we and everyone else here have to run full-out because there's high demand for the products and we're the only places capable of making them. And God help us when a refinery goes out due to a fire or an accident—or in our case, because someone is hacking our control system." His voice tightened in frustration. "We have half the state calling for our heads. I feel their pain because I pay an extra fifty cents a gallon, too. Of course, the other half of the state is cheering because they don't think anyone, rich or poor, should use gasoline at all. Elitist if you ask me because the alternatives are so freaking expensive. But hey, I'm just a middle-class refinery manager."

She sighed. "At the moment all I care about is keeping your refinery safe from any more attacks, finding out who killed Reese, getting an explanation of Arch Webber's murder, and finding and stopping this Cong Li. That's why I'm asking you about it."

He nodded and offered her and Dena cups of coffee. "Let's talk about what we can do and your agenda for the rest of the afternoon. The pipeline inspector will be here soon. He's asked you to accompany him on the helicopter trip to examine our pipeline. Juan will go with you, too."

"Why me?" Lynn said. "What about you and Dena?"

"He wants to meet *you*. The helicopter fits five and then only if one of them isn't as large as Juan, so we have to subtract two. We don't want to press our luck."

Lynn frowned.

"Tell you what, if you spare the time now the pipeline inspector will remember it later when it will do the most good, I promise. He'll return our calls instead of ignoring them," Zhang said.

She checked her phone for the rest of her schedule. "It's tight, but as long as we're not flying more than a few hours I can do it."

Zhang said, "I can't guarantee it, but..."

"But ninety-five percent probability, you'll be back." Dena flashed a hand signal to Zhang and mouthed something. They laughed at an inside joke they didn't share with Lynn.

Annoyance and suspicion flashed through Lynn's mind. She wondered again who Reese had been ready to name as the inside saboteur, filed the thought away for later examination, and said, "What's the joke?"

"We heard about the anatomically-correct female AI robots Kanak's company will be building," Zhang said.

"We wondered who the model was," Dena added.

Juan Rojas, the refinery's safety manager, joined them. He shook his head at Dena. "You cracking jokes in sign language we can't understand? That's against the rules."

Dena looked startled until Juan said, "Kidding. Well, kidding for the office. It *is* the rule in the refinery, especially around heavy equipment."

To understand what she would be seeing from the helicopter, Lynn asked Juan about the pipeline.

"It's monitored electronically by control centers here, in Dallas, and in Houston."

"Safety redundancy?" she asked.

"You got it."

"And like everything else, we've trained local first responders on our procedures, and our folks drill with them to be ready for an emergency."

"How about pipeline corrosion?" she asked, remembering how many industrial accidents occurred when pipes corroded through. She'd had one at one of her own refineries when a rogue, poor-quality, high-sulfur crude had been substituted for better-quality oil by an executive who then pocketed the payoffs.

Juan nodded. News about all refinery incidents, no matter the cause, were circulated throughout TriCoast so similar problems could be rectified in other locations. "We share ownership of the pipeline with two other companies, so we share all prevention costs with them. The pipes are coated to minimize corrosion from the soil."

"The dirt they're buried in can eat through them?" Dena asked.

"Yep. We also have cathodic protection on our systems to prevent corrosion. And we do random flyovers to check for leaks, like we're about to do now," Juan said.

Lynn left Zhang and Dena reviewing material weight balances. Juan drove her to the heliport nearby.

Once they checked in, Lynn introduced herself to the person waiting for them. The inspector was a fit man in his early thirties who immediately mentioned he'd run twenty-two marathons in the previous three years. When she talked about her own running, his first question was about her speed. He nodded at her eight-minute miles and noted his own six and a half minute pace.

"Like a lot of Californians, I'm waiting for the day when the state is hydrocarbon-free," he said.

"You're serious?" She couldn't help shaking her head, but then laughed. "You ready to move back into a cave, cook over a fire, and chop down the old-growth trees to stay warm in the winter?"

"See this air pollution? I want clean air, have ever since I was a kid with asthma who couldn't run so well. That's why I run now."

"I sympathize but you should talk to the coal-burning Chinese. Hydrocarbons—natural gas and oil, not coal—provide over eighty percent of California's energy now. That's a lot of dams, wind farms, and solar farms to build in the next ten years."

"We can reinvent ourselves and the economy. We do all the time," he said, with the certainty of a man who'd witnessed the tech revolution up close.

"Then you'll sure have a big job turning the Chinese economy off coal. It fuels about seventy-five percent of their electricity, which means a dam every few miles on the Yangtze to replace all of it."

He shrugged. "I'll deal with them if I have to when the time comes. Of course, I won't have a job inspecting oil pipelines then, either."

"What will you do instead?"

"California is a big state. There will always be something needing inspection."

She was reminded again of Cong Li, wondering if he was part of the Chinese government or working for it. China needed oil—it didn't have enough of its own. And the country needed to sell its refined products, like diesel and gasoline, because it made too much for its own use. Taking out one or more big US refineries would serve both incentives. China's imported oil would be cheaper, because there would suddenly be fewer other refinery buyers of oil, and there would be more demand for China's refined products if more refineries were offline. This wasn't the first time she'd encountered this risk. *But why us? Why TriCoast*, she wondered. *Or are we just one of many Cong has in his sights?*

They climbed into the agency's helicopter. It was emblazoned with the California state seal and the agency's name on both sides, and presumably also on the bottom.

Once the copter was in the air, she looked back at TriCoast's refinery to orient herself with the accustomed structures of tanks, towers, and white butane spheres. A line of black oil tank cars—pipelines on wheels—snaked at the boundary of the refinery, although rail shipping of oil had declined. *One small upside to low prices.* Shipping oil by rail aboveground was far more hazardous, resulting in more spills and explosions, than shipping by pipeline belowground.

Hillside storage tanks were painted a tawny red-brown. As the helicopter lifted even further, she could see the cedar trees of

Berkeley, Coit Tower defining San Francisco, and on the docks, innumerable big loading cranes looking as if they could walk the sky.

Juan pointed out San Quentin and Treasure Island.

The helicopter flew near the shimmering bay and then headed southeast toward the Central Valley. The land beneath them changed into desert-like scrub, drier than the coastal grass and trees.

She turned toward Juan when she heard his voice through the headphones. "Pipeline monitoring in Dallas says their cameras and meters are showing a leak near our route where the line is aboveground. Houston confirms. Since we're headed over there, I told him we'd check it out."

"They've turned off the flow?" Lynn hoped it was a false alarm.

The TriCoast safety manager nodded. "Rerouted some of it, storing the rest." He gave the helicopter pilot coordinates for the leaking section of pipeline. The pilot told them it was about fifteen miles away.

"Is Genscape reading a heat loss, too?" Lynn asked. From its heat signature studies, the company was often the first to explain where large volumes of oil and gas were going.

"Yes," the safety manager said.

As they got closer, the four of them began searching the ground. Juan pulled out binoculars and handed her a pair.

When she focused them, she said, "I see the spill. What's the group of people doing there? Cleaning up already?"

"I doubt it," Juan said grimly.

As they circled closer, the group unrolled a banner reading "Oil-Free America. Free America from Oil."

"What do you want to bet they punctured the line?" the inspector said. His voice crackled with anger. "That's so fucking dangerous." He asked the pilot to land as near to the site as possible.

They got close enough Lynn could see looks of rage on the faces of several protestors.

As the pilot circled, green light splayed across the windshield.

"Sumbitch! A laser! I don't want it in my eyes. We're outta here," the pilot said. He re-oriented the chopper away from the pipeline. There would be no landing after all. *None too soon.* Lynn could see the group was also preparing to launch a small drone.

The helicopter rose straight up, then reversed course back to the heliport. She bounced against the seat belt.

"Damn it!" The inspector was far more upset than the calm runner who'd introduced himself an hour ago.

His face bright red with anger, the inspector radioed the sheriff's office and gave them the protestors' location. "They flashed a laser at us. Send out a hazmat team with the firefighters, too. It's an oil spill. I'd bet a week's pay they punctured the pipeline to make their stupid point."

CHAPTER 25

PALO ALTO

Lynn, Juan, and the inspector briefed the sheriff and state fire marshal about the pipeline leak. Then Decatur drove Lynn and Dena back to Palo Alto. Kanak had agreed to meet her near Stanford and drive to a hiking trail at the Windy Hill Open Space Preserve. Dena would be talking to Dr. Chin at his Stanford lab and updating him on her Texas electricity grid findings as he'd requested, and then returning to help Kim Garvey in New Orleans.

When Lynn told her plan to Beau Decatur, he cursed. "Thought you were meeting Kanak in a nice safe office."

"I'm dying to get outside."

"'Dying' is not a word I use casually. The trail you're describing is in the Santa Cruz Mountains. Densely populated on the Bay side and as wild as when the First Peoples saw it on the ocean side."

"Wilderness sounds perfect to me," Lynn said.

"It's a ridge, a north-south spine through San Mateo County, with lots of hiking trails like the one you're headed to. You forget you could be a target, particularly if someone with a facial-recognition app who hates energy execs sees you."

"That's true everywhere."

"But this was part of the Zodiac Killer's territory."

"Before my time. Not relevant," Lynn was exasperated with his caution until she remembered the pipeline protestors and the laser.

"Remember that when you find a dead body. Gangs from every city around dump bodies in the mountains."

"You're saying that because you don't like the deviation from the plan."

"Well, there will be another deviation. I'll be accompanying you and Kanak on the hike now."

When Kanak picked Lynn up on Campus Drive near the Gates computer science building, she introduced Decatur and said, "We ran into interference this morning while looking at a pipeline. Beau Decatur will accompany us but he'll stay back behind us to give us privacy."

Kanak shrugged. "Sure. The trailhead is in Portola Valley. Since it's not 9 P.M., let's stop at Bianchini's on Alpine Road for food and water to take with us. It's a combo grocery and farmer's market."

"Sure. But what does 9 P.M. have to do with anything?"

"Sorry, inside reference. On campus and so at all the companies graduates wind up at, healthy food disappears and high-fat food comes out between 9 P.M. and 2 A.M. in the morning. It's the secret to engineers' productivity and one reason all-night coding sessions are the norm."

"I'd be waiting for the fun food, too," Lynn said.

They bought fruit, protein bars, and water at open-air Bianchini's Market. Kanak drove Lynn and Decatur a few more hilly miles to the trailhead.

Houses perched away from the road, each the same distance from the next.

"We're in luck. The parking lot isn't jammed," Kanak said as he turned off his hybrid.

"I have running shoes but not hiking boots. How rough is this trail?" Lynn asked.

"No problem with running shoes."

"And our cell phones will have decent reception, right?"

Kanak sighed and said, "We can go back to the office and talk if you want."

"No way. Since Beau Decatur is with us, we're safe."

"He looks pretty ripped."

"Don't talk about me like I'm not here," Decatur said.

Lynn looked at him and nodded. "And I believe he used the phrase 'Zodiac Killer.'"

Kanak shrugged. "Nothing's a hundred percent safe. So, awesome, a bodyguard! A bonus we haven't thought of. Incredibly expensive here, though. Everything is. Or at least, every*one* is."

Whether or not I'm attacked could help answer the question of whom or what the motive is. So it's a test of the target-Lynn hypothesis.

The afternoon deepened and skies cleared as they climbed the trail past clumped trees and into shaded grottos. As promised, Decatur kept them in sight but stayed about twenty feet behind. After a long walk on one ridge, Lynn snapped pictures with her phone of San Francisco thirty miles to the north, the bay on one side, San Jose thirty miles to the south, and the Pacific Ocean on the other side.

"Can you summarize what you're finding out about who's attacking our refinery?" Lynn asked. *I like the hike but I'm not here for my heart.*

"We looked at all the refineries in your system."

Lynn turned to him. "What?"

"Reese asked us to."

"Before he was killed." The words slipped out before she could stop them.

"Yes, I heard. Incredibly tragic."

Then, despite her sorrow, chilly distrust settled over her that Reese had gone beyond the scope of their investigation. "What did you find?"

"Like any contagion, whoever's gotten into your San Francisco refinery has also worked their way into your Marrero refinery."

"Shit. When were you going to tell us?"

"When we could also tell you where it was from, because that's key to stopping it. I told Dena and I told your refinery manager there, Kim Garvey, and Curtis Zhang, in San Francisco. Kim's already told her people. The four of us outlined plans to shut down and restart if either of the refineries is attacked. Worst case. We need more time to review, but it's a first pass. Kim and Zhang said it's similar to what they do in other emergencies."

Lynn felt her face flush. "Whoa! You shouldn't cut me out of the loop. Ever."

Decatur got closer to them when he heard her raised voice.

Kanak looked chagrined. "I'm sorry. We just figured it out last night. Since I run the company, I'm used to reaching out directly to IT security people."

"But Dena, Kim, and Zhang aren't IT."

"It was four A.M., so I wasn't thinking about organizational protocol."

"I should have heard about the malware infecting Marrero from one of you," Lynn retorted. *I feel like my head will explode. So much for a relaxing walk.*

She stopped and turned to look at him. "I have some questions, even if they repeat whatever was asked at four A.M. this morning." She didn't try to keep the bitterness out of her voice.

Kanak nodded quietly. "Of course."

They stepped off the path. Lynn told Decatur she and Kanak were stopping to talk.

"You'll be preoccupied, so I'll be about twenty yards ahead on the path, checking things out," Decatur said.

Once Decatur had moved into position, Lynn asked Kanak, "How did the malware get into each refinery? Can we stop it from getting into our other refineries?"

"The initial intrusion into your San Francisco refinery was an attack—Cong Li appears to have searched it out specifically and repeatedly probed until he found a weakness. It could have been, probably was, something as simple as someone in the refinery opening a link or an email they shouldn't have. The virus replicates itself and has instructions to send out probes. Do you have communications between refineries?"

"Yes." Lynn and Kanak watched as a couple of college-aged women jogged past.

"It likely piggybacked on either machine or personal inter-refinery communication to get into your Marrero refinery. Once there, it has instructions to burrow in."

"Why haven't you and your company been able to get rid of it?"

"The medical analogy to cancer is apt: it can spread throughout your system—in this case your industrial control system. We have been rooting it out, but the malware can embed in places, or subroutines, we can't easily find."

Lynn wished she had known this sooner. "But you *have* been trying to destroy the malware?"

Kanak blinked. "Yes, of course. However, it appears the malware, once attacked, has instructions to replicate and spread, like spores."

The day felt chilly and cold. "Jeez. The news just gets worse and worse."

"This is stubborn, pernicious coding," Kanak said, with what to Lynn sounded suspiciously like a hint of admiration.

Surely I'm imagining that. We're in so deep. I have to trust Kanak and his company. "What units is the malware targeting? Where are you finding it?" Lynn asked, kicking a rock down the path. One of the women who'd passed them turned and glared at her.

"The malware is attacking the temperature sensors and blocking feedback loops in every heat exchanger."

"Christ! There are dozens of exchangers, hundreds throughout our whole refining system, and probably thousands of temperature sensors."

"Yes. So we require time to examine the control system for each one."

She looked at him carefully. "You have enough people on the job?"

"Yes, but it's why we're making calls at four A.M."

"And why haven't we seen anything going wrong lately in the San Francisco refinery? Not that I want it to. Losing Shirley Watson and her two colleagues was awful." She looked down, remembering Shirley's bereft wife.

"It could have just been a demo." Kanak leaned against a tree. They were quiet as another group of hikers passed them.

Lynn waited until they heard Decatur greet the hikers. "What do you mean, a demo?"

"As we told you, after a lot of work we traced the IP address back to Cong Li, wherever he is in China. So, whoever he's working for, he ran a demo on our refinery to show what his malware could do."

"A freaking demo slaughtering three people! If I ever find Cong, I'll strangle him!"

Kanak nodded sympathetically. "Here's my worry, and it should be yours, too. He's likely sold one or more projects on the basis of the demo."

"And?"

"And as fast as we are rooting out the malware, it's still replicating. And he or the people he works for are likely to trigger something much bigger and much more dangerous. Frankly, an attack could happen at any time."

"What can *we* do to stop him? What are *you* doing?" Lynn wanted to run to her car and start calling and texting, whatever it took to stop the vicious attack that could be delivered at any moment from Cong Li using her own refinery.

"Put out the word to any free IT staff you have—we could use a few more bodies—and just ask your people to stop communicating between refineries. That's how the virus is spreading."

She shook her head. "That's impossible. Our refineries are connected to one another at hundreds of levels, through thousands of people."

"Kim Garvey and Dena Tarleton said they would try it."

"I'll back them up. I'll warn everyone to watch for unusual activity and of course, all the warnings about opening attachments, suspicious e-mails, and even to be careful with communication appearing to be from our own TriCoast people. What will you be doing?"

"After I get some sleep," he yawned, "I'm headed back to work to continue rooting the malware out of the heat exchanger control systems. We've been trying to block Cong's access, but if we're obvious about it, he'll know we've found him and he'll accelerate his plans. My team has also been coming up with what you might call an antidote, or anti-virus software for this particular iteration of Industroyer. So we'll start applying it to your San Francisco and Marrero refineries in the next day or so."

After another mile, they had looped back to the trailhead, Beau Decatur still several cautious yards ahead them.

Lynn wiped sweat from her forehead. Everything Kanak had discussed was worrisome, and his anti-virus was untested. *What if we lose cooling water to the processing units and the safety back-up control systems fail? We'd have hot, massive hydrocarbon explosions throughout the refinery. Even with emergency shutdown procedures, more people could be killed.*

CHAPTER 26

CALIFORNIA, RUSSIA, AND POLAND

After the hike, Kanak Singh had begged off dinner to return to the office, but he'd reserved a table for them at a Menlo Park rooftop Italian restaurant on El Camino Real. Decatur had finished his beef and Lynn her pasta when her phone rang, showing a New Orleans number.

"New Orleans," she told Decatur as she answered.

"O'Shaughnessy, Lynn. The coroner had news you'll find interesting."

"Results from Arch Webber's toxicology screen?"

"Yes," Decatur said. "And if they hadn't been looking for it, they wouldn't have found it—thallium sulfate, apparently dissolved in water. The coroner calls thallium sulfate the poisoner's poison—you can't taste or smell it and it has no color."

"Jesus!" Lynn exclaimed. "How is something like that even available?"

"It isn't. Not in the US. Only in some Middle Eastern countries."

"So Matak Abdullah, the man in Arch's room, must have brought it from overseas."

"Looks like," O'Shaughnessy said. He cleared his throat. "We also got news on Madame Taliesin, something that seems to complicate the timeline."

"What did you learn?" Lynn asked him. She looked at Decatur across the table and mouthed, "A lot of news."

"No water in her lungs."

"So she was dead before she went into the river under the docks."

"Yes. As we suspected from the time we found her body, she died of blood loss after her throat was cut. Whoever did that likely also threw her in the river, just to get rid of the body."

Lynn gasped.

O'Shaughnessy went on. "There's more. She had a deep laceration on her skull and we found bits of glass in her hair. That appeared to have happened well before she died, maybe a few days before. So she was alive for a few days after you last saw her. She died no more than a day before we found her body, maybe less than twelve hours. And the clothes she was wearing were the pants and a shirt of a young man. We asked around—they weren't like clothes she ever wore—always dresses."

"Are you saying someone knocked her out and hid her for a few days?" She put a finger in one ear to block the noise of a car in the alley below.

"That could have happened. Remember she was with your group. Then later that night Gail and Martina separately saw her in the French Quarter with someone, and so did the bartender we talked to, Norman Moore. Only description we have of her companion is a slight young man. Then when Norman Moore was on his second shift that night at Arch Webber's hotel, he swears he saw a man and a woman who wasn't Madame Taliesin but was wearing her clothes go into and out of the hotel. We know the man was Matak Abdullah. The bartender was telling the truth when he said it looked like someone else in Madame's clothes and with her parasol."

"So someone knocked out Madame Taliesin, stashed her, changed clothes with her and took her parasol? Then disguised as her, that person got into or got invited into Arch Webber's hotel room? Matak Abdullah joined up at some point and the two of them killed Arch Webber and took his computer?" Lynn said. "Hard to believe."

"Yet entirely possible. Particularly since we have found two witnesses who saw the real Madame Taliesin the day before or the day she was killed."

"Wow! Where? With the man who took her clothes and parasol?"

"In a bar close to Iberville. Not the same man. The bar was not one she frequented. She was drinking with a big man with a foreign accent. Could have been Russian."

"So he may have killed her? What was his name?"

"Him as the killer does look probable. No information on him yet, though."

"That's a huge amount of news. Thank you for telling me. I hope Madame Taliesin's killer, and this other young man who knocked her out, are identified and found."

O'Shaughnessy's voice was grim. "Oh, we'll find them all right."

After she hung up, Lynn relayed everything she'd heard to Decatur and concluded, "It all sounds so improbable."

"The worst things are," Decatur replied.

Again in Kaliningrad in the small Russian land wedge on the Baltic Sea between Poland and Lithuania, Vikenti Andreev had gathered one of the project coordinators and one of the SVR explosives experts he had contacted in Paris. *Before that too-long trip to New Orleans*, he thought. Despite his urging, the coordinators had been unwilling to attack without him. So after this, he would meet the other SVR coordinator and explosives experts who were waiting near Dunkerque, France at a third regasification terminal.

Cong's harsh words about his sloppiness in Lithuania still angered him. Worse, Cong had been unwilling to front the money for these operations, requiring Vikenti to tighten his budget. He'd wanted to also use the two experienced men who'd been with him in the Klaipėda attack but had had to dismiss them.

In the early morning, the splashing of the fountain in the middle of the Lower Pond covered their quiet conversation nearby. The chilly dawn air was a reminder of the fierce Baltic winter soon to arrive.

They agreed about the need to stop yet another upstart challenge to Russian gas dominance in Europe.

"LNG? Sure we will supply Russian LNG. To Boston in the US, from our own Yamal Peninsula, just as we have," Vikenti said. "An excellent entry into a US region that won't build pipelines for gas from its own states. So instead, the US sends gas Boston won't take to Poland. Poland! And the Polish president bows and scrapes and says how happy he is to reduce reliance on Russian blackmailing. We will show them blackmailing."

The other men laughed at Vikenti's joke. They already knew the mission. They focused on the attack.

"We rented a Skoda Octavia," said the unshaven coordinator. "New. It will go the distance. And we each have a Makarov. They were satisfactory before?"

Vikenti nodded his approval. The Makarovs had performed well. The car would allow them to blend in on Polish roads. They had to drive further and needed reliable transportation.

The snaggle-toothed explosives expert said, "We have Semtex and detonator cord. That's what you used in Lithuania and that's what we recommend again. I obtained it before we arrived here."

Vikenti nodded, not expressing the worry foremost in his mind. They would be only a few kilometers away from Germany in Świnoujście, Poland, and thus not have the easy escape through a less-developed country as they had in Lithuania. Polish security would be high, German border security even tougher. *Only over and back,* he thought.

"Are there ways to return that don't require us to drive?"

The unshaven coordinator nodded and described their route. "Yes by boat, but let me explain. We go southwest on E28, cross the border near Elblag, west for hours on Highway 22, switching off to 24 at Czluchow. I will direct us more as we get closer. We end up on National Road 3."

"We should leave soon. It will require eight hours," Vikenti said, staring at the coordinator's route map. He wanted to get across the border.

The coordinator anticipated his question. "At the border, we will tell them we are headed to Berlin to play the clubs for a few weeks. We have a saxophone, a guitar, and a keyboard and sound equipment. We'll put the guns inside the sound equipment. We packed the explosives and cord into boxes of kitchen supplies, in with waxed paper."

"*Da. Otlichno.*" Yes. Excellent.

The snaggle-toothed explosives expert interrupted. "Instead of going into the regasification plant as you did before, we will get close to the tanks from right outside the fence. Security is tighter. But the prize is bigger. Five billion cubic meters of capacity, enough for a third of Poland's gas demand. All of which they should be buying from us."

The expert showed the other two a picture of the site. "We will attach detonator cord, leave the car, and blow it up remotely, along with the tanks."

"And I have arranged for us to slip onto a boat that will take us to a landing in Sweden east of Trelleborg," the coordinator said.

Vikenti nodded with satisfaction. They had planned well. He looked closer at the picture but he knew what they didn't show because he had studied other pictures. "What about the naval base nearby?"

"We'll be gone before they can get to us."

Vikenti looked at them. "We have a long day ahead before we get to our Swedish beauties. Let us begin. We will take turns driving or sleeping. I will drive first."

They left Lower Pond. Vikenti looked around but saw no one watching them. The other two discarded their burner phones. He tossed his, as well.

Vikenti drove the Skoda and the other men dozed through the morning.

Several kilometers before the border, Vikenti stopped and the three packed their Makarovs inside the padded speaker boxes.

At the border, two guards asked the men to get out of the car. They inspected the Skoda, opened the boxes of kitchen supplies and briefly looked through them.

When they opened the saxophone case, they asked who played. Vikenti froze.

But the explosives expert took the saxophone, warmed up and played several bars of Gerry Rafferty's "Baker Street."

The guards smiled and nodded at the classic, motioning them back into the car to drive on. A few miles further down the road, they stopped and bought gasoline and food, and unpacked their guns. The snaggle-toothed explosives expert took over driving.

Surprised and grateful for the border clearance but not wanting to show emotion, Vikenti fell asleep in the front passenger seat.

They stopped at another gasoline station and changed drivers again. Vikenti kept his place in the passenger seat.

The unshaven coordinator woke him up as they passed through the roundabout that signaled they would soon be at the regasification plant. The road ahead was straight, a set of railroad tracks on one side and forest on the other.

Ahead, a blue and white car pulled to the shoulder in front of them, signaling them to stop. Its flashing light bar was labeled *Policja*. From seemingly nowhere, a second police car pulled behind the Skoda, its lights flashing also. The unshaven coordinator, who was driving, signaled right and drove onto the shoulder. The two police cars blocked them in front and behind.

Vikenti said, "We are better armed than they. Roll down the windows. We shoot as soon as they come to us."

"*Da,*" the other two said, and the driver rolled down all of the windows.

But no one exited either of the police cars.

Vikenti waited as calmly as he could, turned sideways in his seat so he could see both police cars.

Finally, the driver's-side door of the car behind them opened.

"We prepare," Vikenti said.

He was shocked to see two Makarovs aimed at his own forehead and chest.

"*Nyet!* You betray—"

The coordinator and the expert shot before Vikenti finished his sentence. Explosions boomed inside the Skoda.

The two men got out of the car, wiping Vikenti's blood and bone fragments from their clothes. Both raised up their hands as the police officers swarmed them.

"We killed him as we told you we would," the unshaven coordinator said. "He was planning to blow up Poland's regasification terminal."

"Did you like my sax solo?" the snaggle-toothed explosives expert asked. "In exchange for our safety, we will cooperate and tell you everything about Vikenti Andreev's plans, as we promised."

CHAPTER 27

NORTHERN CALIFORNIA

After the walk and discussion with Kanak, Decatur had driven Lynn to a hotel near TriCoast's East Bay refinery. They parted with a plan to meet Curtis Zhang at the refinery the next morning. Zhang would update them on the refinery's cybersecurity progress.

In her room, Lynn saw headlines on her cell phone of a news story from Poland. She conference-called Dwayne Thomas in Pennsylvania and security chief Mark Shepherd in Texas.

"Yes, I just heard from INTERPOL," Mark said. "Damn close. Could have been like Lithuania—a bunch of fireballs. But my sources tell me two of the attackers turned on the third, the leader. Murdered him. All Russians. Two attackers had pre-arranged with the Polish police to kill the third when the police stopped them outside the plant."

"That's where we we're selling some of our export cargoes, right?" Lynn asked Dwayne.

Dwayne seldom swore, but Lynn could tell he was making an enormous effort not to do so. "Darn right. They set sail just two days ago. The Poles even prepaid. Sounds like we got lucky, unlike our cargo going to Lithuania. Kelly is still trying to figure out how to get them the gas we sold them."

"As a condition of assistance from the Polish police, the two other Russians had to spill the beans. My sources tell me the leader they killed and some other men were going after Dunkirk next," Mark explained.

"Are we positive those plans have been stopped?" Lynn asked.

"INTERPOL still has to identify the attackers," Mark said, "but it's likely the two confederates in Poland have already been, let's say, *coaxed* to give up names and comprehensive details by the Polish police or their French counterparts."

"Who's the leader they killed?" Lynn asked.

"INTERPOL's on it. I'll hear soon," Mark replied.

Lynn's cell phone rang at 2 AM. Kanak Singh and Curtis Zhang were on the line.

"Lynn, our refinery is being attacked!" Zhang was trying to keep his voice calm but she could hear it shake. "I've implemented our standard protocol to stabilize and shut down, but it's not working correctly. Our instruments are haywire."

"Zero day attack," Kanak added.

"Zero day?" Lynn asked.

"A unique attack. Some parts of the code your existing security tools don't recognize or can't detect."

"Damn." She was fully awake. "I'm on my way. Kanak, you at the refinery?"

"Yes."

"Curtis, you got everyone you need?" Lynn asked.

"Night shift is here. Juan Rojas is in the room with me. I've called in all of our IT people and I'm calling in part of the day shift now."

Lynn woke Decatur. He drove them quickly through empty streets in the black middle of the night. It wasn't hard to locate the refinery: its hydrocarbon-fed flares lit the dark sky for miles. The yellow and orange flames were much larger than usual—dozens of feet high.

Okay. Lynn thought. *Crude oil and product is being dumped to the flares. That's supposed to happen in an emergency shutdown. At least the flare systems are functioning.*

Electronics and lights at the refinery's gate were out; a security guard shone flashlights on their licenses and checked them in. "You know there's an explosion risk from anything warm, even your car's gasoline tank. I can't let you drive in any further. You'll have to go on foot."

Lynn and Decatur jumped out and began running the half-mile in the direction the guard had pointed them, toward the catalytic cracking control tower.

Everything was drastically, horribly wrong.

Spindly ten-story flare columns roared with flames four stories high as they strained to burn off the thousands of barrels of hydrocarbons being dumped into their systems. The volumes were dozens of times more than usual. The roar was so loud Lynn could only point. Decatur nodded.

Emergency sirens blared over the loud roar of the flames, signaling overloads of hot burning hydrocarbons, enough to send a rocket into space.

She smelled sulfurous gases, gases ordinarily never allowed to escape before their dangerous hydrogen sulfide had been removed.

She pointed to her nose and Decatur nodded. As long as they could still smell the gas, they were okay. If they stopped being able to smell, it meant the concentration was getting high enough to injure or kill them.

To her right, on another asphalt artery, the massive twenty-story distillation column, thirty feet in diameter and the beating heart of the refinery, sprouted an ugly yellow flame at the top, where no flame ever belonged. Black smoke poured up to the sky.

"I can't believe I let you come out here!" Decatur shouted at her.

"Looks like everyone was able to take cover. That's what I care about," Lynn said, a small particle of relief coursing through her that they hadn't seen anyone else, or any bodies on the ground.

They were fifty yards from the control room when they heard another massive explosion. One of the refinery's enormous metallic butane spheres several hundred yards away, but near the bay, shuddered and fractured with a loud crack. Lynn prayed no one was near it. The explosion was likely to send shrapnel whistling in every direction.

Finally they reached the bomb-shelter-strength control room.

Inside, Zhang, Juan, Kanak, and several others huddled over laptops and flashing instrument control displays.

Zhang looked at her, his expression shot through with worry. "It's like the virus has an exact blueprint of our refinery—where the most vulnerable parts are."

"What have you done so far?"

"We were finding the malware and fixing the heat exchanger coding yesterday," Zhang said.

She looked at Kanak and swallowed, afraid to hear his answer. "The Industroyer virus? Did your team come up with the antidote?"

He shook his head.

Juan wiped sweat from his forehead. "Part of our problem is that temperature sensors are disabled everywhere. We don't know when the distillation tower, the coker, the cracker are going to boil over until they do. And the feedback loops that would automatically adjust the volume and steam valves, and the heat exchangers—without temperature sensors, they're not working."

"Christ," Lynn said, unable to imagine a worse scenario.

As if he read her mind, Zhang said, "But it could get worse because some of the safety alarms and the emergency cooling water controls are disabled, too."

Then they heard a *whoosh* and a thunderous explosion outside. When Lynn looked out the window she saw a skinny, multi-story column, one of many ringed with spiral metal walkways, caving in on itself and then toppling over. "Shit. The light ends tower."

Zhang put his head in his hands. "We'll be offline for weeks."

Kanak looked at her. "The weird thing was, everything we debugged *did* help. We could have had even more failures."

Juan shook his head. "But we have safety systems that just failed, never should have. Didn't get their automatic instructions. Inoperable."

"So there's something besides Industroyer or some new nasty variation of it," Kanak explained. "The debugging we were doing must have tipped Cong off. So he decided not to wait any longer. He launched his attack. Remember what I said—this version of Industroyer is much too good at replicating itself and spreading, like spores."

"The nasty code is turning up in places we never expected," Zhang said. He sighed and sat back. "But we almost have the refinery through a staged shutdown. We'll have to buy product for everything that burned so we can still supply all of our customers. But with the refinery almost completely offline, it's safer and we can start to evaluate . . ."

Before he could finish his sentence, the lights in the control room went out and the descending whine of electrical equipment turning off sounded all around them.

"Crap!" Lynn said. "Where's your manual switch for back-up power?"

"Lynn, stay here! They'll handle this," Decatur said, handing out flashlights.

She looked at him. "No."

"I'll resign."

"Fine. You're fired," Lynn said. She turned to Zhang. "Where's the switch for backup power?"

"Come with me," Juan said. "It's not in here. It's in the main control room about fifty yards away. I'll show you." He motioned to two other operators to accompany them.

"Fired or not, I'm coming with you," Decatur said.

The five of them opened the door and ran.

They dodged inside another dark building, one lit only by their flashlights and the tall flares outside. Juan turned in a circle. "I haven't used this in a while. There!"

He spotted a terminal that looked different from the rest and entered his password. "Good. It's on battery reserve storage." After punching several buttons, lights began to flicker on around them.

"Amazing! Thank you! But now we're half in shutdown, half in startup and the temperature sensors aren't working," Lynn said. "Let's go back and see if we can finish the managed shutdown."

As they walked back outside toward the first control room, Lynn saw two huge nearby heat exchangers glowing an ominous red at their flanges. The two-foot-diameter cylinders were riveted at both ends and smaller pipes ran in and out of them. Inside the exchangers' shells, high-temperature, high-pressure steam heated up the heavy oil.

"We need to … "

Without warning, one of the glowing flanges cracked open. Superheated, high-pressure steam sprayed directly at Juan's chest. Since he was closest, his body shielded Lynn, Decatur, and the others from most of the 600-degree vaporizing jet.

Juan screamed in pain as the steam scorched through his shirt onto his skin and condensed, burning him with thousands of BTUs of heat. The 200-pound-per square-inch spray knocked Juan over as if he weighed no more than an empty sack. He tumbled to the ground, unconscious.

Lynn, Decatur and the others scattered to avoid the same burns, then turned around, inching as close to Juan as they could. Decatur ducked under the boiling spray but big splatters soaked his shirt. As the straight, hard steam jet finally subsided to a drip, Lynn and the other men helped Decatur lift Juan.

Decatur maneuvered the big man over his shoulders in a fireman's carry. Lynn raced ahead to open the door of the second control room as Decatur brought him in.

He cradled Juan's head and other people helped ease the big man's body onto the floor.

Lynn gave him mouth-to-mouth resuscitation while Decatur compressed his chest. "Goddamn. His heart stopped. Shock from the high-pressure steam hitting him straight on."

The blare of ambulance sirens interrupted. Zhang met the medics and pointed them to Juan and four other people lying on the floor. One medic took over from Lynn and Decatur, steadily trying to resuscitate Juan.

"Ventricular fibrillation," he said. Two others prepared equipment.

"Step back! One, two, three!" They shocked Juan with a cardiac defibrillator, waited, checked his pulse. One shook his head

"One, two, three!" Another shock. "Epinephrine!"

A second medic plunged a needle deep into Juan's thigh. Lynn clasped Juan's big hand in both of hers.

The medics continued their life-saving treatments, to no avail.

Lynn bowed her head and turned to the other four victims. Two had been killed instantly by a storage sphere of volatile propane that had exploded.

And when two other operators went outside to close valves that their control room instruments showed to be open, they were overcome by poisonous hydrogen sulfide. Fortunately, they had been dragged inside before their exposures were lethal.

Slowly, the medics pulled away from Juan and the other two deceased victims. Others continued tending to those who had survived.

Lynn and the others found blankets and gently covered the three dead men. Curtis Zhang vowed to stay with them.

With their bodies, Lynn thought with a shudder.

CHAPTER 28

NORTHERN CALIFORNIA AND CHINA

Lynn met for hours, first with the families of the victims, including Juan's wife and four children, and then with fire and safety inspectors at the refinery. Decatur finally returned her to the hotel. She took a shower and fell into bed but couldn't sleep, events replaying in her mind. *What did I miss?* She called Kanak, who sounded as sleepy as she felt.

"I'm sorry to disturb you, but I need you to debrief me on what you saw."

"I understand," Kanak said, in a voice that suggested he didn't. "By the way, you should realize that in a sense we are fighting our own fires. Remember I told you our firm is being acquihired by ShireSafe."

"Oh for God's sake! We just lost three more people and two are headed to the hospital. That's all I care about," Lynn tried to keep from sobbing or shouting.

Kanak was quiet, as if he knew the appropriate reaction but couldn't get off his own thought track. "Of course. I was there. Do you want to talk later?"

"No, no, not later. Go ahead, tell me now. Nothing can be as bad as what we just experienced."

Kanak hesitated. "Well, as I told you, ShireSafe is not keen on hydrocarbons, including clients that make them. I've tried to explain, but it's just their corporate policy. They prefer dealing with the federal alphabet agencies, like the FBI, and having them deal with the energy companies. But you can come to our offices and I'll go over everything we found. ShireSafe's building is incredibly secure, a SCIF, like I told you earlier. No more meetings at the Blue Bottle."

Blue Bottle was a Palo Alto coffee bar with a large pay-as-you-went shared workspace and conference spaces that rented by the hour. It took all of Lynn's willpower not to scream at the man. "No way. You come to me."

He sounded chastened. "How about the rose garden near the Berkeley campus? That's not far from you." He named an address on Euclid in Berkeley.

She told Decatur where she was going. "Thank you, again. Thank you for everything you did to save people. You were a hero."

He shook his head. "I wish we'd been able to save Juan and the other two men. And yes I agree, a meeting with Kanak at the Berkeley rose garden is a drive you can handle on your own." He was snoring before she closed the door to his room.

From the hotel, the route to the rose garden took her high through narrow twists and turns on aptly-named Scenic Drive.

Kanak was waiting for her, thinner and paler than when she'd seen him at the refinery. When was that? Last night? Earlier today? She'd lost track of time. They shook hands and stood side-by-side, looking out at the fog in the bay as they talked.

"Kanak, we were attacked by more than just Industroyer, right? Our safety systems were kaput. You called it a zero day event. Could there have been another virus?"

He nodded. "There's at least one out there, Triton, which targets safety systems. Could have been that or something similar."

She shook her head, exhausted to the bone. "I'm going to Marrero as soon as possible in case Cong targeted it, too. What can you tell me?"

"As we discussed, the originating entity is Chinese, apparently led by a man named Cong Li. He could have others helping him, both in China and in Russia. The signature, the mode, et cetera all resembles other Chinese attackers we have seen. The effort has been planned and sustained. The time of day changes matches up with the normal work day in Beijing. They were clearly embedded in your San Francisco refinery system a while. And yes, as I said earlier, possibly our efforts to dislodge the malware caused the perpetrators to burrow in more deeply—as their program is designed to do, and then to launch the attack."

Lynn felt exhausted, and overwhelmed. "One more time. How did they get in?"

"Likely a phishing email or malware someone accidentally downloaded on a home computer. It gets onto a portable flash drive, and when the person brings the flash drive in to work, he or she inadvertently transfers the malware onto your secure refinery system and infects it. Bottom line is someone clicked on a link they shouldn't have."

"Our folks are smarter than that."

"It only takes one slip. And your systems are constantly under attack from the outside. Nonstop. These guys are sophisticated and experienced. They understand certain of your five thousand Tri-Coast employees as well or better than you do. And here's what's different. Another communication initiated from inside the company. Someone clicked on a bogus China Power link. That seemed to start a separate thread of communication."

Lynn thought about what Reese had planned to tell her about an inside traitor, before he had been killed.

"Have you identified who it is?"

"I wish I could say we have. Person's handle is The Viper. The Viper appears to be sharing information. It's encrypted of course. We're trying to break it."

Lynn groaned. *The Viper could be anyone.*

Kanak said, "Your refineries share some common systems, and in particular, the Marrero refinery communicates frequently with this one in San Francisco. So expect those refineries' control systems are infected, too."

"But you just said that trying to dislodge the malware can make it worse."

"Still, what is the saying? Better the devil you know than the one you don't."

"Damn it, Kanak. What are you suggesting we do?" Lynn had no patience for analysis that didn't include directives for action.

"I'm sorry. As we discussed on the hike, I alerted Dena and your Marrero refinery manager, Kim Garvey. She, in turn, alerted all of her employees to the threat. She's already got a small group there scouring their system."

"Yes, I remember. But what else can we do?"

Kanak shook his head. "Step up the pace. All of us. Your plan to go to Marrero is a good one. See if Cong and his viruses can be stopped there. I'll be available by video."

In Beijing, Cong reviewed his goals and his progress, which he considered satisfactory.

His group had hacked into and taken down TriCoast's San Francisco refinery. There had been some casualties, but he expected that. Part of proof of concept. What were a few American lives in the context of his country's billion-plus people? Inconsequential.

Soon he would do the same at TriCoast's Louisiana facility, and at other refineries, natural gas processors, and chemical plants throughout the US. This served two purposes—an increased ability to export China's own fuels and petrochemicals, and the simple but effective display of Chinese power Comrade Jin desired, one that would prove useful in all business and military negotiations.

That left the Viper. It would also be useful to take out Lynn Dayton, but her bodyguard had proved more capable than expected. He would have to make other plans for her.

When the knock came on his apartment door, Cong sent a message containing instructions to the Viper, who would carry on the Second Law work if something happened. It was like backing up a computer, except he was backing up himself.

He pressed a button to put another layer of encryption on everything in his company's computers. His employees wouldn't like it, but trust was not a luxury he could afford.

As soon as he opened the door to his apartment, he knew he was looking at trouble. The two men were likely members of a triad. Everyone, including the government, employed the triads as muscle. So many people could have been displeased or threatened by his abilities, including Comrade Mei Jin.

The torture of an insufficiently patriotic cyberstrike company owner would be a mere afternoon's errand for the men. The only question was how much pain he would have to endure.

The Second Law Project trap had been sprung, just as he had originally feared. Named for the thermodynamics rule that all isolated systems degenerate to chaos, Second Law Projects were typically lethal for all involved.

One of the two expressionless men asked, "Where is your wife?"

"I do not know," Cong said, glad he did not. *Somewhere in the city of New Orleans, Louisiana, United States.*

The jacket of one of the men slid past his waist, confirming his identity. In a leather case attached to his belt was a favorite tool of the triads—a meat cleaver. *Yes, they are prepared to chop me up*, Cong thought. Even if they stopped at cutting off his fingers,

Cong's work was over, his business finished. A voice was a poor substitute for hands.

"Come with us." One waved a gun to indicate the direction he should go.

"Why?"

"You are accused of corruption and theft from the state."

"I have stolen nothing," Cong said.

"You have taken and used numerous state secrets for your own enrichment."

"Who accuses me?"

The men said nothing.

"The Fourth Department?" Cong asked. "Guo An? Comrade Mei Jin?"

Neither answered as they each took one of Cong's arms and led him toward the elevator. A woman hurried by, averting her eyes.

He had no weapons. They would give him a choice of homicide or suicide, after they tortured him.

If Cong got on the elevator with the men, he would exit without fingers, or an arm. Or perhaps he wouldn't exit the elevator at all—his dead body would be left to tell the story, bled out as a warning to others. That's why they'd chosen a semi-public place instead of torturing or killing him in his apartment.

Although they had likely scoped his building, Cong knew it well.

He decided he would complete this Second Law Project, this descent into chaos, on his own terms.

He broke free and ran for the fire stairs. Not all buildings had them—it was easy to bribe a code inspector to overlook such small safety measures—but this one did.

The men chased him. When he opened the door to the fire stairs, yet another man started up toward him from the floor below.

Cong ran up the stairs, gaining two flights by the time his pursuers realized where he was headed.

One more. Just one more flight.

They shot at Cong to wound him, slow him down.

Another shot and his shoulder was on fire. They'd grazed him but they needed to set an example by carving him up. In their minds, that was best done with him alive.

The men were just twenty feet behind him when he reached the door to the roof.

He yanked on it. It stuck at first but then opened.

The smog. The thick smog was his friend. It would obscure Cong from his attackers, giving him just enough time to avoid capture.

He ran to the edge of the building, gathering speed, as if to jump.

Instead, he ducked and grabbed for the outside ladder he knew was there. He swung himself over the building, climbing down the metallic rungs. Any second they would lean over and shoot him and he'd fall ten stories.

Each apartment had a balcony next to the outside ladder.

He scrambled down two floors and a bullet whizzed past. The triad members might just get careless with whether or not they needed him alive.

Shielded by a balcony above him, he scrambled off the metal ladder onto an eighth-floor apartment balcony. He kicked in the glass door, grateful it was a flimsy single pane.

Glass cuts on his arm added to the fire in his shoulder, but he limped through the empty apartment, out the apartment's front door into a hallway just as one of the men came behind him through the glass balcony door.

The hallway, like his two stories above, was a long blank corridor marked only by doors to other apartments.

The elevators would take too long and the men could trap him on the stairs.

Holding his nose, he pushed open the large hinged door of the floor's garbage chute, leapt in, and let himself drop. Miraculously, his fall eight stories to the basement was slowed by several big bags lodged in the chute.

He landed in the rank, disgusting pile of his apartment building's garbage. Scrambling off the top of the smelly heap, Cong Li fled out an open door through narrow *hutong* toward the apartment of his most trusted employee.

CHAPTER 29

NEW ORLEANS/MARRERO

Lynn requested TriCoast's nearest corporate plane. She met the pilot at the Oakland airport and he flew her away from the setting sun toward New Orleans. The plane caught up and passed into evening shadows.

She landed in New Orleans at midnight. The city was already plunged into full darkness except for the twinkle of French Quarter lights. Dizzy with fatigue and sorrow, she called Kim and they agreed to meet immediately at the Marrero refinery to check its control system.

"Dena Tarleton has been helping me. She's fantastic. So have Patrick and a few others. I'll get them to come in, too," Kim said.

As a taxi drove her to the refinery, Lynn dozed, remembering what a business school professor had once told her. *"I've climbed Andean peaks and flown into isolated Alaskan base camps. You don't force your will, you do what the mountain allows you to do… Just as you have to listen to the mountain, you have to listen to the data."*

So what is the freaking data telling me? Lynn wondered. *It's more than just data that I have so many people dead and injured.* She felt fatigue deep in her body. *I'm running out of time. I can't allow people at Marrero to get killed, too.* She longed for Reese Spencer's wise counsel and mourned his death, again.

Lynn spent the rest of the night with Kim Garvey, Dena Tarleton, Patrick Boudreaux, and others at the Marrero refinery.

With Kanak on videoconference and using what he and Lynn had learned from the San Francisco refinery explosion, they checked, changed, and revamped coding throughout the refinery's control system.

"Fucking Kobayashi Maru!" Kim exclaimed.

"What?" Lynn asked, surprised by her Marrero refinery manager using what sounded like an old cult reference.

"Star Trek slang for a no-win situation. I swear we're still in one."

"What do you mean?" Lynn was curious.

"Did we sacrifice one crew at San Francisco for the safety of everyone here? Will I be losing people here to save people at our other refineries?" Kim asked.

"Whoa! We're ahead of the problem here. Nothing has happened and everyone is safe," Lynn said.

"I *still* can't see how that guy, Cong Li, got into our San Francisco refinery to start with unless someone was phished or deliberately made a connection. Kanak said he traced actions on the inside to someone who'd clicked on a bogus link for China Power."

"Yes, it appears to be Cong Li with the help of others, including unfortunately someone in our company," Lynn said. *I wonder what Reese was going to tell me. I wonder who he suspected. God, I miss him.* "So how do we solve Kobayashi Maru?"

"Theoretically, only by cheating or somehow bypassing the structural assumptions." Kim sighed.

They were all exhausted. But together Lynn, Dena, Kim, Patrick and the Marrero employees, with Kanak's help, found and fixed the lines of malicious code that had shut down the San Francisco refinery before it could destroy the Marrero refinery, too. And none too soon. The sabotage, they learned, had been scheduled for later in the day.

From condensation on the windows it was evident the moist warmth of the early morning would become a brittle, unforgiving heat.

"Kanak still isn't certain of exactly how it happened but like doctors, for this moment it's more important that we have the antibiotic. Believe me, Kim, as soon as possible I'll find out who at TriCoast was so *incredibly* stupid." Lynn's eyelids felt sandy. *I just want to sleep. No, I can't. Not until we're absolutely certain.* "Since you always bring me a solution whenever we have a problem, what's your thought here?"

"My after-action review? Curtis Zhang and I approved Kanak's company devising and adding code to the refinery operational systems to root out the malware, keep our two refineries from communicating with unauthorized entities, and blocking intrusions. But they still weren't fast enough to prevent the San Francisco shutdown or else his team didn't completely get the malware completely out and it duplicated itself. Anyway, we started debugging as soon as Kanak called us. Sorry, we didn't get your permission immediately."

Same as what Kanak told me. "You made the right decision," Lynn said. "Did you look at the real China Power webpage?"

"Yes. Weirdly that was a clue." Kim clicked a few keys to bring up the China Power website. Instead of the requisite pictures of clear-running streams producing water power and happy people living near enormous power plants, the page was blank except for an error message: HTTP 451.

"Which means?"

"It's an inside reference—an error code for when a web page is blocked by censorship—or a takedown notice."

"Like in Ray Bradbury's *Fahrenheit 451*," Lynn said. "Someone making a political statement."

Kim nodded. "And we know Cong Li from China is involved. But who else? Damn it! Who else?"

Who in our company? Lynn wondered. *Surely not you, Kim?*

The Viper contemplated the plan for disappearing. Money had been appearing in offshore bank accounts as each task was completed. Finishing the job and wiping the trail clean could take too much time.

In a short message, Cong Li had given a few further instructions about Lynn Dayton but told the Viper his access to the San Francisco and Marrero refinery operating systems was now blocked. Of course, Cong and the Viper had accomplished what they wanted at San Francisco. The Viper tried to forget the faces of the men who had died there.

Cong had also said he was at risk of being killed or silenced, and that the Viper should continue to act in accordance with Second Law protocols. She had not heard from him since.

In a few minutes, the Viper found the new set of TriCoast passwords.

Should he survive, Cong could use them on different TriCoast computers to alter the manifests of tankers unloading TriCoast gasoline and diesel to Caribbean and South American markets, making it appear they had far less product. With the apparent shortage, Chinese gasoline and diesel suppliers could then offer their equivalent but higher-priced products. The Viper smiled. Cong would like this. So would the bosses he sometimes mentioned.

The Viper sat back and remembered the last, bittersweet rendezvous. Instead of fresh and exciting, the dull wear of the hotel room had echoed the depressing breakup. Nicked black wainscoting. Pulled threads in the Berber rug. The bed too squeaky. Dusty windows. The Zen sand garden gone. Women jabbering loudly in the massage area. Pebbles coming loose from the mortar in the bathroom. The same ol' tits-in-the-mist pictures. Apartment-style construction of plywood and stucco showing its age. And the dull, horrible, but oh-so-reasonable final argument.

Disappearing was hard. Telling lies, shading, never quite explaining—all easy enough. But shock and sadness over leaving the old life behind: cell phones with their dopamine-enhancing pops of instant information and computers and email and texts and familiar places and habits. A pro would be more indifferent to the feeling, the Viper knew. The sheer difficulty of continuing to run was surprisingly exhausting. The depressing thought of what's next, and then what . . . and then what? And many people would be looking for the Viper, not just one.

So yes, the Viper had much to do before completely disappearing.

Though the Alpine had no *adhan* to call Liamzon to prayer, the captain allowed him to load a computerized program to broadcast to him and other Muslims on board the daily prayer times, especially important as they crossed time zones. But he woke himself for the *fajr*, or pre-dawn prayer, always kneeling on a rug he placed on the metallic floor. His quarters were in no way plush or comfortable. He had not even a single pillow. Everything was angular, metallic.

After prayers, he verified the location of the phone trigger, still hidden deep in the athletic bag in his locker and not disturbed again since they had killed their fellow Filipino seaman.

He touched the face of his watch. Behind its simple digital display was a tiny compartment with, *Inshallah,* his second ticket to heaven, the heaven to which his entire being was now attuned.

He fingered his license and turned the pages of his seaman's book, thinking of other ships he had worked and where he'd been. Suez. Strait of Malacca. Never had he been shadowed so closely as on this ship. It suddenly felt as if his cousin, whom he'd once trusted, had turned into a small, sullen man with a long knife, behind him in every passageway.

He remembered what Abdullah had told him about Sulaiman, how he had been responsible for Abu Sayyaf's great stature, even leading to the martyrdom of a leader who himself was known as Abu Sayyaf. He would be worthy of Sulaiman and both Abu Sayyafs.

CHAPTER 30

VIENNA

Cong had answered his phone, troubled to hear a synthesized voice speaking to him. "Cong Li, this is Mei Jin. You must tell no one I called you."

"Did your Fourth Department just attempt to kill me?"

"Mistakes get made," was her non-answer. "By you and by others."

Just as he had feared when Mei Jin first approached him, this Second Law project was lethal. "I wish to leave this Second Law Group," Cong said. "It is too dangerous for my health."

"It is not your choice to withdraw," said the synthesized voice. "But you can correct your reputation and remove the corruption charges pending against you if you complete your projects."

Cong despaired, finally saying, "What is it you wish me to do?"

"We are requiring this because you were not successful, and because the Russians are unhappy with us."

"What do you mean?"

"The San Francisco refinery was shut down. We did notice your good work on this. However, the Marrero refinery stayed open, contrary to the result you promised us. The accidents you said were supposed to happen did not occur. Did you know that?"

I was too busy trying to save my own life, Cong thought. "I did not. Surely we can deploy Vikenti Andreev and his men to help finish the job."

"The Russians are angry with us because Vikenti is dead."

"What?" It was true that Cong had not heard from Vikenti Andreev in the last day.

"Two of the men he recruited to assist him in disabling the Polish regasification terminal instead betrayed him and killed him. They then surrendered to Polish authorities, who had full intelligence of their actions."

"I also did not know this. I was running to save my own life."

The weird voice continued. *Is it truly Comrade Jin to whom I am speaking?* Cong wondered.

"More incompetence, although I congratulate you on surviving. You can remedy your social capital deficit by killing the people responsible for thwarting the plans at the second refinery. Start with Lynn Dayton." The voice clicked off.

He wasn't being given a choice.

He called the Viper through an encrypted phone to learn Lynn Dayton's location.

The Viper replied with one word before ending the call. "Vienna."

Cong arranged travel to Vienna. Despite the attempt on his own life and his distrust of Mei Jin and her superiors, he still had colleagues around the world—a sort of hacker collective that was the equivalent of One Belt One Road—upon whom he could rely to capture her.

He made his inquiries, stated his request. The third contact he tried in Vienna agreed to help him. The price was steep, but the price was always steep. They would capture and hold her.

"No marks," Cong requested. The Fourth Department would expect nothing less than for Cong to carry out her killing himself.

He sent a brief message to his friend, telling him that he was leaving the apartment and that it was safe to return.

When he pushed open the door to the *hutong* he saw no one and decided he could risk a stop at his own apartment to pack.

An hour later, the ride service driver arrived at Cong's apartment to take him to the airport.

There had been no chance to rest after fixing the New Orleans' refinery software and preventing another refinery crash that could have killed hundreds.

She had to consider her larger responsibilities to TriCoast. An OPEC meeting in Vienna would allow Lynn to discuss redirecting oil she'd already committed to buy for the now-closed San Francisco refinery to another TriCoast refinery. She would also talk to a Polish deputy energy minister about the shipment of TriCoast's natural gas to its LNG port, the one that had escaped sabotage by a Russian whose name she had just learned, Vikenti Andreev.

Lynn awoke when the plane touched down in early morning Vienna. Sleep deprivation made her feel as if someone had kicked her head. She struggled to clear her mind.

Vienna was located on the divide between eastern and western Europe. The refined city of the Habsburgs had been the spying capital of the world during and since the Cold War. A US-owned Viennese spy center was still reputed to operate there, although the US Embassy said the building was merely an "open source center" for summarizing data already available in newspapers and on the Internet.

Lynn and Decatur checked into rooms at the Hotel Sacher. Soon, Decatur knocked on Lynn's hotel room door as she finished suiting up for the run they had planned. He showed Lynn a picture of a young Asian man and a few paragraphs translated from a Chinese blog. Lynn studied the picture and read the translation.

Renowned computer software businessman Cong Li was found dead on the street outside his Beijing apartment building. His death appears to have occurred as a result of an accidental fall from the building's rooftop. Mr. Li was reportedly snared in a new anticorruption probe.

He was not considered to be in ill health or mentally unstable. Authorities are investigating whether his death was the result of foul play or suicide. Neither the police department nor the regional government authorities, for whom Mr. Li worked, had any comment.

"Our friends at the FBI sent me this, thinking it might be our man, or one of them," Decatur said. "They believe if Cong Li was the center of it all, his death could make things harder because his remaining operatives are now rogue, out on their own. And we don't have a clue about who they are or what they're planning."

"We never have enough information, do we?" Lynn replied. It was a rhetorical question. They never did.

"They also mentioned another possibility—that instead of being killed, Cong has been imprisoned, and this is propaganda to cover it up."

"I wish we knew what to believe."

For safety in a city with a large, conservative Muslim population, Lynn wore a windbreaker over her t-shirt and conservative tights, rather than the shorts and tank top she preferred.

They jogged a few kilometers to Vienna's Ringstrasse, angled along it for a few more kilometers, and then Lynn was ready to return. More and more people streamed onto the street, some looking at her curiously. She turned in what she thought was the direction of the hotel.

Soon all the five-story buildings began to look alike. Lynn took another turn back toward the opera house. They ran toward a dark, elaborate building with a spire, but it wasn't the beacon of St. Stephens she expected. A few people pointed at her and shook their heads. Others pulled out their phones and snapped her picture.

Across one intersection, the character of the streets changed. Everything was new, one or two stories, and constructed of cement blocks. Windows were dusty, a shock compared to the rest of glistening Vienna.

Decatur kept pace. He started to say, "There's a better way—" when Lynn noticed the absence of any women or girls on the street. Men in their teens and twenties gathered in several doorways.

"Uh-oh," she said quietly. Decatur heard.

"I don't like the looks of this bunch either," he said. "Keep an even pace until we're out of here."

The shouts of the group behind them got louder. When Lynn turned to look a couple dozen men were running toward her, some spitting.

"Don't let them surround us," Decatur said. "Turn here!" They dodged right around the next corner. "Now! Pour it on!"

They raced ahead at top speed. A truck roared behind.

"Straight ahead! In there! The open building!"

She had no choice. They ran the last few yards across hard-packed dirt. But Lynn stopped on the steps of the one-story building, her premonition of dread growing. "I don't want to go inside."

"We have to." He dragged her toward the gray, wing-walled structure, which appeared to have been built in the federalist style of an old US post office.

The danger from a group of men who'd signaled displeasure at the sight of an uncovered woman on the street warred with Lynn's premonition that the gray building in front of her was unsafe, a place from a nightmare.

"Run straight through the building," Decatur said. Not a suggestion. An order.

Lynn had the strongest, least rational feeling she'd ever had. *If I go into that building, I won't come out alive.* The menace emanating from its tall, narrow window slits was only slightly less palpable than the danger from the men chasing them.

But Decatur pushed open a door, pulled her through, turned and locked the door, and they stopped to catch their breaths.

"Now what?" She longed to get outside in the sun as soon as possible, even if it meant more running from the angry mob. At least they were a danger she could see and understand instead of this irrational chill.

They were at the end of a gray-floored corridor. "If I see anyone I'll call a car. You ready?" Decatur asked.

"Yes. Let's go!" Lynn couldn't wait to escape the dread of the place.

"We'll run to Volksgarten and then on to Burgring and Openring. Once we spot the opera house we're near the hotel."

The initial charge of adrenaline had subsided. She felt washed out but happy to be outside in the fresh air. They slow-jogged back to the hotel, still looking over their shoulders. No one followed.

Still breathing hard, Lynn said, "Did you see anything odd about those men?"

"We were busy running away from them, not looking at them," Decatur said. "But yes. Here in Austrian neighborhoods like the one we were in, I would have expected a fair number of Afghani, Syrian, and Libyan immigrants."

"Exactly," Lynn said. "And I saw many in that crowd of men whom I would have guessed were from those countries. But the leaders, the ones urging them on, looked and sounded Chinese."

Decatur frowned. "Not the nationality I would expect."

"I don't understand why they were chasing us," Lynn said. *Unless?* "We're lucky we escaped." *Chinese?* "Beau, do you think maybe Cong Li sicced them on us?"

CHAPTER 31

Lynn met with several deputy energy ministers in an anteroom in OPEC's Vienna headquarters. To each whose country supplied oil to TriCoast's San Francisco refinery, Lynn explained the circumstances of the sabotage and negotiated for redirections or delays of oil deliveries.

At a nearby café, Decatur at her side, Lynn met with the Polish energy minister to extend their contract.

"If you like the first batch, we have enough natural gas to sell you some for two decades. We're also supplying the Baumgarten gas storage hub just south of here in Austria. We ship easily out of the US east coast," Lynn said.

He nodded. "You're not the only company with which we're discussing a contract."

"I'm well aware of that. I heard you had a close call with Vikenti Andreev at your terminal."

The man looked shocked that she knew and she explained. "Unfortunately, his name has come to our attention for his destruction of the Lithuanian terminal. Looks like yours was next in his sights."

By late afternoon, she still felt human enough to have a brief dinner with her nemesis, Henry Vandervoost. Vandervoost was in charge of all TriCoast's European refineries and constantly maintained he should take Lynn's place in charge of US refineries, too.

He'd insisted on dinner and an opera as minimum hospitality. *Minimum is right,* Lynn thought. *I'll bet he begrudges us even that.*

Lynn and Decatur met Henry at the heavily-brocaded Hotel Sacher café.

"Eating dinner this early is uncivilized," Henry said.

"Good to see you too, Henry," Lynn replied. Although the man had finally updated his haircut to a shorter, more modern style from the Eighties hairdo he'd long sported, he hadn't updated his general attitude toward Lynn. Typically, he was vocal about his belief that neither she nor any other woman should be running refineries.

Tonight, though, his attitude had apparently softened. With Decatur nearby on watch, she and Henry talked about his use of the gasoline and diesel storage for which she'd just contracted in Curaçao. They discussed whether his refineries could use some of the natural gas and crude oil TriCoast was exporting from the US.

He told her about the best European LNG regasification terminals, saying, "I like the ones in Spain, England, and France. But I agree, the one in Poland is acceptable, too. Too bad the Lithuanians have to rebuild theirs."

The site of the opera lived up to its colorful name as the Golden Hall of *Musikverein.* Inside, big orange abstracts adorned the walls. The opera was a light, popular musical everyone seemed to recognize. A group of four sopranos and a tenor sang short selections, exaggerating their gestures and facial expressions so Lynn needed no translation from the German. A percussionist-jester blew whistles, hammered an anvil, and showed off the conductor's supposed girlie magazine.

After the show, Henry departed with the promise of more discussion—and disagreement—in the weeks ahead.

Decatur walked next to Lynn on the side nearer the street.

As they turned the corner onto a tree-lined boulevard, an Asian man stumbled in front of them.

He turned slightly toward them and Lynn felt a wave of shock go through her body.

"Oh my God! Cong Li! He's alive after all!" Lynn shouted at Decatur.

Decatur jammed his body between hers and Cong's.

Cong put a hand out as if to balance but instead turned and sprang toward them.

Lynn saw he held a pistol. She began to back away. *But I can't leave Decatur alone.*

Decatur was ready. As Cong swung the pistol in his direction Decatur pivoted in and stepped even closer to him.

"Run!" Lynn shouted, barely aware of the handful of other dressed-up concert-goers still on the street.

Decatur seized Cong's wrists.

With surprising strength, Cong swung Decatur around into a long rack of parked bicycles and broke his grip.

"Get out of sight!" Decatur shouted to Lynn.

She ducked behind big white stone pillars at the street-side entrance of *Ringstrassen Galerien* mall just as Cong turned his pistol toward her.

I don't want to die! She froze. *But we have a better chance to take him if I help Decatur.* She squatted so that her head wouldn't be where Cong had aimed. She glanced around the column to see Cong edging closer to her, with Decatur right behind him. She quickly drew back.

Decatur grabbed Cong from behind, putting one arm around the man's neck. With his other arm he squeezed Cong's pistol hand until bone cracked.

Cong screamed and dropped the pistol.

"Get the gun and keep it ready to fire!" Decatur shouted.

Lynn scrambled from her hiding place, kicked the pistol away from both of them and grabbed it. It felt solid, but heavier than she remembered from the Dallas safety training.

She aimed it toward Cong, but even if she had trusted her shooting ability, she didn't have a clear shot.

Decatur dragged the would-be assassin toward the mall entrance pillars and bounced Cong's head against one of them. Lynn heard several sickening cracks.

People walking by stared but quickly looked away, neither wanting to get involved nor understanding who was attacking whom.

The man whimpered as Decatur bent down, looking into his face.

Then Cong rose up and banged his head hard into Decatur's, with a resounding crunch.

Decatur fell, stunned.

Cong Li charged at Lynn. He intended to retrieve the pistol and kill her.

"Oh no no no!" She put both hands on the pistol to steady it. She took a deep breath and aimed at his chest. "Stop or I'll shoot!" Whether or not he understood English, her actions were unmistakable.

In the streetlight, his face showed only cold purpose. He slowed a step and put both arms out to grab her.

"Stop!"

When he didn't, she pulled the trigger. The shot was loud, and the pistol's recoil was a hot, metallic punch into her palms.

He took one more step toward her then fell onto the sidewalk

Blood pumping from a large hole in his white shirt stained the sidewalk red.

Did I do that? Bile rose in her throat. *But it was him or us!*

Lynn and Decatur neared him, Lynn careful to keep the pistol out of reach in case Cong made another grab for it.

"You're Cong Li?" she asked, hoping the man understood some English. *Probably not.* She pulled out her cell phone and set it to record. Maybe they could find someone to translate.

His ear scraped the sidewalk as he nodded.

"Why are you trying to kill me?"

He didn't answer.

"Who are you working with?" Decatur asked, kneeling.

The man whispered and Decatur cautiously bent closer. "Who?"

"Viper," he croaked.

Oh damn. What Kanak told me. The traitor inside our company. Lynn handed the pistol to Decatur who put it in his waistband. She knelt and asked urgently. "The Viper. Who is the Viper?"

Cong stared at her, his mouth slightly upturned. He said something in Mandarin. Lynn hoped her microphone caught the words.

"Cong, who is the Viper?" Decatur said, putting his ear close to the man's head.

But Cong could give no more answers.

After a few minutes of checking to see if his pulse would return, Decatur said, "He's dead, Lynn. We have to file a report."

"I tried to record him. Maybe someone at the hotel can translate," she said. She could no longer avoid the question. Lynn looked at her hands as a slow chill overtook her. "I killed him?"

Decatur stood. "You did. Self-defense. And you just saved your own life. Mine, too."

CHAPTER 32

NEW ORLEANS

After lengthy questioning by the police, Lynn and Decatur were allowed to return to the Hotel Sacher. There the concierge helped them find a Mandarin translator.

Lynn did not explain the circumstances of the recording to the translator. He listened to it several times and said, "This man sounds very sick."

Decatur nodded. "But can you make out what he was saying?"

The translator shook his head. "Not much. A few words. 'Ship.'

'New Orleans,' and strangely, 'Second Law.'"

"Did he say anything that sounded like a person's name?" Lynn asked. *Please, yes.*

"I'm sorry. He did not."

Lynn slept as much as she could during the long flight from Vienna to New Orleans by way of Atlanta. A time or two she looked over enviously at Decatur who apparently had no trouble falling asleep anywhere. When they arrived, Decatur picked up the car he had arranged and drove her to Kim Garvey's office at the Marrero Refinery.

"I'll be outside the door in this chair, sleeping," he said, and to Lynn's amazement, he soon was.

"Heard you had quite a time of it in Vienna," Kim said.

"Some day I'll tell you more. How's everything going?" Lynn wanted to see for herself that the Marrero facility was operating normally before returning to San Francisco to help Curtis Zhang get his refinery online again. More importantly, although she wouldn't tell Kim, Cong's last words had made it sound like the Viper, and Cong's plans, were centered nearby, in New Orleans.

"Really, no problem. In fact, with you here, we planned to have a small celebration among all of us who put in the overtime and stopped the sabotage. Guess we'll have to wait, though. You look pretty beat and Dena, who helped us so much too, left early. She said she had an appointment to talk about a new TriCoast assignment. But I'm due to talk to Curtis Zhang—I know you're headed to see him—about what resources we can offer up for his plant's recovery. Why don't you sit in on the conversation?"

Lynn nodded. It would save time if all they all talked together.

Kim brought up the video conference with Zhang and Lynn thanked him for the chance to sit in. They talked about contractors, timelines, special project managers who could oversee the repairs, and costs. Zhang's eyes were red-rimmed. Lynn knew he felt the loss of Juan and the others as keenly as she did.

Before they ended their conversation, Zhang said, "Is anyone else in the room with you or listening to the conversation?"

"Only Kim, as you can see. Why?" Lynn asked.

"Kanak stopped by," Zhang said. He stopped and bounced a pencil on its eraser which Lynn knew to be one of his signs of anxiety. "He's narrowed it down. He told me the person searching for bidding algorithms and clicking on the China Power link could be Dena or David. There's a seventy-five percent chance every problem that has an inside source can be traced to one or both of them."

"Are you sure? I can't believe it," Lynn said. "They're both loyal." Then she remembered what Cong had said when they'd pressed for the identity of the Viper. *No name. Just New Orleans.* "Kanak doesn't think it's anyone working for you there?"

Zhang shook his head. "But I agree Dena and David seem to have too much to lose. It's hard to believe it would be one or both of them."

Kim added, her eyes flashing as if remembering her military experience, "They wouldn't be the first to appear more innocent than they are."

Lynn shook her head as her thoughts warred internally. "David's been with the company forever. Proved himself time and again. Dena is brilliant and up from nothing, had a hard life. She wouldn't pop a balloon, for God's sake."

"In other words, a lot like you," Kim said.

"I'd pop a balloon," Lynn replied. "I just can't believe it."

"Or maybe, don't want to," Kim said.

"Their appearance of loyalty could be why one or maybe both of them together have been so effective," Zhang suggested.

Lynn felt her face redden. "We need proof before we make accusations. Once that genie is out of the bottle, we have to be right. Otherwise we'll have massive morale problems with everyone else in the company expecting to be accused next."

After she and Kim finished the call with Zhang, Lynn called Dena Tarleton and David Jenkins. She shook her head at Kim when neither one picked up. As Decatur drove her toward downtown New Orleans, she told him what Zhang had said about the possibility that Dena or David was the Viper.

Later at her hotel, Lynn answered her phone, even though she usually never answered unidentified numbers like the one the caller ID showed.

Dena said, "I got your message. Sorry I missed you this afternoon."

As Lynn spoke, she walked next door to Decatur's room and knocked, motioning him out into the hallway so he could overhear the call. "Dena," she said for Decatur's benefit, "I got the good news from Kim about the verified success of our late-night debugging at Marrero. Thanks for your assistance. We couldn't have done it without your insight."

"Did you hear all of the news while you were gone?"

Lynn wondered if Dena knew she'd been in Vienna. *Does she know I was attacked? That Cong Li tried to kill me?* "What did I miss?"

"Kim said she can do a controlled test tomorrow."

But Kim told me she was planning a controlled test next week. And Dena wasn't around this afternoon. Lynn wondered what else Dena would tell her. *I need to encourage her to talk.*

"Fantastic, Dena!" Lynn nodded at Decatur. "Yes, Kim told me today how much she appreciated your help. We're glad to prevent an accident here like the one in San Francisco." Kim had also told Lynn she'd marveled at how quickly Dena had gotten to the source of the problem, and was glad TriCoast hired such brilliant professionals. *Had Dena uncovered the coding problem because she was the one who planted it? Who knew right where to find the bugs?*

Dena said, "Speaking of, I've got an idea about what caused the cyberattacks on our San Francisco refinery, too. Right now I'm with my brother. He's a sous-chef at Delton's in the Quarter on Iberville. It's closed tonight, but he's prepping for tomorrow. Do you want to stop by?"

"I remember where Delton's is. Sure, I can come by. Or do you want to talk over the phone?" Lynn asked.

"Hard to explain on the phone, even if I text or e-mail you diagrams."

"See you in an hour." Lynn thumbed the phone off and turned to Decatur. "Dena's never mentioned a brother. But that's thin gruel given that she almost singlehandedly rooted the malware out of one of the company's biggest moneymakers. Although if she was the one who put it in the system, she sure as hell knew where it was. So this could be our chance to find out if she's the inside source."

"You told me Kanak said the insider was likely Dena or David. Either one of them could be very dangerous. Let's think this through."

Lynn motioned him into her room so their voices wouldn't reverberate down the hallway. "Kanak said seventy-five percent chance. Close enough. In fact, has Munchausen's by proxy occurred to you?"

"You lost me," Decatur said, leaning back in a chair.

"I've heard it from other parents of small children. It's a diagnostic term that refers, for example, to parents who make their kids sick, then take them to the doctor and 'rescue them'. The parents get to feel and appear heroic."

"I see where you're headed. You think Dena infected the whole Marrero control system so she could fix it," Decatur said.

"And Delton's isn't usually closed Mondays," Lynn added. "Almost no restaurant in the Quarter is. They're open every day of the week."

Decatur nodded. "Assume Dena is the insider or one of them, with David. Maybe getting desperate now. What would you do in her place?"

"What?" Lynn was offended.

"I saw it on the training course. There are ways she's more like you than you realize. So again, what would you do?"

I understand how hard-working women always get underestimated, or even slammed. Lynn struggled to clear her mind of the anger she felt at being compared to a possible criminal. "Okay. I'd go to a place I'm familiar with. I'd look for tools. I'd have a way out, and transportation. I'd have enough cash to go off the grid for a while. Fake documents."

"That all makes sense. So we need weapons. No matter how much we plan, things will go sideways the second we walk in, especially if we aren't on our guards. She had the same defense training you had."

Lynn paced. "In one of the finest restaurants in New Orleans. Okay, even though they're always open, let's assume Delton's is closed for some reason. Repairs, maybe.

Decatur said, "You want a gun?"

Lynn sighed. "Damn. If I have one, it's likely to be turned on me."

"Bullshit, Lynn Dayton! I just saw you kill Cong Li."

"I was lucky."

"Maybe. But you were good, too. And I saw Dena at the range. Like I said, she wasn't any better than you were."

"You're the gunslinger," Lynn said. "But okay. I'll take one. A small one that she can't see and grab from me."

Decatur relaxed slightly as he saw her agreeing with the plans. He handed her a holster and a small pistol. "Goes on your ankle. I have one, too. I understand you're loyal to Dena but we have to expect the worst. Jeez, look what just happened with Cong Li, almost out of the blue."

"Dena seemed different," Lynn said, as she fastened the pistol and ankle holster onto her leg. She pulled down the leg of her jeans to hide them.

"So did Ted Bundy." Decatur changed the subject. "You happen to have a thermal imaging app or attachment from the refinery inspection department?"

"I do. Perfect. May help if the lights go out." Lynn dug into the briefcase she'd tossed on the desk, found the thermal imaging camera she used to find refinery hot spots, and snapped it onto her phone.

"Now watch where I hide my weapons. If I go down, get one. I'm putting a mini-revolver on my ankle and this—it's a .357 magnum—at three o'clock on my waist." He put the small revolver into a holster on his ankle and shoved the larger .357 in his waistband on his right hip. He untucked his shirt to cover up the pistol.

He fastened a small tactical flashlight to his belt.

"Dena said she just wants to talk. I wish we could trust her, but we just can't," Lynn said, more anxiously than she intended.

"Yeah, and alligators just wanna swim. It's a trap. Kanak thinks she or David or both could be the insiders sabotaging our company. Look at how many ways we've already been attacked. We're not certain who killed Reese Spencer and who was in the room with Matak Abdullah when Arch Webber was killed, but it could have been her."

Lynn thought about Reese, one of the kindest men she'd ever known and felt a wall of anger. *Did Dena kill one of the best men in my life?* "So what else should I take?"

He gave her a collapsible baton and showed her how to use it. "And, this sounds obvious but it's easy to forget when everything's going down: remember to grab your gun if you need it." Decatur waved her out of the door of her room, then got bulky night vision image intensifier goggles from his room. "Let's catch that ride right now. Think about how she might act, what her motivations might be."

Lynn's face got hot again. "Stop comparing me to her."

"You're both brilliant. Just looks like she's bent, for whatever reason."

As they got into an elevator, Lynn said, "Remember that drill we went through for self-defense? Maybe she wasn't kidding when she said she wanted money and a jet to Belize?"

Decatur nodded. "Hell, we all want money so we can tell the world, 'fuck you.'"

In front of the hotel they hailed a ride and were dropped a few blocks from Delton's. Lynn saw Decatur nod to a couple of plainclothes officers and asked, "Friends?"

"Fortunately for us, yes. We may need them," Decatur said.

"I've been here before," she said, as they crossed in front of the closed green shutters.

"I thought you were a broke student when you lived in New Orleans."

"Recruiting dinners. Someone else was paying."

He stopped her. "Look, I hope I'm wrong and you're right, but it really could be a shitstorm in there." He looked at her. "So try to relax."

She rolled her shoulders. *Telling myself to relax is the worst way to do so.*

At their touch, the door to Delton's pushed open to a brightly lit room filled with tables covered in white tablecloths and set with silver.

However, the lights were glaring construction spots rather than subdued dining wattage. The restaurant was rectangular, with a narrow front on the street and a long expanse toward the kitchen. Past dinner smells of fried oysters, French onion soup, and steak steamed from the walls. Sawdust covered the floors and wires dangled from uncompleted electrical repairs.

Lynn turned on her cell phone video camera with audio and started recording.

"Come back to the kitchen," Dena said.

"Probably cameras all over the front dining room." Decatur whispered to Lynn, positioning her in front of him. "She can see exactly where we are in this room, but not in the hallway."

"Why'd you bring Beau Decatur? I thought we were talking, just the two of us, while we watch my brother cut up vegetables. It's already crowded back here. You need to come in alone, Lynn. That musclebrain can't help us look over these computer instructions." Dena's voice had taken a light, joking tone.

Cameras for sure.

"No need to creep around." Dena sounded oddly cheery.

Despite desperately wanting to believe in Dena's innocence, Lynn slowly edged out of the big dining room and down the hallway, Decatur behind her.

The bright construction lights went out.

It was so dark they couldn't see their hands. Decatur put on night goggles. Lynn turned on her heat imaging camera attachment.

She decided to ask a direct question to see how Dena would respond. "So Dena, what's your idea about stopping the cyberattacks? I can't wait to hear it."

"Oh that." Her voice floated, as if from far away. "I'll send you a link to the person in charge of the ransomware. Tell him—I think it's a him—the Viper referred you, and you'll pay whatever it takes to get him to stop."

"You're the Viper?" Although Lynn was expecting it she was still shocked.

"Awesome, isn't it? Can you believe?" Dena's question ended with an uncharacteristically high-pitched giggle.

"So you want us to pay ransom?" The word caught in Lynn's throat. *Fuck fuck fuck. Kanak's odds were right.*

Decatur whispered to her. "We should leave now."

"We have to stop her!" Lynn whispered back. "She killed Reese Spencer!"

"Ransom? Sure. Easiest thing in the world," Dena's voice still sounded otherworldly. "TriCoast can afford it. Maybe then he'll give back the drilling plans, bid strategy, export plans, refinery configurations, passwords, and everything else he was paying me for. Oh, and as a special favor, our drilling technology. Basically anything I could find to send him about stupid fucking TriCoast."

Lynn felt the hair on her neck prickle but she decided to play along, as calmly as she could. "But there's no guarantee that would stop him."

"Sure there is, once you involve me."

Lynn's anger started spiking and she struggled to keep her voice calm. "What happened to Madame Taliesin, Dena?"

"Ask Arch. He saw her last. Oops. Maybe that was me he saw. Don't you think I look like her?"

Lynn pulled toward the kitchen as Decatur tried to direct her back to the restaurant's front door. "What happened to Madame Taliesin and Arch Webber, Dena?"

A long silence, then a small sob. "Well, Arch, he knew. And then when Matak called and needed to get Arch's computer, the two of us took care of it. Madame Taliesin just came along at the right time. She was a great disguise, don't you think?"

"What did Arch know besides the bidding models, Dena?" Lynn was prepared to wait as long as it took.

Then she realized the restaurant could be booby-trapped.

"Why about me and David, of course!"

"You once told me you had a boyfriend who had little kids. David Jenkins doesn't have little kids."

"So you believed that one? Good. Didn't you ever notice David had no hair in his ears, like all lovers? David, my friend, my lover, my blow-dried liar, my everything until he wanted to be my nothing. So now he is."

Lights blazed back on. Lynn didn't need the cooling readout from her thermal imaging camera to realize that the sliced-up, bloody body ten feet away from them and near the big industrial kitchen prep table was dead. Barely recognizable as David. The man who had been David. Blood pooled out from underneath his body, from gashes on his head and arms, neck and legs. Blood from a deep stab wound stained his chest bright red.

"Oh my God!" Lynn whispered.

"Maybe I'm the real sous-chef." Dena giggled. "I had him investigated. And then I found out everything he was telling me—all the important stuff like leaving his wife and no other girl-friends—it was all a lie. When I asked him about it, he said he wanted to break up. That I was too needy. And then I got angry. Real angry. Angry at him and everyone who knew him and about us and everything ever associated with him."

Lynn and Decatur stood at the opening from the hallway into the kitchen. They still couldn't see Dena.

Lynn thought of their self-defense training. Krav Maga. Try to de-escalate first. Find something in common with your opponent. *What the fuck do I have in common with a murderer? Sympathy?* "Dena, the biggest burdens are the ones we put on ourselves. And you've carried big burdens for a long time."

"Are you always this stupid, or do you save it for special occasions?"

Lynn tried to remain calm. "Is this a side effect of your soccer concussions? Your migraines?"

"You mean my craziness? You were such a sucker for those stories. Just like Reese Spencer."

Lynn felt sick. "You were the killer out in the woods."

"No. Not me. I just told him where to find Reese. And got him the gun. But he shot it. You can't tag me with your special man's death."

"You're responsible! They're dead. You all but pulled the trigger to kill the consultant and Reese Spencer, one of the best men I've ever known!"

Dena went on, proudly. "And at the gun range, I faked incompetence perfectly. You thought I was a hardworking mini-me, growing up to be just like you. Or maybe you thought I was like your naïve little sister. Yes, I found out all about her."

Lynn sensed a movement to her right.

Dena herself faced them. One hand held spray, another a knife. A big butcher knife, a clean one. *Not the one she used on David.*

Two feet to the left of Lynn, Decatur drew his gun from his waistband.

"Yeah, I see that glance between you two," Dena said. "Beau Decatur, I thought I told you to stay away. Now you're going to pay. A shame, really, extra work for me, because the two of you are all that stand between me and freedom."

"What do you want?" Lynn asked.

"Just what I said. A payoff and an escape."

Lynn swore. "We've paid. All of us. You've made us pay. We've paid and paid and paid as you stole our secrets and killed our people. Our *friends*, Dena."

"Ooh. A little heat. I like seeing that from ol' Linear Lynn," Dena taunted. She moved in quickly and squirted her can at Decatur's and Lynn's faces.

Pepper spray seared their eyes.

Dena said, "Is fear the profoundest form of suffering? Or is it physical pain? Or is it guilt? Well, you two are about to find out, aren't you?"

Tears and mucus flooded Lynn's face. She squinted at Decatur. His eyes and nose flowed but he was moving toward Lynn.

Lynn grabbed her baton and turned toward where Dena had been.

Dena grabbed her from behind in a chokehold and held the knife to her neck.

Lynn's vision narrowed. She tried to think but she only felt herself getting colder as blood went to her core. Time slowed. She couldn't hear anything but Decatur's and Dena's voices.

"Let her go or I'll shoot," Decatur said.

Dena's chokehold tightened and the knife started to cut.

"Guess I should have started with you after all, big boy. Go on. Shoot. But Lynn's dead no matter what."

"Let her go now!" Decatur shouted. "One. Two."

Before he got to "Three," Decatur lunged forward and pulled the trigger. The shot was incredibly loud. Dena's head jerked and dropped against hers, brains and blood sluicing out onto Lynn's back.

Dena stumbled and her knife sliced Lynn's shoulder.

But without brain signals directing her muscles, the cut was shallow. Lynn broke free.

Dena mumbled through the blood in her mouth. "Wait until Alpine hits LOOP. You are so fucked."

Dena fell across David Jenkins' body.

Lynn squinted at Decatur, her eyes on fire.

His eyes and nose was still pouring, as was hers.

"Goddamn! She had me," Lynn said. "Thanks, Beau Decatur. You saved me. Jesus."

He smiled grimly. "I owed you one after Vienna."

He hit a button on his phone and plainclothes police officers rushed in.

"Sorry I didn't call you sooner," Decatur said. "This is a tight space, she had Lynn, and it would have been a total clusterfuck."

"She was two seconds away from killing you," he said to Lynn, helping her to a sink.

They flushed their eyes under a faucet.

Lynn leaned back and looked at Decatur. "Oh my God. Is that what Cong meant? He said the word 'ship.' Dena just said the Alpine, and LOOP. LOOP's the offshore port. The Alpine must be a ship. We have to get to it and tell them."

Decatur and Lynn quickly told law enforcement officers what had happened.

Decatur called Mark Shepherd to find out what the Alpine was, where it was, and how to reach them. "Says it's an oil tanker and it's headed to LOOP offshore. He says Patrick Boudreaux has been trying to ring him, so he'll call us back."

They tried to raise the Alpine on their phones but couldn't.

Decatur led her away from the blood-spattered kitchen and toward the front door.

Lynn looked back at the two bodies. Despite Dena's taunts and betrayals, Lynn felt as if a part of herself had died, too.

CHAPTER 33

NEW ORLEANS AND OFFSHORE LOUISIANA

Patrick had been startled by the phone call from his Washington contact. "How good's your intel?"

"It's his suicide video. In Tagalog. Guess our man didn't expect his mother to find it until after his death. She was hysterical, told us what a good son he is."

"Revenge for Sulaiman's death?" Patrick asked.

"Probably. Sulaiman was a major player, Abu Sayyaf's spokesman in the Philippines," the contact said.

"Abu Sayyaf? The head of oil and gas operations for the Islamic State who was killed in a drone strike?"

"Same name, but this was an entire group called Abu Sayyaf. After Sulaiman devised several mass kidnappings and bombings that killed hundreds, including Americans, we thumb- tacked a five-million-dollar target to his ass. Still took years to find him. The Eighth Special Forces finally whacked him."

His Washington contact gave him additional crucial information and he punched in Mark Shepherd's number. Mark wasn't answering, so Patrick kept trying. Finally Mark clicked on.

"We've got to get some folks out to the Alpine ASAP," Patrick said.

"Okay, that's bizarre. I was just talking to Lynn and Beau Decatur and they said the same thing."

"What?" Patrick was stunned.

"Hang on a minute. I'm getting all four of us together on one call to save time." After various clicks, Mark said, "Lynn, tell Patrick what you heard."

Lynn was out of breath, her voice higher than normal. "Long story short, Patrick, Cong Li, head of a group he calls Second Law, tried to kill me in Vienna."

"Jesus."

"From what he said, we figured out his inside source, the Viper, was in New Orleans. He also said something about a ship. Dena—crap this is too long a story—but basically Dena is, was, the Viper and she said the words 'Alpine and LOOP.'"

Patrick sucked in a breath. "Okay, here's what I heard." He explained Abu Sayyaf and Liamzon.

"Who's directing? Why would they get some engine-room greaser to avenge Sulaiman?" Decatur asked, interrupting.

"This man you named, Liamzon, is from the island of Mindanao—" Lynn started.

"—where the Philippine authorities allowed the US Army to train Filipino soldiers to find Sulaiman after he planned the kidnapping of three Americans," Patrick finished. "Sulaiman had a bomb planted on the Superferry. Killed a hundred and sixteen people when it sank. World's deadliest attack at sea."

"So again, why the greaser?" Decatur asked.

"He's licensed for supertanker duty," Patrick replied.

"And you confirmed Liamzon is on the Alpine," Lynn said.

"Exactly. Through interviews with Mommy, airplane passenger files, and ship records, my contact tracked him to the Alpine, which is a crude oil tanker. Those tankers are typically in transit-"

"—between seventeen and twenty days is my experience," Lynn said.

Mark interjected, "So you're saying it's due to arrive at the LOOP offshore Gulf Coast terminal any time now."

"But your contact doesn't know what the plan is, what kind of bomb, who's in charge, who else they've got on board—anything except that this Filipino expects to die," Decatur said. "Goddamn. What about other conspirators? Have you talked to the captain?"

"Not yet, but I will," Patrick said.

"Do this," Lynn said. "Have him ID Liamzon and anyone who's been hanging with him so we can question them first."

"Likely some jihadi group is in charge. Abu Sayyaf has major ties to the bastards," Patrick told them.

"We have to surprise Liamzon," Lynn insisted. "He's the only one who can tell us where the bomb is, what type, and the trigger. The Alpine must be delayed and kept away from LOOP to protect the people there."

"We don't want the crew blown to bits either. We need some Coasties," Patrick suggested. "Got great folks on the roster, including some Iraq war vets." He named Kim Garvey and several others. "All the maneuvers are still top of mind."

"Tell us where to meet you," Lynn said.

"I don't think this is any place for you," Patrick said.

"Patrick. Decatur and I have survived two attempts on our lives in the last twenty-four hours, both led by the same guy who set the Alpine attack in motion. I'm not running away now."

"Still think it's a bad idea. You may be shell-shocked," Patrick said.

"I'm waiting on those directions to the Coast Guard heliport. We'll meet you there for the ride," Lynn said.

Liamzon rubbed sleep from his eyes, surprised to be awakened in the middle of the night for a safety drill. The tanker seemed slow to awake too, creaking and grinding. As instructed, the small crew gathered in the mess. Then the radio was turned off.

Captain Beyer stood somberly in front of them. "We have information that at least one of you has illegal drugs on board. While we question you individually, your quarters will be searched. And give me your cell phones."

Liamzon's heart sank at first and then lifted. If they were looking for drugs, perhaps they wouldn't pay attention to anything else. He was ready with his denials when Captain Beyer selected him for questioning. The second man picked was the one with the fillet knife, his cousin.

The captain demanded their cell phones. At first Liamzon panicked. He was supposed to enable an auto-dialed call to the phone in his locker to close the circuit and set off the bomb.

But then he relaxed. Matak had told him a backup detonator relied only on being near LOOP.

US Coast Guard officers and the tanker's security officer squeezed him into Captain Beyer's cabin. He stared at the position monitor, willing the ship to continue floating toward its target. Four nautical miles.

They began asking him questions. He responded willingly, thinking they might quickly release him. Maybe he could delay them until the bomb detonated.

When the questions took a sharper turn, he knew they would never let him go.

"Who recruited you?"

"Matak Abdullah."

One of the questioners whispered to another. Liamzon heard the phrase *guided missile with no off switch*.

He fingered his watch and turned his head so he wouldn't be seen. For a brief, aching moment, he thought of his mother. He hoped she would get the money.

A blond-haired woman burst in and grabbed his arm, scraping him as she pulled off his watch. "He's got a suicide pill! Don't let him swallow it! He'll kill himself!"

Liamzon fought them, desperate for his glorious exit to heaven.

The guards grabbed his arms and tackled him. Then he looked at the position monitor. Only a few nautical miles from the target. He relaxed.

"Who is communicating with you?" another Coast Guard officer asked.

Liamzon struggled against his handcuffs. "I have continued to receive messages until yesterday."

"From whom?"

"Matak."

The questioner turned back to him, sterner now. "Matak is dead. You must be lying."

Decatur and Lynn had raced away from the French Quarter, desperate to get to the Coast Guard heliport and then find the Alpine's location. Both began calling, and Beau tracked its coordinates to offshore Louisiana. When they tried again to communicate with the ship, they received no answer.

Lynn struggled to concentrate. Her concentration was still scattered as she relived what they had just survived.

"Shake it out," Decatur told her with a nod.

She did.

At the Coast Guard base, Lynn and Decatur met Patrick, Kim, and several others. The pilot flew them over miles of Gulf of Mexico water. As they flew, Lynn took deep breaths to recover from the lightheadedness caused by the adrenaline dump of facing down Dena.

Patrick talked to them through headsets. "We've located the Alpine. I explained to Captain Beyer who we are and that he possibly has a bomb hidden aboard. He authorized the pilots to drop us off. He's still in command of the ship."

The pilot landed on the tanker's helicopter pad. Kim, Patrick, Lynn, Decatur, and several Coast Guard reservists climbed out, ducking under the spinning blades. When they cleared the helipad, the copter took off again.

They raced below deck to the mess, where the crew had been gathered, some clearly just awakened. The captain pointed at two of the men, motioning them away from the group and toward their Coast Guard interviewers.

Lynn looked at the two slight Filipino seamen in front of her. Neither appeared dangerous. They hadn't been armed, though they shouldn't be at this time of night and their rooms had not yet been searched for weapons. The taller one, called Liamzon, was jumpy. The shorter one, identified as Liamzon's cousin, was sullen.

Liamzon was staring at an overhead monitor showing the ship's position five nautical miles out from the Louisiana Offshore Oil Port, or LOOP, terminal.

The six Coast Guards split into two groups, each taking one of the Filipinos. Lynn's group went onto the bridge with the sullen one. The other group crammed into the captain's cabin.

Although every crew member supposedly spoke English, Liamzon's cousin didn't appear to understand the questions she started asking as soon as they closed the door. Where had he boarded? Who had given him instructions? What did he know about a bomb?

The Filipino seaman turned his head, crooked his arm, and coughed into his elbow. His long sleeves hiked up, exposing a cheap watch.

He squeezed the watch and brought his hand to his mouth, continuing to cough. Before Lynn, Kim, or the other Guard members could stop him, the seaman swallowed a pill.

Oh crap! Not a watch. A suicide pill container. Lynn dove for him but was too late. He was focused like a laser on dying.

"*Heimlich!*" She shouted. But the pill was already too far down his gullet.

"Does anyone have an emetic, something to make him throw up?"

In less than a minute he slumped in the chair, eyes rolled back and mouth open. One reservist tried to force a hand into the seaman's mouth to cause him to vomit but the seaman clamped his mouth shut.

Another pressed two fingers to the man's carotid artery. "His heart's barely beating! We're going to lose him!"

"Get the ship's doctor!" Lynn said.

She ran down the passageway and threw open the door of the captain's cabin, desperate to keep the second Filipino from killing himself, too.

She seized his arm as he was lifting it up toward his mouth and yanked his watch off his wrist.

He twisted away and the two Coast Guards grabbed his arms.

Then, surprisingly, he stood still, looked up at the ship's position monitor, and his expression relaxed.

Lynn followed his glance. They were a few miles from LOOP. *Why did the map make him ease up?*

As Lynn entered the mess, she willed herself to appear calm. The Guard's hastily-roused bomb squad appeared taut. Patrick Boudreaux and Kim Garvey were now with the bomb techs, speaking to Captain Beyer. "No info yet but cell phones are the most likely trigger."

The captain raised his eyebrows and rushed away, taking all of the cell phones with him. "I'll put them in a safe."

Lynn glanced at the wrists of each member of the Alpine's crew who had remained in the room. Most were covered in long sleeves. "Show me your wrists!"

Other Coast Guard officers appeared by her side. "Bring me all the watches in the room," she said. She repeated the captain's earlier instructions. "Find any other cell phones that might have been missed or hidden and secure them. Don't let anyone leave. Now!"

Liamzon's watch was the only counterpart to the sullen terrorist's.

An officer waved from the doorway to get her attention. "First man's in a coma and we can't revive him. Medic says he took cyanide."

Back in the cabin with Liamzon, she popped open his watch to reveal a compartment with a small, gray pill. She scrutinized him. His every muscle strained to lunge for the pill.

"A suicide pill if he was caught, like the other one," said a guard.

"Where is the bomb?" Lynn asked. "What is the trigger?"

Liamzon shrugged and shook his head.

"We don't have time for this shit," another guard said.

Lynn grabbed the man's sunburned ear until he winced. She pulled his head close to her mouth and said, "Slay and be slain for Allah."

He spit at her.

"Did you pack your paradise wedding suit?"

He stared at her without answering.

Lynn focused her anger. Anger at this unthinking mule. "If you don't tell us where the bomb is, no imam will say a funeral prayer for you. Your soul will be condemned. Allah won't let you within a million miles of paradise."

She watched as he shook his head violently as if to shut out her words. He was momentarily still, then his eyes widened in panic.

"What is the trigger? Where is the bomb?" Lynn repeated slowly.

"Cell phone primary. Captain has my phone and detonator phone is in my locker. GPS secondary. The bomb is in the engine room," Liamzon whispered.

Oh fuck. "Patrick, call—no don't call—run and tell the captain to stop the ship! We have to turn around! And tell him about the two cell phones. Make sure they can't connect to one another!"

Boudreaux sprinted away.

She spun to Liamzon. "Engine room where? Show us now!"

They paged the bomb squad.

As they ran toward the engine room, Lynn heard the rumble of the tanker's engines stop. The deck's vibration stilled. She sensed a gradual slowing of the enormous tanker and knew Patrick Boudreaux had already reached Captain Beyer. *But stopping this whale will take fifteen minutes we don't have.*

When they shoved Liamzon into the engine room, he pointed in the darkness far behind one of the diesel generators. The bomb was low in a shadowy corner, beneath some pipes.

Fuck. We're paste. Lynn forced herself to be calm. "What sets off the cell phone detonator?"

They could still be drifting into position.

"A preprogrammed call in thirty minutes."

"Secondary remote detonator?"

"What I said. GPS coordinates."

"Damn," she said. "*What* GPS coordinates?"

"I don't know!" Liamzon screamed. "They didn't tell me. I've told you everything. Give me the pill!"

Lynn was desperate. *This man has the answer.* "No imam will say a prayer for you. Matak must have told you something. Something to look for!"

"Lupe." Liamzon looked at the position monitor. Lynn caught his glance. They were a mile away from the offshore terminal.

"LOOP? The terminal? The GPS coordinates are for LOOP?"

Liamzon nodded.

Damn. The ship still hasn't stopped moving forward. She nodded at another officer who ran to tell Captain Beyer to turn away from LOOP.

"If this thing goes off before we disarm it maybe you'll get your trip to paradise," Lynn said. "But we're coming right along with you." They zip-tied Liamzon's feet together and handcuffed his hands behind his back.

Patrick Boudreaux had returned. Breathing hard, he said, "The bomb itself could be booby-trapped."

"You really shouldn't be here, Lynn," Kim added.

"You two are bomb techs?"

Kim nodded. "I've been around way too many IEDs."

"I'll be your second," Patrick said. "Back away, everyone."

Lynn moved back with everyone else while Kim and Patrick focused on disarming the bomb.

Kim squatted next to Patrick. Their sweat and the deliberate pace with which they moved belied their reassurances. Kim described aloud each step of the disarming. As second, Patrick confirmed and supervised.

"Disconnecting wires."

"Affirmative."

At any moment, they could drift into the target zone. Lynn glanced at the position monitor. They were half a mile from LOOP.

Kim Garvey slowly unwound the bomb's red and blue wires leading from the battery.

Patrick exhaled. Lynn unconsciously took a deep breath with him.

"Removing neutron trigger."

"Affirmative."

Kim put on gloves, removed what looked like a small ball and put it into a lead-lined pouch. "Polonium's my guess."

"One-minute break. Stop. Breathe," Patrick said after the pouch was closed. "Breathe again."

Lynn tried to breathe with them but stole a look at the position monitor. *A quarter-mile from LOOP. We could get in range any second!*

"Retrieving conventional explosive. Steady hands."

"Affirmative."

Sweat broke on Kim's forehead. She separated and picked up what appeared to Lynn to be a larger package, and secured it.

"Separating U-235."

The position monitor showed Lynn they were two minutes from LOOP.

If they got too close together, the spheres could still set off deadly radiation. Kim slowly lifted one heavy half-sphere away from its brother. Patrick took and boxed it. Kim boxed the other half-sphere.

Runners left with the two boxes toward opposite ends of the tanker.

Lynn sighed deeply.

Kim and Patrick had disarmed the bomb.

The half-spheres would be kept away from one another and flown in helicopters to different bomb investigation sites.

Lynn took another deep breath, looked around at everyone, and said, "Congratulations to all of you. You're amazing!"

The ships engines grumbled loudly as the tanker reversed thrust. They were one minute from LOOP.

EPILOGUE

Lynn was finally able to indulge a long weekend at home. Three-year-old Matt was spending the night with his grandparents, sure to return with new toys and an even bigger appetite for candy.

At seven in the morning she rolled toward Cy in bed. "We need to make up again for lost time."

They kissed for a few moments. A knock sounded at the bedroom door.

"Damn. I forgot she had a morning game." Cy pulled away.

"At least she knocked."

He got up and unlocked the door for her. "Come in, Marika."

The eight-year-old hopped on one foot toward the end of the bed. Her coltish legs looked longer than they had a week ago. "My game, my game, my game, I can't wait." She kicked an imaginary soccer ball.

"You're turning into such a big kid, Marika," Lynn said. "I think your legs grew overnight."

Marika looked at her father. "Dad's told me what it's like to get older. Was it the same for you? Did your legs get bigger?"

"Yes."

"Your bones got bigger?"

"Yes."

"Your heart got bigger?"

"I hope so.

"Here's what my friends and I can't figure out," she said and then laughed. "It sounds lame. Which part of your body does love come from?"

"All parts, I think. Your heart, your brain. Sometimes I even feel it in my stomach." Lynn exchanged a wink with Cy.

"So when you love enough to get married like you and my dad did, where does it come from?"

"Everywhere," Cy said. He hugged his daughter and said, "Game in forty-five minutes. We'll leave in twenty-five. Go practice your kicks for twenty minutes. Matt's not here to get in your way. Then put on your uniform."

After Marika left, Cy locked the door.

Lynn pulled him into an embrace. "Twenty minutes is plenty of time."

After several local, state, and federal regulatory delays, TriCoast's San Francisco Bay refinery was restarting. In a surprising change, the anti-TriCoast protesters picketing outside the refinery's gates were now being met by counter-protestors with signs that read "Solve energy poverty. Affordable energy for the poor. Save seven billion people from disease & hunger." The groups' occasional conflicts with one another kept the local police on TriCoast's speed-dial.

The dramatic oil price decline continued to burden TriCoast's financial results. New projects were jettisoned.

Lynn fought to save hundreds of jobs with reassignments, training, large-scale safety and maintenance projects, and most importantly, a search for new and expanded markets. Ultimately, the entanglement and deaths of Dena and David caused TriCoast's board of directors to reverse its instructions to lay off thousands. They were finally persuaded that when the cycle reversed, every employee now performing safety and maintenance would be needed for full-time and overtime operations, including plenty of additional jobs in cybersecurity.

Still, TriCoast had to stop its red ink. Mike, Sara, Lynn, and other executives instituted twenty percent pay cuts across the board, starting with their own salaries. Most difficult, Cy delayed his cherished plan of reducing his work hours to spend extra time with Marika and Matt. The union agreed to industry-wide cuts at any company that had already reduced pay for its non-unionized employees, including TriCoast.

Lynn sat at a table in her office with Beau Decatur. Flanking him was TriCoast's chief of security Mark Shepherd and Dallas FBI agent Jim Cutler.

Her phone buzzed with a text. She read it, shaking her head. "Remember the day Reese was killed?"

"I wish I could forget," Mark said.

"O'Shaughnessy at NOPD checked his notes. Dena told us she was at NOPD that day talking to O'Shaughnessy but they have no record of her being in their offices. She *was* helping Reese's killer somehow."

"This whole thing was a group of people," Mark Shepherd said. "Some, like Dena and Cong, had done nothing to get on our radar. Same with Liamzon and his cousin. But Vikenti Andreev was high on our list and Matak hit the top of it once we knew he killed Arch. And as we now know, Dena had a particular grudge against David and by extension, you and all of us at TriCoast."

"Cong Li was the center node," Cutler said. "He ran a company in Beijing that orchestrated cyberattack projects for whichever Chinese government agencies or companies he could sell them to, or that needed them. Mostly for the Fourth Department in China, but also Guo An and some supposedly private companies that in reality are managed by the government.

"Cong recruited and directed everyone. Toward the end, he was caught in a Chinese anticorruption probe but he escaped to confront you and Decatur in Vienna." Cutler nodded toward Beau Decatur.

"I'm glad you had that safety training, Lynn," Mark said. "You okay after killing Cong? Nightmares? Flashbacks?"

"All of the above. But it was going to be him or us," she said. "That's the only way I can think about it."

"The initiator was someone or an agency in the Chinese government, but it's unlikely we'll find out soon. However, in transmissions we recovered, Cong referred to this particular group of individuals as the Second Law group. Mean anything to you?" Cutler asked.

"The second law of thermodynamics. In layman's terms it means everything tends toward disorder, or chaos," Lynn said. "But how did the Filipino seamen get involved?"

"Cong recruited Matak Abdullah from South Sudan, mainly to find them. Cong also asked him and Dena Tarleton, since she was in New Orleans, to get access to TriCoast computers, specifically Arch's bidding program. So they just killed Arch Webber for his computer," Cutler summarized. "Liamzon and his cousin were the only indirect nodes. Matak was the cutout. Matak hired Liamzon and his cousin to carry out the suicide mission of detonating the bomb on the oil tanker once it reached LOOP."

"And we learned a while ago Cong killed Matak in Vienna," Lynn said.

"Cong had as little patience with his recruits as his government employers did with him, especially once Matak was exposed," Cutler said.

"That's when Cong pushed Matak over a bridge in front of a train," Lynn replied.

Cutler nodded. "Yes, and you wound up in his crosshairs. After Cong killed Matak, he stayed in touch with Liamzon, pretending he was Matak. Liamzon couldn't tell the difference since their communication was online. Liamzon and his cousin, by the way, were real prizes: well-trained Filipino seamen who wanted a magnificent jihad. That their families were being paid was just a bonus as far as they were concerned. Apparently the cousin was there as an enforcer, like we see many times."

"Why did Cong attack us in Vienna?" Lynn asked.

"Once you, Kim, and the team fixed the sabotage that was supposed to occur at Marrero, Cong was probably told to make you a target. In the eyes of his bosses, San Francisco was a success and Marrero was a failure. They had identified you earlier as a threat, when they tried to take out you, Decatur, and Rosenberg while you were diving," Cutler said.

"Another close call." Lynn shuddered. "So who was Vikenti Andreev?"

"Former SVR. He was so significant he must have been forced into the group by a Russian-Chinese deal way above Cong's level," Cutler explained. "He was inserted with Cong to help keep Russia's energy stranglehold on Europe."

Lynn nodded. "Russia doesn't want US competitors sending ships full of liquefied natural gas to Europe. Vikenti was the intruder Dwayne caught on camera in Pennsylvania." She remembered his picture on the security video in Pennsylvania. *In our field. Thank God he didn't kill Dwayne.*

"Vikenti Andreev disabled most of the security system," Mark added. "We were lucky Dwayne got even one frame of him."

"He scouted European gas receiving terminals," Cutler said. "Ultimately he and a few men he hired attacked the first terminal in Lithuania. They tried to get to Świnoujście, Poland but Andreev was betrayed and shot by his own men, with the Polish police looking on.

"Vikenti may well have been betrayed himself at the highest levels of government. China has a multi-billion-dollar long-term agreement to buy gas from Russia. The Chinese want to both use the Russians and keep them happy. Once Vikenti started blowing up terminals, the Chinese knew it would drive up the price of the gas they were buying from Russia. At that point, Vikenti Andreev went past his expiration date with both governments. It's likely his subordinates were *told* to kill him."

Lynn shook her head. "So why was Dena part of Cong's group? I thought all she wanted was revenge on David." Lynn remembered with a shudder how David's body looked.

"Dena was quite the special case. Your doppelganger," Mark said.

"How dare you compare me to a murderer!" Lynn glared at Mark.

"You without a conscience. An evil twin. Young, female, brilliant, on the rise." Mark said. "She found David; they both wanted the affair. When he got tired of her or grew a conscience, she decided to kill him. It appears she also wanted revenge on all of TriCoast. Cong found her when she chased his bogus China Power internet link right into his arms. Cong figured out her motivations and the many kinds of inside information she could give him, so she became the Viper. His Second Law group was complete. When Matak showed up to steal Arch Webber's computer, she was assigned to be his partner."

"So the bacon in David's jacket in Pennsylvania . . ." Lynn said.

"She expected a *bear* to kill David!" Mark exclaimed.

"Reese must have learned about the affair," Lynn said. "Dena didn't kill him but you're saying she helped."

"We think it was more basic that that—Reese had probably figured out she was the inside source. It's likely she told Cong Li and Cong sent Vikenti Andreev, a trained assassin, to kill him," Mark explained.

Lynn shook her head, the pang of Reese's loss still taking her breath. "Dena's was the name he was going to give me. He knew I trusted her, so he was trying to figure out how to say it so I'd listen."

"Cong was doing more than coordinating people," Mark said. "He's responsible for sabotaging our San Francisco refinery and trying to sabotage our Marrero refinery. Actually Cong plus Dena. He hacked into the San Francisco refinery's operations and then Dena helped him hack into the Marrero refinery control system."

"Which was why she was so good at fixing the Marrero bugs," Lynn said. "And by unbalancing and damaging the refineries we couldn't make enough gasoline, jet and diesel, so the Chinese expected to sell more of theirs."

"Cong's actions also demonstrated the Chinese could take down critical energy infrastructure at will. That's another reason he likely got the order to kill you when you stopped the sabotage at Marrero," Cutler said.

"But what about the screwed-up auction bids?" Lynn asked.

"Again, Dena and Cong working together. Arch had seen Dena and David together, so he was already one of Dena's targets. Cong and Matak came along at the right time with the right assignment to steal Arch's computer," Mark explained. "First, Dena knocked out Madame Taliesin, stashed her in an empty apartment, changed clothes with ther, and then pretended to be her to get into Arch's room and confuse him. She let Matak in. Helping Matak get TriCoast's bid plans, and then altering them when she was assigned to come up with new ones, was her proof to Cong that he and the Second Law group could trust her. Unfortunately, Madame Taliesin alive was a loose end Cong couldn't take, so we think he sent Andreev to kill her."

The next week Lynn Dayton, Kim Garvey, her Coast Guard crew, Patrick Boudreaux, and the other bomb technicians lined a long table at Café Maspero in New Orleans' French Quarter. Lynn felt Patrick's attitude toward her start to relax when she told him what she knew about his sister's death, and how his sister had saved the lives of many others.

Bowls of chicken and andouille sausage gumbo steamed in front of them. They could smell crawfish pasta and bread pudding being prepared in the kitchen.

The sky was as blue and clear and metallic as hot iron, yet the sun's brilliance somehow felt treacherous, misleading. Lynn shook her head to clear her thoughts. She remembered Arch Webber and David Jenkins. Even Dena. But most of all she missed Reese and his friendship, experience, and good humor.

A trumpet sounded and a bridal jazz parade swung into view. Starting at the cathedral and making a circuit through French Quarter streets, the bride, groom, and wedding party high-stepped past them, waving parasols and handkerchiefs.

Looking around at her group, Lynn smiled and said, "It's true what I always used to hear at Tulane during Mardi Gras."

"Which is?" Kim asked.

"New Orleans is a fever. It enters your bloodstream, and it never leaves."

NOTES

In Ned Cheever's *Nola.com* article about New Orleans streets named for the nine Greek Muses (the goddess daughters of Zeus and Mnemosyne), he reminds readers:

- Calliope is the Muse of epic poetry;
- Clio is the Muse of history;
- Erato is the Muse of love poetry and mimicry;
- Euterpe is the Muse of music;
- Melpomene is the Muse of tragedy;
- Polymnia is the Muse of sacred poetry;
- Terpsichore is the Muse of dancing;
- Thalia is the Muse of comedy and of playful and idyllic poetry;
- Urania is the Muse of astronomy.

Sadi Carnot was a French scientist from the early 1800s who studied at France's esteemed École Polytechnique (or X, as readers may know from **13 DAYS: THE PYTHAGORAS CONSPIRACY**). He is credited as the first to formulate the second law of thermodynamics.

ACKNOWLEDGEMENTS

My opportunity to work with editor John Paine improved this book considerably. Any mistakes are mine alone.

I thank fellow authors and critique group members Gary Vineyard and Art Bauer for their keen eyes and kind words, and lunches fueled by tortilla chips, as they read early drafts.

One need read only a few news stories to know the truth of the vast number of international Chinese and Russian cybersecurity attacks on the US. While **THE SECOND LAW** is not a true story, it follows the arc of global possibility and has been eerily prescient from the earliest draft. The disappearance of Chinese executives who have fallen out of favor is an all-too-common occurrence. Chinese-Russian cooperation and competition is an ongoing fact of global diplomacy, including, according to the *Wall Street Journal*, Chinese authorities questioning the founder of CEFC China Energy after his company agreed to buy a 14% interest in Russia's state oil company PAO Rosneft.

The Sansei Asian oil buyers group is fictional.

At the time I began writing, I didn't know about Russian Internet Research Agency posts on social media against pipelines and US energy to discourage US energy production (which helps Russian energy production.) This has since been confirmed by numerous sources. Since the book's plot follows an economic trajectory, the coincidence is not surprising.

Fellow authors Judy Melinek, MD, and D. P. Lyle, MD provided exceptional medical expertise.

Via the International Thriller Writers' (ITW), I appreciated getting a briefing from the New York City office of the Federal Bureau of Investigation.

Jack Hoban taught the concept of the Ethical Warrior. Allison Brennan, Lee Child, and Grant Blackwood, and many others taught excellent seminars. Thanks, too, to Lee Lofland for his Writers Police Academy.

The energy and business reporting by Rebecca Smith, Spencer Jakab, Alison Sider, Russell Gold, Lynn Cook, and many others at *The Wall Street Journal* filled in gaps or inspired more research. Other energy information resources include the *Oil and Gas Investor*, *Oil and Gas Journal*, Tudor Pickering Holt, and the *Houston Chronicle*. The best energy statisticians, hands down, work at the Energy Information Administration in the US Department of Energy.

Thanks to former police officer Justin Freeman for his article, "How to Respond if Someone Holds a Gun to Your Head."

Tom Miller's book, CHINA'S ASIAN DREAM, provided background on China's ever-growing One Belt, One Road (or New Silk Road) plan.

I appreciated Bill's discussion of antagonists and Kay's insights on Stanford and Silicon Valley. Andy, now Dr. Andy, showed us Blue Bottle. Jeff Champeau explained aspects of energy information security. Jim Kipp identified the relative economies of various countries. He and Susan Paul keep me informed on wider economic issues.

At *CrimeSceneWriter*, thanks to: Robin Burcell, Mark Haile, Wally Lind, Steve Brown, Donnell Bell, Joe Collins, Piper, Orblover, and many others of the group's phenomenal experts.

I appreciate the website expertise of Clara, Carl, and Claude. I also feel fortunate to count marketing pro Diane Feffer as a friend.

Marketing innovation by Texas Association of Authors' founder Alan Bourgeois highlights an array of talented Texas authors.

Tulane architecture professor Richard Campanella's **BOURBON STREET: A HISTORY** explains Bourbon Street's decades-long pull.

There is no Louisiana chain of excellent bars by the name Big Oyster. Nor was there ever a NOLA-in-Exile, although the country's oldest gay bar is New Orleans' Café Lafitte in Exile.

Readers who think oil executives are killed only in fiction are referred to the story of Nicholas Mockford's killing in Belgium by unknown assailants for unknown reasons, as well as numerous stories of contract oil workers kidnapped and killed abroad.

Similarly, there are legions of stories of Russian and Chinese hacking to steal money, intellectual property, or destabilize other countries. Chinese theft of intellectual property has been so extensive it has bankrupted some of the victimized companies.

Dr. Jean Oi, the William Haas Professor in Chinese Politics in Stanford's department of political science, a senior fellow of the Freeman Spogli Institute for International Studies at Stanford University, and the Lee Shau Kee Director of Stanford's Center at Peking (Beijing) University discussed challenges in the Chinese economy.

Palo Alto's Books, Inc. hosted me for a signing of the second Lynn Dayton book, **STRIKE PRICE**.

Huge thanks to Rob Siders and Stewart Williams for their formatting and design expertise. I also appreciated the encouragement of renowned fellow author and former Mystery Writers of America executive vice president Harry Hunsicker.

My friends and readers throughout the world, including those at Goodreads, inspire me. This book is for you.

My parents, husband, and children were kindly supportive of the time, emotion, and energy that writing **THE SECOND LAW** required.

L. A. Starks is the winner of the Texas Association of Authors' 2014 award for best mystery/thriller for her second Lynn Dayton thriller, STRIKE PRICE.

Starks was born in Boston, Massachusetts, grew up in northern Oklahoma, and now lives in Texas. Awarded a full-tuition college scholarship, she earned a chemical engineering bachelor's degree, magna cum laude, from New Orleans' Tulane University, followed by a finance MBA from the University of Chicago. While at Chicago she made time to play for a celebrated women's intramural basketball team, the Efficient Mockettes.

Working more than a decade for well-known energy companies in engineering, marketing, and finance from refineries to corporate offices prepared Starks to write global energy thrillers. In addition to her books, two of Starks' short stories have been published in *Amazon Shorts* and one through Amazon KDP.

She continues to consult on energy economics and investing, often speaking to professional groups for their members' continuing education credits.

She is multi-published on dozens of energy topics at two investor websites: **Starks Energy Economics** and **Seeking Alpha**. Her nonfiction has also appeared in *Mystery Readers Journal, The Dallas Morning News, The Houston Chronicle, The San Antonio Express-News, Sleuth Sayer (MWA-SW newsletter), Natural Gas,* and *Oil and Gas Journal.* She is also the co-inventor of a U.S. patent.

Starks has run thirteen half-marathons. She has served as development co-chair, investment oversight chair, and treasurer of the board of the Friends of the Dallas Public Library.

Visit her online at: http://lastarksbooks.com
and @LAStarksAuthor

Publisher's Note: If you enjoyed THE SECOND LAW, try the rest of the series, 13 DAYS: THE PYTHAGORAS CONSPIRACY and STRIKE PRICE.

CPSIA information can be obtained
at www.ICGtesting.com
Printed in the USA
FFHW02n1743211018

9 780991 110742